To Jackie,

SECRET MITZVAH
OF
LUCIO BURKE

All good things & all the best on a lonely, suddenly day in [...] heights.

A NOVEL BY

~~STEVEN HAYWARD~~

[signature] / 2007

VINTAGE CANADA

VINTAGE CANADA EDITION, 2005

Published in Canada by Vintage Canada, a division of Random
House of Canada Limited, Toronto, in 2005. Originally published
in hardcover in Canada by Alfred A. Knopf Canada, a division of
Random House of Canada Limited, Toronto, in 2005. Distributed
by Random House of Canada Limited, Toronto.

Vintage Canada and colophon are registered trademarks of
Random House of Canada Limited.

www.randomhouse.ca

Library and Archives Canada Cataloguing in Publication

Hayward, Steven
The secret mitzvah of Lucio Burke: a novel / by Steven Hayward.

ISBN-13: 978-0-676-97704-2
ISBN-10: 0-676-97704-9

I. Title.

PS8565.A984S43 2005A   C813'.6   C2005-904049-1

Text design: Kelly Hill

Printed and bound in the United States of America

2 4 6 8 9 7 5 3 1

For Katherine

THE
SECRET MITZVAH
OF
LUCIO BURKE

PROLOGUE

This is a true story. My grandmother told it to me, and for her I suppose it was a kind of love story—a tale about how she met my grandfather one August afternoon after a baseball game. This was in 1933, and the baseball game was in Toronto. At the end of the game, seconds after the final pitch had been thrown, a group of boys who had been watching the game unfurled a massive swastika flag. A riot followed, and in the midst of that riot my grandparents met.

No matter how many times my grandmother told me the story of that day—of those different days—she seemed to think there was no way to make me understand what it had been like back then, and for that reason always included as part of her story a good deal of extraneous material: dates that have been long forgotten, histories of sewers, the names of dead people and what they looked like. And there's no question, parts of it she got wrong. One of the things she got wrong is the name of one of the teams that had been playing that day.

"It wasn't the Lizzies," I told her once. "St. Peter's was there, but not the Lizzies—it was the Harbord Street Playground team that was playing."

"Wait until you're my age," she replied. "Then tell me."

For the most part I haven't changed a thing; this is her story, and I tell it the way she told it, with everything she made up or imagined left in.

Before you read it, though, you need to know she didn't get it all wrong.

It is true that for a brief time in the summer of 1933 young men wearing swastikas could be seen walking through the streets of Toronto. It is true that there was something called the Swastika Club, and that they performed several very public and well-publicized acts of anti-Semitic violence. And finally, it is true that during a baseball game at Toronto's Christie Pits there broke out a riot that would stretch across the city.

But there is no indication, no record, that any of the people my grandmother told me about were there that day—not Lucio Burke, not my grandmother, not even my grandfather, who swore up and down until the moment he died that he was not only there but was there managing a baseball team that did not—as far as I can tell—play at Christie Pits that day. So I suppose I don't believe a word of this story myself.

But I will say this: until my grandmother started talking, I knew nothing about that day at Christie Pits. It seemed impossible to imagine such a thing occurring in Toronto. Like miracles, I thought, Nazis happened elsewhere. And so I suppose I've come full circle. If at the end of the story I've decided, finally, that there is no way I can believe what my grandmother told me, I must confess it was in disbelief that I began, not believing that such a thing as the riot at Christie Pits could happen, could ever have happened, in my own placid, infallibly polite Toronto.

ONE

IT IS THE SUMMER OF 1933. The year of the New Deal. The decade of the night of broken glass. Joe Zangara, a bricklayer from New Jersey, attempts to assassinate Franklin Delano Roosevelt. Instead of Roosevelt, Zangara hits Chicago's Mayor Anton Cermak and Margaret Kruis, a showgirl from Newark. In a frame farmhouse on the outskirts of Callander, Ontario, Elzire Dionne and her husband, Oliva, are talking about having a child. The great dirigible the U.S.S. *Akron* crashes near Philadelphia— falling, say witnesses, like a meteorite. Gandhi starts his fast. And Bloomberg, pitcher of a team named the Lizzies, walks the streets of Toronto, saying he's going to give away a baseball.

That summer Bloomberg is everywhere.

On King and Dundas and Queen and Richmond and Bloor streets. On the Bathurst streetcar. In front of the ferry docks for Centre Island. Underneath the basketball hoops at Bellwoods Park. Outside Maple Leaf Gardens and behind the old Maple Leaf Stadium at the foot of Bathurst Street, where the sharps play dice on sheets of cardboard they fold up when the cops come. At Kew Beach, where there are white signs saying NO JEWS ALLOWED. In line at the St. Matthew Mission on

Morse Street. On Saturdays outside Holy Blossom synagogue. On Sundays in front of St. Patrick's Church. In the foyer of the Ontario Oddfellow's Home and Orphanage on Davenport. Behind the *Encyclopedia Britannica* in the main branch of the Toronto Public Library on Lowther. At the Rose Theatre on College Street, during newsreels.

"There'll be an infield and an outfield," Bloomberg tells people, "and an umpire'll make the calls. It'll be a real game—except there'll be one hit and the guy who gets it gets the ball."

He wears thick bottle-cap glasses that make his eyes seem absurdly large, like the eyes of a fish that lives near the bottom of the ocean; the kind of fish that breathes through its eyes, for whom blinking is a way of taking a breath.

"Single," Bloomberg says, pushing the baseball into people's hands, "double, seeing-eye single, infield dribbler, Texas leaguer, stand-up double, line drive, triple, home run, inside-the-park home run—it doesn't matter. You don't get two balls if you get a double. There ain't two balls. There's one ball, and if you hit it, you get it."

When he finishes talking, he takes the ball back.

He grabs it away, wrenching it out of the other person's hand. It is a calculated gesture; one meant to underline what separates people with baseballs from people without base-balls. It works. All that summer the people of Toronto find themselves staring at their empty hands. There is nothing extraordinary about Bloomberg's baseball, it should be said. It is not gold-plated. It has been autographed by no one. It is not even new. In fact, by the time Bloomberg is ready to give it away, its white leather has turned a dark, dirty grey and its red stitching has started to sag. Still, people find themselves look-ing at their empty hands, thinking about that baseball.

"That's right, it *sounds* easy," Bloomberg tells people, "all you've got to do is hit a Bloomberg Special."

All of this is taking place at a time when Toronto is a city of corned beef and boiled potatoes and soda biscuits. The city is ninety percent British, and Protestant. The Loyal Orange Order can be seen marching twice a year down the middle of the city, down Yonge Street, which cuts the city in two. The Union Jack flag flies over City Hall. Schoolchildren sing "God Save the King." The city's policemen and judges and magistrates and lawyers and most of its doctors and every one of its mayors are members of the Orange Order. The rest of the people are pressed into a dirty corner of the city called the Ward. There is nothing unusual about this designation. Or at least it does not seem so in 1933. Toronto's Ward extends from College Street down to Queen Street and as far east as Bay Street. It is where the Italians and Jews live—the wops and the kikes, as they are mostly called by most of the city—and this is a story about them. Because that is where Bloomberg says he is going to give away his baseball, it begins in the middle of a large, mouse-grey concrete rectangle known as the Elizabeth Street playground.

It will turn out to be a splendid, sunny July day. But even before the sun comes up, the three youngest Bucci children are in line. First is twelve-year-old Antonio, and behind him are his two younger sisters, eight-year-old Giovanna and five-and-a-half-year-old Victorinna. They arrived at six-thirty in the morning, having been up since four, when their parents—who own the Bucci Bakery on Cecil Street—forced all of their children out of bed to help in the bakery. Antonio and his sisters carry pans of dough from the living room of their house (where their mother and two older sisters roll it) into the bakery (where their father and four older brothers bake it). At six they are done for the day, and their mother gives them breakfast, which on this morning is when Antonio says he is going to stand in line to try to hit Bloomberg's baseball.

"How much to play?" asks his mother.

"Nothing," says Antonio.

"Nothing?" says Filomena Bucci, who was born in a town in the south of Italy called Larino, where no one plays baseball or gives anything away. "The truth," she tells her son. "How much?"

"Noth—" says Antonio, holding his hands out like pincers, palms up, as if his mother's obtuseness has driven him to the brink of losing his mind, "—ing."

"*Bene*," says Filomena, "but you take your sisters."

When the Bucci children arrive at the Elizabeth Street playground, it is deserted. The swings have not even been unlocked. The chain is still on the teeter-totter, and the sand-box is covered and padlocked. They sit down to wait and begin eating the buns their mother gave them as they went out the door, watching in silence as the wooden back doors of the hospital across the playground open and two men wheel out two large bins of ashes from the hospital furnace. The men dump the ashes in the middle of the playground and haphazardly spread them around with their feet. Insofar as the playground is immediately behind the hospital, the dumping of the ashes there is expedient; insofar as it is without grass, the dumping of the ashes is altruistic, the idea being that it is more pleasant to fall into ash than onto asphalt. Everything in or near the Elizabeth Street playground is covered with a grey silky film: a grey swing set with three grey swings sits next to a grey teeter-totter and a grey set of monkey bars.

When they have finished eating their buns, the Bucci children make tiny ash pillows for themselves. Lying down, they stare up at the sky, which is already beginning to brighten with weak early-morning light. There is no wind, and it seems that the Toronto streets are taking longer to wake up than they do on other days. The windows of the Hester How School next to the playground are dark, and even St. Patrick's Church, which towers over the playground with its steeple and its stained-glass window showing a portly Saint Patrick leading the snakes out of Ireland, looks as if it has its eyes shut. A lone beggar pushes his cart up Walton Street, and in the distance the creaky brakes of a streetcar can be heard. Soon all three Bucci children are sound asleep.

Meyer Rubin arrives at the playground shortly thereafter, and is dismayed to see the Bucci children already lined up. A small, roundish boy with short-cropped brown hair, Meyer is dressed in brown short pants, a grey shirt and overstretched suspenders that do not entirely hold up his pants. Staring venomously at Antonio and his sisters, he sits down gloomily in the line behind them, cursing his mother for making him wash his face before leaving the house. But then it occurs to Meyer that, if he can manage to place his yarmulke underneath Antonio's head, he will be able to claim that he should be first to bat because his yarmulke is first in line. This seems an excellent plan. He crawls over to Antonio and tries to wedge his yarmulke under the other boy's head, and has nearly done so when Antonio opens his eyes. Meyer panics. He jumps up, still holding his yarmulke, and begins saying something about not trying to jump the line.

Antonio does not hear a word of this explanation. What he sees, or thinks he sees, is Meyer towering over him, brandishing a pumpernickel bagel. Having grown up in a bakery, Antonio has a great deal of experience with how dangerous baked goods can be. He has witnessed his eldest brother, Vince, knock out Guido, his next to eldest brother, with a two-week-old dinner roll hurled from the other side of the bakery. So it is that, when Antonio sees Meyer Rubin wielding something that looks like a pumpernickel bagel, his response is to try and slug him. Being flat on his back, however, Antonio's punch is neither very quick nor very hard, and Meyer sees it coming in plenty of time. He moves easily out of the way and jumps on Antonio, pinning him and then pinching his nose.

"Let go!" yells Antonio.

"What's the magic word?" says Meyer, for some reason in a high falsetto voice.

"Please!" cries Antonio.

So absorbed is Meyer that he does not notice Antonio's sisters are awake. They intervene: Giovanna takes hold of Meyer's ears and pulls; Victorinna bites Meyer's arm. Soon Antonio is sitting on top of Meyer. "Here," says Antonio. "See how *you* like it."

It is at this moment that twenty-year-old Ruthie Nodelman arrives at the playground. Ruthie is a pretty girl with wide, dark eyes, exceptionally straight teeth and long red hair, which she is wearing today tucked up under a red baseball cap that has a large yellow letter C on its front. In addition to the baseball cap, Ruthie is wearing a plain white blouse, a plain black skirt, dark stockings and shiny black high-heeled shoes. These fancy shoes belong to her sister, Esther, who is two and a half years older, not half as pretty and an inveterate reader of *Vogue*. Ruthie disapproves of the shoes she is wearing this morning out of principle. What is worse, with the shoes on she *feels* like her sister. They are the kind of shoes no self-respecting Party member would be caught dead in, which is to say that it seems to her, as she walks, that the people she passes look at her shoes and wonder where she got them and how much she paid. But Ruthie had no choice. In the early-morning darkness of the house she was unable to find her own shoes. She rummaged around in the narrow front hallway of her parents' house on Beverley Street, nearly knocking over the coat rack, and Esther's shoes were simply there. She put them on, for time was of the essence. If she was going to hit Bloomberg's ball, she had to be near the front of the line. The heels might not be the worst thing, thought Ruthie, as she walked down Beverley Street that morning and felt the unfamiliar tautness in her calves, the way the heels caused her to lean forward as she walked— Bloomberg would not expect the batters to be wearing high heels. The heels would unsettle him. Perhaps she would also take her hair down. Let it flow down onto her shoulders. That would unhinge him, thought Ruthie, who had more than once noted the effect taking down her hair had on boys. And then she would hit the ball. That would make people think—when it was Ruthie Nodelman, and not some boy, who got the hit. Not that the world would change right away, but it would be a beginning. Everything had to begin somewhere.

Leaving the house, Ruthie had no illusions about being first in line—the boys in the neighbourhood had been talking about little else besides Bloomberg and his ball. She imagined legions of them arriving at break of day, batters camping out on the asphalt of the playground, and is surprised to find that this is not the case, that the only ones there are four brawling children. When she sees them, she does what any responsible grown-up would do: she breaks up the fight, makes the children apologize to each other and then delivers a lecture on the principles of class warfare.

"Now, Antonio," she says. "What's your father's job?"

Victorinna holds up her hand.

"Yes?" says Ruthie.

"He's a baker."

"A baker," says Ruthie. "And what does *your* father do, Meyer?"

"This is stupid," says Meyer.

"You're stupid," says Antonio.

"Now," says Ruthie, "let's pretend, then, that Meyer's father is a fisherman and Antonio's father is a baker."

"But he *is* a baker," says Victorinna.

Ruthie works as a bookkeeper at Gutman Fur in the Darling Building on Spadina. Mr. Gutman is a distant relative, a cousin of a cousin of her father's, and the job came open just as Ruthie was graduating from Harbord Collegiate. She had taken bookkeeping at high school, as did all the girls (the school routinely "counselled" its female students into such "vocational" tracks), and although she'd graduated near the top of her class, her skills as a bookkeeper had only partly recommended her for the position at Gutman Fur. It was, she knew, her bosom and the way she looked in a skirt that had got her the job; her responsibilities as bookkeeper include the modelling of fur coats. Gutman's clients—most often they are men buying coats for their wives—sit in a chair and watch as she paces to and fro wearing one of Gutman's fur coats. It is usually the case that, after a man sees Ruthie in a fur, he buys it.

She cannot admit this to herself, but the fact that Ruthie spends the better part of every day modelling expensive fur coats is one reason she looks down at her sister's high-heeled shoes with such embarrassment. The shoes remind her that, no matter how many Party meetings she attends, no matter how many times she berates her older sister for wearing fancy shoes, no matter how many leaflets she distributes, she remains a cog in the capitalist wheel. In a perfect world, Ruthie tells herself, she would have a perfect job. But this is no perfect world. And if the imperfection of her situation is only a reflection of an imperfect mode of production, she may as well keep the job.

Although she attended her first Party meeting only a year and a half ago, Ruthie considers herself a born Communist. This is because her parents, Sadie and Abe Nodelman, met in the fall of 1911, when they and twelve hundred other garment workers did their best to shut down the Timothy Eaton Company. And succeeded, more or less, for eighteen weeks. During the early weeks of the strike, Sadie found herself walking in the picket line near Abe, and often beside him. Less than a month later, the two were married on the picket line.

When the strike ended, Abe Nodelman was fired almost immediately. One of the conditions of the settlement had been that there would be no further demonstrations, but on the day the workers returned to the sweatshop, just as they came in through the big front doors of the long grey building for the first time in nearly five months, a shout went up. And that was it. That was enough. Less than an hour later, Abe Nodelman and eleven other men were given their walking papers. He'd been a ringleader, they claimed. Well, it was true. He'd been responsible for making the soup for those walking the line. To Ruthie, the idea of being fired for making soup made complete sense. For surely the strike could not have lasted eighteen weeks if there had been no soup. Unlike her parents, who had found other jobs and had long ago stopped attending Party meetings, Ruthie found this event too romantic, too perfect, to be forgotten. Love and socialism had become hopelessly intertwined in her mind. It was with a sense of disappointment and incomprehension that she often found herself looking at her parents in the evenings—her father reading the baseball scores in the Yiddish newspaper, her mother hemming a pair of her father's pants—trying to reconcile this image of stolid bourgeois existence with the idea of her father heroically *schlepping* soup in the cold Toronto winter to the people who lay down in front of the horse-driven carriages that brought the scabs into the sweatshops. Her secret hope was that something like what had happened to her parents would happen to her. That she would find herself standing in a picket line beside a bespectacled man who would carry her away into the rest of her life.

"So then," says Ruthie, "what we have is a fisherman and a baker."

Victorinna puts up her hand.

"Yes, Victorinna," says Ruthie. "What is it?"

"Being a baker is also my mother's job."

"Excellent point," says Ruthie, silently chastising herself for not having considered this possibility.

Eight-year-old Giovanna puts up her hand.

"Yes," says Ruthie.

"My brothers, and sisters too, everybody works in the bakery, my sisters and my mother roll the dough and my father and the boys do the baking, except for Antonio, who's too little."

"Shut up, Giovanna," says Antonio, and he slaps his sister, hard, on the back of the head.

"We're getting sidetracked here," observes Ruthie.

"She started it," says Antonio.

"Now," continues Ruthie, "we're all workers, we know that. So, what has to happen before we can get those fat cats up against the wall?"

Victorinna puts up her hand. "My cousin Anna Maria had a cat who had babies, and the cat ate five of the babies."

"I know it," says Meyer, "and when you chop off the head of a chicken it goes on running."

"Everybody knows that," says Antonio.

Ruthie soon despairs of teaching them anything, and wonders if, after all, it is possible to convince anyone to become a Communist who is not already a Communist. Certainly if there is ever going to be a revolution, it should be now, during the Depression. Part of the problem, she thinks, as she sits down in the ash that covers the playground and waits for Bloomberg to arrive with his ball, has to do with the words the Party uses, the words the Party says you *must* use: instead of "people" you say "proletariat," instead of "middle class" you say "bourgeois"; strange, foreign words that, no matter how often she uses them, still sound to her as if they were first pronounced a great distance away, by people who have never even seen Toronto.

She listens absently to the children as they debate whether you can indeed make friends with a dog by spitting into its mouth, and thinks back to when she was seventeen and did not consider herself a born Communist. She went to the pictures then without a second thought, and wore shoes like Esther's, and fell in love with John Gilbert, whom Greta Garbo falls in love with at the very same moment that the camera reveals Garbo is falling in love by closing in on her eyes. Ruthie saw *Flesh and the Devil*—in which Garbo plays a woman who is torn between two men, marrying one without being able to stop loving the other—eight times. When the camera closed in on Garbo's widening eyes, the piano player at the Rose Theatre (a man whose face was always turned away from Ruthie but whose worker's cap she could see at the foot of the screen) played a sad, soft melody that clearly implied Garbo would never be happy, despite falling in love. Near the end of the picture, just as Garbo and her lover are about to elope, her husband returns home, catching them in each other's arms, and after that the husband and the lover must fight a duel on the Isle of Friendship, where the three first met. The two men walk out across the ice to the island, not looking at each other, without even seconds to assist, without anything but a small rectilinear box, made of dark wood, containing the pistols.

Back in her bedroom, braless and defiant, Garbo paces back and forth and then, in a crescendo of emotion that the piano player (Ruthie imagined him thin, with clear eyes) rendered as a cacophonic series of ascending minor arpeggios, she throws on her coat and walks out into the winter night in an attempt to stop the duel. She runs down to the icy shore, across the trembling, buckling ice, and falls through it. The two men turn in time to see her pale fingers slip into the dark water, and although they don't kill each other, they cannot save her. Together, the lover and the husband kneel down and stare, silently, at the space in the ice into which she disappeared. It was a terrible, perfect, sad, beautiful thing, and each time Ruthie witnessed it she wept. Until she joined the Party. Now she knows better than to be taken in by such things. She knows that so long as women marry men, so long as women keep going to Greta Garbo movies that make them think they are *supposed* to drown for love, there will be no class equity. And without equity there will be no justice, and without justice there can be no peace. And so Ruthie decided to put Garbo and the rest of it behind her. She stopped going to the pictures entirely, and when at Party meetings Comrade Biro got up and spoke of how carefully you had to watch yourself and the things you wanted, she nodded her approval and felt superior.

It is not quite seven-thirty when Lucio Burke and Dubie Diamond arrive at the playground. They come over the Chestnut Street fence together. Lucio, who is taller, gives Dubie a boost, and then hoists himself up and over easily; Dubie hesitates at the top, straddling the fence as if it were a horse, not quite sure how to make the descent. Finally he jumps down and falls forward, rolling in the ashes. Lucio shakes his head and laughs as Dubie gets up, and then Dubie is laughing also, brushing himself off. Ruthie, who has been staring absently in their direction, tries affecting the blank gaze of the blind, looking straight ahead, but it is too late—they have already seen her seeing them.

Both boys walk toward her, smiles on their faces; they are pleased, Ruthie knows, to find themselves standing next to her in line.

"Hello, Ruthie," says Dubie.

"Dubie," says Ruthie, nodding.

"Hi, Ruthie," says Lucio.

Ruthie smiles a brittle smile.

"You going to bat?" says Dubie.

"You're asking that," says Ruthie, "because I'm a woman."

"I never said anything about women."

"You said something about me," Ruthie tells him. "And I'm a woman, in case you haven't noticed."

"It's just I've never seen you play baseball, is all," Dubie ventures. "I didn't know you liked it."

"That's entirely beside the point."

"If you don't like baseball," says Lucio, "what do you want with a ball?"

"I want to hit it."

"But if you hit it," says Lucio, "you get it."

Ruthie gives him a look. "The point is, if I'd been a man you wouldn't have said anything about my being here, you would have thought it natural I should be trying to hit Bloomberg's ball, wouldn't you?"

Dubie is silent, and Lucio looks down, as if he is ashamed of himself, and finds himself looking at Ruthie's feet. "Nice shoes," he says.

"They're Esther's," she tells him, too quickly.

"They're not baseball shoes, are they?" says Lucio.

"Who says they're not?"

"They've got heels."

Ruthie feels herself blushing, and wills herself to stop. This makes it worse.

"It'll be something if you can hit a ball in shoes like that," says Dubie.

"Yes, it will," says Ruthie. "It will make them think."

"Them?"

"All of them. Even you two."

"Think," says Lucio, looking at Dubie. "That'll be a change."

"Ha," says Dubie, "good one."

Ruthie shakes her head and looks out at the line behind them. There are already nearly a hundred people in it. Most are boys, many with baseball bats. Others have gloves. There is one boy with a snow shovel. Another with something that looks like a butterfly net. But it is not only boys in the line. There are men as well, a threadbare, hangdog look about them, who, having left their homes before first light—as if they had jobs to go to, as if word had arrived of a job coming open in the dead of night—have been wandering around the city aimlessly, and stand in the line because they have nothing else to do, and nothing else to wait for. Near the back of the line is a group of children with tin buckets. Upon first seeing the line, these children concluded that it was a bread line, and ran quickly home for buckets in case soup or milk was being handed out as well. But mostly it is boys who have come to hit the Bloomberg ball, thinking, like Ruthie, that it will be something if they can manage to do that. The sound of cars on Dundas Street can be heard; the city is beginning to wake up. There is not a cloud in the sky. Out on Elizabeth Street a woman in an apron and kerchief hangs the morning wash on a fire escape.

Lucio and Dubie sit down beside Ruthie on the ash-covered pavement. Every few minutes Dubie will look over at Ruthie and then look away, as if she is a statue of a goddess at which it is fatal to look too closely or for too long. Then Lucio will do the same. Ruthie neither reacts to nor acknowledges these stares, treating the two boys, both of whom are three years younger than she, and both of whom she has known since the day they were born, rather like insects that have alighted near her.

Lucio and Dubie are not the first boys to look in her direction. Before them there was Ignatius Au, who lives with his twin brother, Izzy, and his four sisters above his parents' laundromat on Henry Street. Izzy's hand brushed hers one afternoon when Ruthie was in the laundry picking up one of Mr. Gutman's coats, and on the strength of that he asked her out. There was Bloomberg, who allowed his baseball to remain in her hand for an extraordinarily long time before snatching it away. And there was Spinny Weinreb, who insisted on showing her whenever an advertisement appeared in the *Toronto Telegram* for one of his boxing matches. Ruthie allowed Spinny not only to take her out on a date but to kiss her, once, in the balcony at the Rose Theatre while *King Kong* was playing, but then declined to go out with him a second time. Which is what she had intended to do all along. Dating, for Ruthie, is a kind of experiment she uses to test her resolve, her status as a born Communist. It is for this reason that she has managed to reach the age of twenty without ever having gone on a second date. If she never goes on a second date, Ruthie has told herself, she will also avoid a third date. For, as she knows, it is on the third date that things happen. She is determined to stay far away from all those sweaty expectations for as long as she possibly can. Behind her back the boys of the Ward call her a tease and speculate that she may have a thing for girls. But the truth is that she is a beautiful, precise woman whom the boys of the Ward cannot think about asking out without also thinking that she will turn them down. Which is not how Ruthie thinks of herself. Ruthie sees herself as the damsel in a very different kind of story, one in which she goes to a Party meeting and sees *him* sitting there, near the back of the room: bespectacled, serious, unsmiling, a man with callused palms and the thin, tapered fingers of a piano player. A Communist to carry her away.

A little before ten in the morning the Lizzies arrive.

The Lizzies represent the Elizabeth Street playground in the Toronto Junior Baseball League. Even though the team is made up only of boys from the neighbourhood, when the Lizzies play, the people of the Ward come out to watch. And when the boys of the Ward dream their baseball dreams, they do not dream themselves into the skin of the Babe or Gehrig or Greenberg or anyone else whose name everyone will recognize in years to come. But rather into the persons of ordinary schoolboys like themselves. Dubie and Lucio are no different. While watching the Lizzies they'd told each other—while they cheered for boys like Hap Ague, who can throw a ball faster than anyone—that one day it would be *them* on the field. That one day it would be the two of them, rather than Louis Brook and Nathaniel Starkman, turning a double play with the bleachers filled. And then, even when they knew (or thought they knew) that this would never happen to them, that neither of them was Goody Altman and that neither would ever stand under the bright lights at Christie Pits where the Toronto Junior Baseball Championships were held each August, Dubie and Lucio told each other a different story— that they would one day be able to tell their grandchildren what it had been like to watch Bloomberg pitch and, above all, to see the Lizzies win. But that has not happened yet. In the past three seasons the Lizzies have been good, but not quite good enough to make it to the finals. This season it will be different, say people, this time the Lizzies are better than good. This is the year they are good enough. This year, they say, is the year.

The Lizzies begin taking their places on the field. At catcher is Goody Altman. With wavy brown hair and broad shoulders and a badly sunburned nose, Goody is the second-best baseball player the city of Toronto will ever produce. He will go on to play for the Red Sox, playing backup catcher to Johnny Peacock for two seasons before being sent down to the minors and enlisting in the Canadian army, which will send him overseas, where he will lose his right leg. At third is Goody's brother, Mordechai. A sturdily built boy, nineteen years old, Mordechai has short, cropped red hair and watery eyes, and is wearing both a baseball cap *and* a yarmulke. The cap is on his head and the yarmulke is on the cap. He holds them in place with his ungloved hand with ostentatious, unapologetic piety, as if he is daring someone, anyone, but most of all the Nazi thugs who have of late been seen marauding around Kew Beach with swastikas on their shirts, to knock it off.

"Ruthie," calls Goody, as he takes his place behind home plate. "What're you doing here?"

"I expected more of you, Goody," she tells him.

Goody thinks for a moment.

"She means," Dubie tells him, "you wouldn't have asked her if she was a man."

Next to arrive are the Au twins, both of whom are wearing socks so entirely white they seem to glow in the sun. The Au socks have been expertly and excessively bleached the night before by their father—as a message about the treatment all socks receive at the Au Laundromat. With them is Spinny Weinreb, the only boy ever to have kissed Ruthie Nodelman. The fact that she has not expressed the slightest interest in him since has made Spinny worried. Perhaps, he thinks, he is a terrible kisser. When Spinny sees Ruthie he stays as far away from her as possible—on the other side of the field, near first base, which he plants his foot on as if it is the only piece of dry land in the neighbourhood.

In left field is Grief Henderson, whose name, the result of a spelling mistake on his birth certificate, has created in him the ambition to become a magician. Today he is wearing an old black tuxedo and a ragged top hat. Arriving at the playground, he walks straight over to Ruthie.

"What's that?" he asks her.

"Where?" Ruthie says.

"Behind your ear," he says, and pulls out a bouquet of flowers.

"Now if I was a man," she says, unimpressed, "would you do that?"

"Who said anything about a man?"

"How'd you do it?" asks Dubie.

"Secrets," says Grief, "of the magi."

"It's up his sleeve," says Lucio.

Grief wordlessly holds out his arms.

"I guess not," says Lucio.

"And still," says Grief, reaching behind Ruthie's head.

"Here we go," says Ruthie.

"Ta-da," says Grief, pulling a second bouquet out of her ear.

"Enough with the flowers," Ruthie tells him.

In centre field is Vince Bucci, the eldest brother of the three Bucci children, and beside him, in right field, is his younger brother Guido, the fascist—both of whom have just been released from the bakery. Guido stands sullenly in right field, wearing a tight, flour-covered black shirt. A cigarette hangs out the side of his mouth, and he smokes it angrily, as if he is about to eat it.

Bloomberg is the pitcher. He pitches underhand, in the old style. By 1933 almost all major-league pitchers are throwing overhand, bringing their knee up to their chest and firing the ball at the plate as fast and as hard as they can. But there are a few holdouts. A few pitchers who still believe the way to get the ball across the plate is with subterfuge rather than speed. There is Morten Marmorstein of Somerset, New Jersey, who strikes out batters by keeping his back to them until the last minute. There is Hollis Moon, who plays in the Negro leagues down in Kentucky, who stands still as a statue and then tosses the ball up high, in a wide arc. There is Whitey Lippincott, who strikes out batters with a complicated sidearm delivery that gives them the impression that instead of throwing the ball he is going to jump on top of them. And there is Bloomberg, whose weapon is the Bloomberg Special—a devastating pitch consisting mostly of windup.

Bloomberg begins the windup that precedes each Bloomberg Special by windmilling his arm backwards, slowly, as if he is doing the backstroke, until his arm resembles a propeller and he more resembles a biplane than a swimmer—a biplane that has been hit and thrown into a nosedive and is seconds away from crashing into the ground. And even then he does not always let go of the ball. Sometimes, he will hold onto it and his arm will continue to revolve, a sixth and seventh time, and midway through the seventh revolution, most batters find themselves seized by an irresistible desire to swing. When this happens, when Bloomberg sees the batter starting to move, he will let go of the ball, and because the batter was swinging too early, the pitch will get past him. Other times, Bloomberg waits longer. His arm revolves an eighth and a ninth, a tenth, an eleventh, a twelfth, a fifteenth, a twenty-fifth time. On one occasion his arm made ninety-five revolutions before he threw the ball. Such delay has a devastating effect on a batter, who concludes that Bloomberg is never going to throw the ball, or forgets he is up at bat at all. When the pitch finally comes, it comes as a surprise, and the batter looks at it as if it were passing him in a dream, as if the baseball were a figment of his imagination.

Not quite twenty years old, in his last year of eligibility to play in the Toronto Junior League, Bloomberg is wearing his Lizzies uniform, which is black with white pinstripes and has the word LIZZIES across the front in black block letters. He walks into the centre of the playground with the baseball held high over his head, as if it is much heavier than it actually is, as if it is not a baseball at all.

The umpire is Milton Weathervane, whose father changed his name from Weimann the year the bottom fell out of the stock market. A mean, strong boy with a single eyebrow stretching across his forehead, Milton gets into his crouch behind the pitcher and shouts, "PLAY BALL!"

Antonio Bucci, who is first in line despite Meyer Rubin's attempts to oust him, walks to home plate. He picks up the bat—which Bloomberg has supplied—and takes a few practice swings. As he does, a silence drifts over the Elizabeth Street playground. Everyone watches as Antonio—he is small for his twelve years—heaves the heavy bat and steps into the batter's box. Then Bloomberg goes into his windup. His arm goes around once, and then a second time, and after the third revolution Bloomberg releases the pitch. Antonio swings the bat too late, and the ball glances off it, rolling slowly toward third base.

Goody bare-hands the rolling ball, and throws to first.

"Out," calls Milton.

And so it goes. Until Ruthie steps up to bat.

She finds the bat lighter than she expected. She thought it would be heavy, and imagined she would have to ask for assistance in lifting it to her shoulder. But this is not the case. Baseball bats are, she discovers, made to swing. Heavy at the top, light at the bottom. Liable to fall out of one's hands if one is not careful.

Ruthie steps into the batter's box.

Bloomberg blinks his massive eyes and begins his windup. His arm goes around once, twice and then a third time, and at the beginning of each revolution Ruthie tells herself, now, this is when he is going to throw the ball. His arm goes around a fourth and a fifth, a sixth, a seventh and an eighth, and it is then, in the middle of the ninth revolution of Bloomberg's arm, that Ruthie's mind begins to wander. She finds herself looking at the line of people, which now extends well past third base and into the outfield, and thinking, this is what the Revolution will be like. She forgets she is up at bat and begins to imagine the Revolution in the shape of that great line. The people, united. For one thing—not a baseball—for peace. Or justice. Bloomberg's arm is now in the middle of its rotation, still behind his back but beginning its upward motion, passing his hip, the wrist of the hand turning forward. Instead of watching the ball, Ruthie is thinking that, quite possibly, the revolutionary moment—when the proletariat realize they are the proletariat, and therefore capable of bringing about a revolution—could just as well be brought about through a baseball as through anything else—people instead of proletariat, and baseballs instead of bread.

"Strike one," calls Milton.

"No!" shouts Ruthie, when she realizes the ball has gotten by her and is now in Goody's glove. She steps away from the plate and looks down at her shoes. She hits the delicate toe of each shoe—they too are now ash-covered—a single time with the bat, the way she has seen boys do it, and then steps back into the batter's box.

Bloomberg blinks slowly and goes into his windup. His arm goes around a single time and he lets go of the ball, which sails easily past Ruthie.

"Strike two!" calls out Milton.

Suppressing a wild, nearly uncontrollable urge to burst into tears at the unfairness of Bloomberg pitching the ball so quickly, without *any* windup, Ruthie again steps out of the batter's box. Again she taps the toes of her sister's shoes with the bat, but then, just before stepping back into the batter's box, she lets down her hair, shaking it out so that the sun catches its redness as it falls down onto her shoulders.

Bloomberg's huge eyes blink three times, and she winks at him. Let him think about that, thinks Ruthie, recalling the men at Gutman Fur and the way they look at her, and how Mr. Gutman, when he really wants to move a coat, will ask her to let her hair down.

This time Bloomberg's windup begins slowly. To Ruthie it seems for a moment as if he is not pitching at all. As if he, impervious to her charms, is only now waking up after a long nap on the ocean floor. His arm goes around a single time, and Ruthie braces for the pitch that does not come. His arm makes a second revolution and a third, a fourth, and on the fourth revolution Ruthie catches a glimpse of the whiteness of the ball between his fingers. Wait for the ball, she tells herself, wait until you see the white of the ball. And then, as if he knows what she is thinking, Bloomberg smiles. His lips curl back and Ruthie sees his teeth. Meanwhile, Bloomberg's arm is spinning. A fifth, a sixth, a seventh time, then a tenth and an eleventh and a twelfth and a thirteenth, and midway through the thirteenth revolution Ruthie Nodelman, like so many batters before her, is overcome by the urge to swing, and swing she does.

"Strike three!" calls Milton.

The ball is still in Bloomberg's hand.

"Strike three?" says Ruthie. "He didn't throw the ball."

"It doesn't matter," Milton tells her. "A swing is a swing."

"Doesn't he have to throw the ball?"

"Strike three," says Milton, a second time. "Next batter."

"I object," Ruthie tells him. "He didn't throw. A strike is about the ball, not the bat."

"You get one swing," says Milton, "you used it up. You're out."

"You're wrong, Milton," says Goody Altman, taking off his catcher's mask. "The ball's got to cross the plate. Otherwise, it's just Bloomberg standing there and waiting for someone to swing."

"Shut up, Goody," says Milton. "I'm the ump."

"You're only the ump for today," Goody tells him. "If you were really an ump, you wouldn't make a call like that."

"Any more lip from you," Milton tells him, "and you're out."

"For what?" says Goody.

"For grandstanding for some girl."

The line of waiting batters, which had been getting restless, is quiet again. It is watching now, hushed. Anticipating a fight.

"Take it easy," says Mordechai, who has walked over from third base in defence of his brother. "What do the rules say?"

"Rules?" says Spinny. "This is baseball."

"We can know nothing," Mordechai says, "until we know the rules."

"I know one thing," says Milton. "The ump's call is final."

"Is it so written?" asks Mordechai.

"If it ain't written," Milton tells him, "it should be."

"There is no wrong or right," asserts Mordechai, holding his yarmulke in place on top of his baseball cap, "there is only the law. And the law is written."

"Never mind the law," Goody says. "A strike is about the ball, not the bat."

"The batter's got one swing," insists Milton, "and one swing only."

"Ah," says Mordechai, "but is it a strike?"

"If the umpire says it is," says Milton.

"You have the rules?" says Mordechai.

"I don't have them," says Milton, "but I can imagine what they would say."

From the outfield, Little Guido, the fascist, calls in a fascist solution: "It's Bloomberg's ball," he yells, "it's Bloomberg's call."

Bloomberg blinks his magnified eyes and looks at Ruthie. Who does not wait. "Forget it," Ruthie announces. "I'm walking out."

"You can't walk out," Milton says. "Because you've been struck out."

"No, I haven't, and I will," says Ruthie. "I'm not striking out. You can't strike me out, because I'm walking out. I'm on strike."

"There are no strikes," says Milton, "in baseball."

"You think this is right?" says Ruthie, speaking loudly now, to the rest of the line, giddily imagining a huge demonstration over the injustice of the call. "This isn't about baseball," she says. "This is about justice. Without justice there can be no peace, and without peace we have nothing. Is that what you want? I say, is that what you want?" When there is no response, Ruthie throws down the bat, huffs and walks carefully on her high heels toward third base. There she stands, fierce and unsmiling, in protest.

Dubie, who is next in line, walks to home plate and picks up the bat.

"Don't do it," Ruthie calls. "Walk out, Dubie."

Dubie for a moment imagines himself standing under a *chuppa* with beautiful Ruthie, and Ruthie smiling, in a wedding dress—and for a moment he thinks about it. He sees himself giving the speech at their wedding, explaining how it all started when he refused to go up to bat. But the next instant he thinks, there is not likely to be another chance like the Bloomberg ball, which, when he heard about it, seemed like an answer to the most secret of his secret prayers: a chance to do something different. A chance to do something that everyone would talk about after, a way of becoming someone else, a way of *evolving*. "Sorry, Ruthie," Dubie says, and steps into the batter's box.

Bloomberg blinks and goes into his windup.

And that is when the bird lands.

Some, later, will say it was a large crow.

Others will say it was a bird flown down from the wilds of Northern Ontario, where there are animals still to be named.

Still others will say it was a buzzard.

Dubie will say it was a cross between an American eagle and something else, something an American eagle should have kept its hands off in the first place.

The bird's white head is bald and domelike, like a bulbous growth balanced, precariously, at the end of a long stick. Its mouth has lips. After landing, the bird takes a long time getting settled, slowly folding and unfolding its great wings behind its back, then poking its yellow beak under each wing, as if checking for unseemly odours. Its feet look not like a bird's claws, but soft, like the fleshy fingers of a fat man. At the end of each thick finger is a long green fingernail, clearly, almost ostentatiously displayed, as if it has perched itself in such a way as to show its fingernails to best advantage. But its eyes are what everyone will talk about after. They are not at all the black, unseeing eyes of a bird; they are like the eyes of a human being, eyes with pupils and irises and eyelids, that sit in the front of the bird's face.

When he sees the bird, Bloomberg stops his windup.

"What," he says, "is that?"

The bird looks at Bloomberg, and Bloomberg looks back through his pebble-thick glasses, blinking in that slow, undersea manner of his. The bird does not move.

"Dubie," says Milton, "give that bird a kick."

"Good luck," says Dubie.

Milton tries a different tack. "Spinny," he calls, "get rid of it."

Spinny takes a step toward the bird, and the bird immediately turns to look at him. This stops Spinny in his tracks. He takes a step back and says, "Get outta here, you bird."

The bird does not move.

"Maybe it doesn't speak English," says Ignatius Au. He says something to it in Mandarin.

The bird does not move.

"What'd you say?" says Bloomberg.

"I told it to get out of here," says Ignatius, looking at the bird. "I guess," he says, "it doesn't speak Chinese either."

"Birds can't talk," Izzy Au tells his brother.

"Who said anything about talking?" says Ignatius. "They have ears."

"This is true," says Dubie, who has recently reached the end of his third reading of Darwin's *The Descent of Man*. "Birds have ears, it's one of the characteristics of the genus."

"Maybe," ventures Bloomberg, looking pale, "it ain't a bird."

"Not a bird?" says Milton. "That's crazy."

"It's got wings," says Goody.

"So do a lot of things," says Dubie.

"Dubie," says Milton. "Shut up."

"Throw the ball at it, Bloomberg," Spinny calls out.

"Here," says Bloomberg, tossing the baseball to Spinny, "you throw it."

"You do it." Spinny throws the ball back, quickly, as if he is afraid of catching something from touching it.

Bloomberg blinks and then, without windup, tosses the ball weakly toward the bird.

The ball bounces once and rolls forward, stopping just short of the bird. The bird stands up, waddles over and sits down on it.

"Great," says Milton.

"When I said throw the ball," says Spinny, "I meant *throw* the ball."

"Now what do we do?" asks Bloomberg.

"What we gotta do," says Milton authoritatively, "is co-operate."

Milton is now firmly in charge of the situation. He possesses no particular authority, being neither the oldest boy (Mordechai Altman is nearly twenty) nor the best baseball player (Goody Altman) nor the smartest (Ignatius Au, the previous year, memorized over six hundred telephone numbers), but Milton has started to think of himself as in charge because he was chosen by Bloomberg to be umpire.

"So," says Milton, "any ideas?"

Little Guido, the fascist, suggests they try scaring the bird. Dubie gives him the bat and Little Guido waves it, threateningly, in the general direction of the bird. It does not move. He tries it again, this time saying he was not kidding the first time. The bird does not move. Guido gives Bloomberg the bat and goes back to smoking his cigarette, and Izzy asks if the bird's sitting on the ball means the bird is a girl. If the bird were a man, Ruthie tells them, they would have no trouble throwing the ball at it. Dubie then observes, smiling at her (because he is thinking that she is angry at him for not joining her protest), that there are several kinds of birds where it is the man bird who sits on the eggs. Ruthie says that maybe the boys should think about that for a change. Vince Bucci, who has come in from left field to get a better look at the bird, yells at it in Italian, and Ignatius Au asks him what he said. Vince tells him that he told the bird he'd had sex with its mother. When Goody observes that this is a very strange thing to say, Milton says all dagos have a thing for their mothers. Izzy wonders how this is done. Milton suggests he ask Vince. Dubie says the bird looks like a cross between an American eagle and something an American eagle should've kept its hands off in the first place. Nevertheless, the bird does not move. Milton calls it a *schmuck*, and lights a cigarette and throws it. It lands to the left of the bird, who watches it burn down. Ignatius recalls the story of Saint Patrick, who led the snakes out of Ireland by playing on a pipe, and Izzy points out that this is not a snake but a bird that is sitting on their baseball. Still, says Goody, it's an idea, and all the boys join in singing a verse of "Buddy Can You Spare a Dime?" The line is dwindling, many in it having assumed that the ball has been given away.

"Bloomberg," Milton says finally, "somebody's gotta do it."

Bloomberg looks at the bat in his hands.

"Teach that bird," Milton tells him.

"It's only a bird, after all," says Bloomberg nervously. "I think." With the bat in his hands he takes a single step in the direction of the bird, then stops. He turns and looks at Milton. "I don't want to," he says.

"You have to," says Milton. "It's your ball." He gestures at the shrinking line, which is now a quarter the size it once was. "Wait much longer and nobody'll be here at all."

Bloomberg looks as if he's going to cry. "I just wanted to do something," he says, partly to Milton and partly to those still standing in the line, partly to the other boys, partly to Ruthie and partly to the bird.

"You want to do something?" says Milton, cocking his head in the direction of the bird. "Do something."

Bloomberg takes a second step. Then, very quickly, two more steps, his thick glasses flashing in the afternoon sunlight. The bird is looking right at him, and now Bloomberg is close enough to swipe at it at least, to frighten it away, but he does not. He takes yet another step, then he raises the bat over his head. It seems he does not want to simply scare the bird; he wants to kill it, to kill it for ruining his baseball game. He is going to swing the bat and hit the bird's head as if it were a baseball. Bloomberg is still trying to *do* something. But then, just as he leans forward and into his swing, the bird leaps up, pushing off against the baseball with both its feet, sending the ball rolling toward the first-base line, where Lucio is standing.

The bird rears up, unfurling its massive wings, and lifts off into the sky.

"You did it, Bloomberg," says Milton, clapping him on the back. "You did it! Now *that* was a Bloomberg Special."

There is a brief cheer from those left standing in the line.

"You think it was a bird, after all?" says Bloomberg.

"Shut up, Bloomberg," says Milton. "What else would it be?"

"Maybe it was the ball," says Dubie. "The bird thought it was an egg."

"Let's play some baseball," says Milton. "Let's get on with it."

Lucio is about to throw the ball back to Bloomberg when he notices Ruthie looking up at the sky.

"Look," she says.

It's the bird. It's coming back. Heading toward them. It swoops down and flies the width of the playground at eye level, as if it is a dive-bomber plane. Everyone except Bloomberg hits the dirt. At the last second, just when it seems the bird is about to crash into and through Bloomberg's glasses, it pulls up. And as it does, a single one of its green fingerlike claws extends, lifting the glasses off Bloomberg's face. Then it soars up. Milton covers his eyes. Mordechai holds on, with both hands, to his yarmulke, and Dubie screams because he believes the bird has plucked Bloomberg's head clean off his shoulders, like an old apple.

"My glasses," wails Bloomberg, horrified, touching the place where the green claw scratched him. There is a thin gash between his eyes, and it bleeds narrow and red. "My glasses," he says a second time, and looks up at the sky. "My glasses."

The bird is flying up, climbing higher, and is seconds away from never being seen again when suddenly it is hit by a baseball. The baseball strikes one of the bird's great wings, which throws it off balance just enough to cause it to drop the glasses. The glasses fall to the ash-grey playground blacktop, and only after the boys are sure the bird is not coming back, only after they have all run forward to get the glasses (finding them unbroken), do they understand that it was Lucio Burke who threw the ball.

"That's one hell of an arm," says Goody quietly. They stand silent, stunned.

"You knocked it out of the sky," Dubie says, after a moment.

"It dropped the glasses," says Ignatius Au. "But it kept going."

"It was some throw," says Goody. "You could be the next Bloomberg."

"Out of the sky," says Dubie again, as pleased as if he had thrown the ball himself.

Only then do they realize Bloomberg is gone. Without his glasses. Without his baseball. Without a word.

"So I guess," says Milton (who is still, somehow, in charge of the situation), handing Lucio the glasses and baseball, "these are yours."

"I don't want the glasses."

"You want the baseball, you get the glasses," says Milton, looking at the glasses distastefully. Seeing he has no choice, Lucio puts them into his pocket.

Soon the Elizabeth Street playground is empty. Lucio and Dubie walk home, and later that night—after the excitement has died down, after Lucio has taken Bloomberg's glasses out of his pocket and deposited them in his sock drawer, after he and Dubie have told and retold the story of the bird's landing—Lucio takes out the garbage. This is a chore he does every night, after dinner. He goes down the fire escape to the cinder alley behind the house, where the trash cans are kept, and is surprised to find Ruthie Nodelman there, sitting on an over-turned milk carton.

"Hello," she says, lighting a cigarette in the darkness.

"Ruthie?" says Lucio, a little frightened.

"I've been waiting for you," says Ruthie.

"You have?"

"That was one great throw today."

"I didn't know you smoked," says Lucio.

"I do a lot of things you don't know," says Ruthie. "By the way, if you're ever looking for someone to take to the pictures, look me up."

"Look you up?" says Lucio. "You live right here."

"That's right," Ruthie says.

"Like on a date?"

"How about tomorrow?" she says. "Six-thirty, pick me up at Gutman's."

Lucio is unable to speak.

"Fine," says Ruthie, standing up to crush out the cigarette with the high heel of Esther's fancy shoe. "I'll see you then." For a moment she looks closely at Lucio in the half-light of the cinder alley. "You know," she tells him, "Lucio Burke, there's more to you than you think."

TWO

LUCIO GETS UP EARLY the next morning to work the first shift at Michelangelo's Garage. His has been a restless night. A night filled with uneasy dreams of Ruthie, and of menacing birds overhead. Ruthie, too, has been dreaming. Different dreams, but dreams involving Lucio. This is not the first night Lucio and Ruthie have dreamt of each other, however.

Ruthie has known Lucio from the beginning, having been present at his birth, which occurred upon the kitchen table in the Burke household some seventeen years before. Lucio was the third of three children to be born that day, on that same kitchen table, and he slid into the world just hours after Dubie Diamond and Lucio's cousin Dante. Ruthie was three years old, and was present at all three births because her mother, Sadie Nodelman, delivered all the babies.

The Burkes live next door to the Nodelmans on one side and the Diamonds on the other, in the middle of three adjoining houses that, in addition to being identical, are physically linked by a single veranda, a kind of narrow concrete bridge with a black railing and a set of stairs at either end. When they were children, Lucio and Dubie would race back and forth along the veranda, trying to get from one end to the other as quickly as possible. In summertime, to do so involved circum-navigating the various people and pieces of furniture on the veranda. If they began in front of Dubie's parents' front door, the boys had to get around, first, a large green plastic-covered sofa. Dubie's father, Asher, had insisted on the sofa being placed on the veranda because it had been presented to him, years before, by the Halwood Brush and Broom Company, in appreciation of his having sold five thousand brooms. Asher had transported this piece of furniture to Beverley Street at great expense when they'd moved into the house, and therefore it had to be treated with great deference, even by six-year-old boys racing from one end of the veranda to the other. The next obstacle past the sofa was Lucio's *nonna,* who was perpetually sitting out on the veranda; she was against the idea of exercise in any form, and believed the worst thing you could be was out of breath, particularly if you were young. Lucio and Dubie learned how to flatten themselves up against the railing as they passed in front of the Burke house, so Nonna could not grab them. Once past Nonna they were on to the final leg of the race, which required crossing in front of the Nodelman house.

This was the trickiest part, because there were always more people in front of the Nodelman doorway than anywhere else on the veranda. There were, first, Ruthie's parents, Abe and Sadie, ensconced in semi-collapsible beach chairs they had purchased some ten years before in the Better Living Building at the Canadian National Exhibition for a fraction of their retail price. These beach chairs had big, wide arms that were far longer than the arms of the couple who sat in them, arms that stuck out like wooden clotheslines and that had to be avoided to get to the end of the veranda. Then there was

Esther, Ruthie's older sister, always with some catalogue or fashion magazine spread out before her. And at the end of the veranda, Ruthie herself, with a book in her hands, her back propped up against the Nodelman door.

Ruthie was eleven when she began dreaming of Lucio. This was because of a flying leap he took one afternoon from the long veranda. All that week Lucio and Dubie had been jumping off the veranda in a similar manner, their arms outstretched, yelling the name "Lindbergh." Then, one Saturday afternoon while Ruthie was babysitting, Lucio lost his footing as he leapt. He hung momentarily in the air, said "Lindbergh" and fell to the ground with his hands out in front of him. Ruthie screamed and ran down and knelt next to him; he was howling, oblivious of her, his wrists bent in the wrong direction and his face twisted in pain, writhing on the dirty pavement. After what seemed like a long time, he was able to stand, and together he and Ruthie walked to Toronto General on University Avenue.

"Your mother," Ruthie told him later, when they were in the examination room at the hospital, "is gonna kill me."

"I'm sorry," Lucio said.

"Fat lot of good that does me," said Ruthie.

Lucio was sitting on an examination table with his hands stretched out in front of him palms up, as if they'd been knocked unconscious. "I'll say it was my fault," he told her. "That you told me to not do it, but I did anyway. I'll be responsible."

"Responsible?" said Ruthie. "You're eight."

"So?" said Lucio.

Ruthie shook her head. "You don't know anything," she told him. "You think you do, but you don't."

"I know something," said Lucio.

"I remember when I was eight," said Ruthie. "I don't think

you really know anything until you're ten. Ten is when every-thing changes. You'll see I know what I'm talking about when you're ten."

The doctor arrived. "Name?" he asked.

"Lucio Burke."

The doctor looked up from the clipboard.

"In Italian," said Ruthie helpfully, "it means light."

"No," said Lucio. "*Luce* means light, Lucio's just a name."

"It comes from light," insisted Ruthie. "And that's the same."

"You the sister?" the doctor asked.

"She's the babysitter," said Lucio.

"You've done a great job," the doctor told her.

Ruthie hung her head and said nothing. The doctor went to work. Lucio was still sitting on the examination table, wait-ing for the plaster to dry, when his mother arrived.

"Lucio!" cried Francesca Burke, coming into the room. "I was scared to death." She was a tiny, thin woman in a dark green dress; she was a seamstress and had just finished working the early shift at Modern Dresses. Francesca had stopped wear-ing makeup with the death of Lucio's father years before, and although there was a certain gauntness to her face, there was also something striking about her, a mysteriousness that made other people look at her slightly longer than they might have otherwise. Her dark hair was pulled up tight but looked soft, like black wool that had been stored away for some unofficial winter, precariously, as if it threatened at any moment to let itself out of its bun, to cascade over her pale skin.

"Ma," said Lucio, "I'm fine."

The doctor came back into the room and, after setting eyes on Francesca for the first time, forgot for a moment what he had made up his mind to say to her.

"I'm his mother," she told him, looking at the two casts on Lucio's arms, both of which extended nearly to his shoulders.

"Look, I don't know where you're from or what you people do, but children shouldn't be playing unsupervised," said the doctor, recovering himself.

"He wasn't," she replied, looking at Ruthie.

"If I see him here again," said the doctor, "I'll have to fill out a report."

"It won't happen again," said Francesca.

"See that it doesn't," said the doctor. As he was leaving the room, he added, "You've been warned."

When he was out of the room, Ruthie burst into tears.

"It was my idea," Lucio told his mother. "Ruthie told me not to, but I did."

Francesca looked at them both and said nothing. They walked home in silence, and that night Ruthie had her first dream about Lucio Burke. In it, he was falling forward, arms outstretched, and she was watching him, her hands glued to the wide arms of her parents' cheap beach chairs.

Directly across the street from the Burke and Nodelman and Diamond houses on Beverley Street is the Canadian National Institute for the Blind. This is a grey-brick, three-storey Gothic building constructed by the Toronto Benevolent Society near the end of the previous century. It gives the impression that the architect, having been informed that he was creating a refuge for the blind, went about designing a structure that would leave passersby with the impression that the blind were planning to go to war against the rest of the world. There are battlements and turrets, and a series of ventilation shafts resembling the minute openings one finds in the walls of forts, that are big enough only to fit the mouth of a rifle. There is no moat but, as if to make up for it, as if to imply that a moat would not have been a bad idea, there is a rocky granite path extending from the front doors to the sidewalk, like a drawbridge. In the mornings the doors of the College streetcars open and the blind come down Beverley Street, looking preoccupied and sleepy and bored, their white canes clicking on the sidewalk. In early afternoon light it is possible to look out the bay window of the Burke house and see into the windows of the institute. It is a world unto itself. Blind babies touching their mothers' faces with their little hands. Old men, the newly blind, learning again how to tie their shoes and cut their meat.

Next to the institute is St. Patrick's School, which Lucio once attended, for grades one through eight. This is a low-ceilinged, single-storey grey building surrounded on all sides by a concrete yard and then a high chain-link fence, which, if you licked it during the winter, never failed to attach to your tongue. Fence-licking was a practice vigorously discouraged by the nuns and priests who taught at the school, but with little effect. Ruthie, who had gone to the public school down the street and therefore looked on the St. Patrick's kids with unspecified disdain, told Lucio and Dubie that once a little girl who'd got her tongue stuck to the fence had silently frozen to death, unable to speak or even make a sound. By morning she was frozen hard, said Ruthie, with her tongue still attached to the fence.

"That's not true," said Dubie, who was frightened.

"Isn't it?" said Ruthie. "Are you sure?"

"I'm not sure," said Lucio.

"Whether you're sure or not," said Ruthie, "you can still hear her."

"I can't," said Lucio. "I can't hear a thing."

"I thought you said you believed in ghosts," said Ruthie.

"I *do*," said Lucio. "But I still can't *hear* her."

The next day Ruthie told the boys she had made the whole thing up. "There's no girl," she told them, "and there's no ghost—there's no such thing as ghosts."

"I knew it," said Dubie.

"Still," said Lucio, listening, "she could be out there."

"Shut up," said Dubie, who had gone from being scared to being relieved, and now had returned to being scared. "Don't be a *schmuck*."

That night Ruthie had her second dream about Lucio Burke. In it, Lucio had his tongue stuck to the fence and was screaming. Ruthie told him repeatedly that it was not happening.

Lucio dreams of Ruthie also. But his are different dreams. What Lucio dreams of are Ruthie's breasts.

Because he is coming of age in the Depression, the annual catalogue of the Timothy Eaton Company, which arrives each March, has shaped Lucio's imagination. He, like countless boys across Canada, has peered at the advertisements for women's underwear. Up until the spring of 1930, this meant corsets of all shapes and sizes: lightly boned ("for the early part of a lady's day"), unboned ("for bathing at the seaside"), elasticized ("for the equestrian"), and made of jersey ("perfect for riding a velocipede"). And because the corset was so sturdy and self-sufficient a garment, it was often pictured in sober watercolours, disembodied and floating in the middle of the catalogue pages. Still, Canadian boys found cause to linger there. The catalogue that Lucio opened in 1930, however, was a very different matter, for this was the year when the uppermost part of the corset detached and made itself known as the brassiere. Lucio Burke was never the same.

The new garment, readers were informed, was produced by the Corset Company of New York, New York (manufacturers of fine undergarments and rubber products since 1817), which offered customers, among other things, a choice of cup sizes: A, B, C, D and E. When Lucio opened the catalogue that year, therefore, he saw not the expected line of free-standing water-colour corsets, but photographs of fitted brassieres, next to which were photographs of women. These women in the brassiere section were fully clothed, but their photographs had been suggestively placed in such close proximity to the photographs of the brassieres as to make it clear that each of the women had on a brassiere *under* the clothes she was wearing—and that under the brassieres the women possessed breasts that corresponded to one of the brassiere sizes. These pictures sparked a number of debates across Canada, between boys like Lucio and Dubie, having to do with breast size. However much the topic might have been broached previously, it was not until the advent of the Eaton's Spring Catalogue of 1930 that Canadian men were provided with a standardized measurement. Lucio, for his part, found himself looking at the catalogue and imagining the moment when the pictures were taken. What must it be like to be the photographer? You would have to be concerned with how to take the best picture, of course, but also necessarily, with the question of whether the girl was wearing the brassiere the catalogue claimed she was wearing. The photographer would have to see for himself. He would have to put down his camera and check, with his own eyes, that the girl was wearing the right brassiere.

In the dream that Lucio dreams about Ruthie that same night she surprised him by the garbage cans, he is standing on the long veranda in front of the Nodelman door. What he is doing in front of the door, he does not know. He does not knock on the door, but it seems he has just done so and is waiting for an answer. When it does not come, he turns to walk down the Nodelman stairs, and that is when he sees Ruthie. She is walking up the steps, toward him. Lucio then discovers he is holding a camera. He does not own a camera, and does not know he is holding a camera when the dream begins, but now he is holding a camera and Ruthie is walking toward him in a sheer, tight-fitting blue top. That is when he understands that he is supposed to take her picture. As if on cue, Ruthie removes the pale kerchief from around her neck, and is about to lift up her blouse when she stops and asks Lucio if he would make her do this if she were a man.

Which is when Lucio wakes up, wide awake and erect. And that is *always* a problem. Because Lucio sleeps in the same room with his *nonna*. He and his grandmother have, for as long as he is able to remember, slept in identical twin beds on opposite sides of the room. He has always had the worse of the two beds; on his side of the room the ceiling slopes down so much that, when he is lying in his bed, he can lean forward and press his nose against it. This sloping ceiling has caused him a great deal of concern, but never more so than when he was seven years old, and he would become frightened by the sound of animals crawling across the roof. Because the ceiling was so close, it would seem to him as if the animal were crawling across his face. He would wake up in the night and scream, thinking that whatever it was was about to fall through the roof and land in his bed.

When this happened, Nonna would wake up and reassure him by telling him that, if something did fall through the roof, they would just eat it for dinner, like the three little pigs did.

"But the pigs don't eat the wolf," Lucio would say.

"Never mind," Nonna would tell him. "Take a look at the story. The wolf comes down the chimney, into a pot of water."

"But they don't eat him," says Lucio.

"What you think, that the pigs got the pot just for fun?"

"Well," Lucio tells her, "you can't eat a wolf, it's like a raccoon."

"You eat rabbits. What's so big about a raccoon?"

"That's disgusting."

"*Bo*, disgusting—you got it so good. In the old country I'd have a party if my *nonna* gave me a dog to eat."

And sooner or later he would be asleep.

But things are not so simple in the summer of 1933, when Lucio finds himself dreaming of Ruthie's breasts. This night there is no getting back to sleep.

At six he gives up and gets out of bed. He dresses quietly in the semi-darkness of the morning and leaves the house just as the sun is coming up. He walks west along College Street, where a Toronto radial car, the first of the day, comes out of the west carrying people from places as far north as Newmarket. A black Durant, new and clean, its windows opened all the way, passes, going in the opposite direction.

Michelangelo's Garage, where Lucio works, is located at the intersection of College and Clinton streets, in the part of the city where most of the Italians live and the cheapest boarding houses are. Nearly all the boarders in the Clinton houses are male, unskilled labourers from the south of Italy who have come to Canada to work laying bricks or spreading tar on roads or digging ditches. After a few years they will return to Italy, give the money they've saved to their mothers or wives and come back again to America (which includes both Canada and all of South America). There are only two women who live on Clinton Street in the summer of 1933, the first being Lucio's Aunt Carmella, who with Lucio's Uncle Angelo—his mother's younger brother—runs a boarding house at the southernmost end of the street. As with many of the houses on Clinton, the bottom floor of Angelo's boarding house—the floor where the boarders live—has no blinds and no doors, the doors having been removed years before by other boarders for firewood. Angelo and Carmella and Lucio's cousin, Dante, live on the top floor, with a thick deadbolt behind the door that leads up to their apartment. The second woman on Clinton Street is Mrs. Greico, Carmella's blind mother, who is confined to a wheelchair because of her diabetes and lives with her five unmarried sons—Primo (the eldest), Secondo (not quite the eldest), Scevola (who is left-handed), Tommaso (the skeptic of the family) and Quintillano (the youngest). The Greicos live next door to Angelo and Carmella, in the same house in which they have been living for as long as any of the brothers can remember, back to when theirs was one of two houses on Clinton Street. Although Carmella moved into the house next door when she married Angelo, the Greico brothers still regard him as a relative newcomer to the street, and still speak of the day when Nonna and her two children first came to Toronto some thirty years ago as if it were something that had just happened.

Michelangelo knew Nonna from the old country. He had heard she was living alone in New York, with two children. Thinking of her only as the girl he had known years before— the girl he had never quite been able to speak to—he had written her, impetuously, telling her to come to Toronto, where he was a rich man. She had accepted, and Michelangelo had met her, with Francesca and Angelo in tow, at the train station and taken them all to the house on Clinton Street. As they walked through the streets, Nonna was amazed. There was not a single tenement. Toronto was no city of tenements. However small, however rickety or dingy the houses, they would be better, thought Nonna, than the tenements of New York. Although it was nearly ten at night when Michelangelo delivered them, the Greico family was awake, crowded around a wobbly wooden table and making paper flowers. When a paper flower had been completed, the Greico brother who was responsible for it presented it to Carmella for inspection; if it passed, Carmella deposited the flower into a small white sack that was tied to the side of her mother's wheelchair. When Nonna walked in that night, Carmella was in the process of goffering a stray petal, and in order to do this had the flower in her mouth, as if she were about to eat it. After he saw her that night, Angelo liked to say, it was only a matter of time before they were married.

But there are more than boarding houses on Clinton Street. There are other houses, half finished or barely started, belonging to men who plan one day to bring their families to Canada. These houses are for the most part only basements, with tarps for roofs, and cinder floors. On Sundays the men who own them can be seen in their backyards, turning over the soil, planting and watering. This is the one thing that all the houses have in common, no matter how picked over their insides. Their backyards have been transformed into tiny fertile provinces, growing tomatoes and garlic, onions, *lattuga romana*, radicchio, green peas and snow peas and the hairy, sweet *tortarello* cucumbers that come from Bari and are really a kind of melon. On Sundays, when it is illegal in Toronto for any man to do any work, these dirty men come out of their dirty houses at first light, and can be seen driving sticks into the ground for the tomatoes, and laying down old two-by-fours in the soil to make walking in the garden easy, even after rain.

Lucio has worked at Michelangelo's Garage for three years, ever since the summer he turned fourteen and his mother tried to go on welfare. He knows the job is a form of social security, a way for Michelangelo, a rich man by this time, to support his mother and Nonna, who, despite their endless sewing, are never quite able to make ends meet. Michelangelo is a stocky, bald man with hair on the backs of his hands, and a wide grey moustache. He was among the first to leave Italy in the previous century, and before the Depression he was a *padrone*, which is how he made his money in the new world. He had an arrangement with a steamship company in Naples: the steamship company sold tickets on the condition that the men who bought them worked at whatever jobs Michelangelo found for them in Toronto; in return, these men were required to give half their wages to Michelangelo, who in turn gave half to the steamship company. The way Michelangelo saw it, everyone got what he wanted, particularly Michelangelo, who got a little more than everyone else as a result of the arrangement.

Like most Italians at the time, Michelangelo thought of himself as being not from a country but from a town. His town was Mondorio, the same town where Nonna had grown up, which was how Lucio got the job at the garage. He and Nonna (and, by extension, Lucio) were *paesani*, neighbours, which meant that Michelangelo would do anything for Nonna and anyone related to her, while at the same time he was ready to cheat and exploit and refuse the slightest consideration to anyone from any other little town anywhere else in Italy. But in 1929, when the Depression hit, Canada closed its doors to new immigrants and, rich as Michelangelo had become, he needed a new line of work. So he bought an old farmhouse, installed gas pumps at the curbside, put up a sign saying MICHELANGELO'S GARAGE and rented the adjoining barn to bootleggers, who were always of a certain class and always dressed impeccably, as if they worked at the stock exchange on Bay Street. Other than collecting rent, Michelangelo had nothing to do with them. As far as he was concerned, he was running a gas station. He collected rent, looked the other way and that was that; their business was their business, and he never bought a single thing from them. Still, appearances had to be kept up, which was where Lucio and Dante came in—they worked the pumps. Every Saturday morning and every day after school, and every day in each summer since, Lucio has walked west, to Clinton Street, to pump gas.

As he is on his way to the garage the morning after being met by Ruthie down by the trash cans, Lucio passes Altman's Deli, where inside he sees Goody and Mordechai. The brothers are behind the counter, busy in white aprons and hats. Lucio knows he is early for his shift at the garage, and decides to stop in for an egg on a bagel.

The deli is full, as it always is early in the day, with two kinds of people. The first are the men wearing overcoats and dark suits despite the heat, eating breakfast quickly, their elbows propped up on black briefcases. The second are the men in old clothes, with suitcases. These men, Lucio knows, are on their way not to work but to collect their rations at the unemployment office. The first group eats eggs, or bagels and cream cheese, orange juice, coffee; the second group orders coffee and a single doughnut, nursing both for as long as possible before it is time to go and stand outside the office on Teraulay Street to get their handouts. Like the men in the dark suits, these men with their threadbare suitcases know that it is a matter of getting up early, that if they arrive in the middle of the day there will be nothing left.

Lucio stands at the counter. He orders and then asks Goody about Bloomberg.

"Nobody's seen him," says Goody. "Don't even know which way he went. I was looking at the bird."

"He was there one minute," says Mordechai, breaking Lucio's egg onto the grill. "Then he's gone."

"You ask me," says Goody, "he's *meshuga*—first with giving away the baseball. The guy's gotta be a little unscrewed to do that. Then with the bird. He didn't like that bird. I can tell you that."

"He thought it was after him," says Mordechai. "I saw the way he was looking." He flips Lucio's egg and with his other hand lifts a basket of doughnuts out of the deep fryer.

"I gotta tell you," says Goody. "That was some throw."

Lucio shrugs.

"No, really," says Goody. "It's not everybody can throw like that."

"It was lucky," says Lucio.

"Luck," says Goody, "is for *schmucks*."

"What's that supposed to mean?" asks Mordechai.

"You should think about trying out," Goody tells him.

"For the Lizzies?"

"Why not?" says Goody.

Mordechai puts Lucio's sandwich in a bag and hands it to him while Goody rings up the bill. Lucio pays, then turns and is walking toward the door when suddenly it shatters. He covers his face, bringing the bag up in front of him. From outside on the sidewalk there is the sound of a woman getting knocked down and screaming. Then there is nothing. Lucio uncovers his face and sees two boys, one taller than the other, running across the street to the other side of College. The taller of the two—a boy wearing overalls, with closely cropped brown hair—has a limp and an oval face like an egg. Lucio watches him run off down Palmerston Avenue, and then he is gone, ducking, he guesses, into a house or a side alley. Inside the deli, the customers have their heads under the tables. Lucio sees a large stone on the floor with a thick rope around it. The only ones who seem unfazed are Goody and Mordechai. They run out the door and stand on the street, ready for a fight.

"Lucio," calls Mordechai, "did you see them?"

Lucio shakes his head and watches as Goody comes back in and picks the stone up, shaking off the glass and turning it around in his hands. The stone is dark grey and a good fifteen pounds. About the size of a large melon. Goody turns the stone and Lucio sees that something has been painted on its underside. He thinks at first it is a letter, or a set of initials, but then sees it's a swastika.

"Five minutes," says Mordechai. "That's all I'd need."

"Then what?" says Goody.

"Feh," says Mordechai. "Would you stand for it, Lucio?"

Lucio looks at the stone. "I don't know," he says. "I'm not Jewish."

"What's that supposed to mean?"

"Nothing," says Lucio. "I'm just saying."

"Can I get some service here?" says a man at the cash register.

Goody puts down the stone and goes over to the register. Mordechai goes back to the grill, on which a blackened egg sits smoking. Lucio walks out of the deli, but not before he feels the same shaking in his knees, the queasiness in the pit of his stomach, that he always feels when faced with the prospect of violence. He pauses outside and takes a deep breath. Thinking he is going to vomit, he drops the bag with the bagel in it to the street, and watches as a tattered man who has been begging for pennies outside the deli shuffles over to pick it up.

The man has a horsey, weather-beaten face with the puffiness around the eyes of an alcoholic, and a tight, tiny mouth that reminds Lucio of Father Choffe, the priest who was his grade eight teacher at St. Patrick's. A dark-haired man with a tiny bald circle at the top of his head, Father Choffe spoke with a thick Québécois accent and beat the boys in the class with his cedar cane. The blows came hard and fast, and then the boy being beaten would stand up, his face flushed, and return to his seat. He did not cry. Not if he could help it. Lucio believed this was Father Choffe's goal, to make the boy who had misbehaved break down. No matter how many times he watched the other boys stand up, the fear of being beaten himself did not go away. He could not imagine the shame, the terror of waiting to be hit. That it would hurt him, he knew. That he had nothing to fear from the pain, this he knew also. Still, he did not trust himself to walk to the front of the classroom without falling to his knees and begging for mercy. In bed at night, with Nonna snoring in the bed on the other side of the room, Lucio listened to the animals on the roof and attempted to steel himself, saw himself walking to the front of the room, keeping his face as still as possible. When it happened, he told himself, he would be ready. But it did not happen. Lucio graduated from St. Patrick's and, because his mother could not afford to send him to St. Michael's, the Catholic high school, he attended Harbord Collegiate with Dubie and the rest of the boys in his neighbourhood. Just like that, he escaped. But rather than feeling relieved, he felt an even more intense shame, which he blamed on his mother. He believed that she had turned him into a delicate, fearful creature. And that was the way Lucio entered high school—fourteen and uncertain about himself, a boy who thought of himself as not quite part of the world, whose body felt, even at night, entirely untouched.

THREE

WHEN HE ARRIVES at the garage, Lucio unlocks the pumps, sitting down between them and trying to steady himself, and in the quiet of the morning hears the soft rumble of the cows walking north. Soon the cows begin to pass, walking up Clinton on their way to the slaughterhouse on Bloor Street. Sombre and unhurried, with wide, white eyes that make Lucio think they know where they are going. Men with guns march alongside the animals; at the front of the line a great black bull, the Judas cow, its horns clipped.

Working at the garage, Lucio knows, is the best of jobs. He gets ten cents an hour, which, in a year when half the city is out of work, is an exorbitant amount of money. Still, it is never without a twinge of resentment that he shows up for work. This is because, before working at the garage, he was employed by his next-door neighbour, Asher Diamond, Dubie's father. Lucio worked one day a week, Saturday; he was Asher's *Shabbes goy*, and he *loved* working for him.

"There's nothing to it," Asher said, when he came over to offer the job to Lucio. "Turning on lights, lighting candles, opening doors, turning on ovens—that kind of thing. The

Torah says we can't work on the Sabbath, and so we need a *goy*, someone who's not Jewish, to do the work. That's where you come in—you'd be my *Shabbes goy*."

"So," said Francesca, "he waits on you?"

"It's not like that," said Asher. "He helps out, is all."

"If it's not one thing with the Jews," said Nonna, "it's another."

"You'll pay me?" said Lucio.

"Of course," Asher said. "It's a job, but it's more than that—it's a mitzvah."

"A mitzvah?" said Nonna.

"A good deed," said Asher. "It'll get you into paradise. A mitzvah," he explained, "is cleaning up a mess that you didn't make."

"Never mind mitzvah," said Nonna, "you pay him."

The next Saturday Lucio reported next door for work. The door was already open, and Asher stood just inside. "Come in," he said. "How are you?"

"Fine," said Lucio, stepping into the house. Upstairs he could hear Dubie and his older brother, Harold, being told by their mother to be ready in five minutes. They were on their way to see Mazie's relatives, who lived in Richmond Hill, a little town to the north of Toronto. Every Saturday the three of them took the radial car there to see their grandmother.

"How come you don't go?"

"I can't," said Asher.

"You can't?"

Asher shook his head. "The Torah forbids it."

"The Torah?" said Lucio.

"It's like the Bible," explained Asher, "but different. Also, it's not a book. It's a set of rules that say what you can and cannot do. One of them is work, and as far as I'm concerned, going to visit Mazie's parents is work."

"But they can go?" asked Lucio. This was new ground. Lucio knew that Dubie wasn't allowed to eat mortadella or prosciutto and that he didn't have to go to church on Sundays, but he hadn't realized there was more to being Jewish than that.

Asher shrugged, then said, "It's dark in here, no?"

"It's not bad," said Lucio.

"Not bad," said Asher, "but if you were going to read the paper, it'd be dark."

"It would be dark," said Lucio, looking at him.

For a moment neither said anything. Lucio looked out the window at the Institute for the Blind across the street, and Asher made a kind of sucking noise by drawing in air quickly through the sides of his mouth. Dubie's mother, Mazie, came downstairs. She was a compact, round woman with a determined air about her and was slightly out of breath from coming down so quickly.

"Lucio," said Mazie, "what're you doing here?"

"I'm the Sabbath *goy*."

"*Shabbes*," corrected Asher.

"*Shabbes*," said Lucio.

"Is it me," said Asher, "or is it dark in here?"

"Dark," said Mazie, "and cold."

They both looked at Lucio.

"You want me to turn on a light?" said Lucio.

It appeared that neither Asher nor Mazie had any objection. Lucio switched on the light. No sooner had he done so than Asher remarked that the upstairs hallway would also possibly be dark, and that he wouldn't be surprised if the kitchen was as well. Understanding that he was being told to turn on the second-floor lights, Lucio went up, and found Dubie trying to tie a bow tie.

"What're you doing here?" said Dubie, giving up on the tie and scrunching it into his jacket pocket.

"I'm the *Shabbes goy*," said Lucio.

"No kidding," said Dubie, then smiled. "You know," he said, "these shoes could use a polish."

Lucio agreed.

"Well?" said Dubie, holding out his foot.

"Well, what?" said Lucio.

"Well, these shoes could use some polish, no?"

"So polish them."

"I'm not the *Shabbes goy*."

"Are you telling me I have to do it?"

"I'm not telling you anything."

"So what're you saying?"

"I'm just saying," said Dubie, "these shoes could use a polish."

Lucio looked at him.

"Listen, Lucio," said Dubie, "this is how it works. On the Sabbath, Jews can't do any work. What that means is that we can't tell you what to do either. The Torah forbids giving orders on the *Shabbes*. So you have to say everything in a roundabout way, like I observe my shoes could use a polish, and you polish them."

"I do?" said Lucio.

"You're the *Shabbes goy*, no?"

"You got to be kidding."

"I didn't make it up."

"What about walking?" asked Lucio. "Does that count as work?"

"Don't be stupid," said Dubie. "Walking is walking."

"So," said Lucio, "walking is fine but orders are not."

"You got it," said Dubie.

Lucio shook his head.

"There's no right or wrong," Dubie told him. "There's only the law."

"What's that supposed to mean?"

"That in every law there's a loophole. You know that on Saturdays when I crack a nut open I need to make sure I hold the nut over the table, because if I don't, if I don't let it stay on the table, if I catch it in my hands and take out the nut from the shell, it's separating the wheat from the chaff—which the Torah says is work."

"If it's not one thing with you people," said Lucio, "it's another."

Dubie's mother called up from downstairs. "Hurry up, or we'll miss the train."

When they were gone, Lucio went downstairs and found Asher sitting at the kitchen table. He was making coffee. "What?" said Asher, seeing that Lucio was looking at him.

"Isn't that work?"

"You're right," said Asher, making a big deal of snapping his fingers, as if he'd just lost a bet. "I broke the Sabbath."

"You did?"

"I wanted some coffee," said Asher.

"What happens now?"

Asher shrugged. "Depends," he said.

Lucio looked at him.

"Either you can tell Mazie, and be out of a job," said Asher, "or you can sit down and have a coffee."

"I don't get it," said Lucio.

"It's Mazie," said Asher. "I don't want to visit her parents, so I have to make it seem that I'm more devout than she is. Go to Richmond Hill, I tell her, I'll stay here and suffer. My uncle was a rabbi," he said, pouring the coffee, "if you can believe that—so I tell her that I'm more observant. This is what it is to be married. I tell her I was brought up the old-fashioned way, you know, to do no work. I can't help it, I say, you can't teach an old dog new tricks."

"So," said Lucio, "should I go?"

"You go," said Asher, "and it'll give the whole thing away. Your mother'll see you back home and tell Mazie, and Mazie will figure it out. I'll never hear the end of it. No, you stay— I'm paying you, don't forget."

"So," said Lucio, "what am I supposed to do?"

"Nothing," said Asher, "and if you don't say nothing, neither will I."

"Suits me," said Lucio.

"Let's toast to it," said Asher, pouring Lucio a cup of coffee. "*Le chaim*. This is what you say when you make a toast."

"*Le chaim?*" said Lucio.

"It means, 'to life.'"

"To life," repeated Lucio. He raised the cup to his lips, then asked, "Is breaking the Sabbath the kind of thing that'll get you sent to hell?"

"There's no hell," said Asher. "For Jews, anyway."

"No hell?" said Lucio. "Is there a heaven?"

"Of course there's a heaven."

"Then why do anything, if there's no hell?"

Asher shrugged.

Asher and Lucio soon established a routine. Lucio would arrive, and Asher would make a great show of indirectly ordering him to get firewood and turn on lights and open drapes.

When Mazie and the boys left for the day, Lucio would go down to the corner and buy the newspapers. Then he and Asher would sit at the kitchen table. Asher would make coffee, and they would read the papers together. Asher read not one but three newspapers, each of which he engaged in argument, as if the person who'd written the article was right there in front of him. "Listen to this one," he would say, and read the article:

> Provincial Police this morning made one of the largest local seizures of beer when they grabbed some 160-odd barrels, each containing 10 dozen pints of export beer, about 20,000 bottles altogether, product of local breweries, which had been stored under the "camouflage of apples."
>
> The seizure was made at a Jarvis Street address. The load of "apples" had been stored for about two weeks in part of a warehouse, under a fictitious name. Included in the lot were about 15 barrels that really contained apples. The officer believed the beer was being held awaiting a favourable chance to run it into the United States.

"So," Asher asked him that Saturday (it was June 17, 1927), "what did they do with the beer?"

"Maybe they dumped it in Lake Ontario?"

"Maybe."

"That can't be good for the fish."

"You think the cops care about the fish? Good luck. I'll tell you, if you think cops care about fish. Anyways, that much beer would cause a flood."

"Imagine that," said Lucio. "The horses would be drunk."

"Horses can't get drunk."

"Why not? What's so different about horses?"

"You ever seen a drunk horse?"

"No," said Lucio.

"I rest my case," said Asher. Lucio laughed. "I'll tell you what they do with the beer, they drink it. Or sell it. The whole thing's a racket."

"I wonder what happened to the apples."

"What apples?" said Asher.

"The ones that camouflaged the beer," said Lucio. "What happened to them?"

"I'll tell you," said Asher, "those apples are in some room, in some police station, gathering dust and going bad—they're evidence. They should give back those apples," he said. "You know something, Lucio, it isn't right to keep those apples— you got a good head on your shoulders."

And Lucio, who had just learned the word, kvelled.

At noon they would walk down Beverley Street to Altman's Deli, sit at a table by the window and order hot dogs. Lucio would place the order and Goody or Mordechai would bring the hot dogs to the table. When they did, Asher would look over piously behind the counter at Cecil Altman, their father, as if to say, a Jew who made his kids break the Sabbath in such a way couldn't be much better than a goy.

That first Saturday, Lucio took a bite of his hot dog and said, "I love hot dogs."

"So," said Asher, "when's the wedding?"

"What?" said Lucio.

"You said, I love hot dogs, so I said, when's the wedding?"

"What?"

"If you love hot dogs so much," said Asher, "why don't you marry them?"

Lucio laughed.

The following Saturday, Lucio took a bite out of his hot dog and again, without thinking, said he loved hot dogs. And Asher said, "Can I be best man?" Lucio laughed, again. The next week he could not quite keep from smiling as he announced that he loved hot dogs.

"I can't wait," said Asher, "to see what the children'll look like."

But this was one that Lucio, who was just eleven, had to have explained to him.

The weeks passed. One Friday afternoon, when Lucio and Dubie were at the pictures at the Rose Theatre and Dubie said he loved popcorn, Lucio said he couldn't wait to see what the children would look like.

"You sound like my father," Dubie told him.

"It's one of your dad's jokes, actually," said Lucio. "You know, your father's not a bad person—he's funny."

"Now I've heard everything," said Dubie.

So Lucio spent each Saturday drinking coffee and eating hot dogs and reading the paper with Asher Diamond. Near the end of the day, as the sun was setting, when College Street began to get clogged with evening traffic, Asher would talk about his life. He would smile and shake his head, and say that when he was fifteen, if someone had told him he'd get to live in Toronto with a wife and two kids and a house of his own by selling knives, he'd have called them crazy. He had a booth at the St. Lawrence Market, down near the waterfront, where he sold knives that were the invention of Ivor Greenstein, the millionaire son of Sandor Greenstein, who had invented bubble gum. Asher was Greenstein's salesman. There were other products, of course—Greenstein's Remarkable Paper Clips (which were invisible), Greenstein's Unbelievable Telephone (which fit, entirely, into one's ear), Greenstein's Astonishing Phonograph Needles (which, in addition to being indestructible, could also be used to pick locks), Greenstein's Out of This World Page Turner (which you operated with your feet), Greenstein's Magnificent No Mess Apple, Pear, Orange, Carrot, Cabbage, Cantaloupe and Pumpkin Peeler (which you could not operate without gloves) and Greenstein's Incredible Fogless Goggles (ideal for excavations of all sorts)—but there was only a single salesman, and it was Asher Diamond.

"You know," said Dubie, after Lucio had been his father's *Shabbes goy* for a year, "you can quit any time."

Lucio shook his head. "It's a mitzvah," he told Dubie. "It's like cleaning a mess—"

"—you didn't make," said Dubie, finishing the sentence. "Don't believe everything the rabbis tell you."

"I said something about rabbis?" said Lucio.

Dubie looked at him in disbelief. "Listen to you," he said. "My dad's turned you yid."

"Really," said Lucio, "your father's not that bad."

"He's not your father," said Dubie.

Lucio nodded but did not laugh, for the truth was that more than once he had been mistaken for Dubie while he and Asher sat in Altman's. It was the kind of mistake anyone could make. Lucio and Dubie were, after all, exactly the same age. And although he laughed when it happened, he carried those moments of mistaken identity inside him, gingerly, and allowed himself to dream of what it would be like to find out that he was, in fact, Asher's son. That he was really a Jew, one of the chosen people who had been chased out of Egypt and had not given up being Jewish no matter how hard it got. It could have happened; babies were switched and mothers and fathers got confused. Look at Moses. It had happened to Moses.

But every so often Lucio would look out the window of Altman's Deli and see a red DeWitt streetcar lumbering along College Street, with its conductor hanging off the back. He would watch the doors of the DeWitt open and the driver come down the steps with the heavy metal rod Lucio knew was called a switcher, to pry the track from one side to another. He knew the switcher was called a switcher the way he knew the driver of the College streetcar had to switch the track twelve times during his route: at Dufferin, at Dovercourt, at Ossington, at Clinton, at Manning, twice at Bathurst, once at Brunswick, at Robert, twice more at Spadina and here at Beverley, at the intersection right in front of Altman's, which was where Lucio's father, Andrew Burke, had been killed. Run down by a man asleep at the wheel. Killed instantly. Lucio knew the route by heart because he had started to ride the College streetcar back and forth, alone, without telling his mother or anyone else. He could say the names of the stops along with the driver, taking care always to sit at the front so he could watch the driver take the switcher from behind his seat and go down the steps, wedge it between the metal tracks and shift his weight to lean against it. His own father must have done the same thing a thousand times. Lucio would sit on the streetcar and try to picture his father in his uniform and cap, his hair slicked back under the cap, not at all the awkward, smiling man in the faded orange daguerreotype of his wedding. It was not quite a memory, this vision of his father with the switcher, and it was more than a habit, for a habit accumulated over time and could be broken. This was something else. Something heavy, with sharp edges that had been pressed into Lucio; he didn't know where the memory ended and he began.

Asher did not realize that Lucio was thinking such thoughts. Despite the amount of time the two spent together, he thought of Lucio hardly at all, and he seldom spoke to him outside of their Saturday mornings, even when Lucio was over at his house with his son, for to do so, he thought, would be to ruin everything. Mazie would start to ask questions, and questions were critical to avoid in a marriage. But one afternoon, for all his studied indifference, he saw Lucio had fallen silent and was staring absently out the window of Altman's.

"What's the matter?" he asked.

Lucio looked at Asher and said, "You were here?"

"Here?" said Asher.

"When it happened," said Lucio. "When my father was killed."

Asher looked at the half-eaten hot dog on his plate, and then at his cup of coffee, and back at Lucio.

"Not here," he said. "I was back at the house—with Mazie and the baby."

"You didn't see it?"

"Nobody saw it."

"No, but afterwards," said Lucio. "You saw it."

"There was nothing to see."

"You saw the car," persisted Lucio. "You must have seen the car."

Asher pointed out the window. "Right here," he said. He was pointing to a telephone pole that stood just to the right of the window. "It was that pole. Not actually that pole, because it broke in two and had to be replaced, but right there."

Lucio looked. His father had come down the steps of the streetcar with his red and black uniform on, and his hair slicked back beneath his cap, the switcher in his hand, and had been moving the track when the car had come into the intersection.

"People say it was quick," said Lucio.

"It must have been," said Asher.

Then Lucio asked Asher something he had never asked anyone before.

"They say the driver was asleep," he said, "but how do they know? How do they know he was asleep if no one saw him?"

Asher's eyes widened, and his face changed. "There were no skid marks," he said simply, after a breath.

Lucio looked at him.

"The driver didn't touch the brakes," said Asher. "He didn't even try to."

"So he must have been asleep?"

Asher shrugged.

Lucio looked out at the telephone pole and tried to imagine the car drifting dreamily into the intersection.

"I've got a new one," said Asher. His face had a worried look.

Lucio did not think Asher was talking to him.

"I said," said Asher insistently, "that I've got a new one. Knock-knock."

"Who's there?" said Lucio, half-heartedly. He knew what Asher was trying to do and wanted nothing to do with it. He wanted to sit there and stare out the window.

"Eskimo Christians," said Asher.

"Eskimo Christians who?"

"Eskimo Christians," replied Asher, "and I'll tell you no lies."

Lucio did not laugh. Dubie was right, he realized; Asher Diamond was not his father.

His father was another person entirely.

Andrew Burke had been an iceman. He'd had a horse and a cart, and in the back of the cart had been an insulated carton in which the ice was stored. One cold morning he saw a crowd gathered around a streetcar driver who was trying to switch a frozen track. The driver must have been at it for some time, because the conductor was offering a dollar to anyone who could pry the track loose. The dollar was the reason for the crowd. Andrew waited his turn, then stepped up, crossed himself and, miraculously, switched the track.

The conductor handed him the dollar and asked his name.

"Burke," said Andrew.

"You Scottish?" asked the conductor.

"Irish," said Andrew. "By birth only."

"What line you in?"

"Ice," said Andrew.

"How'd you like to be in the streetcar line?" said the conductor, smiling (it was a kind of joke to call the streetcar business the streetcar line). "Come into the shop if you're interested, and I'll see what I can do."

"The shop?"

The conductor said he meant the TTC headquarters on Dufferin. "I'm Cobb," he said. "Tell them Cobb told you to come in."

The next day Andrew did this. "Cobb?" said the man at the front desk. He stood up and went through a door at the back of the room.

A moment later Cobb walked out. "Burke," he said. "Irish by birth."

"Now," said the first man, "you need to fill out these forms."

"We'll take them with us," said Cobb.

The two walked up Dufferin Street to the Sapphire Restaurant, and as they walked, Cobb told Andrew he'd seen him make the sign of the cross before switching the track, and that was how he'd known he was a Catholic. Cobb said he knew what it felt like to be a Catholic in this Orange town. To knock on doors, for people to take one look at you and say they couldn't use you even when there was a sign in the window. Ninety percent Protestant, said Cobb, saying he'd read it in the paper the other day as if it were a brag. Things would change, he said, but they hadn't yet, and that was why he'd changed his name from Cobh to Cobb and invented himself a barrister uncle in County Clare, a citizen of the Empire, to write him a letter of recommendation. There'd been no questions. They needed men and that was that. Andrew wore no cross around his neck, noted Cobb, but there was the matter of the box on the form. A box for Protestant and a box for everything else. Cobb told Andrew that if he checked the second box, there was nothing he could do for him. He could go back to the ice business. And if Burke repeated a word of what he'd said, Cobb would call him a liar, and that would be the end of that.

"Now," said Cobb, "what's all this about being Irish by birth?"

Andrew explained about his being an orphan. That he had been born on an Irish steamship called the *Nativity*, which had been hit by typhus. Both his mother and father—about whom he knew nothing other than the fact that they had written down "Dublin" as their home on the ship's manifest, and that their names were Candida (which in Latin means "white") and Andrew Burke—had died soon after his birth. When the ship arrived in Halifax, a middle-aged couple named Lindstrom had adopted him. The adoption of an infant had a predictable effect on the Lindstroms—it made them homesick. And so, forgetting that they had left Sweden because it was so cold and because the land had been impossible to farm, they headed for the part of Canada that most resembled the frozen wasteland from which they had come. They moved to Timmins, Ontario. As it turned out, there were a number of Swedes and Finns already living there, working in the mines, and so Andrew's adoptive father, who'd been a banker, went into mining, and remained in mining for nineteen years, until he coughed himself to death. Mrs. Lindstrom soon followed, leaving Andrew once again alone in the world. After his mother's funeral, he packed his things and went to the city, to Toronto, and took a job delivering ice.

"You could do better," Cobb told him. "You could have a proper apartment and money in your pocket besides. Still," said Cobb, "there's the matter of the box. If you're a man of religion, I'll respect that. We'll say thank you very much, and that'll be that."

Andrew looked again at the form and checked the Protestant box.

"You'll start tomorrow," Cobb told him. "There'll be a week of training, and then you'll work with me on the College car."

There were two parts to the training. The first part involved learning how to operate the streetcar controls; the second part involved memorizing the rules and regulations of the Toronto Transportation Commission. Neither was difficult. There was not much to be said about streetcar controls, and there was only a single rule.

"Rule Number One," Cobb told him, "the driver never leaves the streetcar."

"Got it," said Andrew.

"There's no Rule Number Two," said Cobb. "There's no leaving the streetcar, and that's the end of that."

"That's not hard to remember," said Andrew.

"We'll see," said Cobb, ominously.

Having started as a driver himself, Cobb knew from experience that it was not easy to adhere to Rule Number One. For in a streetcar you are neither here nor there, but hurrying through the middle of things. Known and strange things pass, said Cobb, and come at you sideways and catch your heart off guard, and blow it open.

In the eight years Andrew Burke drove the College streetcar, he disobeyed Rule Number One only twice.

The first time was when he met Lucio's mother, Francesca.

At the time Francesca was living on Clinton Street, and on her way back from the Bucci Brothers Bakery on Cecil where she had gone to buy flour because her mother's friend Michelangelo—who was in those days the kind of man who always had something on the boil—had arranged it so that Guido Bucci would sell it to her for fifty cents cheaper than she could buy it anywhere else. The transaction was completed, as usual, in the alley behind the bakery, and Francesca lifted the twenty-pound bag onto her shoulder and walked out onto College Street, where she waited for the streetcar. As she heaved the bag up she noticed that it had a slight tear in it, and that some flour had spilled out onto her dress. She pinched the tear closed with her free hand, and kept walking.

By the time she boarded the streetcar, the wind had blown a good deal of the flour out of the bag and into her hair. She got on the streetcar at the back, giving the conductor a dime for a nickel fare. Cobb accomplished the operation of giving her change with a swiftness that was nearly robotic, holding out a nickel before she had produced her dime, so that Francesca got nervous and attempted to give him her dime and take his nickel simultaneously. This caused her to lose her grip on the bag of flour, which began falling forward. Francesca chased it, and very nearly had it, when the driver put the streetcar in motion. It lurched forward and then backwards, causing her to fall backwards, and the bag of flour to fall on top of her. The people on the streetcar laughed. Covered with flour, and not knowing what else to do, Francesca picked up the bag and sat down in the seat behind the driver.

The streetcar moved west along College, and at every stop Andrew Burke looked at her in the rear-view mirror, wanting to see at which stop the flour-covered girl would get off. She did not. Not even when the streetcar reached the end of the line and changed direction at Dufferin.

At some point, Francesca began to cry.

"Excuse me, ma'am," said Andrew, turning around. "Which stop?"

"Clinton," she told him.

Her face was covered in flour, white except where her tears had been.

"Don't worry," he said.

At Clinton, Andrew applied the brake and opened the front doors. He picked up the bag of flour and started walking. Francesca followed him, and soon they were walking together down Clinton Street. It took Cobb nearly a minute to realize what was happening, but when he did, he got off the streetcar himself and yelled out that Burke was in direct contravention of Rule Number One.

"Are you going to be fired?" asked Francesca.

"I might," he said.

"You can't do that," she told him.

"Too late," he said.

The two walked down Clinton toward the house and, one by one, all the boarders in all the houses came out and watched as Andrew carried the bag of flour up the front steps of the house. The unmarried Greico brothers were playing *scopa* down the street, but even they put down their cards and looked as he got down on one knee and laid the flour at Francesca's feet, as if he were proposing.

"Thank you," she said.

"I'm Andrew," he told her.

"I'm Francesca," she told him.

"I should get back," he said.

To Andrew's surprise, the streetcar was right where he'd left it.

"You get one chance with Rule Number One," Cobb told him.

The next day, the flour washed out of her hair, Francesca went to the streetcar stop. She brought Andrew a bowl of spaghetti with tomato sauce. These were the last tomatoes of the season, she told him, and she had made the sauce and the pasta herself. Andrew Burke uncovered the bowl, and for a long moment said nothing. He had never seen pasta before.

"This is lovely," he said, picking up a strand with his fingers.

Francesca took a fork out of her pocket.

"This," she told him, winding the pasta around the end of the fork, "is pasta."

Francesca was twenty-four, with big dark eyes, and when Andrew took the fork from her she ran her hand through her dark hair, which she wore loose, down to her shoulders. Andrew watched her, and Francesca saw that she was being watched, and looked straight back at him.

That was the first time he left the streetcar; the second would be the day of Lucio's birth.

Lucio's Saturday mornings with Asher came to an end in the spring of 1930, when Modern Dresses on Spadina went out of business and both Lucio's *nonna* and his mother found themselves out of work. He went with his mother to the Welfare Office and filled out an application. A woman with silver hair behind a wooden desk looked at it disapprovingly and informed them that someone would be sent to the house in a few days. As they walked home to Beverley Street, Francesca instructed Lucio to tell no one about their visit to the Welfare Office. Lucio did not need to be told. He knew what it meant to be on the dole. He knew which kids at St. Patrick's wore charity shoes, knew the smell of the old fruit in their lunches, knew that these were the children whose parents did not get up and go to work in the morning but instead sat on the benches on College Street, looking at the street, waiting for nothing. These people were ghosts. This was what Lucio's Uncle Angelo called the threadbare, thin men who had started to arrive in Toronto the summer before. Young men and old men from little towns where there was no work and no food, leaping off the backs of trains, living in makeshift encampments to the west of the city that people called jungles.

"Listen, Burke," Angelo told him. "You look too much at a ghost and he stops being a ghost. He starts to change, at least in your head. Once you start thinking ghosts aren't ghosts, you want to give them things. And a ghost's got nothing, you know what that means?"

Lucio said he did not.

"It means, Burke, you can give everything you got to a ghost, and he'll still be a ghost. *Capisci?* It's not nice, I know that, but it's the way things got to be. You don't even look at them, not if you can help it. It's like killing a chicken. You got to be careful to not look at it, because when the time comes, the chicken's got to go. The chicken is a chicken; a ghost's a ghost."

"Burke" is what Angelo calls his nephew. Never by his first name. It is in this way that Lucio's uncle says Lucio is not quite Italian enough. That he is a *mangiacake*, a *mezzo-mezzo*. Angelo regards the boy as a kind of half *paesano*, prone to being influenced in the wrong way—someone who has something inside of him not quite right.

The following weeks were a horrible time of stillness and anticipation. Lucio and his mother waited for the visitor from the Welfare Office to arrive, and as they waited she insisted on the house being spotless. She would yell at him if he left a dish unwashed, or left his socks out to dry on the radiator or a book on the kitchen table. "Lu-ci-o," she would yell, her voice stretching his name into three syllables, and he would come running. But never was the visit discussed openly. This was because Nonna knew nothing about the trip to the Welfare Office, and most surely would have objected if she had. To Nonna, going to the government for help was like going to the police if you had a child who'd stolen a radio or killed someone; say what you want, but don't hand things over to the *strangeri*.

One night, the doorbell rang. They had just sat down for supper—for *olalia*, the simplest and cheapest of all pasta dishes, made with only olive oil and garlic. Lucio saw the look on his mother's face and knew she had said nothing to Nonna about their visit to the Welfare Office. He understood that—just as he had sat as still as possible at his desk in Father Choffe's class, fearing the day when he would be forced to walk alone to the front of the class—his mother had been hoping it would all just go away.

Lucio went to get the door.

The Welfare Lady was a thin woman in a white dress that looked like a nurse's uniform but was very clearly not a uniform. The kind of thing put on by someone who wishes she had a uniform to put on. The woman walked past Lucio, very quickly, and up the stairs to where his mother and Nonna were still sitting at the table. She was clearly determined to get into the house as quickly as possible, as if she was trying to catch the people upstairs in the middle of something. He closed the door, but not before looking out to the veranda. He saw Ruthie's parents sitting in their cheap chairs, looking very sorry for him. Lucio knew it was the first time the Welfare Office had visited one of the three houses joined by the long veranda, and that they did not like it. He closed the door but felt no better for having done so, imagining that all along Beverley Street people were looking out of their windows at the Welfare Lady, and then looking away.

Upstairs, the Welfare Lady was getting down to business.

"Now," she said, sitting down at the table without being invited, "I have here as residents Lucio and Francesca Burke."

"Correct," said Francesca.

"*Bo*," said Nonna, "what's this?"

"Is this the grandmother?" asked the Welfare Lady. "Does she live here as well?"

"Back there," said Nonna, motioning toward the hallway.

"Then," said the Welfare Lady, "who filled out this form?"

Silence.

"It was me," said Lucio.

"If there are any further fabrications, I will have no choice but to deny your application. It is a serious matter to lie on a government form. You realize this?"

When no one replied, the Welfare Lady stood up and began making her way through the house. She opened and closed kitchen cabinets. She looked beneath the sink. She flushed the toilet and lifted off its top to see if there was anything hidden in it. She checked between mattresses. She went through closets and dresser drawers. She walked back to the kitchen and lifted up the forty-inch statue of San Bonorio that sat in the middle of the Burkes' kitchen table, took it in her arms and shook it up and down roughly, knocking its underside against the top of the table.

"*Aspetta*," said Nonna. "That's valuable."

"How valuable, exactly?" said the Welfare Lady. "If you're to receive any aid, it'll have to go."

"San Bonorio," said Nonna, "go? *Madonna!*"

Oblivious to the significance of the recommendation she had just made, the Welfare Lady sat down again at the table.

"Now," she said. "I've a few questions about your finances."

Francesca's face had turned a sickly pale colour, as if she was about to faint, and she stared blankly ahead. She'd thought applying for welfare meant filling out a form and getting a cheque in the mail.

"Have you," said the lady, "any property, either in this country or anywhere else, any jewellery or stocks or bonds?"

"*Bo*," snorted Nonna.

"What did she say?" said the Welfare Lady. "*Bo?*"

"It's a short form of San Bonorio," explained Francesca. "The patron saint of our hometown in Italy."

"The one," said Nonna, standing up and pointing to the statue, "you wanna get rid of."

"Have you," asked the Welfare Lady, ignoring her, "any works of art?"

"What?" said Nonna. "You miss the *Mona Lisa* when you come in?"

"This is your last warning," said the Welfare Lady.

The doorbell rang.

Lucio got up. He went downstairs and opened the door to find Michelangelo standing there in a white suit, with a bouquet of flowers.

"*Buon giorno*, Lucio," said Michelangelo. "Your *nonna* here?"

Lucio led him upstairs.

"Ah-ha!" said the Welfare Lady, turning around in her chair when Michelangelo entered the kitchen. "And who are *you?*"

"I'm Michelangelo," he told her.

That was the last straw.

A week later, Nonna told Lucio she had got him the job at Michelangelo's Garage.

FOUR

LUCIO WORKS AT THE GARAGE until three in the afternoon, and at three his cousin arrives to relieve him. Dante finds Lucio sitting on the curb, propped up against one of the gas pumps, sound asleep. Dante is short and squarish, with an angular protuberant nose. Most days he talks incessantly to Lucio about girls. Which girls he has porked. Which girls he plans to pork. Which girls he will never be able to pork. Which famous girls he would pork if he had a chance. Which famous girls he would not pork even if they came and begged him to do so. What to say to a girl if you want to pork her. What not to say to a girl if you want to pork her. What girls have said while he's been porking them. But today Dante has other things on his mind—he wants to know about the Bloomberg baseball.

"So, Burke," says Dante loudly, prodding Lucio with his foot, "you got it?"

"What?" says Lucio, opening his eyes.

"You bring it?" says Dante. "The ball?"

"No," says Lucio, reaching into his pocket. "But I got his glasses."

"Where's the ball?"

"At home."

"You left the ball at home but brought the glasses?"

"I thought maybe Bloomberg would come looking for them," says Lucio, and hands the glasses to Dante. With their dirty thick lenses and faded black frames, it seems somehow as if Bloomberg's eyes are still attached to the glasses—as if somehow Bloomberg is still able to see through them.

"So it's true," says Dante. "It was you who threw it. I mean, I heard it. Everybody's heard it. But I thought they were kidding us. Some guy came by saying that you had whipped the ball and knocked that thing out of the sky, easy as pie, like you'd been doing it all your life, but I said no way. So did my father. We said there was no way you could throw a ball like that."

"Well," says Lucio, "that's what happened. Where were you?"

"The hockey game," Dante says wearily. "Where else?"

Lucio knows that Dante was at the hockey game at the insistence of his father. His Uncle Angelo was, some two years earlier, one of the workers employed to construct the new Maple Leaf Gardens on Carlton Street. This seemed an excellent job, at least at first. But then Conn Smythe, the team's owner, announced that he wouldn't be paying his workers in cash; they would receive, instead, lifetime hockey tickets. Each man would get two tickets per game, and when the man died, his children would inherit the seats. They and their descendants, Smythe told his workmen proudly, would never want for a hockey game to go to. The response to Smythe's proposal was less than enthusiastic. The workmen were, for the most part, Italian and had only the vaguest idea of how hockey was played. You don't want the seats, Smythe told them, I'll buy them back at the end of the year, after the revenues from the season have come in. Anyone wants to leave, he told them, should leave now, and there'll be no hard feelings—otherwise they should get back and finish the job they'd started. No one left.

To Angelo, the offer of hockey tickets was a remarkable thing. Angelo liked Conn Smythe personally, had shaken his hand and looked straight into the taller man's eyes and had seen there not a trace of guile. Moreover, he respected the man's energy and vision—that he wanted to do something and knew how to get it done. But at the same time he hated the *idea* of Conn Smythe, the idea of a man who, after being fired as the head coach of the New York Rangers with twenty thousand dollars' severance pay in his pocket, had come back to Toronto and bet it all on the Canadian Olympic hockey team. And won. And then, as if that weren't enough, had staked his winnings on the Toronto St. Pats to beat his old team, the Rangers, and again won. With his winnings he had bought the St. Pats himself, changing their name and changing the team insignia to a maple leaf, which tied in, in some indefinite way—in a way that exceeded the red capital C on the jerseys of the Montreal Canadiens—to people's idea of what it meant to be Canadian.

But it was not Smythe's business sense that bothered Angelo. It was his overconfidence, his carelessness. This, to Angelo, was astounding. At Sunday dinners he told and retold the story about Smythe, shaking his head each time with a new vehemence, as if Smythe's offer of hockey tickets instead of wages was truly beyond the realm of belief, like the Gordon Sinclair stories the *Toronto Daily Star* printed each week about mummies in Egypt whose blue eyes had been miraculously preserved over thousands of years. But he did not quit. Every Monday he got up and went to work, sawing and planing and hammering into place the boards that would make up the sixteen thousand seats in Maple Leaf Gardens, and as he carried the planks up the cement stairs to nail them in place he looked around the building, at the wide arc of its incomplete ceiling, and the thought of Smythe sitting in an office on the east side of the city galled him to such a degree that he would spit on the floor, where one day he knew the ice would be. But then Smythe himself would show up, and offer Angelo a cigarette, or shake his hand because he was doing good work, and all would be forgotten. Angelo would see Smythe looking at the new building and would know that the other man was seeing not discontented men but a great notion taking shape, that he understood these men to be taking part in a holy task that had to be carried out whether or not there was a depression. Smythe would walk around the floor, slapping his workers on their backs, and for Angelo, who had been born on the sixth floor of a tenement in New York City, this ungainly venture was his first experience of what it meant to be a Canadian. As a consequence, Angelo makes—demands that—Dante go to the hockey games with him, in the hope that his son will see on the ice something of what Smythe saw when he looked out across his unfinished ice rink.

"Anyway," says Dante to Lucio, "that must have been one hell of a throw."

Lucio shrugs.

"Yeah, right, be modest," says Dante. "It knocked that thing right out of the sky."

"It was a bird."

"That's not what they're saying."

"It was a bird," says Lucio. "I saw it."

"I heard it spoke Chinese," says Dante.

"That's bunk, it was a bird. It sat on the baseball like it was an egg."

"Now that," says Dante, "is crackers."

"Not for a bird."

Dante thinks about this for a minute, then says, "Still, it was one hell of a throw, you gotta say that."

Lucio nods in a noncommittal way.

"What's the matter?" Dante asks.

"Nothing. I don't remember doing it, is all. I mean, I know what happened—I remember the ball rolling my way, and picking it up, and throwing it, but it wasn't like I aimed it or anything. I just threw it."

"What did Bloomberg say?"

"Nothing."

"Nothing?"

"He was gone. He was there one minute, the next he was gone."

"And no one saw him?"

Lucio shakes his head.

"That's strange," says Dante. "Did anyone else disappear?"

"Just Bloomberg."

"Strange again," says Dante. "What're you gonna do?"

"Do? With the glasses?" says Lucio. "Nothing; they're Bloomberg's. He can come and get them if he wants."

"Maybe he doesn't know where they are," says Dante.

Lucio nods, then says, "You know, I don't remember throwing it. There I was, holding the ball, and then it was in the air."

"Never mind," says Dante. "You'll get used to the idea. Soon you'll be beating them off with a stick, the dames. They love a man who can throw a ball."

Lucio says nothing. He's still making up his mind what he thinks about having thrown the ball the day before, and is still somewhat shaken by what happened earlier at the deli. But about the stone and the swastika, the way the glass door shattered just as he was about to walk through it, he says nothing to Dante—who he knows would never understand what it feels like to be so helplessly afraid. The fear, like the throw itself, was a reflex. Like when he had the casts taken off his arms after his flying leap off the long veranda; the doctor knocked on his elbow with a rubber hammer and his arm leapt forward, but the movement had nothing to do with him. It was a lucky throw, and Lucio knows it, knows he would not be able to do it a second time. Like any seventeen-year-old, he has secretly been waiting for something, for some piece of news about himself to arrive. But to find, suddenly, that he is able to throw a baseball with extraordinary speed and accuracy runs so contrary to the current of his life that it makes no sense. It robs the moment of any joy, and makes him regard the mystery of that throw and his impending date with Ruthie as a predicament, as something needing repair.

Just then, as Lucio is standing up to leave, Ruthie herself walks by. Dante sees her first, walking down the other side of College Street, looking tall with her red hair down. She is wearing a tight black skirt that ends mid-calf, and a thin green blouse that shows off her breasts. She carries a large brown bag in one hand and a white slip of paper in the other. In the bright stillness of the summer afternoon she looks entirely out of place, which Lucio guesses is the point of the green blouse.

"Hello, Lucio," she says.

Although he is not looking at his cousin, Lucio can feel Dante staring. Ruthie's eyes are flecked green; she looks elegant, but also like she's just come from somewhere illegal.

"Hi, Ruthie," says Lucio. "What brings you this way?"

"I'm showing a coat on Palmerston," she says. "Poor man—he's too sick to leave the house but he wants to get something for his daughter."

Dante is staring.

"You know Ruthie," says Lucio, seeing his cousin's expression. "Ruthie—who lives next door."

"Of course he does. I was there, after all, when you were born," she tells him, and smiles at him appealingly, snapping her head to sweep her long red hair off her shoulders.

Dante is still staring. "Ruthie?" he says. "Ruthie the Commie?"

"Ruthie the Commie," says Ruthie.

"Wow," says Dante.

"Wow what?" says Ruthie.

It is plainly not the first time Ruthie has seen such a reaction, not the first time she has not been recognized, and again no one seems to know what to say. An old woman in a wheelchair inches by them on the sidewalk, leaning forward in the chair, using her toes, which barely touch the ground, to propel herself. The woman has a wristwatch on each arm—large, dirty silver circles that seem to remind Ruthie she has an appointment to keep.

"Are we still on for tonight?" she asks.

"Gutman Fur," Lucio says, "six-thirty."

"See you then." She smiles lightly and walks on.

"*Madonna,*" says Dante, when she is gone. "What I'd give to slip her the sausage."

"Take it easy with that," says Lucio.

"*Bo,*" says Dante. "I wonder what the children'll look like."

At twenty-five to seven that evening Lucio finds himself on the third floor of the Darling Building, facing a door in the top half of which is a frosted glass window with the following words inscribed in ornate black letters:

Leonard Gutman Furs
"We don't just sell fur, we make it."

Under which, in smaller, less ornate letters, is written:

FUR, LEATHER, STORAGE,
CLEANING, FUR BEARS, FUR HATS

Lucio stands for a moment and stares at the door. It does not seem possible to him that Ruthie Nodelman is on the other side of that door, waiting for him. He is five minutes late, and for a moment he imagines that she is already gone. That she waited, got fed up and left in a huff. He has seen Ruthie yell repeatedly at her sister, and knows this is a distinct possibility. After she became a born Communist, the two had the most terrible arguments, and Ruthie would call her sister a slave to the capitalist machine. That was exactly the phrase she used: "You," she told Esther, who had come home with a new pink hat, "are a slave to the capitalist machine." This, Lucio reminds himself, is the girl waiting on the other side of the door for him. He nearly leaves. But then he knocks once and turns the knob, entering the offices of Gutman Fur.

What he sees is a large room divided into a series of cubicles. There are six cubicles in all, each with a desk and a chair and a typewriter, each separated from the others by frosted glass partitions five and a half feet tall. Directly in front of the door is a receptionist's desk, which is where Ruthie sits during the day. For nearly a minute Lucio stands there, then closes the door behind him, staring at that desk as if to convey that his ambitions extend no further. In one right corner of the desk sits a telephone; in one left corner, a narrow canister of meticulously sharpened pencils. Immediately in front of this canister are a check protector and staple driver; on the other side of the desk, in front of the telephone, sits a pile of carefully stacked ream paper. In the dead centre of the desk, a typewriter. Lucio is entirely frightened by what he sees on this desk, by the care that has been taken with the placement of these items. The typewriter, most of all—it appears to have been placed in the dead centre with utter deliberation, and it does not take much to imagine the exactitude of whoever placed such a typewriter in such a manner. This is Ruthie Nodelman's desk, he thinks, and it corresponds exactly to the impression he has had of her ever since that day when he broke his wrists. The more he thinks about this precision the more it frightens him, and he finds himself thinking it entirely possible that the typewriter's owner, if she is still here, will accuse him of touching something, of disturbing the perfect order she has brought to the world. This leads Lucio to consider what he and Ruthie have in common; he realizes, with a start, that despite living next door to her his entire life, other than the fact that she is a Communist, he knows next to nothing about her.

Directly behind the receptionist's desk is a tiny enclosed room built entirely out of frosted glass. Unlike the other cubicles' half-walls of frosted glass, the walls of this glass room go all the way up into the ceiling. There is a frosted glass door on the frosted glass room, with a frosted glass doorknob, and on the door the word GUTMAN has been printed in the same black ornate script that Lucio saw on the outside door. Behind this office are rows of fur coats hanging from large metal poles stretching the length of the room; each of the hangers is attached to a tiny silver rollerskate-like device that allows it to slide easily along the poles.

In the centre of the room, framed by a large three-sided mirror, stands Ruthie, with a fur coat on, as if Lucio were a prospective customer.

"So," she says, "what do you think?"

Lucio does not know what to say.

"Don't worry," taking the coat off. "Mr. Gutman isn't here— he closes up early on Tuesdays. We've the place to ourselves."

"Ready to go?" says Lucio.

"I'm fine," she says, with ironic formality. "And how are you?"

"Fine," says Lucio. "You ready to go?"

"Go?"

"To the pictures?"

"Want to dance?" She smiles at him in the half-light of the store, which smells like new shoes. "Two years ago I swore off dancing. You know that? I told myself that it was one of the things that had to go. That and the movies."

"I'm not much of a dancer," says Lucio.

"The movies can wait," Ruthie tells him. She has a sweet kind of unpretending elegance about her, and although Lucio has known her for as long as he can remember, it seems to him that she is only now speaking to him; for the first time looking at his face. "And I find myself dying for a dance. I don't know why that should be. Maybe I'm weak, a bad Party member. The type of girl who's part of the problem. Do you think that could be it? That I'm part of the problem?"

"What problem?" says Lucio.

"Exactly, that's exactly right." Ruthie laughs. She is now standing very close to him. Behind the fur coats, big glass windows look out on Spadina Avenue. Through them the streetlights shine up, like stars that are somehow underneath them.

"You know," he says, feeling bolder, "this isn't the kind of place I'd have expected a Communist to work."

Ruthie sighs. "The fact of the matter," she tells him, a little sharply, a little like her old self, "is that it's a perfect job—you work and you get paid and there's a lot of sitting around. I do the books for Mr. Gutman, but there's only so many figures to add up in a given day. And only so many coats to show. The rest of the time I have to myself. Let me tell you a secret. While I am sitting at that desk I'm reading Karl Marx. That's why it's a good job for a born Communist like myself. Right here, right in the middle of this fur store, in the middle of capitalism itself, I'm doing the work of the Party. This summer alone I've read Das Kapital twice."

"Is that right?" says Lucio.

"In a perfect world, in the world after the Revolution," says Ruthie, speaking quickly now, saying something that she has long said to herself and longed to say to another person, "the world will be a different place. Everyone will work as much as they want—no, not as much as they want but as much as they need to, as much as they need to work to feel themselves productive, and the rest of the time they can read. Or dance. Or do whatever they want."

"Sounds all right," says Lucio.

"It *is* all right," says Ruthie emphatically, and takes a step toward him, kissing him sweetly on the mouth. "How do you like that?" she asks him.

Lucio is dumbfounded.

"So," she says. "How about it—the movies or dancing?"

"I don't know how," says Lucio. "I mean, I don't know how to dance."

"Here," she says, "I'll show you."

He steps back.

Ruthie pushes out her lower lip and studies him. "Let's start with the waltz," she says. She places his hand on her shoulder, and his other hand on her back. "Now," she tells him, "the basic step is to go forward with your left foot, and then slide over with your right, and then over with your left. And then back with your right, and then over with your left. And then you start all over again."

For a brief moment they are dancing; then he is lost.

"What is it now?" he asks. "Is it back with my left?"

"My left," says Ruthie, "your right."

"Got it." He steps back with his left foot.

"You're doing wonderfully. Now it's time to learn to turn," and she steps back from him with her arms extended as if he were still in them. "Left foot—this is what you'll do, it's *your* feet I'm talking about—and then slide over with the right, and then plant the left when you're over there, and soon you'll be twirling around the room."

Lucio looks down.

"Never mind your feet," says Ruthie, "look at me. Here it is again," she says, and again demonstrates the step. "That's what's called a box step. You try now, I'll watch."

"OK," says Lucio. "Forward with the left."

"What about the arms?" asks Ruthie.

"What about them?"

"They should be out—you forgot all about your girl."

"Sorry," says Lucio.

"Quite all right." She makes a curtsey. As she does, she lifts her skirt up, and Lucio sees the beginnings of her knees. "Try it again." He does so, and after a few more tries Ruthie tells him he is ready to try it with a partner. She walks over and stands next to him, and he puts his right hand in her left hand, and his arm around her back, and feels, under the white cotton of her sweater, her brassiere. "All right," she says. "You ready?"

"Ready," says Lucio.

Just then Ruthie leans forward and kisses him. Softly, and only once. But on the lips.

"That's for luck," she says. "One, two, three," she counts, and soon they are dancing. Through the window come the sounds of Spadina, mingling with the sound of sewing machines from the sweatshop on the floor above them. They move back and forth across the room with some difficulty, turning sloppily and not without Lucio stepping on Ruthie's feet. The turning is the most difficult part, and is always done at her initiative—she presses her thigh against his, which makes him draw back his leg at the appropriate moment.

When they are finished Ruthie looks down at her shoes, and says they are a mess.

"I'm sorry," says Lucio, "did I do that?"

"You did. What are you going to do about it?"

"If you give them to me, I could give them a shine."

"You can give them a shine," says Ruthie, "but I'm not about to give them to you."

"I'll give them back."

"They're my sister's," says Ruthie. "So I think I should keep them close. She might ask me, and then what would I say? That Lucio Burke's got my shoes? I don't think so. If you're going to give them a shine, you'd best do it here."

Lucio shrugs. The shoes are fancy, but they don't look to him to be all that expensive. But what does he know about shoes? "If you want," he tells her.

"Over here," says Ruthie.

He follows her to the receptionist's desk. From a drawer she takes two blackened rags and a can of shoe polish. "I keep this on hand," she says, "in case this kind of thing happens. Mr. Gutman is very strict. Before I go out in front of a client, he gives me the once-over. If I've a torn stocking, or a hair out of place, he sends me home and I don't get paid that day. Right down to the shoes. My first week, I got sent home every day." With this she hands him the polish and the rags and sits down on the wooden swivel chair behind the desk. She lifts her right foot onto the desk in front of her and looks at Lucio expectantly. "Well?" she says.

"Well, what?" says Lucio.

"What about that shine?" Ruthie points to her foot, resting on the desk.

"Your shoe's still on. Take it off and I'll polish it."

"Would you ask me that if I were a man? When you get a shine, do you?"

Lucio admits he doesn't.

"So?" says Ruthie.

He kneels down and takes her shoe in his hand. She is wearing clear, shiny stockings, and when he kneels in front of her she lifts her skirt so he can see that the stockings end somewhere around the middle of her thigh.

"Are you having trouble getting started?" she asks him. And with this she draws her skirt up over her knee. Lucio looks at the knee and then up at Ruthie, and sees she is waiting. He gets to work on the shoe.

What do you think?" asks Ruthie.

"Nice," he says.

"Of the shoes."

He feels himself blushing.

"*The Missing Rembrandt*'s playing, you know, at the Rose."

"What?" asks Lucio.

"*The Missing Rembrandt*," says Ruthie. "The new Sherlock Holmes picture."

"It's over by now," says Lucio.

"I'm not talking about tonight."

He finishes the shoe.

"That looks good." She leans forward to inspect his work. She switches feet and he starts on the second shoe. "Hold on," she tells him, lifting her skirt again. "There you are," she says.

Lucio seems to be focusing considerable attention on the second shoe.

"You could ask me, you know, if I want to go. To the pictures. I mean, we didn't get there tonight, and although *The Missing Rembrandt* will wait, it won't wait forever."

He looks up at her then, past her exposed knee and into her eyes. He feels as if he is proposing. "Ruthie," he says, "do you want to go to the pictures with me?"

"I thought you'd never ask. How about Friday?"

He looks at her shiny right leg out of the corner of his eye. "Friday, then," he says and, standing up, he feels his knees shake; she is still looking at him, and he notices suddenly, ashamed, that he has an erection. He feels it pressing against the inside of his pants, urgent and helpless. There to be seen. But Ruthie does not seem to notice, or mind. She stands to kiss him, but before she can he steps away from her quickly. He says he will see her Friday, and a moment later he is out of the office, closing the door behind him. He runs down the stairs and out onto Spadina into the summer air, where he discovers that his knees are still shaking.

This is not the first time Lucio has wanted someone. When, after grade school, he was sent to Harbord Collegiate because the Catholic high school was too expensive, he found himself surrounded by girls he had never seen before, many of whom he wished would think him wonderful in some unstipulated manner. But his first two years of high school were uneventful in this respect. Although Dante opened his locker each February fourteenth to find a number of unsigned valentines spilling out of it, Lucio received only three valentines in three years of high school, all from a tough-looking girl named Harriet Bennet who sat behind him in geography. Lucio did not want Harriet Bennet, whom the other boys called Hairy Bennett because of the thick black hair that grew on her fore-arms, and had hardly ever exchanged more than a glance with her. When the first valentine came, he even had to ask Dante which girl Harriet was, and then tried to think what could have possibly prompted the valentine. All he could come up with was that, one rainy afternoon in his first semester at Harbord, he had seen Hairy Bennett waiting for the streetcar. He'd said something about the weather, and kept walking. That, evidently, had been enough. Harriet had fastened on him with a tenacity that, when he mentioned it to Dubie, Dubie compared to the giant lizard called the Gila monster, which he explained was native to Mexico and killed its prey by biting into it and not letting go until the other animal died. So it was with Harriet: without fail, every February fourteenth, Lucio would open his locker to find an elaborately signed, brightly coloured missive from her. The one saving grace was that she seemed no more eager than he to let the rest of the world know about her feelings toward him. Lucio would walk into geography class and see her looking up at him expectantly and patiently. Then he would sit down at his desk and neither one of them would mention it. Lucio hoped that Harriet would get over her feelings sooner or later, rather as she might recover from a bad cold she had unaccountably contracted.

No, Lucio did not want Hairy Bennett. He wanted Rachel McHugh, the dark-eyed girl with long dark hair and a rosebud mouth who sat at the back of his English class and had a thrilling way of never looking at him directly. Before Ruthie, he imagined himself in love with Rachel, by which he meant that if he happened to be in a room with her alone, and if he was certain that no one would ever find out, he would kiss her. Lucio knew, in some measure, that he wanted Rachel simply because she was tiny and perfect, and when he imagined kissing her it looked in his mind's eye very like the way a valentine looked—pink and fully clothed. Rachel had curled hair, and when Lucio thought about kissing her he heard music playing, the way it did in movies. The prospect of his ever having an erection to do with, much less in the presence of, Rachel McHugh, seemed to him sacrilegious, the kind of thing for which you could be sent to hell, even after you married her.

But with Ruthie everything is different. Lucio knows this right away, and as he runs, frightened, onto Spadina, and hears around him the noise of the city, he knows he will never again think of Rachel McHugh's eyes. He knows what is happening, but he does not know how to respond, and he has no idea what is going to happen next. He also does not know *why* any of it is happening. Why the beautiful and severe Ruthie Nodelman would want to dance with him. And he does not know which is worse, the not knowing or the not knowing why.

After Lucio runs out on her, Ruthie stands for a long moment in the centre of Gutman Fur, looking at herself in the long mirror as if she does not quite recognize her own reflection. Then she smiles, picks up her purse and leaves the store, locking the door behind her. As she walks home, she tells herself that she knows exactly what she's doing: she's testing herself. She watched Lucio pick up the ball out of the corner of her eye, and she saw him throw. He was calm and strong. Decisive. Not at all like the boy who'd grown up in the house next door. He looked like someone else completely. The ball leapt out of his hand and, just like that, Ruthie knew she wanted him.

It was a strange sensation, something hard and intractable within herself, and even afterwards, after she tries telling herself that she is not feeling it, she knows she is. What does she care if he can throw a baseball? What does that have to do with anything? It is irrational. Still, she waited outside in the cinder alley for Lucio to bring out the garbage. Then she threw herself at him, the way Garbo throws herself at both her lovers in *Flesh and the Devil*. Lucio, she can tell right away, is both confused by her and interested in her, and she knows he wants her from the way he cannot look at her.

That Friday, when Lucio arrives at Gutman Fur for their second date, it is Ruthie who does all the talking. Again, they do not go to the pictures. Ruthie makes him dance with her, kissing him when she wants to kiss him. She is the one in charge. She knows exactly what she is doing. But when she kisses him, when she feels Lucio's arms around her waist, when she looks into his clear eyes, something happens. The kiss does not, as she thinks it will, cause her desire to evaporate. It makes her want to kiss him again. And Ruthie, who does not know why she is doing it and cannot stop herself, touches Lucio's face, pulling him toward her. And (again despite her firmest resolutions) she kisses him again. Then kisses him again. And is in the middle of kissing him a fourth time when she draws back and tells him he will have to leave. That is exactly how she puts it: "Lucio," she tells him, "you'll have to leave."

"Sorry," says Lucio, not knowing what he's done wrong but thinking it best to apologize all the same.

"Yes," says Ruthie.

"Leave?" says Lucio.

"Yes," says Ruthie, suddenly very formal, as if Lucio is someone she's hired, "thank you."

Lucio looks around the room, and then at Ruthie, as if he is waking up after falling asleep in a strange place. He and Ruthie have been dancing in the middle of the showroom, in the big open space in front of the mirror where she models coats during the day. Now, having stepped away from him, she stands with her back to the mirror, leaning up against it with an air of inconvenienced impatience. When he looks at her, he can see his own reflection beside her in the mirror. He has on his green work pants from the garage, and a dirty white shirt that has not been ironed in some time. In his left hand he holds a felt cap, which looks matted and old in the bright white lights that hang above. The first time he came to the store, Ruthie was standing under those lights, and it seemed to him that he was walking into a page in a magazine, dancing with the kind of girl whose picture soldiers carried with them into the trenches—who were only allowed to carry such pictures because they might die at any minute.

Now those bright lights are like spotlights, something beaming from the top of a turret. They shine down on Lucio ironically, reminding him of the Hap Kvidera pictures his mother took him to when he was a child, before talkies were invented. Kvidera was perpetually falling in love with the kind of girl he had no business falling in love with. The way you could tell this in the movies, even before you knew anything about the girl, had to do with the way the girl was covered in whiteness: her dress, her shoes, even her skin emitted a white glow as she went about doing the beautiful things she did each day, arranging flowers or, if she was a maid, bringing in tea. Because he was constantly being pursued, Kvidera found himself hiding in unusual places, and often it was while he was in those places that he looked in through open windows and found himself confronted by the sight of a girl he had no business falling in love with. Inevitably, Kvidera would find himself tumbling into the girl's world, and this was always a shocking, incongruent moment that was made to seem more so because he looked so dirty in the whiteness of her white world. Before this happened, or on the way to it happening, it was not uncommon for him to get run over several times by cars, or to be dropped from a great height, or to have a house fall on him, or to ride accidentally backwards on a horse, or to douse himself with a firehose—and indeed, if he somehow looked refreshed by these calamities, they also left him much dirtier. Such is the paradox of the Hap Kvidera picture—the hero who finally is allowed into a clean white world is, at the moment he enters it, made conscious of his own filthiness, of the extent to which he will never fit in.

Lucio is no Hap Kvidera, and certainly it would be difficult for Ruthie to behave in a manner more unlike the heroines in Kvidera movies, who immediately rush to the hero's side and cook him dinner. She leans up against the mirror, watching Lucio warily, as if he might at any moment lunge at her. He stays where he is, however, and looks at her, and as he does he sees reflected back at him his own confused stare, and his hands, his dirty fingernails, his right hand upturned as if he is looking for a handout. Looking at himself, he realizes with a start that he is being made a fool of. Ruthie has led him to think all the wrong things, and he has thought them. It would have been better, he tells himself, to have just put the garbage in the can that night and gone back into the house.

"You want me to go," says Lucio, "I'll go."

"What's that supposed to mean?" says Ruthie. "If I say that's what I want, it's what I want."

"You say that now," says Lucio. "But first you ask me to come here, and then you tell me to go."

"You didn't seem to mind." She shakes her head, and something in her face changes. She takes a step toward Lucio. "It's just that my sister is coming," she tells him, speaking quickly. "She's working the late shift and needs me to walk her home. Why she can't walk by herself," she says, laughing a shrill, artificial laugh, "I don't know. But she said to my father, tell Ruthie to wait and walk home with me. What choice do I have? So you have to go."

Lucio says that he can wait, he'll walk the two of them home.

"No," Ruthie tells him. "That won't do. I mean, I wouldn't care, but if Esther were to come and see you here, I mean, what would she say? No," she says, now firmly. "You'll have to go. If Esther shows up and sees you, it'll be like having our picture in the paper."

Lucio knows Ruthie doesn't mean his picture will actually appear in the paper, but all the same he finds himself imagining it: the two of them photographed in Gutman Fur, having been surprised by a newshawk at the end of a dance, just as Buster Crabbe, who replaced Johnny Weissmuller as Tarzan, was surprised a month ago by a photographer who found him in a hospital closet with Myrtle K. McGraw, a young nurse. Crabbe had come to the hospital to get an eyebrow stitched, and one thing had led to another. Dante pointed the photograph out to Lucio, and told him to take particular note of the way it had been cropped; it was of Crabbe's face, framed with broom handles and cleaning supplies. That look, said Dante, meant that the photographer had caught Crabbe and the nurse doing it, or doing something like it. Somewhere, Dante said, someone had the whole photo, and that someone was a rich man. Lucio looked at the paper and tried to imagine the rest of the photograph, but found he could not, as if there was something inside him, some deep hesitancy or delicacy, that prevented it. He knew Dante was probably right; that however shocking the alliterative headline that accompanied the picture (CRABBE CAUGHT WITH CANDYSTRIPER), however suspicious Crabbe's raised eyebrows, however damning the sight of broom handles standing in such close proximity to the star's face, none of these amounted to an incriminating photograph. But to Lucio there was something terrible about the picture, something about the look on Crabbe's face that he could not think about without imagining himself in a similar circumstance, wide-eyed and unprotected. So it was that, when Ruthie kissed him and pulled away, he felt relieved. It meant he would not have to do anything. But to *tell* him to leave—that is a different thing entirely, and he feels obliged to say something. And so, as he turns to leave, he makes a joke.

"Too bad," says Lucio, "you're not a man."

"What?"

"There would be nothing for Esther to say then."

"Esther?" says Ruthie. "What are you talking about?"

"It's a joke," says Lucio. "I was making a joke. It's something you say a lot is all—about not being a man."

"So I do," says Ruthie, and laughs.

He tells her goodbye.

"Well," says Ruthie, "I'll see you."

"Maybe one day we'll make it to *The Missing Rembrandt*."

"How about Monday?" says Ruthie.

"Fine," he tells her. "Monday it is."

"Pick me up here."

On his way out the door, Lucio walks past the desk at the front of the office. It is in as perfect order as it has ever been, now with a copy of *Das Kapital* in its blue and white dust jacket sitting in the exact centre of the desk.

"Monday," he says, turning around one last time.

"Monday," she repeats, and then waves demurely, as if she is standing on a railway platform and Lucio is on the caboose of a slowly receding train.

After he has closed the door, Ruthie remains still for a long time, listening, making sure he is really gone. Then she leans forward, puts her head in her hands and begins to cry.

She *did* want him to go, but told him so in such a bald, ham-fisted way, cackling inanely and making up such a stupid excuse, that he probably saw through it on the spot. Even if he believed her, he will find out soon enough that she was lying. He is sure to walk home and find Esther sitting on the veranda. What he will think then, Ruthie can only imagine. As she replays the scene in her mind she slumps forward, unable even to pretend she has just been testing herself. No, she *has* tested herself. And she has failed. Before Lucio arrived, Ruthie thought differently. She told herself she'd passed. Before he stood there looking at her with those blue eyes of his, she had resolved to end it with him. She would dance with him, perhaps kiss him, no more than once—and then send him on his way. She would be firm: it would not work, she would tell him; there were more important matters to attend to, the Revolution was not going to come about by itself, after all. No matter how much she liked him (Ruthie had imagined herself standing a safe distance from him as she said this, with her hands on her hips so he wouldn't think of touching her and she wouldn't be able to touch him), it would have to end. She had imagined he would protest, or argue with her about the possibility of the Revolution ever occurring. But she would have none of it; she would say to him (she'd seen herself putting up her hand like a traffic cop and looking into Lucio's clear blue eyes with the same resolution that was on Garbo's face in *Flesh and the Devil* when, tragically and too late, she made her decision to walk across the ice) that it was over. That would silence him. And in the silence that descended between them in that awkward but necessary moment, they would be able to hear, Ruthie had imagined (for she had imagined it all that afternoon, when the girls in the sweatshop on the floor above were working at full speed, and she could hear nothing but the mechanized rattle of Singers and the garment trucks being rolled through rows of sewing machines) the sound of those poor women working late into the night—without any rights, or a minimum wage, or any protection whatsoever from anything that might be done to them—and that would make her point more eloquently than anything she might say.

But that was not what had happened. It was not even close.

Until then, Ruthie had never wanted to kiss a boy more than once. She'd kissed Spinny Weinreb that single time in the balcony of the Rose Theatre. And once had been enough. The kiss had been a brief, awkward and moist affair, and Spinny, in addition to smelling vaguely like gefilte fish, had had a peppermint Life Saver in his mouth at the time. She had taken it upon herself to kiss Spinny right after the projector had started rolling, so as to get it out of the way. She had firmly put her hand on his large, smooth cheek, turned his face toward her and planted her lips on his. Finding not the least urge to repeat this act, she had felt free to enjoy the picture—*A Farewell to Arms*, starring Helen Hayes and Gary Cooper. Spinny, who was optimistic that Ruthie's quick work was indicative of what the rest of the date would hold, had removed the Life Saver from his mouth and sat in rigid expectation. But Ruthie did not kiss him a second time. Not even later that night, after Spinny had walked her home and was leaning forward with his eyes closed. Ruthie had stepped away, and Spinny had felt his hand being shaken.

Ruthie's kiss with Lucio was quite different. She did not pull back. Indeed, *she* was the one to lean forward, closing her eyes as if Lucio were an ambulance driver and she a smitten nurse fighting in the Spanish Civil War, perhaps never to see each other again. Then they danced, slowly, as Bing Crosby crooned away on Mr. Gutman's old DeForest Everyman. She felt Lucio's breath on her neck and right then knew that everything she had meant to say had gone out the window.

Ruthie does not really care what people say about her, but the more she thinks about it, the more troubled she becomes. No one knows about Lucio, and she likes it that way. Not that anyone would disapprove. Though if they did disapprove, that would be fine. Lucio is not even a fascist, like so many of the other Italian boys in the neighbourhood. It would be much better if he were, thinks Ruthie. Were Lucio a fascist, were there something unreasonable or fanatical about him, something for Ruthie to reform, that would be better. The two of them would parade up Beverley Street with Lucio wearing a red baseball cap and everyone would understand. But that is not Lucio at all. He is no fascist. He isn't even entirely Italian. So if the two of them were to walk hand in hand down Beverley Street, people would merely think he was wearing the red baseball cap because she had asked him to. And worst of all, that she had asked him to wear it because she loved him. The two of them would be the picture of stolid bourgeois civility, of love overcoming all, and everyone would forget about politics. No one would disapprove. They would think it funny. Quaint. It would allow the people of the Ward, the boys who called her Ruthie the Commie behind her back, the men at the Party meetings who tolerated the presence of women but really felt that, after the Revolution, having a more equitable distribution of wealth would mean more women having more babies—it would allow all of them to think that they'd always been right about her: that at bottom she was a girl like any other. And that Ruthie cannot allow. Any more than she can bear the wry smiling and whispering, and everyone asking each other, who'd have thought it would be Lucio Burke who got to Ruthie Nodelman? Was it that throw? Does she, like the girls who sat behind the bullpen when the Yankees came to town, have a thing for boys who throw baseballs? Ruthie herself cannot say. Lucio has blue eyes like his father, and dark hair like his mother, and when he smiles you can see that his two front teeth are slightly too large and too far apart. He is tall, taller than most of the boys in the Ward, but he is shorter than Spinny Weinreb, who Ruthie is fairly certain can lift more than Lucio (Ruthie knows nothing about such things, and indeed, until she wonders what she sees in Lucio, she has wondered about them not at all). But that is not it either.

It has to do with how careful Lucio is. With how he seems always to be standing at a distance from her. Ruthie watched him throw the baseball that day, and saw how afterwards, after the ball knocked the great bird askew in the sky, he looked at his hand as if it had nothing to do with him. There is a nervousness to Lucio that makes him different from other boys. It is also what makes him different from her—and that, thinks Ruthie, with all the naïveté of a Communist in love, is the remarkable thing about it. Lucio Burke is the last person she should want anything to do with.

And now there is a third date.

She more than agreed. She asked for it. It was her idea.

The third date, as Ruthie well knows, is when things happen.

The next Monday, when Lucio arrives at Gutman Fur, he knocks three times, sharply, which is very different from the two previous times he has knocked. This, thinks Ruthie, is the knocking of someone on his way to a third date. She gets up from behind her desk and opens the door.

"Hello, Lucio," she says. "Come in."

"Thanks," he tells her. "How're you?"

"Fine."

Lucio nods, as if Ruthie has just made a telling observation that would not have occurred to him. He looks down shyly at his hands, and seems to notice that he is carrying a flower.

"I brought you this," he says, handing her a single red rose.

"Oh my," says Ruthie.

"If you don't want it," says Lucio, "I can get rid of it."

"No," says Ruthie. "It's lovely." As if to give evidence of this, she brings the flower to her nose and inhales deeply. "Lovely," she says again.

"Good," says Lucio.

The rose was Dante's idea, Dante being something of an expert, if not an actual encyclopedia, on the subject of how to deal with women. Dante lost his virginity when he was fourteen, to a cigarette girl who worked at the Sunnyside Amusement Park. He told the girl she looked like Jean Harlow, and after that it was only a matter of time. The details of the encounter he has supplied to Lucio on several afternoons when the two were manning the pumps at Michelangelo's Garage. Lucio knows that Dante walked up to the girl and came right out with the compliment. He saw the girl himself, afterwards, when she came by the garage to see Dante, and was surprised to find that she looked nothing like the actress. She did not even have blond hair. Dante told him this was exactly the point; she'd never heard that one before. So it was that, when Lucio told Dante about his imminent third date with Ruthie, Dante advised him against showing up for a third date without a rose.

"So," Lucio asked, "I just walk in and hand it to her?"

"You have it behind your back," said Dante. "And when you step in, before you say anything else, you say, I got this for you, and you hand it over."

"So I have it behind my back."

"Behind your back, behind your ear, up your ass—it doesn't matter. The important thing is that you got the rose, and that you give it to her. Then you can give it to her, if you know what I mean."

"What if I say, thanks for having me on this date," said Lucio, "and then hand her the rose?"

"Don't thank her," said Dante. "Why would you thank her?"

"I don't know," said Lucio. "For going out with me."

"She was the one that did the asking."

"And I was glad she asked me."

"Listen," said Dante, "don't do any thanking her. You come in and hand her the rose."

"Can I ask you a question?"

"*Bo*," said Dante, "what am I here for?"

"Why do you think she wants to go out with me?"

"Because of the baseball," said Dante. "Didn't I tell you you'd be beating them off?"

"You think so?"

"What does it matter? I don't know why the broads that go out with me go out with me. You think I look in the mirror and think about asking *me* out? It doesn't work like that. They look at us and we look at them, and whatever happens happens. The important thing," said Dante, "is that you're finally getting laid."

"Laid?" said Lucio.

"*Bo*," said Dante, "why do you think the third date is called the third date? Think about those little pigs, the first one with the straw, then with the sticks, then with the bricks. Don't tell me you think those pigs are building houses."

"They're trying not to get eaten," said Lucio.

"They're trying not to get screwed by the wolf," said Dante, shaking his head.

"Where is that in the story?" said Lucio.

"Lucio," said Dante, "you read that thing again, and tell me where it *ain't*."

Lucio was still thinking about this when he realized that Dante was shaking his hand, pressing a tiny square packet into it.

"Remember," Dante told him. "You ain't shooting blanks any more."

Lucio went home and was faced with the question of what to wear. He had initially imagined himself wearing his suit, a pinstriped number he had inherited from Dante, which Dante had inherited from Quintillano, the youngest of his mother's five unmarried brothers. But maybe, he thought, there was something presumptuous about a suit. No, he should put on a clean white shirt and leave it at that. But no sooner had he taken the clean shirt out of the closet than he imagined Ruthie looking at that shirt, thinking it bourgeois and sending him on his way. No, he told himself, better to show up for the third date in work clothes, as if he thought there was nothing momentous about the occasion, as if he didn't know or, better, didn't care whether anything happened. This struck him as such an excellent idea that after he had put his work clothes back on, he took the condom that Dante had given him out of his back pocket and hid it outside, in the eavestrough. He was dimly aware that there was something irrational about taking the condom out of his pocket before going on a third date, but once he had done so he felt so much better, so much safer, that he walked straight out of the house and directly down Beverley Street, where he realized he was late, and had to run in order to make it to Harrimen's Florist on Augusta Street before it closed. He bought a single rose for a nickel. By the time he arrived at the Darling Building, he felt so shaken and harassed as a result of carrying it—as if his cousin had forced him to march down Spadina while holding aloft any number of products made exclusively of rubber—that he almost turned around and went home. But when he handed Ruthie the rose and she made a very un-Ruthielike cooing noise, Lucio was glad he had followed his cousin's advice.

"So," he asks her, "are you ready?"

"Ready?" says Ruthie, alarmed.

Lucio nearly blurts out that he does not have the condom with him.

"For the movie," says Ruthie, standing up. "Of course."

"Yes," says Lucio, "for the movie."

"Fine," she says, nodding for no reason. She is wearing a yellow blouse with shiny brown buttons in the front, and a black skirt. "So," she says, as they walk toward the door, "how's the dancing?"

"What's that?" says Lucio, stopping.

"The dancing," says Ruthie. "Have you been practising?"

"A little," says Lucio, and then, as if to demonstrate, he extends his arms as if she is in them, and moves his feet—left foot forward, forward with the right, then the left—just as Ruthie showed him.

"Very impressive," says Ruthie.

"Do you think it's better, really?"

"Hard to tell from here," she says, moving toward him. "All right," she says, pressing up against him, standing close enough to smell the gasoline on his clothes. "One, two, three," she counts.

And once again Lucio and Ruthie are dancing.

"Wonderful," Ruthie says, and her arm slides farther around his back.

Lucio can smell perfume. Ruthie the Commie, he thinks to himself, is wearing perfume. They take a couple of steps and turn, and Lucio gets lost, falling out of step and causing Ruthie's thigh to brush against his crotch.

"I'm sorry," he says, pulling back.

"You know what we need?" says Ruthie.

"Yes," says Lucio, cursing his stupidity.

"Music."

"You're right!" exclaims Lucio, as if he is a balloon popping.

Ruthie goes into Mr. Gutman's office and brings out the old DeForest Everyman. She puts the radio down on the floor, turning the knob until she finds some music.

The voice of Bing Crosby fills the room. Crosby's voice is raspy and rough (for this is the summer of 1933, before he has become much of a movie star, before MGM has tried to insure his throat and the doctor has found nodes on his larynx and forced him to take singing lessons, which smooth and change his voice), and the roughness sounds desperate to Lucio, as if the singer, like Lucio, is an underdog and about to go home alone.

But then Ruthie gets up. She takes Lucio's hand, and he feels transported somewhere indistinct, outside of himself.

"Now," she tells him, unbuttoning her blouse. "This is where you put your hand."

Lucio does not stop her.

On the radio the song ends and another begins. Guy Lombardo and the Royal Canadians play "Charmaine."

"We need to be careful," Ruthie tells him. "Do you understand that?"

Lucio nods.

"Do you like that?" she says.

"I do," says Lucio, as if it is a wedding.

A few minutes later, Ruthie tells him, "One day I'd like to do something."

Above them the sweatshop sewing machines are rattling. When Ruthie speaks she looks up at the ceiling. As if the sweatshop upstairs is what she is talking about.

"What do you want to do?" says Lucio, who expects her to say something like see the Leaning Tower of Pisa.

"Something about the world, to change things," says Ruthie. "You know, I showed up that day at the playground for a reason. I thought it would be something if I hit that ball, a little thing, but something—the kind of thing that could change people's minds, if they thought about it long enough and in the right way. I think there's something out there waiting for me that I have to do. I mean, look around—the world's changing, and now's the time, if you're ever going to do anything."

Lucio looks at her and smiles.

"Go ahead and laugh if you want," says Ruthie. "But it's true—people are starving everywhere, whether or not I say they are. You think that someone like Mussolini or Hitler just comes out of nowhere? He doesn't, I'll tell you that. It's what they call the historical imperative asserting itself. The world is a desperate place," she says, excited. "There are a lot of people who need a way out, a lot of people at the end of their rope."

"And that's a good thing?" says Lucio.

"That's a great thing," says Ruthie. "Not that people are hungry or poor—I mean, not that I'd wish such things on anyone, but certain things have to happen before the Revolution can take place. Things have to get a lot worse before they get any better, and that's what's happening right now. Things are getting as bad as they can get, and when they can't get any worse, things will change. It's not easy, you know. Today when I was walking here, I saw a woman and two kids sitting on the side of the road. Dirty, lousy, and I had a dollar bill in my pocket. I don't know what came over me. I just gave it to them."

"And that's a bad thing?"

"It's nothing," says Ruthie. "Worse—it's part of the problem. I didn't help today with that dollar. Maybe in the short run, but not really. Maybe I avoided a little misery today, but I didn't solve anything. I slowed things down."

"What'll it be like after?" says Lucio. "You know, after the Revolution?"

"See," says Ruthie, as if she is talking at once to Lucio and about Lucio, "this is the problem—you can't see what's going to happen after on the basis of the way things are before. It'll all be different, including the way you think about those people who had to go hungry in order that things could change."

"I know what it's like," says Lucio, "to wish things were different."

"There's going to be a straw one day," says Ruthie, "that breaks the camel's back."

"What's the camel, again?"

Ruthie laughs. Then she says, "This, capitalism, you and me, everything."

"And you," says Lucio, "want to be that straw?"

"A straw," corrects Ruthie. "You can't decide to be *the* straw"—and here she pauses, wondering if this is true.

"So," says Lucio, "what'll be your thing?"

"I don't know," Ruthie tells him. "I used to think it'd be something I'd write, but now I don't know. I sit here with *Das Kapital* open and listen to the sewing machines above me, and I think of all those poor girls working away for nothing at all, and the feeling wells up inside of me. That is what Marx is writing about—them. It's like I have something to say, but when I go to write, nothing happens. Lately, I've been thinking I need to *do* something. You know that shop above us—McMullen Fabrics, or whatever they're calling themselves now—they've closed down and declared bankruptcy more times than I can count, which is so they don't have to pay anyone, not even their employees. I saw one of the girls outside and asked her if she was in a union, and she looked at me like I was crazy."

"Maybe she didn't want to risk it."

"Anything worth doing is dangerous. You know when their shift started? Eight this morning. You know when they shut off? At eleven. That's a fifteen-hour shift. You call that right?"

"I'm not saying that," says Lucio.

"Then?"

"I don't know," says Lucio. "I never really thought about it."

Ruthie looks at him. "You know," she says, "you're right. I shouldn't think about it."

"I'm not saying that, either."

"No," says Ruthie. "I've done my thinking. I know what I think. I have to stop thinking."

She looks at Lucio and sits down beside him under the lights, then turns and looks at their reflection in the wide mirror, and she notices for the first time that while she is dressed finely, in a sheer yellow blouse and stockings, with her hair down, Lucio's dirty clothes make him look as if he has been working all day with his hands. There seems to Ruthie something pleasantly appropriate about the picture; its appropriateness is all the more striking because it is unplanned, and it makes her think that there has been something guiding her toward Lucio all along. She turns toward him and looks into his eyes. "You know," she says, "I see what you've been trying to tell me all along."

"Me?" says Lucio.

"Tell me what you were thinking that day when you knocked that bird down."

"Nothing," says Lucio, telling her the truth. "The ball rolled toward me, and I picked it up, and I saw the bird. Then I threw it. There's not much more to say than that. I wish there was. I wish I could do it again, but I can't."

"No," says Ruthie, standing up. "And that's the point."

"The point?"

Lucio stands up also, and before he knows it, Ruthie has put her arm around him. Once again they are dancing.

"Now I know what you're doing here, Lucio Burke," she tells him.

"That's good," says Lucio, who doesn't feel relieved in the least.

Tuesday afternoon, at the garage, Dante wants to know what happened. "*She* did it?" he says, when Lucio finishes telling him. "She unbuttoned her *own* blouse, and did it *herself?*"

Lucio nods.

"She got *your* hand," he says, "and put it on *her?*"

Lucio nods.

"And what did you do?"

"I let her."

"*Mamma mia*," says Dante, and pretends to faint.

The following evening, Lucio knocks again at the door of Gutman Fur. He goes in to find Ruthie sitting behind her desk, a brown felt brimmed hat pulled down low over her face.

"What's this?" says Lucio. "You're a movie star now?"

She removes the hat, and he sees that her left eye is swollen and blackened.

"Ruthie!" Lucio is shocked. "What happened?"

"I went up." She nods toward the ceiling. The rattling of the sewing machines seems louder than ever.

"Up there?"

Ruthie smiles. "Mr. Gutman went out yesterday, for lunch. He always does. He walks to Altman's, and he doesn't come back, most days, until after one. Every day I just sit here, but after the other night—after what you said—I went up. I know the Party wouldn't agree, but who cares? Anyway, I waited until some of the girls went down for lunch, and I got talking to them, and went up with them and walked in."

"And that's when you got your shiner?"

"Shiner," says Ruthie. "It makes me sound like a boxer."

"Well?"

"You wouldn't believe it," says Ruthie. "It's a huge place up there that takes up half the whole fourth floor. A field filled with sewing machines. It's nothing like Weiss Clothing, where Esther and my mother work. This is a factory. When one girl drops, and I bet they drop all the time in that sweltering place, they replace her with another. Anyway, I got up there and saw the foreman looking at me, but I hung my head in that kind of hangdog way they all do, and I started talking. I sat down at a machine and I was pumping the pedals with my feet. I've no idea what I was saying, but they were listening to me. The moment I started talking, everyone got quiet, and I could tell that none of them were saying anything out of fear, not knowing what the rest of them would say. But then one of them I'd never seen before said it wouldn't be a bad idea to have a union. All of them agreed—just like that, spontaneously, the way Emma Goldman says they ought to—but then I turned and saw the foreman standing there."

"Did he hear you?"

"Standing right over me," says Ruthie. "Like he was going to scare me."

"Weren't you scared?" says Lucio.

"A little, not that it matters—he knew what I was doing there, whether or not he heard me, and whether or not I was scared, it didn't matter."

"What did you do?"

"I said I was going to leave, and he grabbed me," says Ruthie, taking a handful of her long red hair and holding it above her. "Just like that." She seems unbothered—rejuvenated—by the recollection. "He picked me up as if I were a teapot. It hurt like the dickens, I can tell you that, and I must have screamed, because all the girls stopped sewing and looked. The room went all quiet, and the foreman dragged me out the door. I thought he was going to push me out with a kick, you know, the way Hap Kvidera always gets kicked around by the police, he had me bent forward so. But then he stood me up and asked me if I was alone. I said nothing, I just looked back at him, right in the eyes, and that was when he hit me."

"My god," says Lucio, looking at her eye. When he tries to touch it, she pulls back. "Did you put ice on it?"

"Ice," says Ruthie, shaking her head. "I'm fine."

"It'd take down the swelling, at least."

Ruthie is agitated, excited. "Anyway," she says quickly, "I'm fine."

"This time," says Lucio.

Ruthie looks at him.

"What did you tell Gutman?"

"Nothing," she says. "I said I opened the door the wrong way."

"And he bought it?"

"Sure he bought it. As far as he's concerned, I was here the whole time."

"You should have said something. He wouldn't have fired you, and besides, maybe then he would've gone up and given that foreman a taste of his own medicine."

"Then he would have been going up for the wrong reasons. Mr. Gutman can hear those sewing machines up there just as clearly as we can, and still he's done nothing about it. He'd go up because he wanted to think of himself as brave and chivalrous, or even just because he wanted to get the foreman back for slugging me."

"What's so bad about that?"

"What would that have to do with anything?"

"It would have to do with you."

"Listen, Lucio, if I thought there was a chance of Mr. Gutman looking at my black eye and marching up to negotiate a more equitable contract for those girls, I'd tell him the truth in a second. But as it is, if he or anyone else"—and here Ruthie looked at Lucio, as if to warn him—"went up and did any kind of grandstanding, it would erase, just like that, any of the good I've done."

"At least you should be careful. That's all I'm saying."

"Is it? Is that *all* you're saying?"

Lucio opens his mouth to speak, and then stops.

"What?" says Ruthie.

He looks away.

"Anyway, I won't be going up there any more."

"Good," he says, looking up at her, feeling he has made his point.

"No," says Ruthie. "And that is where you come in."

"Me? I'm not going up there, I can tell you that."

Ruthie decides to ignore this. "It's simple," she says, and tells him that what she has in mind is a kind of general strike, a mass demonstration. If she cannot get onto McMullen Fabrics herself, if she cannot speak directly to the girls whose sewing machines punctuate and sometimes drown out her reading of *Das Kapital*, she will communicate with them in other ways. She will go into every dress shop on Spadina, and spread the word that on a particular day there will be a walk-out. The walkout will be Ruthie's message to those girls on the floor above her, a sign to them—but not just to them, to them all, to all the girls in all the non-unionized shops who think they've no choice about working sixteen hours a day—a sign of what is possible, a sign that there is nothing to be afraid of. On exactly the same day, Ruthie tells Lucio, at exactly nine in the morning, all the girls, all the finishers and sleeve drapers, all the alteration hands and stenographers, all the pressers and stock girls and dressmakers and buttonhole-machine operators and cloakmakers and embroiderers and trimmers and body makers and drapers, and all the girls who work in the flower and feather factories on King Street, and the paper-box makers in the Empire Building near Dundas—she has been drawing up a list—all of them will walk out, all at once. No whistle will blow, no announcement will be made. At nine they will stand up and walk out, and Spadina will be filled. And then the girls in the sweatshop upstairs will look out the window, and the sight of the crowd in the street will be enough.

Mr. Gutman is going away to England, says Ruthie, leaving her in charge of the shop, to model and sell the coats on her own. He just told her about the trip this afternoon, and she hit on her plan right away. It seems to her that history is lining things up, the way Lucio lined up the bird in his sights that day before throwing the ball.

"I still don't get what this has to do with me," says Lucio.

"You're going to run the shop," she tells him.

"This shop?" says Lucio. "Gutman's?"

"There's nothing to it," says Ruthie. "You sit at this desk, and tell whoever comes in that I'll be back soon."

"What about my job at the garage?"

"What about it?"

"Well, how can I do the two?"

"Lucio," says Ruthie. "This is important. Ask Dante to cover for you."

He looks at her. "You think you've thought of everything, don't you?"

"That's because I have," says Ruthie. A moment later she says, "Just ask Dante, and see what he says. Will you do that for me?"

Thursday afternoon, when Dante shows up at the garage to take over for him, Lucio puts it to him.

"You've got to be crackers," says Dante.

"OK, if you won't do it, you won't do it—but at least I tried."

"Hold on," says Dante. "Let me get this straight. I work your shift, and you work hers, and she goes around planning some parade."

"It's not a parade," Lucio points out. "It's a walkout."

"If they didn't want the jobs, they shouldn't have taken them in the first place."

"You're right," says Lucio. "They take the job, then complain about it."

"If they don't like it, they should quit," announces Dante. "Nobody forced them, and there's enough people that'd jump at the chance."

"You're absolutely right."

"I get it," says Dante.

"Get what?"

"You've gone over to the Communism."

"No, I haven't," says Lucio. "And besides, you don't say *the* Communism, you just say Communism."

"See, what'd I tell you about hanging out with that red broad?"

"You never said anything about it."

Dante considers this, and admits it is true.

"So," says Lucio. "The answer's no?"

"Sure, I'll do it."

"You will?"

"Of course."

"You want to think about it for a bit?"

"I said I'd do it."

"It might be for a while," says Lucio. "I don't know how long it'll be for."

"Never mind," says Dante. "I'm your cousin, and that's what cousins are for."

Lucio sighs. It seems there is no way around it.

"You better be getting it, is all I can say," says Dante.

Lucio says nothing.

"You're *still* not?" Dante shakes his head. "I knew it."

No, Lucio and Ruthie have not done it. They have not done it on Ruthie's desk and they have not done it behind the frosted glass windows that enclose Mr. Gutman's office. They didn't on the table in the back of the shop where the alterations are done. They didn't in front of the three-sided mirror. They didn't under the bright lights above the mirror that Ruthie stands under when she models the fur coats for rich old men. They didn't leaning up against the big windows that look down on Spadina, where the lights shine up like stars beneath them, where Ruthie touched Lucio through his rough workman pants for the first time. They didn't when Ruthie straddled Lucio on a narrow chair under the ventilation shaft, through which nothing but the rattle of sewing machines could be heard, with her skirt off. Lucio has perfected the pinch that springs open a brassiere, has slid his right hand over Ruthie's top and felt her nipples hard against the fabric of her blouse, and still they have not done it.

"Soon," Ruthie tells him, as if she is talking about the Revolution itself.

FIVE

THAT FRIDAY, THEREFORE, Lucio wakes up early and goes to the garage as usual but stays just long enough to be seen by Michelangelo. At nine-thirty, when Dante arrives, Lucio takes the College streetcar to Spadina and walks down to Gutman Fur, where Ruthie is waiting. When he gets there, she is changing into a plain grey dress she sewed herself the week before—like the dresses the girls at the shops wear: crude, handmade, formless productions entirely unlike the clothes Mr. Gutman requires her to wear while she is modelling the fur coats. Lucio sits down in a chair and watches her, and when she is finished her undressing and dressing he watches her pull her hair up so tight it makes her eyes water. She has skipped breakfast, she tells him, to make it look as if the drudgery of the sweatshop has changed even the colour of her face. Despite her paleness, she seems to Lucio completely happy, her eyes dark and sure, her whole face glistening, as if she has never wanted and would never want anything else in the world. Since coming up with her plan, she is like a different person; instead of being guarded and edgy she has been excited and giddy, on the inside of something mysterious and dangerous and necessary.

The change was apparent to him almost immediately. That first night after she got her shiner and decided to stage the walkout, the two of them stayed late at Gutman Fur, talking about the walkout and how best to make it happen. The main problem was the leaflet Ruthie needed to hand out to the shop girls—how to distribute it, but also the more urgent, difficult question of what it should say.

The puzzle of how to get the leaflets into the hands of the girls was solved easily enough. It was Lucio who suggested they could be folded; once they were squeezed into tiny white squares, Ruthie would be able to press them into the palms of co-conspirators and then those co-conspirators could press them into the hands of other co-conspirators, until all the girls in all the shops had seen, if not touched, one of them.

But what the leaflet should say was a real problem. It had to be elegant, Ruthie told him, moving, but not confusing—a beautiful, direct plea for a display of solidarity. She sat down resolutely at her desk and went to work. A few minutes later, she held up a piece of paper for Lucio to see.

WALK OUT
9:00 A.M.
AUGUST 11, 1933

"What do you think?" she asked him.

"It's perfect," he told her.

"It could be better."

Lucio looked again at the paper and said nothing; Ruthie, he could tell, had already made up her mind.

"It's like I'm saying, walk out or else," she told him.

"You sound just like a boss."

The two looked at the leaflet again, then Ruthie crumpled it up in a conclusive way and threw it into the trash can. "I'll give it another try."

"Not as easy as you thought, eh?" said Lucio.

"I never said it would be *easy*," Ruthie told him. "Did I sit down here and say, this'll take a second? This'll be easy?"

Lucio started shaking his head.

"There's nothing easy about doing this. You can't just sit down and write the first thing that comes into your head. It doesn't work like that." She sat back down and took out a fresh piece of paper, placing it in the centre of the desk.

Lucio attempted to remain as still as possible.

"It's not just me." Ruthie put down her pencil. "It's not like it's my problem, like it's just me wondering how to do it, you know, how to write something that will make people want to change their lives—it's a big problem, the whole problem. That people should cooperate, everyone knows that. But why? Why should they stop what they're doing and do something else?" She looked up at Lucio, who attempted to show that he didn't have an answer to this by raising his eyebrows, shrugging his shoulders and shaking his head at once. "You have to convince them, of course—and what do you have to convince them with?" Lucio now made a low whistling sound, to convey his mystification. "With language," she said. "But as soon as you begin to talk, everyone starts getting confused, and you have to ask what So-and-So meant by a certain thing, and nothing gets done, like at the Party meeting—" She stopped talking, shook her head and then—for no reason at all, for she had yet to write a single thing on it—turned the paper over.

Lucio tried not to breathe. "Without communication," she told him fiercely, as if he had been arguing with her the whole time, "there's no cooperation." With that she raised her pencil, stopped again, crumpled up the paper and burst into tears. "I'll never do it," she told him. "I can't."

Lucio went over and knelt in front of her. "Don't give up, the first one was good."

"You thought so? I mean really?"

"When I saw it," he told her, "I wanted to head right out there."

She stopped crying. "You did not."

"Maybe not right then, but eventually."

She smiled and wiped her face. "It's got to be catchy. Think of something catchy."

Lucio got up and went back to the other side of the desk and sat down in the chair. Neither said anything for a long moment. Ruthie picked up the pencil and bit the end of it.

"'All of Me,'" said Lucio suddenly.

Ruthie looked at him.

He sang, by way of explanation.

"You're right," she told him. "That *is* catchy."

"You should make up something like that," he told her. "That makes you want to dance, right?—you need to do something like that, only instead of dancing it's got to make you want to get up and walk out."

"It's easy to make people dance," said Ruthie. "*Anyone* can make anyone else dance." And then, because it was Lucio who was there with her, with his beautiful eyes, and because she inexplicably wanted very much to dance, she started to sing, and as she sang she got up from behind the desk, stood him up and took him into her arms.

"All right," said Lucio. "I think you're getting sidetracked."

Ruthie laughed and kissed him. Then she went back to the desk and sat down, and a moment later she was writing. She held up the paper a second time. "Here," she said. "What do you think of *this*?"

Hope Begins
9:00 A.M.
August 11, 1933
Stop Work, Stand Up, Take Spadina!

"Well?"

Lucio replied without thinking. "It's good, I'd do it."

"I would too," she said, and looked again at the paper, as if she had not been the one to write the words on it.

"How'd you think of it?"

Ruthie didn't reply; she had stood up and was again moving toward him. She turned off the lamp at the edge of the desk, and suddenly it was dark except for the glow of Spadina beneath them and the moon above, which shone in through the windows, a narrow bit of light on a wooden floor.

So it is that on a sunny day in July, with Lucio behind the desk at Gutman Fur and Dante manning the pumps at Michelangelo's Garage, Ruthie begins her campaign of infiltrating the sweatshops and handing out leaflets. She starts at the south end of Spadina, in a paper-box shop on the eighth floor of the French Building, south of Richmond Street.

The conditions in the shop are far worse than anything she has ever seen. However remote her job modelling fur coats is from such places, Ruthie is no stranger to the inside of a sweat-shop; before Mr. Gutman hired her, she, like her mother and sister and most of the women on Beverley Street, worked in a number of the semi-legal, non-unionized sweatshops along Spadina. When a few days earlier she entered McMullen Fabrics for the first time, and tried to talk to the girls there, the dank, airless scent of the sweatshop, the numbingly monoto-nous sound, the crushing sameness of posture and task were familiar to her. But even steeled, even expecting the worst, when she enters the paper-box shop, she is shocked.

There are about thirty girls, she guesses, all of them crammed into a room not much larger than her living room. At one end of the room the door is propped open, and at the other a window has been swung wide to let in as much of the weak summer wind as possible. There is not a single chair in the room: it seems the girls are expected to stand the whole time, at one of several four-foot-long tables. They are organ-ized into human assembly lines. At the far end of the table stands a girl who extracts sheets of paper from a chugging, dangerous-looking electric paper-cutter. Once the sheets are cut, the setter-upper, as she is called, hands them to the strip-per, who separates them and throws the excess paper into a bin behind her and hands the pieces to the turner-inner, who gives the box to the paster, who glues the bottom on and deposits the finished box into one of the large bins that sit at the end of each table. When the bin is full, a man comes and wheels it away. The names and functions of the positions Ruthie will discover later, after she becomes practised at infil-trating shops and friendly with a number of paper-box girls—but about the men there can be no question: they are there to keep order.

After standing outside and looking in, Ruthie finally steps inside. She installs herself at the end of one of the tables, beside a paster, a girl of about seventeen with long, dirty brown hair.

"Are they treating you well?" begins Ruthie, without introduction, assuming it will be plain to the girl what side she is on.

"What d'you want?" calls another woman. She stands at the other end of the table, next to the machine, which chugs along noisily. "Who're you?"

"I'm a woman," Ruthie says loudly. "Like you."

"What?" she calls back. "She's your sister?"

One of the men at the front of the shop has noticed her, and Ruthie sees him begin to move in her direction. She tries to shake the girl's hand, to press one of the folded leaflets into her palm. But the girl wants none of it, and steps back quickly with her hands up.

"Go on, take it," mutters Ruthie, and tries again to shake the girl's hand. The girl backs farther away, her hands still up.

"What's all this?" The man stands alert, ready for trouble, near the door.

"Nothing, sir," says the girl, speaking for the first time. Ruthie is surprised by the sound of her voice—it is thin and high, reedy like an oboe.

"Back to work," says the man. He looks at Ruthie. "What's your name?"

Ruthie looks down shyly, mutters something and walks quickly past him, out of the shop. She knows he is following her, and once in the hallway she starts to run, ducking into a latrine. He does not follow her in. Why, she doesn't know—perhaps he is waiting outside for her to come out. Inside the latrine there are no cubicles, merely three granite toilets lined up. Two girls are sitting on the toilets closest to the door, one smoking and the second apparently asleep. The smoker looks at Ruthie when she enters, and watches as she crosses the room to the toilet farthest from the door. Ruthie hikes up her dress, sits down on the third toilet and notices she is trembling. That she is afraid surprises her. She was so calm that other day— even when the foreman hit her, she was not really frightened. She knew that if something did happen to her, people would come to the Darling Building looking for her, asking questions. But this is different. Now she is in danger, not in control of what will happen next, and at the mercy of strangers. No one knows she is here—not even Lucio. She didn't tell him where she was going so he wouldn't be able to follow her and intervene if anything happened. Slowly Ruthie gets control of herself, calms down, and it is only then that she realizes the two other girls in the latrine are laughing at her.

"Who you meeting afterwards?" says the smoker.

Ruthie looks at her. "No one," she says.

"Could have fooled me," says the one who was asleep, and laughs again.

It takes Ruthie a moment to understand that the girls are talking about her underwear. Under her grey dress she is wearing rolled silk stockings with frilly black garters that end about six inches above the knee, and black lace panties. The stockings, like the panties, were Mr. Gutman's idea, so she would feel glamorous when modelling his coats. She did not refuse, on the grounds that her underwear had very little to do with her. That morning when Lucio arrived, she changed her dress but did not think to change what was under it. While she changed, he straddled the chair behind her desk and watched her fold the skirt, and watched her look at herself in the mirror. This plain dress, she told him, is indispensable. If you want to speak to these girls, you have to do it while you are standing with them, while their hands and your hands are busy, while you and they are wearing the same clothes. She knows she is right to think this, but as the two girls laugh she sees how incomplete her transformation has been, despite her best efforts. And perhaps it will always be incomplete. Perhaps her willingness to conform to the chorus-girl stereotype for Mr. Gutman has changed her. Why does she wear such things? And why did she allow Lucio to watch her change? Some part of her, she knows, enjoyed standing nearly naked in front of Lucio, who will never touch her if she does not touch him first.

Eventually Ruthie gets up and leaves the latrine. Finding the hallway empty, she runs down the stairs and is soon out on Spadina, short of breath but safe. She walks aimlessly for a long while and returns to Gutman Fur only at the end of the day, so Lucio will not know the day has been such a failure. Upon arriving, she discovers that he is also at the end of his rope. After only a single day of sitting behind her desk and watching the door, he is unsure he'll be able to go through with it. He's spent this first day staring at the word GUTMAN on the frosted glass door, waiting for it to open, waiting for Mr. Gutman to walk in and call the police.

"You ask me," he tells her, "I don't need to be here at all."

"What if someone came?" says Ruthie.

"Then they'd find the place closed."

"Look," says Ruthie. "You want out, just say it."

"I'm not saying that," says Lucio. "I just don't know why anyone has to be here."

"You have to be here so I know if someone does come by—if the wrong person comes by, the jig's up with Mr. Gutman. You're here to tell me if they do."

Lucio says nothing.

She takes her hair down in a preoccupied way.

"What am I supposed to tell them?" says Lucio suddenly.

"It doesn't matter, just tell them that I'm not here, and neither is Mr. Gutman."

"I could say I'm his nephew," says Lucio.

"You could," says Ruthie. "It doesn't matter."

"But what if they know his nephew? What then?"

"Then," she says, "the jig would be up."

"Maybe, then, saying I'm the nephew isn't a great idea?"

"Bingo."

Lucio paces the floor in front of the big mirror.

"Listen," says Ruthie. "You worry too much. There's nothing to worry about. No one is going to grill you. They'll come in and you tell them that I'm not here, or I'm sick or whatever. And that I'll get back to them, and that's all you have to say. Don't say anything you don't need to say. Just act normal and they'll act normal. Like I said, it doesn't matter what you say. Just tell them you're some kid who's minding the place, and I'll be back soon."

"But you won't be," says Lucio, who has spent the day telling himself that Ruthie is going to be right back.

"The point is to get them *not* to stay."

"What if they don't go?"

"Don't worry," says Ruthie. "Nobody's going to come in. You want to know something? I worked here last summer. Every day I was behind that desk, rain or shine—no one came in. Not a single person. You have nothing to worry about, really."

Lucio looks away, petulantly. "Still," he says.

"OK," she says. "You want to worry, worry. If you want to call it off, call it off. I've said what I can say, now it's over."

"Come on, Ruthie," says Lucio. "Don't be like that."

"It's a store that sells fur coats," she reminds him impatiently. "Who thinks of a fur coat in the summer?"

Lucio says nothing.

"Would you?"

"Then what am I doing here?" says Lucio.

"You're the lookout, that's all—just be yourself, or someone else. Make up a name. I don't care."

"You're sure?"

"Go home," she tells him.

"Home?" He has seen her hardly at all. But he knows better than to argue. "Fine," he says, and gets up to leave.

When he is gone, Ruthie changes out of her grey dress and walks home alone. Their leaving separately has become an expected thing. Nothing is planned out, but Lucio always goes first and then, after a decent interval, she follows. Why this should be is never discussed, but it is as if a fragility hovers around them at all times, as if to tell anyone about their being together would be to risk breaking apart everything. So they are careful. Lucio leaves for home first and is never anywhere to be seen by the time she gets to Beverley Street. This night is no exception. It is past eleven, and as she nears the three houses across from the Institute for the Blind, she is surprised to see people on the veranda. Her mother and Francesca, Lucio's mother, are out sewing. The stillness of the summer evening and the sight of the two women working so late combine with Ruthie's dark mood and make her feel overwhelmingly beaten. The houses behind the veranda, like the veranda itself, look to her dreary and solemn, the type of buildings that will one day be demolished by men with more money than her family will ever have, to pave the way for the future. Hope is there in the beginning, she thinks cynically, but it also ends; her mother still has to sew in the poor light for pennies.

But as Ruthie nears the houses she sees that the two women are laughing—they are sitting out late because they want to. As she reaches the veranda steps, her mother and Francesca look up and smile and laugh again, at something Ruthie knows has nothing to do with her. Their familiarity feels jarring now—that Lucio's mother and her mother should be such good friends—but of course it is that way, she reminds herself; she and Lucio have only remade each other, the rest of the world is still the same.

Francesca and Sadie Nodelman have been friends for nearly twenty years, and have lived next door to each other for most of that time. Ruthie knows it is because of Sadie that the Burke family came to live on Beverley Street in the first place. This happened some eighteen years ago, just before Lucio was born, and when she was just a baby. Francesca and her mother were working together at the Timothy Eaton factory on Front Street, the same factory her father helped close down in his little way by serving soup in the fall of 1911. After the strike, after her father was fired, Sadie stayed—the strike had made it a better job. It was around that time that Sadie found herself sitting beside a pretty girl named Francesca DiFranco. The two became friends, and after Francesca married Andrew Burke, about six months before Lucio was born, Sadie told her about 187 Beverley being for sale.

At the time, Francesca and Andrew were living in a perfectly serviceable apartment on Sherbourne Steet, the same small one-bedroom apartment Andrew had occupied before they married. There were windows that looked out onto the street, and in the mornings the living room was full of light. The icebox did not leak, and the little kitchen was equipped with the newest kind of gas stove. If the kitchen was far too narrow to hold a table, this was made up for by the fact that the living room was large. In the evenings, Francesca and Andrew ate dinner on fold-out wooden tables and listened to Andrew's phonograph. The couple lived there happily up until the time when Francesca concluded she was pregnant, something she had done just hours before Sadie mentioned the house being for sale. But Francesca had not yet confided this news to her friend, so when Sadie told her about the house she spoke casually, in the tone of voice she might use if she were remarking that it looked like rain.

"Who's selling?" asked Francesca (who was in the process of sewing an inseam).

"The owners," said Sadie (who was in the process of sewing a hemline).

"The owners?" said Francesca, looking up from her sewing machine. "Who?"

"Old," said Sadie, not looking up from her sewing machine. "*Goyim.*"

"I want to see it," said Francesca.

"What for?"

"I said I want to see it," Francesca repeated.

That night, instead of going home, Francesca went with Sadie to take a look at the house. They walked up from Front Street and had just crossed Dundas when they saw a woman in a watermelon hat.

"Look," said Sadie. "That's her."

"Her?"

"Mrs. Comstock," said Sadie. "The one who's selling the house."

The woman in the watermelon hat walked slowly and stiffly along Dundas Street facing straight ahead, her back rigid. Francesca knew better than to read any significance into the stiffness with which Mrs. Comstock walked; it was impossible to walk any way but stiffly while wearing a watermelon hat. Reaching the zenith of its popularity sometime in the spring of 1915, the watermelon hat was a large, heavy helmet with a sheet of clear plastic at the front and a heavy mesh brim at the back. It had been created to solve the problem of automobile exhaust, the idea being that the headpiece—which resembled a fireman's hat—would prevent fumes from reaching the hair of the woman wearing it. Since it was designed to be worn while sitting in an automobile, any woman who wore a watermelon hat while she was walking had, out of necessity, to assume an upright posture not unlike that of a tightrope walker, and a rigidity of gait that was often confused, particularly by women who owned watermelon hats, with a regal bearing. Because it was impossible for her to see either her feet or to her left or right, Mrs. Comstock walked cautiously up the front steps, and stood there for a long time trying to find her keys. Finally she lifted her purse up over her head, and the keys—which seemed to be the only thing in the large black bag—fell out, bouncing off the top of the hat. It was apparently not the first time; Mrs. Comstock caught the keys as they bounced, with a practised hand.

"Good luck," said Sadie, giving Francesca a nudge.

"You're not coming with me?"

"Do you want the house or not?" said Sadie. "If you do, don't say you know me."

Francesca walked across the street alone and rang the bell.

Mrs. Comstock, when she opened the door, turned out to be a pale woman in her late sixties. Expensively but inelegantly dressed, she looked at Francesca with a disapproving lipsticked mouth. Francesca was marshalled into the front room, where, sitting upright on a daybed, reading the *Telegram*, was Mr. Comstock. He was shaped like a smokestack: tall, bald, thin, with a shock of perfectly white hair at the top of his head that he continually marshalled from the front of his head to the back, with one or the other of his thin hands. When his visitor entered the room, Mr. Comstock folded the paper deliberately and put it down on the coffee table before him. He did not nod or smile or otherwise move in the slightest, performing the task only with his hands, and in a way that suggested they were simply going about their own business, which he had elected not to inquire into.

Francesca introduced herself.

"Burke," said Mr. Comstock, in a British accent. "I once knew a fellow named Burke in finance, of the Leeds Burkes."

"My husband," said Francesca, guessing his meaning, "is an orphan."

"An orphan," said Mr. Comstock, and frowned, as if it were indecorous of her to bring it up. "Unfortunate."

Francesca shook her head, and so did Mr. Comstock. This operation caused him to turn around completely in his chair and to stare pensively out the big front window at the institute across the street. Then he began nodding, and nodded solemnly, as if the thought of Francesca's in-laws dying had caused him to reflect on his own mortality, which in turn had caused him to reflect on the transience of all things, and in so doing had rendered any discussion of the sale of the house not only impossible but pointless. The Comstocks had not introduced themselves, but neither seemed to regard it as strange that Francesca knew who they were. She perceived that they were the kind of better people who believed that all people were (or should be) born knowing who the better people were. He sat like that for some time, until Mrs. Comstock suggested he give Francesca a tour of the house.

Mr. Comstock got up from his daybed and began telling Francesca how, in a fortunate convergence of circumstance, he had been offered the house on terms that were most advantageous. An Englishman named William Patterson with an acute olfactory sensitivity had constructed the three linked houses all at once in the latter half of the previous century. This, explained Mr. Comstock, accounted for their peculiar construction, for the fact that the kitchen was on the second floor and the washroom on the third—all the rooms that could be expected to smell were as far away as possible from the rooms that could be expected not to smell.

Mr. Comstock's tour concluded with the bathroom, at the very top of the house. Francesca discovered that it took up the most of the third floor, which was a kind of attic up to which pipes had been run and into which a toilet, a sink and a bathtub had been wedged. Things were so tight because a big window, which looked out on St. Patrick's Church, took up an entire wall. When Francesca looked out the window, she had a clear view of the church's big stained-glass window showing Saint Patrick leading the snakes out of Ireland. As if to signal the end of the tour, Mr. Comstock flushed the toilet ironically, at once demonstrating that the house was in good working order, and that those who needed this demonstrated were of a class with which he did not often associate.

"It's a wonderful house," said Francesca, when they were back downstairs.

"It is," said Mrs. Comstock. "Or was."

"Was?" said Francesca.

"The immigrants," said Mr. Comstock, in his British accent, "ruin everything."

"Five hundred?" said Francesca.

"Five hundred," said Mrs. Comstock, her pink lips pursed. "Cash."

As she walked back to her perfectly serviceable apartment on Sherbourne, Francesca found herself unable to think about anything besides the difficulties of having a baby in the tiny place. Where would the crib go? And what about the playpen? It would be difficult, she told herself, but it could be done. They would be together, very close together, but they would be happy. The baby would be fine. With such a resolution she believed she had put all thoughts of the house on Beverley Street out of her mind, but by the time she reached Yonge Street, and found herself confronted with the sight of the longest street in the world, she had decided that it was uncaring and possibly criminal to raise a child in the confines of a perfectly serviceable apartment. A child needed a house with a backyard. A child needed a room of his own. A child and his mother needed a kitchen table.

Thus it was that she burst in on her husband, who, having just got home from working a double shift, was asleep on the sofa.

"Andrew," Francesca told him, "I've found a house."

"Who do you think I am?" Andrew Burke said, trying to make a joke. "Timothy Eaton?"

Francesca burst into tears.

Afterwards, after she had told Andrew about the baby and the house, there was still the problem of the money.

"We'll borrow it," said Francesca. "You must know someone."

She was right. Andrew did know someone. Alex Cobb, Conductor Cobb, who had got him the job on the streetcar and was still his boss. The thin Welshman, with his sprawling white moustache, and bushy eyebrows that curled downwards as if they were trying to find their way into his nose, had become his best friend. Cobb lived alone in a flat on the second floor of a square building on Gerrard Street. In terms of family, Cobb was wholly alone in the world; he had never spoken even once to Andrew about his family, as if he had somehow shaken himself free of them when he'd changed his name years before. That night, Andrew found Cobb exactly where he expected to find him—eating pork and beans in the window of Ford's Kitchen, a restaurant on Albert Street where Cobb took most of his meals.

"Burke," said Cobb when he saw him. "Fancy that."

"Cobb," said Andrew without ceremony, "I need five hundred."

Cobb at first said nothing. Then he asked, "What's it for?"

"For a house," said Andrew.

The next day Cobb gave him the money, and the Burkes moved into the house between the Nodelmans and the Diamonds.

SIX

IMAGINING HER MOTHER YOUNG AGAIN, and invested with the graces of youth, makes Ruthie feel sorry for herself, and she realizes what she is missing because of her solitary job at Gutman Fur. She worked in a sweatshop for a time, but not for as long as her mother did—and certainly not long enough to make a friend. Ruthie always thought of the sweatshop as a temporary thing, as something to be endured and overcome— a kind of personal version of capitalism itself. That her mother and Francesca are able to laugh puzzles Ruthie, who is unsure whether that laugh is genuine. She is confident that if her mother could look at her life as a whole with the same clarity that, years earlier, led her to the picket line, she would stop laughing. Still, the laughter of the two women makes her feel friendless and cut off. She attempts to go straight inside, but in order to do so has to cross in front of her mother. And that is enough—Sadie manages to get a look at her. "Ruthie," she calls, looking up from the pants she is hemming, "what's the matter?"

"I'm fine," says Ruthie.

"Ah-ha," says Sadie. "Do you hear that?"

"Could I miss it?" says Francesca, sounding very Yiddish—which she does, Ruthie has noticed, whenever she speaks to Sadie.

"Any moment," Sadie tells her daughter, "you're going to cry."

"Me, cry?" Ruthie hardly recognizes her own voice. The two women laugh at the sound of it. "Don't laugh at me," she says bitterly, and immediately they stop. "I'm not crying."

"So, Ruthie—is it a boy?" asks Sadie.

"You think I'm that stupid?"

"You could be."

"Everyone is," says Francesca. "If not, life would be easy."

Ruthie nods, as if Lucio's mother is speaking from experience, an acknowledged authority on such matters. But Ruthie has never seen her with any man. Too young to remember what Lucio's father looked like, Ruthie grew up thinking it an impossibility that Francesca would ever marry again, and now finds herself wondering why that should be the case, why there are not even any interested men around. Ruthie knows from experience how difficult it is to avoid such things: there is always someone trying to kiss you or shoving his baseball into your hand and letting it remain there for an unusually long time. Francesca is somehow exempt from all of that. There is old Michelangelo, who comes around, always in a white suit and always with flowers, but everyone knows that both are for Nonna, whom he has courted for years. Like everyone else, Ruthie knows the story of the reckless letter Michelangelo sent years before that brought Nonna and her family to Toronto in the first place. Why nothing has come of this eternal courtship Ruthie doesn't know for sure, but she imagines that it had to do with the fact that by the time Nonna got off the train that night, both she and Michelangelo were no longer as young as they had been in the old country. Or perhaps they had changed in other ways. Perhaps neither was looking for anything requiring consummation. Whatever the reason, to Ruthie, Nonna and her daughter are as unlike as any two people could be. Where Nonna is broad-shouldered and squat, with a pinched dry face, Francesca has the same dark hair and eyes, the same perfect ankles and waistline as she must have had that day when she walked onto Andrew's streetcar. The story of that day Ruthie has heard many times, and has no trouble believing—Francesca still looks like the kind of woman who could do that to a man. But something has closed in her, and perhaps men sense this and keep their distance. Ruthie watches Francesca hold a lacy bra—the clasps for which she has just sewn on—up to the light, but clinically, as if such a garment never had and never would have anything to do with her.

"So, Ruthie," Sadie is saying. "If not a boy, what?"

Ruthie decides to tell her mother the truth, or something like it. "Today, after work," she begins, "I went to a shop—you know, to talk to the girls."

"Ah," says Sadie. "You mean to organize them."

"They didn't want anything to do with me," Ruthie goes on, answering her mother's question not at all. "I had leaflets, and tried talking to them, but I couldn't give away a single piece of paper. One girl wouldn't even touch me. I was leaving, and went to shake her hand, and she backed off"—Ruthie demonstrates, raising her hands as if she is being held up—"like I was Dillinger. You should have seen how she looked at me."

"Don't take it so personal," says Francesca.

"It's for her own good," protests Ruthie.

"Not if she gets caught with that paper," says Francesca.

"It's the oldest trick in the book," Sadie tells her daughter. "Shake her hand—who're you trying to kid? They're not born yesterday either, those girls."

"Still," persists Ruthie, "I thought I could talk to them, that they'd listen."

"This, people have thought before," says Sadie wistfully.

"So how does it happen, then?" Ruthie faces her mother. "How does it *ever* happen? If no one listens to anyone, how does anything ever change? That big Eaton's strike, when Daddy made the soup, back then you could make them listen."

"You could never *make* them; they either would or they wouldn't," says Sadie.

"Still," interjects Francesca, "your father made them."

"What'd he do?" Ruthie says derisively. "He made the soup—but by then they were already on strike. I'm not talking about making soup. Once you're on strike, anyone can make soup."

"Is that what you think?" says Francesca. She looks at Sadie. "Is that what your parents told you?"

"It was Abe told the story," says Sadie.

Francesca shrugs. "Anyway, you're right about that, it wasn't the soup that did it—it was the sandwiches."

"Sandwiches?"

"In the shop, he made sandwiches—with sardines."

"He's a presser."

"He's a presser now," says Francesca, "but back then, he worked in the kitchen." She stops speaking abruptly—as if she has already said too much, as if she has just resolved to keep her nose out of Nodelman family business.

"What's she talking about?" Ruthie asks her mother.

"Before your father was a presser, he worked in the kitchen," explains Sadie. "Like Francesca says, he made sandwiches. So it's like this—one day he finds he's out of paper. This is trouble because it's his job to make sure the paper is there, so when he sees it's gone, he runs around looking for something to use to wrap. He decides he's got to go buy something, you know, on the quick, and when he steps outside there's a man there with a stack of papers. Your father thinks he's dreaming, and tries to buy the papers. Forget about it, the man tells him, these you can have. So your father takes them and wraps the sandwiches. That's how it starts for him—the papers were union membership, and he wrapped the sandwiches in them."

"He didn't know?"

"He didn't know then."

"But he found out," says Francesca.

"Imagine." Sadie shakes her head.

"What'd he do?"

"He did it again the next day. He found the man, and got more."

"But why?"

Sadie shrugs. "He knew it had to be done, that it was the right thing to do—this was how everybody got the forms. Before long we were unionized, and once that happened, well, you know the rest. After the strike was over and he got fired, everyone knew why. Some of the men taught him to be a presser so he could earn a living, because after that no one would hire him as a cook."

The Nodelman door opens and out steps Abe. From the look on his face, which is strangely sheepish, it is plain he has been listening. He goes over and sits down in his cheap beach chair. "So," he says to Ruthie, "there it is."

"Why lie about it?" Ruthie asks.

"If you found out, what would you want to do with the Party?—nothing. You'd grow up hearing about making sandwiches, another story with a punchline—a joke. Better to have a presser who's done some thinking for a father."

Ruthie says nothing for a moment. Then she has an idea. "How do you make them?" she asks.

"Make what?"

"Sardine sandwiches."

Abe tells her: how to remove the head and tail of the fish, how to break open the body and remove the spine, to use a pickle jar when she crushes the fish into a paste, to use white bread, not to be shy about the butter. "Then," he says, "you have to wrap them. That's the hard part; there's a special way." He stands up and feels in his pockets for some paper with which to demonstrate.

"Here," says Ruthie, giving him one of her leaflets. "Use this."

He unfolds it, and in the poor light of the veranda it is necessary for him to take out his spectacles. "Ah," he says, after a long moment. "This will do." He kneels down next to his daughter, as he might have years before when teaching her to tie her shoelaces, and shows her.

The next day, when Lucio arrives at Gutman Fur, he finds Ruthie making a great quantity of sardine sandwiches. "You butter the bread," she says, and tells him the story of her father and the sandwiches. She crosses the room and kisses him once, hard, as if she is biting him. She is in the process of mashing the sardines into a paste, her hand all the way inside a big pickle bottle, hammering away with a wooden spoon, like someone making a bomb. Once the sandwiches have been made, she changes into her plain grey dress. Lucio watches her as she takes everything off, pulling on a pair of heavy linen underwear, rough and unsexy, formless.

Soon it's routine. Lucio arrives early, helps make the sandwiches and waits for Ruthie to undress. And Ruthie lets him. She does not know what to think of her own simultaneous eagerness and reluctance to please him. To give him what he wants. Not to go near him, but to show him everything, to willingly put herself on display, standing before him with a studied nonchalance, like the girl on a playing card she found once in the backyard the three houses share.

That is how it begins. It is how such things always begin. This is a simple story, despite the complications, with a predictable beginning, a certain muddiness in the middle and a happy ending. Or at least it should be. From here the story of Lucio and Ruthie might have moved along the tracks that such stories usually move along. A first kiss, a second kiss—and then, history. And it nearly did. If not for Dubie Diamond cutting off his index finger a week later, the two very well might have lived happily ever after.

It happens at the St. Lawrence Market.

Dubie is pitching Greenstein's Remarkable Knives. A crowd of about forty people are watching him. They stand in rapt attention, hanging on his every word, but Dubie is bored. He is bored because the pitch has nothing to do with him. Every word, every gesture, has been planned in advance by his father, Asher, who devised a foolproof way of selling Greenstein's knives before Dubie was even born.

Asher met Ivor Greenstein in Toronto's Union Station

when Asher was living in Richmond Hill, where, along with Mazie and Dubie's older brother, Harold (who was then a chubby three-year-old), he constituted half of the town's Jewish population. Most of the time Asher was out on the road, selling brooms. When he reached a new town, he would take his brooms out and go to work, and when he finished a demonstration, whether or not he sold any brooms, the floor in front of him was impeccable. Greenstein happened to be walking by when Asher was in the midst of demonstrating a new variety of straw broom. He was impressed, not by the brooms Asher was selling but by the cleanliness of the floor. Asher clearly knew what he was doing when it came to using a broom. It was on these grounds, when the demonstration was over, that Greenstein offered him a job.

"I've already got a job" was Asher's response.

"Brooms," said Greenstein, inventor and manufacturer of the Remarkable Knives, contemptuously, "shrooms."

Asher had to agree. Selling brooms was not much, but it was what he did. As a teenager he had travelled the country with his own father, Jakob, who had also been a salesman. Jakob had come to America midway through the previous century with his father and elder brother, both of whom had been rabbis. They had come for the brother's marriage, which Asher's grandfather had arranged transatlantically from a synagogue in Hungary, through a series of cagey, formal Yiddish letters exchanged with the daughter of a rabbi on New York's lower east side. Jakob had come to serve as his brother's best man, and then—for a number of reasons, some of which had to do with the dowryless girl who lived in a Mott Street tenement and would later become Asher's mother—had decided to stay. Knowing he'd not been cut, as he liked to say, out of rabbi cloth, Jakob had looked for another line of work. Partially out of expedience and partially because Jews at the time were implicitly (and often explicitly) barred from doing most everything else, he went into sales. His connections with rabbis meant that he started off in Yiddish typewriters. He soon exhausted the supply of rabbis in New York, and hit the road, travelling all along the east coast of the United States and into the Midwest, looking for rabbis without typewriters. As he travelled, he picked up other products to sell, and in the year of Asher's sixteenth birthday he came home and picked up Asher. For eight years the two travelled together, selling everything from orange peelers to brooms to plastic fruit that smelled identical to real fruit, to vacuum cleaners, to bathtubs, to a kind of inverted bicycle you pedalled with your hands.

One of the places they stopped was Richmond Hill, a tiny town on a great hill north of Toronto, where Jakob sent Asher to knock on the door of the one Jew in town, to ask if he needed a Yiddish typewriter.

"Good evening," Asher said to Mr. Feldman when he opened the front door. "Need a typewriter?"

"A typewriter?" asked Mr. Feldman.

"A Yiddish typewriter."

Mr. Feldman looked at him.

"A man like you," said Asher, "can always use a typewriter."

(One of the things Jakob had taught him about pitching typewriters was that people always liked to hear that they were the kind of person who could use a typewriter.)

"One second," said Mr. Feldman, closing the door. A moment later he opened it and pushed a tough-looking girl out onto the veranda. "This is my daughter," he said. "Mazie."

Asher asked for Mazie's hand after they had been dating for two years, and after she had informed him that she wouldn't complain if he did so. He put on his suit, knocked on the Feldmans' door, revealed his purpose to Mr. Feldman and was led into the living room, where he sat down across from Mazie's father and where, after a good deal of murmuring, his request was granted. Mazie ran into the living room, and her mother and sisters also came into the room, and they all burst into tears.

Taking Asher's hand, Mr. Feldman said the most affectionate thing he would ever say to Asher. "Asher," he said, "call me Dubie."

"Dubie," said Asher. "What's that short for?"

"For nothing," he replied. "It's not short."

Mazie then threw her arms around Asher, and he kissed her in front of her father, and almost immediately found he was no longer happy selling brooms. Still, he continued doing it for nearly two years. Then came the day when he met Ivor Greenstein in Toronto's Union Station.

"I can sell anything," he told Greenstein. "What've you got?"

"Not sell," said Greenstein, "pitch."

"Pitch?" said Asher.

"Salesmen sell anything," Greenstein told him. "Pitchmen tell the truth."

The two sat down on a concrete bench, and Greenstein explained the difference between a pitchman and a salesman. A pitchman began by mastering the device he was selling. This was not always easy, and seldom did it involve the same pitch twice. Each product was different, had its own secret. Indeed, every product, if it was not *chuzzerai* (to use the word Greenstein used, the Yiddish word for trash, candy floss and gimmicks that served no other purpose than to make those who sold them rich), held within itself, within its design or shape or the way it moved, something that made it worth buying. It was the job of the pitchman to find that secret, and to show it to others. There were no mirrors involved, no impossible promises. A pitchman did not talk anyone into anything. Greenstein said he believed the same thing to be as true of people as it was of products: the world's problems were a result of the wrong people doing the wrong things, of carrot peelers being used to shovel driveways or washing machines being used as wineglasses.

"You sound like Karl Marx," said Asher.

"Who?" said Greenstein.

Then he took out the knives. It was now nearly five o'clock, early in the fall of 1915. Somewhere, the world was at war. Greenstein took from under his arm a black bundle that had two knives in it. He unfurled the black cloth on the bench and the knives shone even in the dim light of the train station. Asher picked up one of the knives and drew his thumb across the blade and found it extremely sharp. He then pointed the knife down and pressed and found that these knives were amazingly flexible. Then he turned his attention to what was remarkable about the knives: instead of a handle, each knife had at its end a metal shaft—a hand—that was a foot and a half long, and tapered off into three equidistant, fingerlike metal prongs.

"When can you start?" said Greenstein.

A week later, Asher, with Mazie (who, because she was pregnant with Dubie, threw up five times during the hour-long train ride), Harold and the bright green plastic-covered sofa he had received for selling his five-thousandth broom, arrived in

Toronto. They deduced that their next-door neighbours were named Burke; the woman, Francesca, was pregnant with her first child, who, as both sets of parents soon realized, would likely be born at about the same time as Mazie's child. Once they had arrived, Asher set about crafting the pitch that Dubie would still be using some seventeen years later, when he cut off his index finger.

This perfect pitch that Asher created begins with the pitch-man producing a pineapple—an impossibly tropical fruit, which most Torontonians had never seen, much less tasted—from a black sack that has the name *Greenstein* embroidered on it in red and yellow thread. Using the metallic hands that are at the end of each of Greenstein's Remarkable Knives, the pitchman places the pineapple atop an eight-foot wooden pillar that Asher constructed himself for the express purpose of holding a pineapple.

"In a moment," the pitchman says, pointing to the pine-apple but not saying the word *pineapple*, "I'll get to *that*."

Next, the pitchman takes a number of carrots out of the sack, which he peels and chops while discussing the many virtues of Greenstein's knives. They are durable. They are easily cleaned. They never need sharpening. They never need ironing. They need not be plugged in. They will never break. They are like an extra pair of hands. They *are* an extra pair of hands. When he is finished peeling each carrot, he plunges the knife he is using into the chopping board in front of him and leans on it, bending the knife almost in two to demonstrate its remarkable flexibility. When confronted by the sight of the pitchman bending the knife, many in the crowd cannot help ducking out of the way. But the knife never snaps in two, and when it does not snap in two the crowd is suitably impressed.

(That the crowd is suitably impressed does not impress Dubie. The crowd is always suitably impressed. This infuriates him all the more because it is a testament to his father's ingenuity.)

"Now, before I get to *that*," the pitchman tells the crowd, when he finishes enumerating the virtues of the knives, pointing to the pineapple but not saying the word *pineapple*, "I'm going to really show you something."

Next: from the black bag he pulls four turnips. But not all at once. He takes out the turnips separately and slowly, as if the bag were the black hat of a magician and each turnip were a white dove. Because he is moving very slowly, the appearance of the turnips has a calming, hypnotic affect. When enough turnips have come out of the black sack, the pitchman looks gravely at the crowd and goes to work with the knives. He prods and gouges and cuts with increasingly broad and rapid strokes, until he holds up a turnip transformed into an exact likeness of Queen Victoria. The second turnip he turns into an exact likeness of Sir John A. Macdonald, the third into a clown face and the fourth into a tulip.

The crowd bursts into applause.

The pitchman takes a short bow, bending low at the waist.

(After Dubie finishes taking the bow, as he is straightening up, he sees Ruthie Nodelman near the back of the crowd. She is wearing a plain grey dress and her hair is up. In her hand she carries a brown bag.)

"Now," says the pitchman, pointing to the pineapple, "I'm going to get to *that*. But first, I'm going to show you what these knives can really do."

Then: out of the black bag the pitchman takes a large book. The book itself does not matter. (On that particular day Dubie takes out *The Complete Works of William Shakespeare*.) He puts the book on the chopping block in the centre of the podium before him, holding it in place with his left hand. In his right hand he has the largest Greenstein Remarkable Knife. It is a carving knife with a receding half-moon blade that looks very much like a guillotine. Now a real silence falls over the crowd, and with this silence all around him the pitchman lifts his right hand and the knife in it over his head and, just for a moment, he hesitates and looks out into the crowd.

(And when he does this, Dubie sees Ruthie standing there, smiling. He smiles back, and brings the knife down on his finger. Blood is everywhere. Ruthie drops her bag and runs through the crowd to Dubie with a handkerchief, which she presses down on the empty space between his thumb and middle finger.

"Dubie," she says, "are you all right?"

That is when Dubie comes right out and says he loves her.)

SEVEN

DUBIE HAD BEEN DISTRACTED from the beginning. He would say later that it was as if the deck was stacked against him. That the universe, or history, or fate, or all three, had it in for him. That cutting off his finger was something he had always been meant to do. The kind of thing that happened for a reason. But that was afterwards. He thought nothing of the sort at the time. So it has always been; turning points are only visible in retrospect. Unlike people, Dubie told himself, all moments are created equal.

He knew this better than anyone, or so he believed. He had arrived at the age of seventeen with a profound desire to be someone else. There is nothing uncommon about such a desire; in Dubie's case, however, because there exists a strong resemblance between him and his father (whom he concluded at an early age to be entirely average), he has become convinced that what it means to be someone else starts with his being *different* from his father. As it happens, this conviction took root when he was listening to Mr. Booth, his biology teacher, explain the concept of natural selection. The teacher started by drawing a picture of the sun in the uppermost corner of the blackboard, under which he wrote the word SUN; next, he drew an arrow to the right, and a picture of a flower under which he wrote PLANT. Then there was another arrow, a picture of a rabbit and the word HERBIVORE. Finally a fourth arrow, the picture of a wolf and the word CARNIVORE.

"Evolution," Mr. Booth told the class, "turned rabbits into the kind of animal that eats plants, and wolves into the kind that eats rabbits. It hasn't always been that way. It's something that's happened over time, over millions of years."

"But why," said Dubie, putting up his hand, "why did it happen like *that*? What happened to the plants?"

"Why what?" replied Mr. Booth.

"Why don't *they* evolve?"

"Because they can't," said Mr. Booth. "Part of what makes a rabbit a rabbit is that it has to stop where it has to stop. A rabbit is something that has to stop at being a rabbit."

"How do you know?"

"It's all in Darwin," said Mr. Booth, who could no more imagine rabbits turning into wolves than he could one of his students reading Darwin. "Read your Darwin."

Later that same day, Dubie took out his first book from the Toronto Public Library, a Modern Library hardback edition of *On the Origin of Species*. So irreverent did the book seem to him that he hid it in the eavestrough outside his window, where Harold kept a pack of playing cards with dirty pictures on the back.

That night Dubie got out of bed, opened the window and began to read Darwin by moonlight. He noiselessly turned the pages, his back to the window. It was not easy going. Those first pages in particular, where Darwin's circuitous, ambling Victorian English combines with a conspicuous indirection of argument, were hard to get through. But Dubie persisted, mostly because it sounded as though Darwin was saying exactly the kind of thing he wanted to hear. Darwin, at least, was on his side; here, finally, was a book written for someone like him, someone intending to evolve. He clutched the Darwin to his breast and told himself that he had been mistaken that day in Mr. Booth's class, when he'd seen himself years in the future, bent and smelling like his father, selling Greenstein's knives at the same booth in the St. Lawrence Market. It is not going to happen to me, he thought; I am one of the buds that do not do what they are told. A peach bud that produces a nectarine. A moss rose. Dubie had never seen a moss rose and had no idea of how it differed from a common rose—but the name itself told the whole of the story, that it was infinitely preferable to be a moss rose. Which was what he would do. He would refuse to be a rabbit. He would not marry his mother. He would *evolve*. And Darwin would tell him how.

It was not long before Dubie understood that *On the Origin of Species* was not that kind of book. It was a book about evolution, but not about *how* to evolve. It was a book about why the red grouse is native to Britain, about why *prodromus* should not be understood as being a member of the oak family, about the connections between woodpeckers and mistletoe, about the role of bees in producing Dutch clover rather than red clover, and about the reasons for the decline of insectivorous birds in Paraguay at the end of the nineteenth century. But nothing about the *business* of evolution, about how to do it for yourself, to yourself. He kept reading all the same, believing that at any moment he was going to turn to the page that contained the answer. But one day, after eighteen pages devoted solely to enumerating the differences between black and pied and green woodpeckers and whether or not the variations between them could be grounds for considering them different species, he lost patience. He threw the book down on the floor, where it landed with a bang that woke up his brother.

"What the hell is going on here?" said Harold.

"I'm reading," Dubie said, bitterly. "Darwin. You know— about evolution."

But Harold was already asleep.

The next chance he had, Dubie confronted his biology teacher.

"What are you looking for exactly?" Mr. Booth asked.

"I don't know," said Dubie, "something about people."

"People?" said Mr. Booth. "You're reading the wrong book. What you're looking for is in *The Descent of Man*."

Once more Dubie was back at the library, and gradually he came to understand how it was that evolution occurred. Wanting had nothing to do with it. Thinking had nothing to do with it. Knowing about evolution had nothing to do with it. It was called survival of the fittest, but it had nothing to do with knowledge or practice. It had to do with where you were, with conditions, with the environment. When one kidney ceased to function because of disease, said Darwin, the other grew in size. Bones increased not just in length but also in thickness from carrying a great weight. Soldiers were shorter than sailors, watchmakers were nearsighted and Australian Aborigines far-sighted. This was the way things happened. This was the key. So Dubie decided that if he didn't want to end up like his father, he would have to put himself into different circumstances. He would have to do the kinds of things his father never did. Dubie would need to become famous or rich or prime minster, or climb Mount Everest, or ski, or tame a lion or marry a starlet. Such heights seemed impossible to him, so he resolved on the next best thing—he would do something extraordinary. By getting people to think about him differently, he would create the conditions whereby he could evolve. The only problem was how. What was he to do?

Convinced the answer lay somewhere in Darwin, Dubie read *The Descent of Man* through to the end, and it was while he was doing this that the idea of going to the Riverdale Zoo occurred to him. He remembered reading in the *Toronto Daily Star* about the arrival of the cheetah, an animal that quite clearly had resolved not to be a rabbit. Perhaps if he sat for long enough in front of the cheetah, just as Darwin had sat for hours on the deck of the *Beagle*, watching the world around him and coming up with the idea of evolution, perhaps he would get some idea of how to evolve. Soon Dubie was in the habit of going off alone to the zoo. He would lie to Lucio about having to work, and instead would walk east along Gerrard Street and down into the valley to take up his vigil in front of the cheetah cage.

One afternoon Lucio followed him. He remained at a distance, and watched as his friend sat down on the bench in front of the cage and took a thick book from his backpack. He watched for the better part of an hour, as Dubie opened and shut his book but mostly just looked at the cheetah pacing back and forth in its tiny cage. At last Dubie returned the book to his backpack and got up to leave.

"Dubie," said Lucio, surprising him just outside the zoo gates, "I thought it was you."

"What're you doing here?" asked Dubie, too quickly.

The two boys stood in the middle of the sidewalk.

"What're you doing?" asked Lucio.

"Looking at the cheetah," Dubie said, before he could stop himself.

"At the cheetah?" said Lucio. "What for?"

"Because I feel like it."

Dubie was telling the truth. He had been opening and closing *The Descent of Man* as if it were a bible, because he was still trying to think of the great feat that would set him apart from his father forever and for good. But he had become convinced that, whatever he did, it would involve the cheetah in some way. He would let the cheetah out, but keep it on a leash and take it home. The zoo would discover it was missing, call the police, and soon the search would be on. At the last moment Dubie would arrive with the cheetah and be declared a hero. This seemed a good idea at first, but it soon seemed both impractical and dangerous. How would he get the leash over the cheetah's head? While it was in the cage or after? What kind of leash? He thought a very large dog leash would do, but then he heard that Mrs. Cohen on Cecil Street had tried putting her cat on a leash in order to take it for a walk, and had only got as far as the bottom of the veranda before the cat managed to slip the leash. If Mrs. Cohen's house cat could do such a thing, thought Dubie, so could the cheetah. And there were other problems, besides. How would he get the door to the cage open? And what if the cheetah got away? What if it ate someone? What if it ate his brother? What if it ate his parents? That would not be half bad, and people would feel sorry for him. Which just might cause him to evolve. But then, people might also find out that he had engineered the whole thing, and he would have to do hard time, which, even if he was sent to Attica, seemed like the wrong kind of notoriety. No—whatever he did, it would not involve the cheetah. And it was that very day, just as he had decided that his plan with the cheetah was fundamentally flawed, that he and Lucio walked out of the Riverdale Zoo and ran into Bloomberg.

"Hey," called Bloomberg. "Want a baseball?"

"You're giving it to us?" said Dubie.

"Not you specifically," said Bloomberg, and told them how it would work. "That's right," he said when he had finished, "it *sounds* easy—all you've got to do is hit a Bloomberg Special."

It seemed the answer to Dubie's prayers. The thing he had been waiting for. The event that would cause him to evolve.

But then Lucio got to keep the ball.

And Dubie was fine with that, because even though he had not thrown the ball, even though it had not been him everyone stared at that day in disbelief, he had been right there beside Lucio. The throw had been so unlikely—so incongruous and so amazing—that Dubie had already decided it must be evolution. And because he had told himself that being around people who were evolving was the best way to evolve, Dubie had decided that Lucio's getting to keep the Bloomberg ball was a good thing.

Until he cut off his finger, that is.

Earlier that morning, before his accident, Dubie had opened his father's booth the way he always did. He had walked into the low-ceilinged building that housed the St. Lawrence Market and had seen that it had already started to fill with the early-morning bustle of produce arriving and ice trucks unloading and the haggling of shoppers. Dubie went in and removed the white sheets his father had placed over the booth the night before. Dubie, like his father, called the tiny rectangle that Greenstein rented for the family a booth, but it was actually nothing of the sort. It was a large, podium-like chopping board, a wide wooden contraption that could tilt forward toward the audience so they could see the pitchman use the knives. Beside this podium, also covered with a long white sheet, was the tall, whitewashed pillar on which the pineapple rested for the duration of each pitch, as the pitchman threatened to cut it. Each evening Asher insisted that both the podium and the pillar be covered, claiming that people were less likely to stand and watch a pitch if they could come and look at the podium any time they liked.

The unveiling done, Dubie crossed over to the side of the market where the produce was sold, and purchased the turnips and carrots he would need for that day's pitches. Then, at eight-thirty, when he was just about ready to begin the first pitch of the day, he placed the pineapple atop the pillar. This was never an easy thing to do, for the pillar was eight feet tall, and Dubie, like his father, could only reach the top of it with the aid of the tiny metallic hands at the end of Greenstein's knives. After this was done, he turned around to see a woman and two dirty-looking children, a girl of about eight and a little boy who was not more than three, watching him. They looked at him in a shy, indirect way, as if they expected to be shooed away at any moment. Probably, thought Dubie, they were used to such treatment. The mother had a drawn, humourless face, and the little boy had close-cropped hair, which made Dubie think that he'd been recently deloused. The little girl was dressed in a blue dirndl skirt and white blouse, very plain and not at all new.

"If you hang around," he told them, pointing to the pineapple but not saying the word *pineapple*, "I'll get to *that*."

They moved closer.

Dubie smiled, as if to suggest he hoped they would. As if to make them think he believed they were every bit as likely to buy a set of knives as the next person. In fact, he thought they looked stone poor, and as if they'd been that way for a long time. And when he stepped up and began slicing the carrots into the narrow, perfectly straight orange sticks his father insisted upon, the first thing he did was to spear one of the sticks and, with an inviting smile, hand it to the little girl. He did the same with the little boy, leaning all the way down with the carrot at the end of the long knife, smiling generously with a flamboyant big-heartedness that caused two passersby to stop and watch. Then he gave the mother a carrot stick for herself, and by that time two more people had stopped to watch. Dubie speared more carrot sticks and tried to give them to the newcomers, two nurses and a young couple wheeling a baby carriage—people he considered potential customers—and although they refused at first, he insisted, and soon all seven were chewing carrots.

"If you hang around," said Dubie, pointing to the pineapple, "I'll get to *that*."

Soon a crowd had gathered, and Dubie was ready to start the first demonstration of the day. At the end of it, he sold a set of knives to a man in a light grey suit and a straw hat.

Not bad, thought Dubie; it was only nine in the morning and already he had made a sale.

He knew he was getting better as a pitchman, but he was most impressed by his own ability to gather a crowd. Like his father and older brother, he possessed the ability to smile in just the right way—as if he were a person's perfect friend, someone glad to see them but asking nothing—and it was that smile that always lured people in. And luring people was half the battle. It *was* the battle. Dubie found that what his father always said about crowds was true. That the only way to gather a crowd was to begin with a crowd. That people would always stop to look at what people had already stopped to look at. So he did not send the woman and her children away; he gave them carrots. He knew what the beginning of an audience looked like when he saw it.

At nine-thirty Dubie began his second pitch of the day, and at ten-thirty his third. After the third pitch he sold two sets of knives to a puffy woman dressed in a dark blue tailored suit who had a dozen dangling strands of artificial pearls around her neck. After the twelve-thirty pitch he sold a set of knives to a reporter from the *Star* who said his name was Callaghan, and another to a man with a British accent and a monocle who spoke in a low voice, saying the knives were not for him but for his mother, who, as far as he was concerned, had more knives than she knew what to do with.

Through it all, the poor woman and her children stood by and watched. Each time Dubie was getting ready to begin a pitch, they would step forward and put out their hands. He continued to hand them carrots with the same showy munificence, and the crowd remained large. During the pitches the three stood attentive and near the front, and clapped at the appropriate moments, then slipped away at the end, when it came time to buy the knives. Dubie did not mind, and even felt grateful for the fact that it was only three people who had their hands out this morning. There was no shortage of such people in the city. People who had nothing to wait for and nowhere to go. One afternoon a crowd of twenty homeless men, having heard about the free carrots, had swarmed Dubie and made it impossible for him to give his pitch.

Much to his surprise, after the one-thirty demonstration the woman stepped up and pulled out a dollar bill from somewhere inside her grimy dress.

His first impulse was to hand the bill back to her. To tell her she should use the money for something else, to buy some clothes for the children, or a hot meal. But he did not. However unlike his father he wants to be, he is, in the end, Asher Diamond's son. This means that he never asks himself the kinds of questions salesmen should ask themselves. When the woman held out the money, it was after only the most minute of hesitations that Dubie took the bill, and shoved it into his pocket.

"Congratulations," said Dubie (for this is what his father insists he say to each person who buys a set of Greenstein's knives), and he reached into the black bag for a new set.

Taking the black box that had the knives in it, the woman moved to one side. Kneeling down so her children would be able to see, she opened the box. The overhead lights in the market glinted off the knives and shone up into their faces. He watched, and found himself thinking of the war monument on Queen Street, outside the provincial courthouses, which showed three soldiers kneeling over a fourth, fallen comrade. These three, however, were kneeling over a set of Greenstein's Remarkable Knives, and seemed much more pleased than the soldiers. Dubie looked at them, and wondered if his father's work might be a good thing. Someone had to give the people what they wanted. If Dubie and his father could make a buck from it, so much the better. The woman probably could have used the money for better things, but what they wanted were the knives. What they believed would make their lives better were the knives, and by the look on their faces, the knives had done exactly that.

Dubie was feeling a shifting of sorts within himself, which, if he had not looked up and seen Goody Altman, the second-best baseball player the city of Toronto would ever produce, standing in front of him, he might have called evolution. He nodded to Goody, then saw that he wasn't alone; with Goody was his brother, Mordechai (who was wearing a fedora with a yarmulke on top of it, making it seem as if a fabric mushroom were growing out of the top of his head), Grief Henderson (who was wearing a Lizzies cap on the side of which he had sewn stars, as if it were not a baseball cap but a magician's robe) and Milton Weathervane (who still had his arms crossed, as if he had never quite stepped out of the position of authority he had assumed that day when Bloomberg named him umpire at the Elizabeth Street playground).

"To what do I owe the pleasure?" said Dubie.

"Dubie," said Goody, cutting to the chase, "have you seen Lucio?"

"Lucio?"

"Listen, Dubie," said Milton. He took a step forward so that he was standing very close to Dubie. "There are two ways for this to go, the easy way and the hard way—it's your decision." Milton had one eye slightly larger than the other, and when he looked down at Dubie, the eyelid of the smaller eye fluttered.

"I haven't seen him," said Dubie. "Not for a while, anyway." As he said this, he realized it was true.

"When last?" said Mordechai, who had not seen Lucio since that day in the deli.

"Last week," said Dubie. Up until that moment, he had supposed he'd seen Lucio every bit as much as he always had—which was all the time, every day. "I don't know," Dubie said nearly to himself. He stared off in the direction of the crowd, which was melting away, and found himself looking at the woman and her children. They were sitting on a dilapidated wooden bench, and the woman had taken one of the knives out of its case. She held it up for her children to see. Catching the light, the blade of the knife threw a tiny luminescent square on the forearm of the boy, who tried to catch it in his fingers.

Mordechai looked over at the woman and her children, and shook his head. "I see business is fine," he said.

"I can't complain," said Dubie. "It's been a good day."

"Doesn't it bother you? Most of these people come up here to get their fruit and vegetables, and they see you work your magic and they walk out with cockamamie knives."

"Listen, it's my father's magic—all I do is do what I'm told."

"What kind of magic are we talking about?" asked Grief Henderson, touching one of the stars on his baseball cap.

"There's no magic," said Dubie, sounding very like his father. "No tricks. I just make the pitch, I tell the truth."

"Do you swallow the knives?" asked Grief. "Because if we're talking about swallowing them, then I'll take a set right now. But if you can't swallow them, I'm bringing them back for my money back."

"You try swallowing them," said Dubie, "and you won't be back for your money."

"And that'd suit you fine," said Mordechai, still looking at the woman who had given her last dollar to Dubie. "Grief'd be in the hospital, and you'd keep the money."

"I was joking," said Dubie.

"You won't be joking if you don't tell us where Lucio is," said Milton, trying to sound as thuggish as possible.

"I said I don't know. What'd you want with him anyway?"

"The fact of the matter is," said Goody, "we need a pitcher."

"A pitcher?" said Dubie.

At first, said Goody, after Bloomberg disappeared, the Lizzies were not worried. Particularly Goody, who thought he knew Bloomberg best. But when Bloomberg did not show up for the Lizzies' practice the day after the bird had carried away his glasses, and when he didn't show up for a second practice, they started to worry. Now, with the first game of the Toronto Junior playoffs just a day away, they needed to find another pitcher—quickly.

"To make a long story short," said Goody. "We play the Vermonts tomorrow and we need Lucio."

"You try the garage?"

"Every day this week," said Goody. "Lucio's taken the week off."

"Taken it off?"

"That's what Dante told us," said Milton. "But he could've made that up just to get rid of us. Because another time he tells me we just missed him, that if we'd been there a minute before, we'd have caught him."

"What about the house?"

"I sat all night on the steps of the blind institute," said Grief. "I didn't see him."

"But," said Milton, "you were asleep."

"Five minutes." Grief was defensive. "I shouldn't have told you anything."

"Five minutes," repeated Milton, shaking his head.

"No," insisted Grief, "I was there the whole night, and didn't see him. It was like he was invisible."

"What about in back?" said Dubie. "Was one of you watching the back? He probably used the fire escape. The kitchen window opens, you know."

"Ah," said Milton to Grief, "you think of that?"

"I thought he was doing it another way," replied Grief.

"Another way?" said Milton. "That he was invisible, that's what you thought?"

"I didn't *think* that, I considered it as a possibility." Grief touched one of the stars on the side of his baseball cap.

"I'd have looked at the fire escape first," said Milton. "That's all I'm saying."

"Well," said Grief, in his own defence, "Moses parted the Red Sea."

"Lucio Burke," said Mordechai, "is no Moses—he's not even Jewish."

"Neither was Jesus," observed Grief.

"He started off Jewish," countered Mordechai.

"You know, Mordechai," said Grief, "there are more things in the world than you think, even when you're trying."

"Anyway," Goody intervened, "we're still looking for Lucio."

"And," said Mordechai, "you and he were born on the same kitchen table."

"And on the same day," added Milton, as if he were amassing evidence against Dubie.

"What's that got to do with anything?" said Dubie.

"People like that," said Milton, "stick together."

"But why wouldn't I tell you where Lucio is? Don't you think I want the Lizzies to win?"

"Why don't *you* tell *us*," said Milton. He finally had Dubie where he wanted him.

"Maybe you want us to win," said Goody, looking closely at Dubie. "But maybe you don't want Lucio to pitch."

"Have you ever," broke in Grief, before Dubie could reply, "witnessed Lucio disappear? He might be standing here right now, invisible to our mortal sight, moving among us like a shadow, a wisp of air."

"All right," said Goody. "Let's go."

"You see him," said Milton, "you tell him the Lizzies need a pitcher." When he said this, Milton stepped close to Dubie and poked him in the soft place just above his pectoral muscle, a sharp, short stab that was meant to hurt.

"What does Lucio know about pitching?" asked Dubie.

"You saw that throw," Goody called back over his shoulder.

"What if he doesn't want to do it?"

"Want to?" replied Goody. "Who wouldn't want to pitch for the Lizzies?"

As Dubie watched them walk away, he wondered about what Goody had said: who would not want to be pitcher for the Lizzies? Certainly *he* would. Who would not want to be Bloomberg, he wondered, as he stood in the St. Lawrence Market, about to repeat the same pitch his father had come up with years before. Who would not want to be on the mound at Christie Pits? Who would not want to be at the centre of the story? Did he really not want it to be Lucio?

Dubie readied the carrots and turnips for the final demonstration of the day. A crowd began to form, and although he smiled the same smile, the thought of his friend in a Lizzies uniform now infuriated him. If the Lizzies won the championship, a picture of the team would appear in all five Toronto newspapers. Throughout the city people would be wishing they were Lucio, the boy in the centre of the photograph. The one with the ball.

Dubie started the demonstration. He worked automatically, thinking not at all of what he was doing. In the pit of his stomach he felt the beginnings of something hard and bitter. It should not be happening this way, he thought; it wasn't fair that Lucio got to evolve. Dubie spoke to the crowd in words that his father had put together before he was born, telling them that if a truck should run over one of Greenstein's knives, the knife would still be able to slice melon to an airy thinness, and he realized that he'd been completely wrong about evolution. There was nothing you could do about it. You couldn't bring it on. Changing your environment didn't matter. Doing extraordinary things was beside the point. You remained, at the end of it, the same. Evolution was a sudden, pointless thing. A leap in the dark. It picked you up and threw you in some direction. There was nothing you could do about the direction, or whether or not it happened.

Dubie understood that he had been wrong also about himself. He had imagined himself *Homo sapien*, who was pictured in the books standing triumphantly at the top of the evolutionary tree. No, he thought, he was *Australopithecus africanus*, the apelike creature that looked much like a human but could not use tools, and lived in the trees like a monkey, with arms too short to hold its own children. Because it walked upright on two feet the *Australopithecus* was ranked with the hominids, but like Neanderthal man—who had a thick skull and a tiny brain—it would never be a human being. Dubie recognized that he was something left behind. A curious relic, which people would find long afterward and think interesting because they'd forgotten about it. He carved a turnip into a likeness of King Edward, and knew that despite his friendship with Lucio, despite having been born on the same kitchen table on the same day, he would never be able to throw a baseball with one ounce of the speed and accuracy, the preternatural facility, with which Lucio had thrown it that famous afternoon. Lucio had evolved.

It wasn't fair and it made no sense, thought Dubie, as he handed a turnip rose to a pretty nurse. Dubie was *Megalotragus*, the giant antelope that once roamed the steppes of Africa, or the shamanu, the smallest wolf ever known; the mammoth, the Parisian wild violet, the giant beaver, once native to Southern Ontario, that was more than six and a half feet long. Dubie found himself thinking of the tiny arms of *Australopithecus*—before, they had seemed to him the result of poor judgement, of stupidity, an example of exactly the kind of thing *he* would avoid, and he was hardly able to not weep. But this was the apathy of evolution, he thought. And it had already started: Lucio was doing something Dubie considered nearly unthinkable—taking a week off work.

A week off! Lucio had said nothing to him about taking time off, so when Goody had said it, Dubie's first response had been to think it a lie, to think that Dante was covering for Lucio at Michelangelo's Garage, or that Goody was saying it just to make Dubie tell him where Lucio was. But who would make up such a thing? It could mean only one thing: that Lucio was, in fact, not going to work. No one could possibly hope to fool anyone by saying such a thing, with the entire country, with the world, out of work. Perhaps Lucio's mother had made him go with her, a second time, to the Welfare Office. But then why would Lucio miss work? And where had he gone? Why had he not told Dubie? They had stuck up for each other, always. Lucio had told him about the first time they'd gone to apply for welfare, and the forms they'd had to fill out, and how the Welfare Lady had stormed out of the house when Michelangelo told her his name. He and Lucio had laughed about it one night, when they'd snuck into the cinder alley behind their houses to smoke cigarettes together.

Lucio had told Dubie, and Dubie had kept quiet about it, and when people said that Lucio's mother was on the dole, Dubie told them they were wrong. This was how it had always been between them. It was the way Dubie had thought it always would be. People born on the same kitchen table stuck together. At least they should. It wasn't being related, but it was like it. It was more.

But now things had changed, or so it seemed. Perhaps, he began to think, Lucio had come to the same conclusions about him as he had arrived at himself—that he was heading nowhere, an atrophied, inconsequential limb on a forgotten tree.

Such were the thoughts running through Dubie's mind as he went through the pitch for the ninth time that day, speaking words he did not even have to think about. Words he had said so many times before that they felt almost like a prayer. Words that spilled out of him with an automatic eloquence, in a voice that seemed to him not to be his voice at all. It must have to do with me, he thought, as he took *The Complete Works of William Shakespeare* out of the black sack. He placed the book on the chopping block. He would confront Lucio. He would make Lucio say what he was up to. He would refuse— unlike *Australopithecus*, who had been content to stay up in the trees—to be left behind.

So angered was Dubie that he said the word *refuse* out loud, repeating it under his breath as he raised the big knife.

That was when he saw Ruthie. She was wearing grey, a lovely grey flash near the back of the room. It seemed to him she must have felt his stare, for she stood there and looked at him, and she smiled.

Dubie smiled back, and brought down the knife.

What he felt first was a weak tingling. He saw the blood, and his finger lying on the dirty market floor. But it was as if he were watching it all from high above, with the kind of perspective, he thought fleetingly, that the great bird must have had of the Elizabeth Street playground that day. He looked at his severed finger, half covered by sawdust, bloody at one end and too white at the other, and understood what had happened. What he'd done. But at the same time he felt it had nothing to do with him. He had cut off his finger—this was a piece of information that was true, and that he knew to be true, and that had no bearing on his life. There was no pain. This surprised Dubie, who had stood, years before, on the other side of the black railing and watched Lucio take that flying leap from the long veranda. After he'd hit the ground and snapped his wrists back all the way, Lucio had opened his mouth to scream, and nothing had come out. It was as if any sound, even a scream, would be inadequate. Slicing off a finger, thought Dubie as he went into shock, was much easier. It was then that he looked up and saw Ruthie coming toward him, saying something he couldn't hear, taking out her handkerchief and pressing it down on his hand, the blood soaking through it in an instant.

Dubie, watching her, comes right out and says he loves her. "I love you," he says.

"Don't worry, Dubie," she says, "it'll be all right."

"I love you," Dubie tells her again. "Ruthie, I love you."

Ruthie looks at him through a tangle of red hair. The next thing he knows, she is pushing him through the crowd and into a taxicab. "Don't worry," she tells him. "I've got the finger."

He smiles. This seems to him an entirely appropriate thing to say.

When the taxi arrives at Toronto General, Ruthie gets out first, and when he seems unable to figure out how to do the same, she comes over to his side of the car and drags him out. She stays with him the whole way, with his severed finger in the pocket of her grey dress, and when the doctor comes in, she lays it on the examination table, beside where Dubie sits smiling, and tells the doctor that he has to try to reattach it, that she knows—she has read it somewhere, in the papers—that this kind of thing was done all the time in the Great War.

"We'll see what we can do," says the doctor, and takes her out to the waiting room.

When the doctor, who has a bad limp, comes back into the room, he unwraps Dubie's hand and shakes his head, telling him it's not possible to save the finger. Dubie says this is fine. The doctor nods, turns around and opens one of the wide metal drawers on the other side of the room. He takes out a syringe and injects Dubie with something. He takes the hand-kerchief off and begins cleaning the wound and Dubie feels the pain then, for the first time. As he works, the doctor tells Dubie how he was in the Great War, how he lost his leg in a town near the French border, whose name he cannot now recall. He'd been shot and the gangrene set in. They used a saw and it hurt like the dickens, says the doctor, what you've done with your finger's much cleaner. I couldn't have done it better myself. If only we'd had one of those Remarkable Knives in the trenches. The doctor smiles when he says this, and although Dubie knows the doctor wants him to laugh or smile or cry, or say something tough, he cannot quite make himself do it.

"Sometimes," says the doctor, in a different voice, "I still feel it. I look down and look for the leg and it's gone. What I'm saying, I suppose, is that everything happens for a reason. If I hadn't had my leg amputated," he tells Dubie, "who knows what would have happened to me?"

The doctor works quickly, and soon Dubie is on his way out to the waiting room, where his parents are waiting. "Did Ruthie go?" he asks.

"Yes," says Mazie. "She was very worried. We all were."

"But she left?" asks Dubie.

"Never mind that now," Mazie tells him. "Let's get you home."

"What are we going to do?" says Asher, too loudly. He is thinking of Dubie but also of his business, of his perfect pitch, and is asking himself who will want to buy Greenstein's knives after this, no matter how remarkable they are.

"All right," says Mazie, putting her arm around Dubie, holding him as if she is going to pick him all the way up, the way she did when he was a baby.

"I'm fine," Dubie tells her. "I can walk."

Despite the doctor's warning that it might happen, when Dubie wakes up in the middle of the night with a pain in his hand, he goes to put ice on it, thinking the pain is from catching a baseball the wrong way. It isn't until he turns on the kitchen light that it comes back to him. He is still standing in the kitchen, looking at the bandage covering the empty space between his fingers, when Harold comes in and asks what is the matter. He felt nothing, Dubie tells Harold, when the blade passed through his finger, it was as if the knife were travelling through water, not even a sound. No crunching through bone, no difficulty in raising the knife afterwards.

"A Greenstein clean slice," says Dubie, as if he is trying to sell a set to his brother.

EIGHT

IT IS RUTHIE who tells Lucio what has happened.

For the past two weeks, while Ruthie distributes her leaflet-wrapped sandwiches and Dante fills in for him at the garage, Lucio has spent his days behind the desk at the front of Gutman Fur. Most of the time he is alone and, just as he did when working for Asher as his *Shabbes goy*, he reads the paper, buying all three morning editions of each of the Toronto papers on his way to Gutman Fur. As he reads through the papers, Lucio begins to think that Ruthie may be right, that the world is heading toward a turning point. That everything may be changing. He reads of how Liggett Drugstores, with over four hundred and fifty stores in Canada and the United States, has declared bankruptcy. Of how Alice Kenny Shiffer Diamond, one-time wife of noted gangster Jack "Legs" Diamond, has been shot in the head while appearing in a vaudeville act involving a mock electric chair. Of how Prime Minister Richard Bennett, carefully using the past tense, has declared that Canada had weathered the Depression better than any other country in the world. The next day, Lucio reads that the Ministry of Labour reports that over a million Canadians, more than enlisted for the Great War, are on welfare. He sees a grainy photograph of a hundred men and boys in black shirts parading down Mansfield Avenue in Toronto, giving the fascist salute. Of the drought in Saskatchewan and Alberta; even in the tiny photographs of the prairies in the paper, he can see the hushed look that the frame houses and the stone barns wear, with their windows boarded over like bandaged eyes. He reads that the new Chancellor of Germany, Adolf Hitler, had celebrated his forty-fourth birthday in April. The *Toronto Daily Star* has a man, Van Paasan, in Berlin, and each day's headline is worse than the one before: the liquidation of Jewish businesses; the discharge of Jewish reporters and editors from German papers; a resolution at Munich University to dissect only Jewish cadavers; the exclusion of Jewish students from German universities; the announcement of Hitler's plans to sterilize Jews, along with the mentally ill and physically handicapped. In the middle of it, the *Star*'s rival, the anti-Jewish *Telegram*, runs a story saying that none of this is true. There were a few isolated incidents, says the *Tely*, and a few Jews against whom Hitler's followers had personal grievances were hurt.

Lucio also reads of how there is a group in Toronto calling themselves the Swastika Club, who are sticking up swastika flags and anti-Semitic signs along the Beaches, a lakeshore neighbourhood in east Toronto. One morning he reads that, the night before, a gang of Jewish boys went down to the Beaches looking to remove a number of swastikas that had been posted there—and that a violent confrontation between them and the Swastikas was narrowly averted.

Lucio spreads out the paper on Ruthie's desk and reads the article out loud to the empty shop.

BALMY BEACH DANCE HALL CLOSED
TO AVERT SWASTIKA ROW

The Jews arrived on the scene in a large transport truck, and left by the same medium. Although police were on the job prepared for trouble, there was none, the Jews going in an orderly manner when requested to do so by the police. And the police did not interfere with the Swastika Club as they marched up and down the boardwalk. Had the Swastikas been organized when the Jews arrived, there would have been the opportunity for the two parties to start trouble. As it was, they did not actually meet. But that there is considerable feeling in the matter was evidenced by the numbers in the Swastika parade.

Lucio is amazed, but not by the threat of violence—by the fact that he heard nothing about it. The boys were from his neighbourhood, no question. But the paper says nothing specific—it gives no names and includes not a single photo. Maybe Goody was there, or Mordechai or Milton. Maybe even Dubie. The thought of Dubie there—ready for a fight, looking around for Lucio and wondering, maybe even asking people if they've seen him, not wanting him to miss it— makes Lucio feel trapped, suckered by Ruthie. It is not the first time Lucio has second-guessed himself in this way. More than once, while sitting behind the desk at Gutman Fur, he has felt guilty about Dante, but his cousin seems somehow convinced that Lucio spends his every moment in erotic

embrace—and Lucio's silence on the subject seems more deli-
cious to Dante, more wicked, more tawdry, more furtive,
more eloquent about the secret reaches of Ruthie Nodelman,
than anything he would be able to say about the crossing and
uncrossing and unrolling of Ruthie's silky loveliness. So he
has not thought too hard about what he is doing or why he is
doing it. He tells himself it is about justice and the more
equitable distribution of resources, but at the same time
Dante's persistent questions and eye-rolling have left him no
illusions about the extent to which Ruthie has infected his
imagination.

But this is different. Because it is all already over—because
nothing happened—Lucio is free to picture himself joining
ranks with the Jewish kids in his neighbourhood without hesi-
tation. Lucio imagines what it must have been like in the
Ward the night before, when word of the swastika signs having
been posted went out, like a dare. All along Beverley and
College streets people would have been talking about it—first
in hushed tones, unbelieving whispers, but before long the
shouting would have started and someone would have resolved
to do something. A crowd would have formed, perhaps outside
Altman's Deli. And all at once they would have started to walk
east, toward the Beaches. Not walk, Lucio thinks, march—like
an army. And if he had been there, he would have been one of
them—resolute, unafraid. Ruthie herself looking at him with
approval, with pride, from the Beverley Street sidewalk as he
walked past, shoulder to shoulder with Mordechai Altman,
wearing his own yarmulke.

The front page of the *Telegram* the next day makes it sound
as if the volatility of the situation is the result of Jewish intoler-
ance: TORONTO "SWASTIKAS" AROUSE JEWS.

Accompanying the article are a number of pictures: one of the swastika signs that were posted along the waterfront; a sweater with a swastika sewn onto its centre; a larger picture of girls lying in the sun on the Toronto waterfront, wearing bathing suits with swastikas stitched into their suits in the space between their breasts, as if daring someone to rip them off. The article includes a statement from the club defending its right to demonstrate, and claiming to have no connection to any political or racial organization, claiming that the swastika emblem was chosen because it is "a symbol of luck."

This defence seems to Lucio so outlandish, so flimsy, that when Ruthie returns from the shops he shows her the paper, expecting her to laugh with him at the Swastika Club's stupidity—but Ruthie does not think it funny in the least.

"They know what they're doing," she tells him.

"You think this'll fool anyone?"

"They don't want to fool anyone, they want to get away with it."

"But they're not getting away with it."

"They're not in jail. What they want to do is make it seem like it's the Jews who are making the whole thing up, it's the Jews who can't take a little parade."

"No one thinks that," insists Lucio.

"It doesn't matter what anyone thinks, it's how it looks on paper, in the paper."

The papers are soon debating the question of whether a swastika must always be seen as anti-Semitic. Lucio learns that the word *swastika* comes from Sanskrit, and that the symbol has been found on any number of prehistoric artifacts—the association with Hitler's National Socialism is a recent thing. It can also be found on a number of ancient Hindu tombs.

How can anything found on an ancient Hindu tomb be anti-Jewish? This is a question in a *Telegram* editorial.

"They shouldn't be allowed to do it," he tells Ruthie. "The cops should go in there."

"And do what?"

"Make them stop."

"What if they won't? Put them in jail? Round them all up, take them away?"

"If they have to."

"You sound like one of them."

"I sound like one of *them?*" says Lucio, too loudly. "I do? It's not like a flag, the swastika, you know, it's not like they won the Olympics or something—waving around the swastika, it's like shouting, 'Down with the Jews.'"

"Shouting isn't against the law."

"That makes it OK?"

"That makes it different."

Lucio shakes his head. "Now who's sounding like a Nazi?"

"Shut up," she tells him, abruptly in earnest. "Just shut up before you say something really stupid."

Lucio turns, surprised, and walks to the other side of the room. Watching him, Ruthie thinks of calling him back, of saying she knows it was a joke, that he meant nothing by it. But she doesn't; she is still too angry, and besides, she wanted to hurt him. She is growing tired of Lucio's outrage, his opposition to the Swastika Club, which he seems to have adopted as a cause. Ruthie does not buy it—not entirely. There is something overdone about his rage, as if his anger is supposed to make up for the fact that he isn't a Jew—as if it is his way of showing Ruthie he isn't like his Uncle Angelo. She knows there is nothing unusual about such a stance; for most of the people on Beverley Street, opposing the Swastika Club is a popular cause, a rallying point, an excuse for a brawl. She has even heard Asher Diamond—who once seemed so resigned in his belief that anti-Jewish feeling was a fact of life—talk about the Swastika Club as an aberration, a toxin that has to be expelled at any cost. If the club will not take down its swastikas, she's heard him say, someone will do it for them. Ruthie thinks this a kind of tribute to the Swastika Club, that there is an element of fear in such declarations. The fear is not without cause: every day the headlines describe the deteriorating situation in Germany. At such a time, could the appearance of a swastika, anywhere, not be taken seriously? No, it *is* serious. And it must be stopped. Ruthie knows this, just as she knows that what is at the heart of her annoyance with Lucio is that she *does* think the Swastika Club has a right to protest.

While reading the newspaper reports about the Nazi demonstrations in the Beaches, she feels a strange kinship with them—they have the right to demonstrate, just as her girls have the right to stand up and walk out into Spadina to make a statement. She wants Lucio to see this as well, to not have to tell him so, not have to point out that freedom of speech isn't a cab you take to where you need to go, then get off. But Lucio doesn't see the connection, and that disappoints her—it's something that shows him to be, at bottom, completely ordinary.

"So," he says a little while afterwards, changing the subject. "What does the Party say about all of this?"

"About the Swastikas?"

"About the strike."

Ruthie looks away. "They don't know about it."

Lucio nods. He asked the question on purpose. He knows she has not told her comrades in the Communist Party what she is planning. She still attends Party meetings, but the walk-out is a secret from them. This confuses Lucio, who thinks that if anyone can be counted on to be in support of a walkout, it is the Communists. "What if someone comes by from the Party?" he asks, pressing her. "What do I tell him?"

"That won't happen," says Ruthie.

"What if it does?"

"Then," she tells him, with real firmness, "you keep your mouth shut."

"OK," says Lucio. "Take it easy."

"It's not a secret, it's just they don't need to know."

"Wouldn't they *want* to know? Wouldn't they help?"

"More people means more problems."

"Don't you want more people? Isn't that what a walkout is about? The more people, the better the walkout."

Ruthie does not know quite what to say to this. It is not an easy question to answer. From the first she suspected that the Party would not approve of what she is doing, and earlier that week she saw for herself that this was the case, when, at a Party meeting, Comrade Biro held up one of Ruthie's flyers between his thumb and forefinger—delicately and at a distance from his face, as if it were a thin, unsanitary shoe—and denounced the walkout. "I trust," he told the assembly in his Hungarian accent, "none of you are behind this."

There was a good deal of confusion. Until that moment, Ruthie knew, many of those present at the meeting had assumed that the Party—perhaps even Comrade Biro him-self—was behind the action, and had themselves worked to spread the word of the walkout. "No, I have nothing to do with it," he announced, "and neither should any of you—this is an action unapproved by the Party. This is not the time for

such a thing. What we need now is not melodrama but unity."
Bringing down a gavel and calling for order, he made again
the same point that he had been making at Party meetings for
the past six months, ever since it had become clear that the
rise of Hitler and the Nazi Party had to be stopped, above all
else. Initially, like the Comintern, he had believed the Nazis
would hasten the Revolution by breaking the back of the
German middle class, but he had recently decided it was time
to change strategies. Rather than fostering revolutionary
upheaval, he told them, the Party now needed to change the
system from within, by having progressive candidates elected
to Parliament and using their influence to further the cause.
"If we cannot have the Revolution now," he explained, "what
we need is to build alliances, to work in the system and not
against it. We must think of ourselves as parents and of the
masses as babies taking their first steps. It will take time. It
will require patience. But one day the child will learn to walk.
To do the opposite, to force the child to stand, to prop it up
and let it go, will produce nothing lasting—and the child may
not ever walk."

"Never walk?" called out someone from the back of the
room.

"What I am telling you is what I have told you before," he
went on, as if without interruption. "Different times call for—"

"I ask you again," persisted the voice, that of a woman,
speaking with the measured, composed voice of an orator.
"Does your child never walk?"

At first Comrade Biro was intent on ignoring the question,
but when the woman began making her way through the
crowd, which parted slowly at first, and then more quickly and
with much fanfare as she was recognized, he knew he had to

stop and speak to her. She now stood in front of the podium—not quite sixty-five, short but sturdily built, wearing tiny round spectacles. "Once more," she said composedly, waiting for a reply, "does your baby, Comrade Biro, this child that is made to stand before its time—does it ever walk?"

"Emma," he replied. "How nice it is to have the famous anarchist grace us with her presence."

It was the first time Ruthie had ever seen Emma Goldman, and she stood up, out of her chair, to get a clear view of her. Red Emma—who had been exiled from America for speaking out against the Great War and then, after two disheartening years in Communist Russia, had come to live in Toronto. Ruthie had been only a girl when Red Emma first came to the city, but she'd heard her father's stories about the lectures Emma gave when she arrived. They were widely publicized, well-attended events at which Emma spoke passionately about the mistakes Lenin had made, the poverty and corruption she had seen, which were no different at bottom from the czarist regime she had suffered under as a child, the Bolsheviks turning their rifles on the very proletariat who had helped bring about the Revolution in the first place. She had left and come back to Toronto many times since then, leading a restless, nomadic life, and had recently returned in order to complete work on her autobiography, the first draft of which was rumoured to be more than three thousand pages. It had been common knowledge that she was back in the city, but no one had seen her. The book was long overdue, and it was said she had received an ultimatum from Knopf so devastatingly severe that she had sequestered herself in order to complete her task. But even if she had seen Red Emma, thought Ruthie, she would not have recognized her. Now an old woman with a permanent stoop, her brows arched into a perpetual wince, she was not at all the clear-eyed firebrand Ruthie remembered from the photographs she had seen in her father's copies of *The Daily Worker*. Red Emma was famous, and certainly a kind of ally of the Party, but her relationship with Comrade Biro—who made much of his connections with Lenin—was not likely to be any simple matter, despite all his talk of building bridges. "The child," Red Emma asked again, over the din of the crowd, "how does it get around? Does it crawl?"

"Child?" said Comrade Biro, seeming to have forgotten his own metaphor.

"The people," she reminded him. "You are the parent."

"What I was saying—"

"My question is," she broke in, "does this refusing to walk, does it last forever?"

Comrade Biro laughed, shaking his head. But the room had become silent. He looked down at Ruthie's flyer on the lectern—the one he had held up with such distaste minutes before—and suddenly crumpled it, and looked for a moment as if he would fling it in Red Emma's face. Then, merely wincing as if finding himself at a dead end he had seen before, he took a deep breath and let it out again, and uncrinkled the flyer, smoothing it on the podium as if he were planning to iron it. "No," he said finally. "You have me, Emma. The child would walk. One day it would."

Shouts of approval from the back of the room. Ruthie was shouting herself. "Hope begins," she called out, "and it walks—on its own legs."

Red Emma continued to speak. "What if you took the child and bashed its brains out? Would it walk then?"

"Still with the child?"

"The child I'm speaking of is socialism itself," she told him. "At its birth, it declared war on injustice, whatever its shape. It always *has* walked before its time. And it always *will* walk before its time."

There were more shouts of approval. Comrade Biro held up his hands for silence, but it did not follow. Emma went on speaking, raising her voice—people had started to call out, some of them in support of her, others trying to drown her out. "The truth is," she went on, "that all politicians, no matter how sincere, are but petty reformers, perpetuators of the present system—abortionists of a great idea." As she listened to Red Emma, Ruthie felt overcome by an urge to join her, and she got off her chair, walking out into the aisle toward the front of the room, ready to confess that it was she who had been behind the distribution of the leaflets, ready to allow herself to be taken into the bosom of Emma's approval—to be seen, at last, as a woman of vision who sought to preserve liberty and combat the phantoms that had long held ordinary girls like herself captive. As she made her way to the front of the room, she saw that Emma was still speaking to Comrade Biro. "Will it not?" she was still asking, but now more quietly, a terrified look on her face. "Will the child *not* walk?" Ruthie saw then that this was a real question—that something had happened, or was happening, to the older woman, that Red Emma had despaired and had started to think nothing would ever change. Emptied of conviction, Emma seemed to Ruthie isolated and without a home—exactly the sort of person she didn't want to end up as.

Standing there, Ruthie was close enough to see the look on Comrade Biro's face, to see that he was not at all cowed by Emma's sudden appearance, that he refused to forgive her outburst. "We must agree," he told her, very simply, "before it's too late."

Ruthie waited for Red Emma's reply, but it did not come. Comrade Biro got down from the podium and walked away, leaving Red Emma standing alone in front of the noisy room. Emma turned then, looking right at Ruthie, but she walked past her and said not a word.

The meeting broke up soon afterwards, and despite Ruthie's resolution to continue spreading the word she was unsure, for the first time, if she was doing the right thing. Still she did not confess. She went back to her seat and sat still and said nothing, firm in the knowledge that she was doing something wrong and was going to do it anyway.

Three days later, after a day of handing out her sandwiches, Ruthie went to the St. Lawrence Market at the end of the day to buy more sardines. She walked in just as Dubie was reaching the climactic moment of his pitch. He raised the knife and she saw him seeing her—and she smiled.

Meanwhile, as Dubie is beginning to bring down the knife and sees Ruthie smiling at him, Lucio is asleep in the chair behind Ruthie's desk at Gutman Fur when the door opens and in walks a squat, red-faced man. The man closes the door behind him and sits down in the chair on the other side of the desk. Taking out a handkerchief, he unfurls it, takes a breath and pretends to sneeze.

Lucio wakes up with a start.

"So," says the man. "Good morning."

Lucio has never seen him before. "Can I help you?"

"Well, yes, in fact," replies the man. "I'm here to see Gutman."

"Gutman," says Lucio, "I mean, Mr. Gutman's not here."

"Ha," says the man. "He's got you trained, I can see that. You tell him anyway. I'm here to take him to lunch, actually, so stand up, knock on that door and tell your boss that Leo Bernstein, of Queens, New York, is here to see him."

"Actually," says Lucio, "he's my uncle."

"Uncle?" says Leo Bernstein.

"That's right."

"Gutman is your uncle?"

"That's right, and I'm his nephew."

"I'm sorry," says Leo Bernstein. "That's impossible."

"Damn," says Lucio, before he can stop himself.

"The fact of the matter," Leo Bernstein tells him, "is that Max Gutman is the only sibling of the girl they used to call Susie Gutman."

Lucio feels the blood drain out of his face.

"Which means that any nephew of Max Gutman would need to be Susie Gutman's son. You're with me?"

"Yes," says Lucio.

"Now, Susie Gutman has been married to yours truly, Leo Bernstein of Queens, New York, for the last thirty-five years— which would mean you would have to be my son. And you are not my son. Further, and if you don't mind my saying, you look nothing at all like any Gutman who has ever lived. Tall they are not. Blue eyes they do not have. You may be many things, but you're not Gutman's nephew."

Lucio looks down and Leo Bernstein stares at him expectantly. Lucio tries to think of something to say. Nothing comes, and he decides he must tell the truth.

"Ah-ha!" exclaims Leo Bernstein, before Lucio has a chance to speak.

Lucio jumps.

"Never mind," he tells Lucio. "I got it."

"You do?"

"Never mind," he says, winking at Lucio. "The details, I don't need. You ask me, worse things he can do."

Lucio, who has no idea what Bernstein is talking about, nods.

"Not that I'd do the same, mind you," he tells Lucio. "Only it hasn't come my way, if you know what I mean. Never mind, you know what I'm saying."

"Mr. Gutman," says Lucio, "went to England."

"Mr. Gutman," says Bernstein. "That's good."

"It is?"

"I see it now," he tells Lucio, looking at him. "You *are* a Gutman."

"No, I'm not." Lucio feels the truth is sliding away from him. "He's in England," he says. "He won't be back until it's winter, until it's time to sell the coats again."

"Ah-ha!" says Leo Bernstein. "We'll play it like that, good—your father would be proud."

"You knew my father?"

"Knew, know—he never let on, not once. His sister wouldn't like it, but there's plenty, I can tell you, his sister doesn't like."

"But Gutman's not my father," Lucio tells him.

"Ha," says Bernstein, making a sharp, choking noise that Lucio understands is a laugh. "I got another one for you."

Lucio looks at him.

"A joke," says Leo Bernstein. "Knock-knock."

Lucio stares at him.

"So?" says Bernstein. "Say it."

"Who's there?"

"Not now," says Leo Bernstein. "Let me start it again." He clears his throat. "Knock-knock."

"Who's there?"

"Fanny."

"Fanny who?"

"Fanny body calls, I'm out," says Bernstein.

Lucio pretends to laugh.

"What? You heard it before?"

"No," says Lucio.

"Well, you didn't laugh."

"Sure I laughed," says Lucio.

"No you didn't," says Bernstein. "You pretended to laugh. There's a difference. Don't think I can't tell, because I can. Here's another. Knock-knock."

"Who's there?"

"Abyssinia!"

"Abyssinia who?"

"Abyssinia behind bars one of these days!"

Lucio tries to laugh.

"You're a tough one, you know," says Bernstein.

"I laughed."

"Don't do me any favours."

The door opens and in walks Ruthie, looking shaken.

"Ruthie," says Lucio, springing up out of his chair. "This is Mr. Bernstein from New York."

"It's OK," says Ruthie. "I know Leo, he was a friend of my grandfather's."

"Benny Nodelman," said Leo Bernstein. "Now that was a man who knew a joke. The kids today, Ruthie"—he glances at Lucio—"feh."

"So," says Ruthie, "what can I do for you?"

"I'm here to see Gutman," he says. "But this one here says he's in London."

Ruthie tells him Lucio has told the truth.

"So what am I supposed to do? How about you, Ruthie"— and Leo Bernstein leans way over and flicks an imaginary ash off an imaginary cigar, as if he is Groucho Marx—"can a guy buy a girl a hot dog?"

"Why don't I meet you there?" says Ruthie.

"Meet," says Bernstein (still as Groucho), "shmeet."

"Lucio," says Ruthie under her breath, hardly opening her mouth. "I have to tell you something."

"What is it?"

Leo Bernstein takes her arm. "Come on, Ruthie," he says.

An hour later, Ruthie returns to find Lucio looking very pleased with himself. At first, he says, he felt intense relief, as if, against all odds, he'd made a miraculous escape. Just as quickly, however, that feeling of relief disappeared as he imagined rumours rippling across the city, people shaking their heads at the thought of Mr. Gutman having an illegitimate son who secretly ran his fur business. Lucio realized, as this occurred to him, that he knew nothing at all about Mr. Gutman. Did he have children? Might they think Lucio was out to take their inheritance away, like in *Amazing Stories*—several copies of which Lucio has discovered in one of Mr. Gutman's desk drawers—where illegitimate heirs wrought disaster only to be eventually punished in the most brutal manner? But Lucio then realized that Mr. Gutman was, after all, brother-in-law to Leo Bernstein, and that any blemish on Gutman would be a blemish on Bernstein—so no matter how bad Gutman's sin, Bernstein could surely be counted on to be quiet about it. So Lucio concluded he was safe. In fact, as he says to Ruthie when she returns, he has been ingenious. At the time it seemed a terrible mistake to have claimed to be Gutman's nephew, but it turned out to be perfect, the one thing he could say that would save himself and Ruthie from exposure.

But Ruthie does not seem at all happy.

"What's the matter?" says Lucio, suddenly afraid.

"It's Dubie," she says.

"Is he all right?"

"I think so. I left the hospital before he came out."

And she tells him what happened.

NINE

"THERE'S ONE MORE THING," says Ruthie, when she finishes the story. "He said he loves me."

"What?"

"After Dubie did it, after he cut off his finger, he saw me and just came out with it."

"You sure that's what he said?"

"You don't miss something like that," says Ruthie.

"He said it more than once?"

"How should I know?"

"I thought you said you don't miss something like that."

"I was thinking of other things by then," says Ruthie. "I was looking for the finger."

Lucio moves away from her and she sits down at the desk. If only she'd kept walking, she tells him, none of it would have happened. And none of it would have happened, she says, if she were a man. When a girl cuts off her finger for a man, everyone agrees the man should run in the other direction. But when it's a man, it's a romantic, tragic thing. Ruthie tells him she cannot be sure how many people heard Dubie's declaration—whether it was only the people closest to the front, or whether his words echoed through the market, as they seemed to her to do. It was a declaration, though; Dubie did not whisper. He looked directly at her, and came out with it.

Ruthie shakes her head, and gives the side of the desk a swift kick, causing Lucio to jump like a frightened animal. "Listen, Lucio," she says, with a decisiveness that makes him think she understands all this very clearly. "You should go home, and I should go home, and then we should go at different times to the Diamonds' and see how Dubie's doing."

"Why don't we go together?" he says. "We could see him together."

"No," she tells him. "It would be too much for Dubie—who knows what he's thinking?"

"But he doesn't know about us."

Ruthie nods but says nothing. She stands up and takes her clothes off the hanger, changes quickly, and then Ruthie and Lucio do something they have never done before: they leave Gutman Fur together. They walk together down the Darling Building stairway, and out onto Spadina. It is eight o'clock and the street is filled with people: men coming home from the factories on the outskirts of the city, from the slaughterhouses and soap factories, still in their work clothes; sleek men with slick pale faces; and loud boys heading to the poolrooms and dance halls. Ruthie and Lucio walk quickly through the crowd, preoccupied and not speaking, and at the corner of College and Spadina, while they are waiting for the clang of the traffic signal, Lucio reaches out and takes Ruthie's hand in his.

"Don't," hisses Ruthie. She pulls her hand away, and the signal changes. He feels her looking at him and he turns away so she will not be able to see his face. But she is still looking, and keeps looking at him until he looks at her.

"Fine," he says, "go."

Ruthie takes a breath, as if she is about to say something, but instead of speaking she exhales, like someone giving a demonstration of how to be quiet. Then she turns and crosses the street.

Feeling foolish and dispensable, Lucio sits down on the steps of the darkened Bank of Montreal building and puts his head in his hands. He knows he should have said something, but he can't imagine what this would have been. When he tries to imagine the scene that should have taken place between them, it is melodramatic and strained, like a silent movie. He watches her walk away and then, oblivious of the world around him—and, most particularly, oblivious of Harold Diamond, who is watching from the other side of the street— buries his head again in his hands. Had this happened anywhere else in Toronto, had Ruthie torn her hand away from Lucio's on Queen Street, or Bathurst or Dundas, or even Harbord—which are all wide streets, but not nearly as wide as Spadina—it is likely that Ruthie or Lucio, or both, would have felt themselves being watched, and looked up and seen Harold standing there. They would have noted the boy's already pronounced paunch, and the fact that he looked very like Asher Diamond, standing just five feet tall; would have noted his unremarkable flat face; perhaps, if he'd called out, would have heard the booming voice and realized that they were being watched by Dubie's older brother.

Like Dubie, Harold perceived at a very early age the strong resemblance between himself and his father, and for Harold it came as a great relief. He knew himself to be a poor to middling student, and not particularly witty. A greater impairment, perhaps, and a more serious worry (as far as

Harold was concerned), was that he had discovered he was not particularly interested in anything at all. By the time he was in the eleventh grade—the age at which Dubie would begin staying up late with a flashlight and reading Darwin—Harold was hearing all around him talk about careers and getting the best start in life, and the fact that the first Jewish doctor had recently graduated from the University of Toronto, and what happiness Harold would bring his mother if he was a doctor too. But Harold wanted none of it. He *liked* pitching Greenstein's knives, liked the way the pitch his father had invented thrilled people each time, and the way the crowd got silent just before he sliced the book in half at the end. He loved the way people handed him their money. It did not matter to Harold if he was selling a knife or an apple peeler or an ointment that cured baldness. Each time was as thrilling as the first time had been, when at the age of twelve he had sold his first set of knives. The excitement of changing another person's mind, and taking his money. The fact that he had not invented the sales pitch himself, that it was his father's words he repeated day after day, bothered him not in the least. Dubie went on and on about the unfairness of this, and would often try to incite Harold to a similar rebellion.

"Don't you see?" Dubie said. "It's fascism."

"I don't know about that." Harold had a very approximate idea of what fascism was. "I don't think it is, exactly."

"People think fascism is not being able to say what you want to—that's not it at all," Dubie replied. "Fascism is you have to say what they want you to. You have to lift your arm when the dictator says lift your arm, you have to laugh when the dictator says laugh—you have to cut up the carrots the way the dictator wants the carrots cut up, or else you're kaput. This is a fascist state, and our father's a dictator—he's Il Duce, only with knives."

"Who's Greenstein, then?" Harold asked. "He makes the knives—he made up the knives in the first place."

"Greenstein?" Dubie did not know what to say. "He's no better."

"So he's the dictator of a dictator?"

"Never mind Greenstein," Dubie told him. "The point is, we shouldn't take it."

Harold did not see it this way. He had never wanted to do anything different, or anything other than what his father did. On the rare occasions when Greenstein came out with a new product, Harold hated learning the new pitch. What he wanted was to sell the same things he had always sold, and to sit on the veranda in front of his parents' house beside Esther Nodelman, Ruthie's older sister, for the rest of his life.

Harold had recently made some progress in the Esther Nodelman department, having presented Esther with a pair of new shoes, from the Eaton's Spring Catalogue, that he had overheard her admiring. Esther had pointed out the shoes and then Ruthie had called them bourgeois. Harold wasn't sure what Ruthie meant, but he asked to take a look, and the catalogue was passed to him accordingly. He feigned indifference, but took the opportunity to memorize the order number, looked at his mother's shoes to figure out the size, and right away posted a letter to Eaton's with a money order inside. When the shoes came a week later, he waited until Esther was alone on the veranda, and presented them to her wrapped up like a Christmas present (something neither of them had ever been allowed by their parents to give or receive).

"Oh, Harold," said Esther. "What's this?"

"It's a present," Harold told her. "A Christmas present."

"It's July," said Esther. "Christmas isn't for a while yet."

"I know."

Esther looked at him in a puzzled way.

"It's for you," he said.

"Should I?" said Esther.

He nodded.

"Oh, Harold," she said, after she'd opened it. "How did you know?"

"Remember the other day?" said Harold, unable to contain himself. "With Ruthie and the catalogue?"

"That's sneaky," said Esther, punching him on the arm.

"Well?" said Harold, after a moment. "You going to try them on?"

"Right here?"

He waited and they both looked at the shoes. Then Esther stood up and stepped out of her flat felt shoes, which she always wore for the walk to and from work at Weiss Clothing, and put on the new leather shoes, with their high heels and rounded toes.

"They're nice," she said, looking at him. "They fit good."

"A nice girl should have nice things," he told her.

"What a nice thing to say," she told him. Then she looked at him again, this time seriously. "Do you think so, really?"

"I do," he told her.

"So do I," she told him.

"I think, basically," said Harold, "that people would be a lot happier if they had nice things."

"So do I," said Esther.

"Want to go to the pictures tomorrow night?" said Harold, suddenly.

"Yes," said Esther.

The following night Harold and Esther went to the Rose Theatre to see *The Missing Rembrandt*. They sat in the balcony, near the back, which was where couples sat who knew they would not be watching much of the movie.

"This will never work, you know," Esther told Harold, as they waited for the lights to come down.

"It won't?" said Harold, looking back at the projectionist.

"Not the movie," whispered Esther, "us."

"Why not?" said Harold, who was already considering the two of them more or less married.

"Our parents, I mean. Think about it. Your father's a pitchman and mine's a Communist. They're complete opposites. They'll never allow it."

"But they're friends," said Harold. "They live next door to each other, practically."

"In these kinds of things," said Esther, "none of that matters."

"Your father's not a Communist any more," Harold pointed out. "He's a presser."

"Well, maybe not the way he was, but back when he met my mother, it was a different story. Anyway, he's in a union."

"Everybody's in a union."

"*You're* not."

"You're right."

Esther gave him a meaningful look, and the movie began, the projector behind them making a loud clicking noise as it whirred into motion.

"Maybe it won't work," whispered Harold.

"I don't care," she whispered back.

"Me neither," said Harold, not at all whispering.

Having reassured themselves of the fact that they were

about to do something their parents would disapprove of, as the lights of the Rose Theatre began to fall, Esther and Harold kissed each other for the first time, and did not stop kissing until approximately halfway through the second reel, when a boy with mousy brown hair and a pinched face in the seat behind them suggested they get a room.

"*You* get a room," said Harold (later he would tell Esther that he had just come up with that on the spot).

This reply had a predictable effect. The boy stood up. Which prompted Esther and then Harold to stand up. There was a brief scuffle, and two bouncers were soon escorting both boys and their girls, hastily and by the elbow, out of the theatre.

"That was very brave," Esther told Harold, when they were out on the street.

"You think so?" said Harold.

"Yes," said Esther, and kissed him again.

"Careful," said Harold, "someone could see."

"You're right. Let's keep our love a secret."

"But not forever," said Harold. "Right?"

"We'll see. We might *have* to."

"I hope not."

So began the tempestuous secret romance of Harold Diamond and Esther Nodelman. Although they could just as well have met in the light, the couple would meet in darkness every Friday, in the balcony of the Rose, where they would begin kissing almost immediately and continue right through the newsreel and the movie, and then, because they nearly always bought tickets to double features, through another newsreel and another movie. Then they would leave the theatre and hide in an alley off Spadina, where they would continue to kiss.

The night of Lucio and Ruthie's sidewalk melodrama is one of these nights. Harold and Esther are on yet another clandestine date, and because Harold has spent the greater part of the evening in the movie house and has not been home, he knows nothing about Dubie's accident. Certainly he knows nothing about Dubie's unprompted and unprecedented declaration of love for Ruthie. When he sees Lucio and Ruthie, Harold and Esther are in each other's arms in the alley off Spadina.

"I don't know," Esther is saying to him. "I can't find the shoes—the only one they'd fit would be Ruthie, and what would Ruthie want with shoes like that?"

"Maybe she tried them on and liked them. Maybe she took them."

"She thinks they're bourgeois."

"Whatever that means," says Harold. They both laugh, and as they laugh he looks out onto Spadina and sees Ruthie. "Look," he says. "There she is now—Ruthie."

"My Ruthie?" says Esther, turning. "Oh, you're right."

They watch as the boy next to Ruthie reaches out and tries to take her hand. She pulls away and the boy looks in the other direction.

"Is that Lucio?" says Esther. "Lucio Burke?"

Ruthie crosses the street and the boy sits down, putting his head in his hands.

"Look at that," says Esther. "It *was* Ruthie. I'm sure of it."

They look again, but the boy is gone.

"Lucio and Ruthie," says Esther, shaking her head. "It can't be."

"These things don't always have to make sense," says Harold, looking at Esther meaningfully. "Sometimes you might just, you know, *want* a person."

Esther is not quite listening. "You know," she tells Harold, "I'll find out. I'll ask Ruthie if it was Lucio and she'll tell me. She'll have to."

"You mean," asks Harold, "you'll *make* her admit it?"

"I mean she won't be able to deny it. I'd like to see her do it, actually. I'd like to see her try."

Esther returns home to find Ruthie in her bed with the light on and *What Is To Be Done?* open in front of her.

"So," says Esther. "Who were you out with tonight?"

Ruthie looks up from her book, and her cheeks redden. "What are you talking about?"

"On Spadina," says Esther. "I saw you. Harold and me were there, and we both saw you."

"Harold?" says Ruthie. "Harold Diamond?"

"Don't try to change the subject, I know you were there."

"I assure you I wasn't on Spadina tonight," says Ruthie. "No matter what you and your boyfriend think you saw."

"He's not my boyfriend," says Esther. "Not yet, anyway. All the same, we saw you."

Ruthie's cheeks now most undoubtedly redden. Still she denies it. "Sorry to disappoint you," she says to her sister.

"Then why're you blushing?"

"I'm not."

"You are," says Esther. "Don't try to tell me you're not blushing when you're right there, blushing."

"Esther, go to sleep."

"Blushing," says Esther. "Blushing, blushing, blushing. I'll wake Mom and Dad up if I need to. They'll say you're blushing, and then let's see what you say to that."

"If you want," Ruthie tells her sister. "But I'm telling you I've been here all night. I mean, haven't you heard about Dubie?"

"I know it wasn't Dubie," says Esther. "But if I can't make you tell me, I want you to know you don't fool me. You think you're smarter than me, with all the books you read and the fancy men you stand in front of in those fur coats, but for all that you're still my little sister, Ruthie, and when you were three and got kissed by Mordechai Altman on the teeter-totter at Bellwoods park, you turned red as you are now. You probably forgot that, and a hundred other things, like when Daddy said you were beautiful in your white dress before Harold's bar mitzvah and you blushed then. But I was there and I saw you the way I can see you now. So you can say whatever you want, but don't tell me you're not blushing because I can see for myself that you are."

Ruthie looks away.

"And if you want to know," says Esther, "if it'd been any other day, it would have killed me to go to bed and have you not tell me it was Lucio. Not that I'd tell anyone. Or maybe you'd say you don't care about that sort of thing. But I know as well as you that you could kiss anyone you like, that when the boys knock on the door they're looking for you and not me."

Ruthie tries to object.

"No," Esther tells her, "don't say it isn't true or whatever you're going to say. Because it's true and tonight it doesn't matter. Tonight I was out with Harold Diamond, who you've probably decided is a bit of a fool. And it seems to me that Harold really *does* like me; he isn't one of those boys that come over and take me out just so they can get a better look at you. And that's why I don't care who you've been kissing. But don't tell me you weren't, and don't tell me you're not blushing."

With that, Esther stands up and goes upstairs to the washroom. Turning on the light, she opens the medicine cabinet and takes from it a green bar of Palmolive soap, which she's recently purchased on the strength of an advertisement in the *Daily Star* revealing that Ruth Chatterton, star of stage and screen, keeps her youthful complexion through a combination of bending exercises and washing daily with Palmolive. Esther has been using Ivory ("sensitive skin and pure Ivory agree") after a brief, disastrous experiment with Lava Soap, but when the Palmolive arrived in the mail she took the cake from its wrapper and held its greenness to her face, wondering if it might really be the soap she was looking for. She is always on the watch for the soap that will transform her too round, too plain face into the kind of face someone might wish for, a face like her sister's. But not tonight, about which Esther wants not a single thing changed, not even herself. And so she shuts off the water and puts away the soap, going back to the bedroom, where Ruthie has turned out the light. From her sister's shallow breathing, Esther knows Ruthie is only pretending to sleep, and not doing a very good job of it.

Meanwhile, two doors down, Harold arrives home.

"You're his father," Mazie is telling Asher. "You've got to do something."

"I've got to do something?" says Asher.

"Something to cheer him up," Mazie insists.

"So," says Harold, coming in, "who're we cheering up?"

"Your brother," says Asher.

"Dubie?"

"Your brother," says Mazie, "cut off his finger."

"All right already," Asher tells her. He glares at Harold.

"What?" says Harold. "Why'd he cut off his finger?"

"It was an accident," says Mazie. "It was only a matter of time. Didn't I always say I didn't want the children selling those things, didn't I always say?"

Asher says nothing. The truth is, he has not said a single word about the accident to Dubie since it happened. He does not know the details, and does not want to know them. He does not want to have to do his pitch—his unchanging, perfect sales pitch—while thinking about Dubie's severed finger.

"What we need," Mazie tells them, "is to think about what would be best for Dubie."

"You could take him to a baseball game," says Harold. "The Lizzies are playing tomorrow—first game of the playoffs, against the Vermonts."

"He won't be in any shape for that," says Mazie.

"What?" says Asher. "You want to lock him up?"

"The boy has just cut off his finger—he should be in bed."

"Good," says Asher, ignoring her and speaking to Harold. "You take him, if he's all right."

"How about," says Harold, "I take your shift and you take him?" Asher just looks at him. "Fine," says Harold, "but I won't like it."

There is a knock at the door. Asher goes to answer it and finds it is Lucio. "How is he?" asks the boy.

Asher shrugs. "Not good." He leans back against the door so the veranda light shines into his face, and Lucio sees that it is gaunt and pale. He looks to Lucio like someone who has run a long way without stopping. "Harold's taking him to the Lizzies game tomorrow," he says, and brushes an invisible speck from his dark suit jacket. The movement of his hand, the brisk futility of the gesture, is something Lucio has never seen Asher do before. "Why," Asher says, "why would he do it?"

"He did it on purpose?" says Lucio.

"Who knows?" says Asher. "He never liked pitching those knives in the first place."

Across the street, the darkened windows of the Institute for the Blind reflect back the lighted windows of the Diamond house.

"It's not your fault, Asher," says Lucio, suddenly calling the older man by his first name, the way he would on those Saturday mornings long before. "Dubie cut off his own finger."

"I know that," Asher says, shaking his head again. "Still."

"Still what?"

"Still," says Asher, "it should've been my finger."

"It was an accident."

"Anyway," says Asher, "Harold is taking him to the baseball game tomorrow—to cheer him up. Maybe you should go too."

"I have to work," lies Lucio. He has already decided he will turn up the next day at Gutman Fur as if nothing has happened between him and Ruthie.

"What if I could fix it?" says Asher. "You know, talk to Michelangelo—he'd understand, Dubie being your best friend and all."

"No," says Lucio quickly. "Don't talk to Michelangelo. I'll do it."

"Thank you," Asher tells him. "It's a good thing you're doing—a mitzvah."

"Cleaning up a mess I didn't make," says Lucio, almost to himself

As Lucio is saying this, Harold, at his mother's behest, is going upstairs to see his brother. He walks into the bedroom he and Dubie share to find him fully dressed, lying atop the covers, staring at the ceiling.

"So," says Harold, attempting a joke, "what'd I miss?"

Dubie rolls onto his side and faces the wall.

Harold takes off his tie and hangs it carefully in their little closet. He knows that he and Dubie have always wanted different things, even that Dubie has always hated the things Harold wanted most. When Dubie was young, Harold was responsible for teaching him their father's Greenstein knives pitch. He noticed the way Dubie took no pleasure in it. Not in slicing the carrots with precision, not in carving the turnip busts, not even in chopping *The Complete Works of William Shakespeare* in two. Unlike Harold—who, after his father taught him to carve a turnip tulip, practised for days until he had it exactly right—Dubie was content to do as poor an approximation as he could get away with. Despite Harold's best efforts, he seemed only marginally interested in the work. At first Harold explained away Dubie's inattentiveness as a result of his relative youth, but the older Dubie got, the more distracted he became.

Eventually Harold gave up trying to understand his brother. Especially after he happened one night to see Dubie leaning out the window to retrieve a book he'd hidden in the eaves-trough. This, at first, reassured him. He had done similar things when he was Dubie's age. The next day, with something approaching affection for his younger brother, he opened the window and took Dubie's book out of its hiding place. He was shocked to find himself holding neither a dirty magazine (he had owned, for a brief period of time before selling it to Norman Ravvin on Hayter Street, a black-and-white publication that bore on the front cover the frank title *Breasts*) nor a pornographic book (he kept his copy of *A Man with a Maid*, the story of a young, wilful woman who falls into sinister hands, under his mattress) nor even a pack of playing cards with girls on the back (he owned a pack displaying variously shaped nude girls engaged in various kinds of secretarial work). Instead, he found *On the Origin of Species*. This was the last straw. As poor a student as he had been, he recognized the title. What was Dubie doing hiding Charles Darwin in the eave-strough? In a last-ditch attempt to find something he could understand about his brother, Harold opened and closed the thick book several times, hoping that pages had been cut out to make a place where photos of girls copulating with horses and sheep could be hidden (Harold owned, for this purpose, a copy of *Middlemarch*). He found nothing of the sort. Hearing the sound of the door downstairs, he opened the window and replaced the book in its hiding place. A moment later Dubie walked into the room, and Harold could not speak to him. This was not the kind of thing, he felt, that he and his brother could or even should talk about. Pictures of naked girls playing badminton you could talk about. Books about girls being abducted by Germans and forced to strip while being interrogated you could talk about. Playing cards with pictures of coy women you could talk about. Boxes of rubbers you could talk about. But not *On the Origin of Species*. Since that day, Harold has treated his brother with a new aloofness. Now Dubie has cut off his own finger, and Harold is not surprised. On any other night he would have told him as much—that, as far as he was concerned, Dubie had never been as careful as he should have been. But on this particular night, the success of his date with Esther Nodelman combines with the worried look on his mother's face and he decides that, no matter how strange Dubie is, he has lost his finger and he, Harold, will do his best to make his brother feel better.

"So," says Harold. "I heard what happened."

"No kidding," says Dubie.

"Did it hurt when you did it?"

"Shut up, Harold."

Harold decides to ignore this. "You'll never guess who I was out with tonight," he says.

"Esther Nodelman," says Dubie.

"How do you know?"

"I saw you a month and a half ago, necking in an alley."

"You did?"

"Everybody did."

"Everybody?" says Harold. "Did Mom and Dad?"

"How should I know?"

"Did they say anything?"

Dubie shrugs.

"What about the Nodelmans—do they know?"

"Harold, listen, I said I don't know. I've had a hard day."

"Did anyone forbid it?"

"Forbid what?"

"Our love?"

"Goodnight, Harold," Dubie tells him, and rolls onto his side so he is facing the wall. Harold flings himself down on his own bed. He imagines his mother and father drawing up the ultimatum they will give him in the morning. Break it off with that Communist's daughter, his father will tell him, or else. Harold stares at the ceiling and contemplates his fate. Has it, he wonders, already been decided? But then he has an idea. "You know," he says, "tonight when Esther and me were at the Rose, we saw Ruthie."

"Ruthie?" says Dubie.

"That's right, Ruthie Nodelman. None other."

Dubie sits up. "You did? What'd she say?"

"Say?" says Harold, and slightly alters the facts. "She was too busy *doing* it."

"Doing it?"

"In an alley."

"Ruthie doing it in an alley?" says Dubie. "You're wrong."

"Fine," says Harold.

"No, really," says Dubie.

"I'm just saying I saw what I saw."

"You saw it?"

"Plain as day, on Spadina."

"Who with?"

Harold smiles, happy that he has hit upon something that has caused Dubie to so completely forget his severed finger. "I don't know for sure, but Lucio, I think."

"Lucio?" says Dubie. "Doing it with Ruthie? Dry out."

"I didn't want to look," says Harold. "But I did—not too close, but I looked, and it looked like Lucio."

"Figures," says Dubie, with real bitterness.

"Maybe because he's so bourgeois."

"You don't even know what that means," says Dubie.

"Anyway"—Harold stares at the ceiling again—"you can ask Lucio himself tomorrow—he's coming to take you to the Lizzies game. Won't that cheer you up? And you can get the whole coozie story."

Dubie has stopped listening. He lies down again. "Lucio and Ruthie." He closes his eyes, then says again, "Lucio," and finds himself thinking of the extinct rook snake, which Darwin was never able to see, and which had markings on its back that people believed were indistinguishable from the black eyes of birds.

And, at about the same time, next door, in the house that stands between the Nodelman and the Diamond house, Lucio sits down at the kitchen table.

At one end of the table is Nonna, making gnocchi. She performs this operation by rolling dough into a long, skinny, snakelike roll, cutting this into small pieces with a sharp knife and then pressing the gnocchi into shape with her thumb, rolling the bits of dough sideways like Jimmy Cagney giving reluctant and defiant fingerprints to the police in *The Public Enemy*. At the other end of the table sits Lucio's mother. She is sewing a black clasp onto the back of a black brassiere. This is what she calls finishing. Once a week Harry Rothenberg, owner of Perfect Clothing and Accessories, drops off brassieres (and their unattached clasps), or new, unbelted smocks (and their unattached belts), or zipperless rubber jackets (and their unattached zippers), or sleeveless shirts (and their unattached sleeves), or a hundred other things (with a hundred and often two hundred unattached things) at the house, and he comes back the next week to collect them. There may be a depression on, Mr. Rothenberg has told Francesca, but so long as there are people willing to pay good money for handmade clothes, there is always work for anyone who wants to work with her hands.

"Dubie," Nonna is saying, "he's never going to be the same."

"*Bo*," says Francesca, "don't say that."

"Say it or not," says Nonna, "I've seen it before."

"You don't know," Francesca tells her mother.

"Back in the old country," says Nonna, "Ezio DeAngelo had

a sheep bite off his finger. Just like that, out in the field—and then that's the end of it."

"The end of what?" says Francesca, holding up a finished brassiere. Each time she finishes a brassiere, she holds it up in front of the statue of San Bonorio and his chicken that sits in the middle of the kitchen table, as if looking for the saint's approval.

"They found Ezio," says Nonna, "the next morning, sleeping like a baby, only with no eyebrows, no hair, no nothing."

"What happened to him?" says Francesca.

"He pulled it out," says Nonna gravely.

"What for?" Francesca asks her.

Nonna shakes her head, as if to say that such things are beyond explanation.

"So he was bald?" says Lucio.

"Look who's here," says Nonna, turning toward him theatrically, as if she's been unaware of his presence.

"This one must be my son," says Francesca. "I'll tell you something, you're working too much—I never see you. You go so early, and come back so late. I'm telling you, it's going to catch up."

"I'm all right," says Lucio.

"You heard what happened to Dubie?" says Francesca.

Lucio nods.

"It's a terrible thing," she says.

Nonna shakes her head. "He ain't ever going to be the same."

"Dubie's going to pull out his hair?" says Francesca.

"How should I know?" says Nonna. "But Ezio—"

"Who?" says Francesca.

"The one with the sheep," says Lucio. "Back in Mondorio."

"*Bo*," says Nonna, "nobody's listening to me."

"All right, Mamma," says Francesca, "tell us. Why did Ezio pull out his hair?"

"He got nervous."

"About what?" says Lucio.

"Nervous," Nonna says with great severity, "and he was never the same again."

"Don't scare the boy."

"*Bo*," says Nonna. "He needs to know."

"Enough," Francesca tells Nonna. "We don't need any fairy tales around here. The old country is the old country. It's not the same here. Here people don't go crazy and pull out their hair." She is threading a needle with a placid, detached look on her face, as if she can barely hear what she and Nonna are arguing about.

"*Bene*," says Nonna, standing up now. "That's what you think. In that case, it's only going to be a few years before you put me away."

"Put you away?" says Francesca. "Who said anything about that?"

"Who?" says Nonna, not knowing what to say but indignant beyond repair. She stands up and leans across the table, placing one hand on the head of San Bonorio, and swears that it is true without a word of a lie that Ezio DeAngelo, after having his finger bitten off by a sheep, pulled out all the hair on his body.

Had Lucio and his mother not been present on so many occasions when Nonna had sworn on the statue, and many other occasions when, after receiving bad news, she attempted to destroy the statue in one way or another, they perhaps would have been more impressed by her pious gesture. But both know that she has a complicated relationship with the patron saint of her hometown, and that more than once she has tried to hurl him out the window, or to flush all three and a half feet of him down the toilet. In the end, she always comes back to San Bonorio. She has surrounded herself with images of him—in addition to the statue in the centre of the table, there is the pendant she wears around her neck, and the painting that hangs over her bed in the room she shares with Lucio. In all of these, San Bonorio is depicted holding a chicken, and Lucio knows the one thing he cannot ask is why. Ruthie's father, who as a Communist looks at all matters religious in a particularly unsentimental manner, once offered the opinion that the chicken was connected to a folk tradition in which chickens, notoriously stupid animals, are always thinking the sky is about to fall. Nonna replied to this conjecture by standing up, saying something derogatory about Moses and stomping off. Although Lucio cannot subscribe to Abe Nodelman's atheism, it does seem to him as if the chicken has very little to do with any of San Bonorio's miracles. But this, he knows, is not the way Nonna or anyone born in Mondorio thinks about it. His grandmother seems to see the chicken as a necessary conduit, a feathery antenna without which the Lord would be unreachable.

"So," says Francesca, turning to her son. "Where have you been?"

"Been?" says Lucio. "Working."

"Working?" says Francesca. "What's her name?"

Lucio shakes his head but cannot quite stop himself from smiling, and for a moment he thinks he might say something. Not about his clandestine mornings or Dante filling in for him at the garage. But about Ruthie. About her determination to change things, and something else, something hard to say and having nothing at all to do with the class struggle. And he almost does. He is about to speak when he realizes that it is not as simple as all that. That nothing is as simple as it might have been yesterday, before Dubie cut off his finger. Now he and Ruthie are a complicated, illicit matter. Now he would never dare. Who knows if Dubie was telling other people of his love for Ruthie? Lucio decides he needs to know, and understands that he will have to be at that baseball game tomorrow. Ruthie will be waiting for him, of course, back at the shop. The strike is only two weeks away, and there is a very real chance of Leo Bernstein coming by again, so she will need him more than ever. But he has agreed to spend the day with Dubie, and Asher has slipped him a fifty-cent piece, saying he should take Dubie to breakfast at Altman's Deli. That means Lucio will have to stand Ruthie up. She will be angry, but he will explain—or try to. How simple it would be, he thinks, if he knew Morse code and could knock out a message on the kitchen wall, and in that way tell Ruthie—whom he imagines sitting, at this very moment, on the other side of the wall, at her own kitchen table—that he will not be there tomorrow. It's Dubie, after all, and she will understand. That day when he broke his wrists, it was Ruthie who took him to the hospital, but Dubie wanted to come, crying himself, as if his own wrists had been broken. Or will she understand, he wonders, and just like that the smile dies on his face, with such queer abruptness that neither Nonna nor Francesca has any doubt that Lucio is in love.

"So," says his mother again. "What's her name?"

Lucio shakes his head, as his face reddens. "There's no one," he says. "That's the truth."

"Sure," says Francesca, "tell it to San Bonorio."

Lucio looks at the statue—at the old saint from the old country, an old man with very little hair, clinging to a chicken. "By San Bonorio," Lucio says, reaching over to put both his hands on the saint, "I swear there's no one."

"I suppose," says his mother, pretending to be absorbed in her sewing, "it must be true."

TEN

DUBIE WAKES UP THE NEXT DAY to find the glow of trauma has worn off.

The day before, the world was bright; Ruthie had sat beside him in the taxicab, and he'd felt euphoric, as if everything—as if he—was starting to change.

To evolve.

Dubie had not expected it would feel like this. What he'd imagined was a series of calculated and gradual transformations, a series of excellent judgements. But not this. He had been picked up and hurled, like a baseball. But then it came back to him that the dinosaurs had been obliterated in a single stroke. Wiped out by a meteor shower. This was his meteor, a directionless, violent thing. He'd been mistaken about what Darwin was saying, but that was fine. Because it was happening. He was glad to have Ruthie there with him, though: a witness, and more than a witness. The girl he would talk to years later about it, with grandchildren who would look nothing like him.

Through it all, Ruthie stayed by his side. Even when the nurse told her she had to wait in the waiting room, he could hear her voice outside, echoing through the hospital corridor, telling the doctor he must reattach the finger. This was just like Ruthie. Always thinking the world could be different. Whether it was loss of blood or something else—that some part of him had been shut off as the knife slid through his finger—he could not recall much about what had happened next, other than the doctor saying that everything happened for a reason. This accorded so wholly with what he was thinking himself at that very moment that Dubie watched with placid, nearly disinterested equanimity as the doctor deposited the handkerchief that held his severed finger into a bright metal can that sat in the corner of the room. He was given a needle then, and as its contents spread through his bloodstream, it occurred to Dubie that he'd not even known he was in love with Ruthie until the instant he'd told her. And indeed, when he thought of her he could think of nothing in particular, no moment when he'd been drawn to her. But he had cut off his finger, and said he loved her, and that, he told himself, was the shape of the deal. The price of the arrangement. And now that it was done, it made complete sense. It fit him like a glove. A four-fingered glove he thought, without bitterness. Something meant to be. A kind of sacrifice. A trade. A finger for a girl. And what a girl! Any animosity he felt about the Lizzies wanting Lucio to pitch evaporated at that moment. Lucio could have the Lizzies; he had bigger fish to fry. Ruthie was no consolation prize. Let Lucio try his luck on the mound. Looking at the bandage on his hand, Dubie felt foolish for having cared about baseball so much. Not that it was unimportant, but it was a childish thing and should be put away.

The doctor finished with his hand, and when the morphine wore off, the nurse took Dubie into the waiting room, where he was disappointed not to find Ruthie waiting. What had he expected? For her to be still sitting there, puffing expectantly on a cigarette, like a starlet? For her to embrace him in front of everyone? When they arrived home, Dubie leaned on his mother and walked stoically past the crowd that had congregated to catch a glimpse of him: Ruthie's parents ("Chin up, Dubie," Abe Nodelman said), Lucio's mother and Nonna (he saw Nonna look at him and shake her head, as if he were returning from his own funeral), Grief Henderson (back on the steps of the institute, still waiting to catch Lucio coming home), a rabbi and Cecil Altman, who just happened to be walking down the street with the rabbi when they saw the cab pull up in front of the house and, expecting a big shot, stopped to look. But not Ruthie.

Dubie felt betrayed. After what he'd done for her, he believed himself entitled to more. At the last moment he thought he'd been mistaken, and tried to turn around, but his mother caught him by the shoulders and shepherded him inside, taking him up to his room and insisting that he lie down. She closed the door behind her, and a moment later, or what felt to Dubie like a moment later, she was setting down a bowl of soup next to the bed. How long he'd been lying there, whether he'd been asleep or awake, he had no idea, nor, until his mother wiped his face, that he'd been crying.

"Dubie," she told him, sitting him up, "eat something." He looked at the bowl and lay back down. Once again his mother closed the door, and once more she was back, saying this time that she wanted to look at the bandage. Then she was gone and the door was opening—this time Harold, who seemed intent on cheering him up with his report about Ruthie and Lucio. This to Dubie was worse than betrayal. It was unforgivable. While he'd been getting his hand bandaged, while he'd been think-ing that Ruthie was sitting waiting, full of concern, she had, in fact, been with Lucio. Dubie imagined them together: Ruthie like a cheap cigarette girl fallen on bad days, on her way to the back of a playing card. Harold turned off the light, but Dubie did not close his eyes, and then, in the middle of the night, he sat up and it all came back in a single cacophonous recollection. And just like that, he put it together: the Lizzies hadn't been able to find Lucio because he'd been with Ruthie.

"Lucio," Dubie said out loud, "is fucking Ruthie."

He discovered that he was crying, a sharp, clipped sobbing, a kind of coughing sound. Harold woke up, and their mother was suddenly back in the room, sitting Dubie up and knocking him in the middle of his back as if he had something caught in his throat. Dubie let her, as if he were watching the whole thing from a great distance. What a fool he'd been, to tell Ruthie he loved her; his own presumption infuriated him, and he felt an overpowering urge to do what people were saying Bloomberg must have done—to disappear, to pull up stakes and get on a train to another place, losing his papers in a dank boxcar corner and taking up residence in a hobo jungle. His mother laid him down and sat beside him, at the end of his bed, and the next thing he knew it was morning and she was knocking at the door, saying that Lucio was downstairs.

As he dresses, Dubie struggles with the buttons on his shirt. Downstairs he can hear Lucio talking to his mother, waiting for him, and he finds himself thinking of them in that alley, like dogs, Ruthie arching her back so Lucio can put it in from behind, needing to bend, thinks Dubie, like a bitch in heat. Lucio stupidly pumping away. There is a knock on the door.

"Dubie?"

"I'm fine," he calls, unnecessarily shouting through the closed door.

The door opens anyway, and Mazie Diamond comes in, her face full of concern for her son. "Let me help you," she says, thinking the flush on his face is from his frustration with his shirt buttons.

"No, Mum!" He pushes her hands down, fumbling with the buttons himself.

Mazie takes a step backwards and goes out of the room.

Lucio is standing there, in the front foyer—open-eyed, playing the innocent, thinks Dubie, the cheerful sidekick. Tonto to his Lone Ranger. No, thinks Dubie resentfully, the other way around.

"How're you feeling?" says Lucio.

Dubie shrugs.

"I came last night but you were passed out or something."

"They gave me something, I guess—at the hospital."

"That good, eh?" says Lucio.

Dubie laughs in spite of himself, and Lucio laughs also. It is like old times. Dubie's mother exhales, relieved, as if she has brought Dubie safely into port. She goes into the kitchen.

"So," says Lucio. "Where's Harold?"

"Harold?"

"He was supposed to be here."

"Ma," calls Dubie. "Where's Harold?"

Mazie calls back that Harold has gone to work.

"Work?" says Lucio. "He told me he was taking the day off."

"The day off." Dubie nods. "You'd know about that."

Lucio looks at him.

"I guess you're stuck with me," says Dubie, after a moment.

"Story of my life," says Lucio, smiling.

The two leave the house and walk toward Altman's Deli. Ahead of them on the street is a girl wearing a green blouse. It shimmers in the morning sun in a way that makes it look like one of Ruthie's blouses. The girl is walking briskly, far ahead of them, and neither can be sure if it is Ruthie or not. But both see her at about the same time, and are aware of each other looking in the same direction at the same girl.

"Is that Ruthie?" says Dubie.

"Don't know," says Lucio. "She's got a blouse like that, I think."

Dubie lets out a snort. Lucio ignores this.

"You know," says Dubie, "I think it *is* her."

"You might be right."

"Nice ass," says Dubie.

"What?" says Lucio.

"That Ruthie," says Dubie. "She's got a nice ass. A fine ass."

Lucio lets out a low, ambiguous grunt.

"I take that back," says Dubie. "Ruthie's got a great ass. One of the best asses in the world. For sure, she has the best ass of any Commie I've seen."

Lucio tries to smile.

"And what is more," says Dubie, "the best two proletariats I've seen."

"The best what?"

"Proletariats," says Dubie, his two hands out in front of him as if he is cupping his own enormous breasts.

"I get you."

They walk a little farther.

"What?" says Dubie, hitting Lucio on the arm. "I'm joking."

"Right," says Lucio.

"Can a guy joke?"

"Sure," says Lucio. "I just didn't get you is all."

Dubie looks at him and stops walking. "Proletariats," he says, reaching forward as if he is grabbing ahold of Lucio's imaginary breasts and fondling them.

"You feeling all right, Dubie?"

"Me?" says Dubie. "I can't complain—other than the finger, of course. Other than the fact that I chopped off my finger yesterday, I'm fit as a fiddle. What about you, Lucio?"

"Fine," says Lucio.

"You sure?" says Dubie.

"Sure I'm sure," says Lucio.

"Good," says Dubie, walking again. "That's settled."

Lucio suspected that Dubie would act strangely, but not like this. He expected him to be silent and engulfed in self-pity, disoriented by the loss of his finger and unsure of himself because, even though he has told Ruthie he loves her, she has told him nothing. But he didn't expect this. Dubie has never been one for such garrulous vulgarity. Neither has Lucio. It's one of the things that has bound them together. Just as they live in identical houses, they have led identically tongue-tied, exclusively masturbatory existences that consist of watching wordlessly—nearly deferentially, if not quite innocently—as Ruthie comes and goes. He and Dubie have never had a conversation like this. Lucio feels vaguely that it is wrong to talk this way about people you actually know. You can talk this way about the girls with alarmed eyes and massive breasts pictured on the front covers of *Amazing Stories,* or about Milton Weathervane's imaginary girlfriend in Niagara Falls, who Milton claims got on a swing for his benefit. But not Ruthie. Ruthie they know. Ruthie watched them being born.

But there is also something fiercely proprietorial about

Lucio's sense of the impropriety of Dubie's comments. Ruthie is *his* girl, after all, and he feels like telling him this, whether or not Dubie knows it. It is not jealousy, for the idea that Dubie could have a chance with Ruthie seems so improbable to Lucio that it does not occur to him to see his friend as a rival. Lucio's discomfort surprises him, however, and he wonders if, in the days before he came outside to find Ruthie waiting for him by the garbage cans, he would have had any objection to what Dubie is saying. Maybe he has said such things himself. He cannot recall. Everything is so utterly changed. He tells himself to act normal, but finds himself not able to recall what normal is like. He checks his watch. It is ten; at Gutman Fur, Ruthie will have finished making and wrapping the sandwiches and will be changing into her working-girl costume, looking at her own watch, wondering where he is.

"What?" says Dubie, seeing Lucio look at his watch. "You got a date?"

"Yeah, right," says Lucio as they enter Altman's Deli, in a self-deprecating way that makes him feel so entirely superior to Dubie that it fills him with pity, "me."

The deli is half full. Mordechai is behind the grill and Goody is behind the counter, taking out the food, making out bills and working the cash register. Neither of the brothers sees Lucio and Dubie come in.

Lucio follows Dubie to a booth near the window.

"Have what you like," says Lucio. "It's on me."

"No kidding," says Dubie, unimpressed.

"Asher," says Lucio, "is taking care of it."

"Asher," says Dubie, and shakes his head.

"Your father's really not so bad," says Lucio. "You know what he told me? That he wishes it was his finger."

"Yeah, well," says Dubie. "We'll see."

Lucio puts his hands on the table.

Dubie looks out the window at College Street. "You know," he tells Lucio, "I would have thought that, when someone cut off their hand, the bleeding would be slow at first, and then quicken, the way a water leak is when the water pushes itself through an opening. But it's not like that."

Lucio nods, unsure of what Dubie is trying to tell him.

"The blood," Dubie is saying, "comes in a quick spurt, all at once, and then later more slowly, until it stops on its own. As if it just decided enough is enough. I didn't feel a thing, you know that? I cut off my finger, and I didn't feel a thing. You know what that does to you?"

Lucio shakes his head.

"It makes you think," says Dubie, "that you can do any-thing. You know what that's like?" Before Lucio can speak, Dubie says, "No, I don't think you know what that's like, I don't think you ever looked at your own hand and thought, if I can do that, I can do anything."

Lucio observes that he works pumping gas, not pitching knives.

"That's not what I'm saying," says Dubie. "I mean, it would be the last thing you'd do, wouldn't it?"

"You sure you're feeling all right?" says Lucio.

"You know who, seriously," says Dubie, "made me do it? It was Ruthie."

"Ruthie?" says Lucio, suddenly interested.

"I was there, you know, doing the pitch. The way I do it all the time, every day, over and over again, the same stupid pitch my father made up all those years ago and that god forbid we should change, and I look up and there she is."

"Ruthie?"

"Ruthie," says Dubie, more distantly now. "There she is, perfect, walking through the market—and she turns around and smiles."

"Smiles?"

"At me."

"And then it happened?" says Lucio.

Dubie raises his eyebrows, but before he can say another thing, Goody Altman walks over, wearing a white apron and a white paper hat, with a pad in his hand.

"Dubie, Lucio," says Goody. He turns toward Lucio. "Long time no see."

"I guess," says Lucio.

"You been away?"

Dubie snorts.

"I've been around."

"You're not an easy man to find," says Goody. "Sorry about your finger," he tells Dubie.

"What?" Dubie asks Goody. "You running for office?"

"I heard you had an accident, is all," says Goody, looking at the bandage on Dubie's hand.

"That's the thing," says Dubie. "It was no accident."

"What?" says Goody.

"You heard me."

Goody looks at Lucio, who says nothing. "You meant to do it?" he asks Dubie.

"I didn't say that," says Dubie. "But it was no accident."

"Goody," shouts Mordechai from behind the grill, "ask him, already."

"Ask me what?" says Dubie.

"Ask Lucio, actually," says Goody apologetically.

"Ah-ha," says Dubie, "Lucio Burke. Go ahead, ask him, make like I'm not here."

"What is it?" says Lucio.

"We've been looking for you everywhere this past week. Where you been?"

Dubie brings his unhurt hand down on the tabletop. The loud smacking sound causes everyone in the diner to jump, as if another stone has just been thrown through the window. Goody stares at him. "What's your problem?" he says.

"What colour," says Dubie loudly, "does a guy have to be to get served in here?"

"Hand or no hand," threatens Goody.

"Go ahead," says Dubie, looking back at him. "Take your shot, kike."

"Kike?" says Goody.

At the grill Mordechai looks up for a moment, looks around. "Ask him is all," he calls over to Goody, and goes back to what he's doing.

"Never mind," says Lucio. "He's had a rough couple of days."

"What'd he say?" calls Mordechai.

"Give me a minute," Goody tells his brother.

"So you going to take our order, or stand there jerking off all day?" says Dubie.

Goody takes out his pencil. Dubie orders scrambled eggs with sausages, and Lucio says he'll have the same. Goody writes this down, then tears off the slip and goes over to stick it up in front of the grill. Mordechai reads it, reaches beneath him and, while he is flipping sausage with one hand, cracks the eggs with the other.

"What's the matter with you?" says Lucio when Goody is

gone. Dubie shrugs. "You don't watch it," Lucio tells him, "people'll be saying you're a loon."

"Let them."

"You say that now," says Lucio, "but that's because you're hurt. You're not thinking straight, you can't—remember when I broke my wrists? For a whole week after, I couldn't make myself touch that railing, because I thought it had pushed me. After, you'll feel better, and not think the same—then you'll wish you'd kept your mouth shut. You don't know it because you're the one that's not thinking straight, but take it from me. You're acting crazy."

"And you can tell?" says Dubie.

Goody comes back and throws the cutlery down on the table in front of Dubie, and leaves.

"*You* can't tell," says Lucio. "Besides, what're you talking about? What kind of a guy cuts his own finger off? A lunatic is who."

"I never said that," said Dubie.

"Then how isn't it an accident?"

"It was one of those things that happen for a reason."

Lucio shakes his head, and Dubie picks up one of the knives that Goody left, digging it into the tabletop.

"Don't do that," says Lucio.

"What?"

"That," Lucio says. "With the knife. Goody'll have a fit."

"Let him," says Dubie.

"Here," says Lucio, reaching for the knife. But Dubie leans backward, so that his good hand, the one with the knife in it, is nearly touching the ear of the man sitting in the booth behind him. The man is reading the paper, and he turns around when Dubie's hand brushes against his hair. "Watch it," he says.

"It was a trade," Dubie tells Lucio.

"A trade?"

"The finger," says Dubie. "It was a trade."

"With who?" says Lucio. Dubie looks at him. "With Ruthie?"

"Ah-ha," says Dubie. "So you know."

"I heard some things," Lucio says quickly.

"I thought you might have," says Dubie, pleased even at the thought that Ruthie has been talking about him. "You know, after I did it, Ruthie came running, and took out her own handkerchief, and she held it down tight on my hand. I looked at her and smiled, and she smiled back. And that's when I knew. I mean, I thought it before when she smiled at me, and before that, that day at the playground when she walked out on Bloomberg and refused to let him strike her out, and it was me she wanted to walk out with her."

"She asked everyone—that was the whole point."

"You're wrong, but in any case, when she grabbed my hand at the market that day—I knew right then."

"Knew what?" says Lucio.

"That I had a chance."

"At what?"

"Like I gotta tell you."

"Maybe," says Lucio, "she was just smiling to make you feel better."

"That was before," Dubie snaps at him, again digging into the table with the knife. "I was doing the pitch, and I look up and there's Ruthie giving me one of those looks. Before I did it. She looked my way before *any* of it. But that's part of it. It's not the same thing, but it's part of it."

"Now it's a look," says Lucio. "I thought she smiled."

"That's right," says Dubie. "It was one of those smiles, and you know it. You know what I'm talking about. If anyone knows, it's you. Don't act like you don't." He is still digging into the table, and not looking at Lucio. "When a girl smiles at you like that," he says, "you know."

"Maybe," says Lucio again, "she was just smiling."

"Maybe, well, it doesn't matter—not now."

"You mean now that you've cut off your finger?"

"I said," Dubie tells him in a loud voice, "I didn't cut off my own finger. Why do you keep saying that?"

"Who was holding the knife, then?"

"I was, it was me who did it, but it wasn't me. I didn't mean to do it. But just because I didn't mean to do it doesn't mean it was an accident—it doesn't mean it didn't happen for a reason."

"Give me that knife," says Lucio, reaching forward.

"What're you going to do?" says Dubie, leaning back again. The man at the table behind him turns around again.

"See what you did," says Dubie to Lucio, viciously.

"Me?" says Lucio. Then, to the man: "I'm sorry, sir."

The man turns back, and Goody arrives with their meals. "There," he says, putting down the two plates.

As if in defiance of Lucio, with the knife in his uninjured right hand, Dubie stabs the sausage and puts it into his mouth, then chews it, mouth open, continuing to stare right at Lucio. Goody watches him, then turns to Lucio.

"Listen," he says. "You know the playoffs start today—anyway, the Lizzies have been talking."

"Goody, cash," calls out Mordechai from behind the counter. Goody turns around and sees two men standing at the cash register. "I'll be right back," he says.

"It was like a ballet," Dubie tells Lucio, with his mouth full, as if he's been interrupted in the middle of a story. "You know, she came over to me with her handkerchief, the way she floated over to me, it was like that."

"Except there was blood everywhere."

"Why'd you have to say that?" says Dubie. He is looking at the white bandage on his hand. At the way its whiteness loops around his wrist twice and then through the empty space between his middle finger and thumb. "I know you're jealous."

"What are you talking about?" says Lucio. "Jealous of what?"

"I bet she can't stop talking about me," says Dubie. "It was worth it."

"What was? This trade was worth it? Did Ruthie know about it?" says Lucio, suddenly angry. "I mean, did you ask her first?"

Dubie is cutting up his eggs with his knife, shovelling them into his mouth.

"Did you ask her if she wanted your finger?" says Lucio, very deliberately.

"I knew you wouldn't get it," says Dubie. "You never get it. It wasn't a trade with her. It was a sacrifice. A gamble. Only it wasn't, because I wanted to do it. I didn't see it at first, but now I do. Clear as day. Things happen, and when things happen other things happen."

"What happened?" says Lucio.

Dubie smiles. "Don't tell me you wouldn't do the same," he says.

"No," says Lucio. "I wouldn't do it. Not in a million years."

"You wouldn't do it," says Dubie. "You really wouldn't. Not for Ruthie, not for anyone. Not for anything."

Goody comes back to the table. "Listen, Lucio," he says. "We play the Vermonts tonight—"

"Maybe this is the year you go all the way," says Lucio, grateful for a change in topic.

"Ask him, already," calls Mordechai.

"Bloomberg's gone," says Goody. "We need someone on the mound."

"You want me to pitch?" says Lucio.

"You'd be Bloomberg's replacement," says Goody.

"I don't know," says Lucio, not quite able to stop himself from smiling, imagining himself borne aloft on the arms of his neighbourhood, victorious, knowing he's made it into the record books. It's not the first time the thought has crossed his mind, but this is different. This is Goody Altman (the second-best baseball player the city of Toronto will ever produce) asking him to do it.

"We all saw you throw that ball," says Goody. "I've told you that."

Lucio looks at Dubie, and sees he has pushed his plate over to one side and is again digging into the table with the knife. Goody is looking at Lucio expectantly, waiting for an answer, and Lucio, seeing pinstripes under Goody's apron, knows that the other boy is wearing his Lizzies uniform. He thinks, we will go there from here—if I say yes, I will be on the mound in an hour. "What do you think?" he asks Dubie.

And Dubie tells Lucio that he knows he's fucking Ruthie Nodelman. "Lucio," he says, "I know you're fucking Ruthie Nodelman."

Lucio shifts in his seat.

"Don't deny it," says Dubie. "Harold saw you last night. Doing it in a back alley."

"Where?" says Lucio.

"Where?" says Dubie. And right then Lucio knows that he has said the wrong thing. That "where" is, quite precisely, the worst word he could have chosen. "*Where?*" says Dubie to Goody. "Get a load of this guy—*where?* You can't narrow it down?"

"I mean," says Lucio, "it wasn't me." But it is already too late.

"It was in an alley," Dubie tells Goody.

"An alley?" says Goody, impressed. "With Ruthie the Commie?"

"He had her bent over," says Dubie. "He was giving it to her from behind."

"*Oy vey,*" says Goody, truly amazed.

"There was no alley, no nothing; it didn't even happen. Harold's making it up."

"All of it?" says Dubie, and Lucio looks away. "Let me tell you something," says Dubie. "She deserves better."

"What's that supposed to mean?" asks Lucio.

"And she's going to get it. I've seen to that. Let's see you get on top of that girl when she's thinking of me and what I did for her."

"So," says Mordechai, coming over from behind the grill, "we got a new Bloomberg?"

"Lucio," says Goody, "was doing it with Ruthie the Commie last night."

"*Oy vey,*" says Mordechai. "What about Spinny? Didn't he go to the pictures with her?"

"He kissed her once," says Goody. "Now she's on to Lucio."

"You're crazy," Lucio says. "All of you. But mostly you, Dubie—what the hell are you talking about? A trade? I expected you'd be strange, but nothing like this. You cut your finger off on purpose—where'd you get it in your head that it works like that? It doesn't work like that. You're a lunatic, and if you don't watch it, if you don't keep your mouth shut, they'll be carting you off."

"Yesterday at the market," Dubie tells the Altman brothers, speaking very evenly now, in a monotone that makes it seem as if Lucio is the one out of control, "Ruthie came running over to me, and she grabbed my hand, and I said I loved her. And she said the same. Right there in the market. Everybody heard it."

"Now," says Goody to Mordechai, "Ruthie is on to Dubie."

"She said it back to you?" says Lucio. "Bullshit."

"You asked her?" says Dubie. "I knew you would."

"Bullshit," says Lucio.

Dubie cocks his head to one side.

"This is Ruthie the Commie we're talking about?" says Mordechai.

"Dubie cut his finger off, and Ruthie was there," says Goody. "And Dubie said he loves her, and she loves him."

"What about Lucio?" says Mordechai.

"She came to help you," Lucio is telling Dubie, not listening to what the Altman brothers are saying. "She told me. There you were, bleeding all over the place, and she came to help you. You just came out with it: 'I love you Ruthie,'" says Lucio, mimicking Dubie, in a monotone, a dull-sounding voice that comes from the back of his throat— "'I love you, here's my finger, I cut it off for you.'"

"Shut the hell up," says Dubie.

"Just don't break anything," says Goody, reaching between the two and removing the plates from the table. Under Dubie's plate, Goody finds, someone has carved a swastika. "What's this?" he says. "Look at this," he says to Mordechai.

Mordechai looks.

"When'd they do this?" says Goody.

"I should know?" says Mordechai. "They came in and did it. They didn't check with me."

"Nobody did it," says Dubie. "I did it."

"You?" says Goody.

Dubie shrugs, as if to say it matters not at all.

"Dubie," says Lucio, "there's something wrong with you. I don't know how and I don't know what, but it happened."

"You dickless wop," says Dubie.

"I don't have to listen to this," says Lucio.

"You're wrong." Dubie stands up. "It's me who doesn't have to listen to this; it's you who brought me here. It was your idea."

"You," Mordechai is saying to Dubie, "*you* drew this? Why would *you* draw this?"

"Asher was crazy to think a baseball game would make you feel better," says Lucio.

"Asher," says Dubie, with real derision. "He's not your father. No matter what you do, it's not going to happen. You'll never be me. You can live on our street as long as you like, but it just ain't going to happen. I'm sorry to tell you, Lucio."

Lucio stands up.

"What? You want to hit me?" says Dubie. "Go ahead, wop, give it your best shot—"

Before Dubie can quite get to the end of the sentence, Mordechai hits him in the face. Six inches taller and nearly twenty pounds heavier than Dubie, he sends him backwards into the table behind him, where an empty plate and coffee cup tumble down on top of him. Forgetting about his finger, Dubie sticks out his left hand to break his fall. The tape that holds the bandage in place gets caught on the side of the table and is ripped off, leaving the bloodied stump on his hand exposed. "What do you want to do that for?" says Dubie lamely, before he notices that the bandage is gone.

But Mordechai, like Lucio and Goody, is staring at Dubie's hand. As remarkable as Greenstein's knife was, as cleanly as it sliced through telephone books and turnips and nearly everything else, Dubie's wound is not at all the clean, cartoonish affair that the doctor described in the emergency room. Not at all a neat, bloodless stump. The knife hit bone, and did not come cleanly out the other side. Mordechai, his hand still raised, looks at the jagged wound, and lets his arm fall to his side. Wordlessly, as if he is the sad clown at the end of a silent movie, Dubie gets up, picks the bandage up off the floor and covers his hand. He goes to say something and the bandage slips off, falling to the floor. He bends, tries to catch it but cannot. Stumbling, he picks it up once more and presses it onto his wound, as if he is trying to get it to stick there.

Goody speaks first. "Dubie," he says, "you should go to the hospital or something, and get them to do it up again. And maybe lie down or something. I know you've been through a lot, but you can't just come into this place and start putting swastikas all over."

"Shut up, kike," says Dubie.

"What are you talking about?" says Mordechai, "You're a Jew. When you call him a kike, you're calling yourself a kike."

"And when you knock me down," Dubie tells him, "you're knocking yourself down."

"It's not the same thing, Dubie," says Mordechai, unfazed, in a level voice.

Dubie looks out the window at the College Street traffic. "Doesn't make sense," he says very quietly, half to himself. "You think you can tell me what makes sense and what doesn't. This *goy*," he says, pointing to Lucio, "is fucking Ruthie."

"I'm not," says Lucio, before he can stop himself.

Dubie is about to say something, but stops. "You aren't, are you?" he says. "No—*oy*, how long have you *not* been fucking her?"

"Dubie," says Goody, and takes a step forward, taking him by the arm.

"I'm not talking to you," says Dubie, and pushes past them all, toward the door. "It doesn't matter. I'm leaving—go take your baseball and shove it up your ass. I know what you're thinking, that this is the way it's always been. Read your Darwin and shut up—one thing leads to another and some are left behind, and that's the way it goes. But you know, it isn't true. And it isn't fair."

Lucio puts up his hands as if to surrender.

"What's he talking about?" Mordechai asks him.

"Never mind," says Dubie bitterly, opening the door, with a strange look on his face, as if he has not quite believed a word of what he's been saying. "You know, Lucio," he says, turning around, "it's just not fair. No matter what they say. It's not a straight line, but that doesn't make it any easier."

There are tears in Dubie's eyes, and a moment later he is gone, running down College Street.

Goody turns toward Lucio and says something about the playoffs, but Lucio is not listening. He pushes past Goody and goes out the door himself, walking the other way, toward Spadina.

Mordechai looks at Goody.

"What?" says Goody. "I asked him."

"We're going to have to do more than ask him," says

Mordechai, who is also wearing his Lizzies uniform under his apron.

"No time for that," says Goody, taking off his apron and throwing it behind the counter. "Looks like you're pitching."

"Me?" says Mordechai. "Why me?"

"Someone has to," says Goody. "You can't not have a pitcher. Not if we're going to make it to Christie Pits this year."

Mordechai shakes his head, and then also removes his apron. "Where's Dad," he says.

"Don't worry," says Cecil Altman, walking out of the back room. "I'm here."

Goody reaches behind the counter for his glove and catcher's mask, and gets out Mordechai's glove too, flipping it to his brother.

"Win," Cecil Altman tells his sons, as if he is talking about much more than just the start of the Toronto Junior playoffs. For a moment he stands there, watching them run down the street, thinking of how the three of them, a month before, had crowded around the radio and listened as Max Baer, a Jew, beat Max Schmeling into submission in the centre of Madison Square Garden, in front of the whole world.

ELEVEN

BY THE TIME LUCIO REACHES the Darling Building, it is almost one in the afternoon. He takes the stairs two at a time, flinging open the frosted glass door.

"Hello, Lucio," says Ruthie.

"Ruthie," says Lucio, out of breath.

She is sitting behind her desk, the way she used to. Her copy of *Das Kapital* is in front of her, closed, and Lucio sees that everything he had pushed to one side during those days he kept his vigil in Gutman Fur has been put back, that the desk has been restored to its perfect order.

"I was wondering when you'd show up," she says.

"It was Dubie," says Lucio.

"What about Dubie?" says Ruthie. "Is he all right?"

"He knows everything," Lucio tells her. "The whole thing."

"The whole thing?" says Ruthie. "About the walkout? What did you say?"

"Not about the walkout," says Lucio. "About us."

"What does he know?"

Lucio tells her about Harold seeing them in a back alley.

"What?"

Lucio looks earnest and panicked.

"First of all," says Ruthie. "I don't know what you're worried about. Whatever Harold saw or thinks he saw, whatever he said to Dubie to get him riled up—he didn't see us. As far as I can recall, you and I haven't copulated in any back alley."

Lucio turns and walks to the far corner of the room. He runs his hand through his hair and looks out at the street. Behind him he hears Ruthie standing up.

"We haven't even done it," he says sullenly.

"Is that the problem?" asks Ruthie. She is behind him. "What else did he say?"

"That you told him you loved him," says Lucio. "When he cut off his finger. He told you, and then you said you did too."

"You believe him?"

Lucio shrugs, still with his back turned.

"I understand," she says, kissing him on the back of the neck.

Lucio stands still and feels her hands on his chest. Then she moves away, and he turns around. She is over at the coat racks at the rear of the store, taking the fur coats off their hangers one by one and laying them on the floor.

"What're you doing?"

"Making a bed," she tells him.

"A bed?"

"That's right."

"On the coats?" says Lucio. "Won't they get wrinkled?"

"Wrinkled?" says Ruthie. "Is that what you're worried about?"

Lucio's mouth is dry.

"What's the matter?" she says. "I thought this was what you wanted."

"But now?" says Lucio. "Why now?"

"Because this is what happens next," says Ruthie, coming toward him. "You have something, right?"

Lucio freezes. "I do," he says, "but not here."

"Not here?"

"Back at the house," sputters Lucio, thinking of the condom Dante gave him, which is still in its hiding place out in the eavestrough. "I'll get it."

Before Ruthie can reply, before she can say anything at all, Lucio is out the door, running down the steps of the Darling Building, on his way to the house on Beverley Street.

Lucio goes up the fire escape to the second floor, in through the kitchen window. Lowers himself onto the white tiled floor. There he stands, listening. The first thing he hears is voices. It seems to him that the voices—and there are many of them, a whole crowd of people—are coming from the living room, and for a moment he worries he will be stopped. But there is also a distant, muffled quality about the conversation, and he realizes that people are talking on the veranda. He steps out of the hallway and turns, taking a couple of steps in the direction of the little room he shares with Nonna, telling himself he will be out in a second. Once in his room he will shut the door, open the window and get the condom out of the eavestrough. Then he will be back down the fire escape. But before he can get very far down the hall he hears the sound of a voice out on the veranda below that makes him freeze in his tracks. Despite its being muffled, he recognizes the accent of someone from Queens, New York. He turns and walks into the living room, looks out the window and down on the long veranda and sees he is not mistaken. At one end of the veranda are Dubie's parents.

Asher is sprawled on the green, plastic-covered sofa and Mazie is sitting next to him in a stiff-backed wooden chair—Lucio knows she cannot stand the feel of the plastic against her skin. At the other end are Ruthie's parents, Abe and Sadie, in their wide-armed beach chairs. In the middle of the veranda sits Francesca Burke, slim, with her long black hair pulled up into a bun, wearing a black dress, black stockings and black shoes, sewing a black clasp to the back of a black lace bra. On the sidewalk in front of the veranda is Dante's blind, diabetic grandmother, Mrs. Greico, with her two eldest sons, Primo and Secondo, on either side of her. They have, it seems, stopped by for a visit. Mrs. Greico sits in a massive wooden wheelchair, and even from the upstairs window Lucio can see her eyes rolling from side to side as usual, with a fierce randomness, like flies in the early evening light.

And in the middle of the sidewalk stands Leo Bernstein, telling a joke.

"So," Leo Bernstein is saying. "Here's another one."

"Wait," says Asher. "Have a seat."

Bernstein declines.

"Feh, Leo," says Asher, "have a seat."

"I'll stand," says Bernstein. "It's for the joke."

"What is?" says Asher.

"The standing."

"What kind of a joke is it that you need to stand?" says Asher.

"If a man wants to stand," says Abe Nodelman, who remains a staunch defender of liberty, "that's his right. His unalienable right."

"If you want a guy to sit," says Primo, "hit him in back of the knees."

"Primo," Mrs. Greico tells her son. "Be nice."

"No, Ma," Secondo tells his mother, "Primo's right. It don't take a second. You go sideways with the hand"—he demonstrates—"then we'll see."

"Feh," says Asher provocatively, glaring at Leo Bernstein as if to say he hopes such measures are unnecessary.

"Why don't you see," Mazie tells her husband, "this is about the plastic on that sofa? Who wants to sit on a plastic-covered sofa? I've said it a million times: take the plastic off. Throw it in the garbage. I tell you, I've stopped trying. With that plastic there's no getting comfortable. What do you want to keep the wrapping for, I say."

"It's not wrapping," says Asher. "It's a covering."

"Wrapping," insists Mazie.

"You can see through"—Mrs. Greico's tone is that of a woman who is accustomed to having her pronouncements acted upon—"then it's no wrapping. You give that thing to somebody, they're gonna know it's a couch."

"I rest my case," says Asher.

"See?" says Mazie, gesturing expansively toward the sky, as if to invoke a divine perspective on her situation.

"Feh," says Asher, also staring heavenward and gesturing, as if to ask whatever divine perspective Mazie is invoking to see it his way for once.

Upstairs, Lucio hears a sound. Behind him, in the kitchen. Then he hears it a second time, and a third. Someone is in the kitchen. He lies down behind the couch, flattening himself against the floor so he can see under the sofa. He finds that he can see the doorway but not into the kitchen. It is Nonna, he thinks. Then the kitchen light comes on and there is the clattering sound of drawers being opened and closed.

"Here's the joke," Leo Bernstein is saying. "A man comes in and sits down at a bar. He orders a drink, picks up a peanut, and just as he's about to put the peanut in his mouth, the peanut says, 'That's a wonderful tie, it's perfect for you, and I don't say that to everyone, by the way.'"

"This is what the peanut says?" says Asher.

"This is what the peanut says," says Leo Bernstein. "It likes the tie."

"Some peanut," says Asher.

Lucio hears more movement in the kitchen. Someone is picking things up and putting them down. He hears the clank of dishes being placed on top of each other. A sharp intake of breath. The dull thud of something heavy being dropped clumsily on the floor. Lucio tries to think what this could be, what in the kitchen could make the heavy sound. Then it occurs to him. San Bonorio—someone is moving the statue.

"So," says Bernstein, "this man, he puts down the peanut and orders another drink."

"What?" says Asher. "Just like that?"

"No, not *just* like that," Bernstein says. "There's a little time that goes by. He looks at the peanut that liked his tie, thinks about it, drinks a little, thinks about it a little more and then orders another drink and takes another peanut. Just when he's about to put this peanut in his mouth, the peanut says, 'I love that suit, that's the best-looking suit, it fits you so nice.'"

"This is the same peanut?" Mrs. Greico interrupts to ask.

"Yes," Primo tells his mother.

"No," says Leo Bernstein, "this is a different peanut."

"Another peanut?" says Primo.

"*Madonna!*" says Mrs. Greico, as if to say that there are entirely too many characters in the story to follow.

Lucio hears his mother. "It's only a joke. They aren't real peanuts."

"It's an honest question," says Abe, who is still enough of a Party member to be in favour of a little questioning. "It could've been the same peanut."

"I'm gonna say it again," says Leo Bernstein. "That first peanut is out of the picture. Forget about it."

"Please," says Abe, who is still enough of a Party member to know how to determine the order of speakers. "Leo is the floor."

"Has the floor." Lucio recognizes the voice of Sadie Nodelman.

"Leo," says Abe, as if he cannot get a word in edgewise, "talk."

"So," says Leo Bernstein, "to make a long story short, the man at the bar puts down the peanut and calls the bartender over. He says, 'What's the story with these peanuts? They love my tie, my suit.' 'Sure,' the bartender tells him, 'they're *complimentary*.'"

Upstairs, crouched behind the sofa, Lucio is thinking that it's an animal, one of the things he used to hear crawl across the roof. There is scratching now, rhythmic, and he wonders if it might be something strange—a monkey, perhaps a beaver.

"I'm curious," Asher is saying below him. "What part of that joke you just told did you have to stand for?"

"Take it easy," says Abe. "Everybody's friends here."

"Easy?" says Asher. "Who's taking it easier than me?"

There is the sound of a car pulling up in front of the house. Thinking, irrationally, that it may have some connection with whatever is scratching away in the kitchen—that it may be a truck from the Riverdale Zoo come to recapture a monkey, or the police to arrest a burglar—Lucio lifts his head to peer over the windowsill, and sees that a taxi has pulled up. First the driver's door opens and the driver emerges, pivoting on his heel and opening the passenger door in a single movement. He makes a low bow and extends a gloved hand and then, from inside the taxi, there emerge five ruby-red fingernails, which take the proffered hand, and then a single, stubby stockinged leg. The leg reaches tentatively for the curb and the skirt covering the leg hikes up, exposing a plump knee. The driver stares at the leg routinely, as if this is part of his job.

As does everyone on the long veranda. But not because the emergence of the knee is particularly provocative; everyone on the veranda is staring at the plump, not particularly provocative knee because they have already guessed to whom it belongs.

"Look," says Asher, "it's Esther."

Lucio watches as Esther herself emerges, wearing a light blue dress and a matching hat. Harold, who has got out of the other side of the taxi, is wearing tartan trousers with a matching hat, which those watching can only assume Esther picked out for him.

"Hello, everyone," says Esther.

"What a beautiful day," says Harold, taking his wallet out.

"And Harold," says Asher.

"What a surprise," says Abe.

After paying the driver, Harold takes Esther's arm. It seems he is intent on walking her to her door, despite the number of people on the veranda. The couple proceed first to the stairs in front of the Diamond house, making their way around Mrs. Greico's wheelchair and Primo and Secondo, up onto the veranda and past Asher and Mazie and the green plastic-covered sofa, past Lucio's mother. Just as they are about to reach the Nodelmans' door, Harold halts abruptly and addresses Esther's mother.

"Well," says Harold, "it looks like there's a real gusher here."

"A gusher?" says Sadie.

"Right here," says Harold, "right here on this veranda."

"Are you absolutely certain?" says Sadie.

"A gusher," says Harold slowly, by way of explanation. "A real gusher."

Realizing finally that she is being flattered, that Harold is comparing her, in a favourable way, to an oil well, Sadie Nodelman smiles. Which prompts Abe Nodelman to stand up and thank Harold for the compliment, and to recommend that, when attempting to flatter in the future, he should, if at all possible, avoid alluding to oil wells, and in particular avoid the word *gusher*.

"Gusher," Abe Nodelman tells him, "is open always to misinterpretation."

"You think so?" says Harold, worried.

"Don't mind Daddy, he's always got something to say," says Esther. "I better go."

"What, go?" says Asher Diamond, from the other end of the veranda. "Sit down awhile."

"No, thank you, Mr. Diamond," says Esther.

"Call me Dad," says Asher. There is great laughter and much blushing after this.

"So," says Harold. "Saturday?"

"What'll we do?" says Esther.

"Whatever you want," says Harold.

"Pick me up at five," says Esther, opening the door. Then, just as she is about to go inside, she turns and looks back at Harold. "Harold," she tells him, "I thought gusher was charming."

"You did?"

"I did," says Esther. "I was charmed."

"You were?"

"Entirely," says Esther.

"Entirely," repeats Harold.

"Yes," says Esther. "It was very, very nice."

Lucio stops listening to their conversation—the scratching coming from the kitchen has changed and he realizes that it is not an animal but someone trying to light a match. Someone is trying to burn down the kitchen, he thinks, and a chill runs through him. He edges forward on his hands and knees, toward the kitchen door. The scratching continues, now more frantically, as if someone in the kitchen desperately needs a smoke but can't light a match. Then all at once the scratching stops. Lucio is inches from the doorway. There is silence and then the abject, unmistakable sound of someone crying softly. Lucio stretches forward and peers in through the doorway.

What he sees is Dubie, weeping over a pile of wrecked matches.

"Dubie?" says Lucio.

Dubie jumps and lets out a little scream. It takes him a moment to figure out where the voice is coming from, to see Lucio on the floor, his face in the bottom left corner of the door. But then he shakes his head and stares back at Lucio, surprised but also not surprised, as if he's been expecting him to show up. As if thinking to himself that he's been foolish to think he'd be allowed to leave Lucio out of anything. It is the bitterness in the way Dubie looks at him, the resentment, that makes Lucio understand that Dubie is trying to burn the table, and thereby bring about a kind of divorce between the two of them. That he is trying to change the past by burning the table upon which they were both born some seventeen years ago.

"What's the matter with you?" says Lucio, standing up.

Dubie backs away, and a moment later he is pushing himself out the window.

"Wait," says Lucio, grabbing him by the leg.

"Let go of me!" screams Dubie, and the sound so surprises Lucio that he does. A moment later Dubie is gone, having run down the fire escape.

Lucio looks at the pile of matches, and thinks he must get rid of them. As angry as Dubie may be at him, as much as his life would be easier right now without Dubie, Lucio's impulse is still—lending credence to Milton Weathervane's claim that people born on the same kitchen table on the same day stick together—to cover for Dubie. He gathers the matches and shoves them into his pocket. Then he starts putting things back on the table, which is what he is doing when he hears above him the sound of a toilet flushing. Nonna, he thinks; she has been upstairs the whole time. He replaces things as fast as he can. A spoon. A half-full bottle of Scoll's Emulsion Vitamins. Salt shaker. Pepper shaker. His mother's sewing box. Nonna is now on the stairs, taking each one slowly. He is trying to remember how things were arranged when he left this morning on his mission to cheer Dubie up. A half-eaten piece of toast on a dirty white plate. A copy of the previous day's *Toronto Daily Star*. Two empty glasses. Nonna is now halfway down the stairs, now nearly in the hallway. A box of Cook's baking powder. A McIntosh apple. Drying cucumber seeds. A rolling pin. And then, as he hears the doorknob turn, he pushes himself up onto the drainboard and out through the window, landing on the fire escape with a deep, metallic bang. He runs down, then along the cinder lane, running toward Ruthie but with the image of Dubie and his defeated matches in his mind. He realizes then that Dante's condom is still in the eavestrough, and panics at the thought of having to return to Gutman Fur empty-handed. But he recalls a store on King Street called Nowlan Rubber, where, according to Dante, you can put your money down and they hand you a rubber. And then—just as he is reaching the end of the cinder alley, where it becomes Baldwin Street—Lucio stops. He knows he cannot go through with it. He thinks of Dubie's bloody hand, and of the awful look in his eyes. It's a mess he didn't make, but he's got to clean it up anyway. He knows he must say something. What he has to do is go back to the veranda and tell Asher that something is wrong with Dubie. That something has happened. That Dubie is not thinking clearly and something must be done before he does something desperate. As he walks, Lucio puts his hands in his pockets and finds them filled with Dubie's bent matches. He turns the corner at Baldwin and Beverley, and a moment later he is there.

Leo Bernstein is about to tell another joke. "Here's one," he says.

"Just a second," says Lucio, cutting him off.

"Lucio," says his mother. "Don't be rude."

"Ma," begins Lucio.

"Ma?" says Leo Bernstein, looking first at Lucio and then at Francesca.

"I'm sorry," Francesca says.

"It's all right," says Bernstein, with a wink at Lucio.

"Do you know my son?" says Francesca.

Just then the front door of the Burke house flies open. Nonna steps breathlessly onto the veranda. And screams.

Her scream is a low, long sound that issues from somewhere deep inside her chest. But she is not in any pain, it is not that kind of scream. Instead, it is the kind of scream that people scream when they find themselves confronted by the miraculous.

"San Bonorio," says Nonna, and stops, and turns around and goes back inside.

Everyone follows her upstairs into the kitchen.

"He walked from here," says Nonna, pointing at the tabletop, "to here," pointing to the middle of the floor, where the statue is standing.

"Maybe it fell," says Asher.

"It didn't fall," says Nonna.

The statue, Lucio notes, is exactly where Dubie put it. In the corner of the kitchen, facing the wall.

"This kind of thing," says Mrs. Greico, nodding and looking right at the statue, "used to happen all the time in the old country."

There is a silent moment when everyone in the kitchen turns to look at Mrs. Greico and realizes that, in addition to getting out of her wheelchair and walking up the stairs to the second floor, she has regained her eyesight.

TWELVE

FATHER McELARNEY, pastor of St. Patrick's, hears about the miracle on Beverley Street two days later, and quite by accident. He has just finished saying morning mass to a very meagre collection of parishioners. Even for these irreligious times, when people are blaming God for everything, the congregation was sparse. It consisted of four hobbled old men, two old women, a middle-aged man in a wheelchair who slept soundly for the duration of the service, and three flour-covered children. After a quick final blessing the old priest walks into the sacristy, and he is just beginning to remove his vestments when he hears a knock at the door.

Opening it, he finds himself confronted by the three children.

"I'm Giovanna," says the tallest of the three. "This is my brother Antonio, and my sister Victorinna. Our father's Guido Bucci, the baker."

"That," says Father McElarney, "explains the flour."

The three children carefully dust themselves off, scattering flour in every direction.

"What seems to be the problem?"

"No problem," says Giovanna. "We have a question."

Father McElarney gestures expansively.

"It's about the window," says Giovanna.

Father McElarney sighs. "Which window?" he says, although he already knows what the answer will be.

"Over here," says Giovanna. She turns and walks back into the church, where the man in the wheelchair is still sleeping.

Father McElarney and her siblings follow her.

"This one," says Giovanna, pointing.

"Ah," says Father McElarney, "Saint Patrick."

All four look up.

Dressed entirely in green, with a quiver of arrows slung over his back, Saint Patrick is located in the exact centre of the big stained-glass window above the altar. It is not, of course, the first time Father McElarney has been asked about this window. Nor is it a new addition to the church. The window has been there for years, was already in place when he arrived, some thirty-six years ago, from Dublin. Since then, most of the questions he has received have been about this window. Many members of the parish are convinced that the green figure is not Saint Patrick but Robin Hood, or perhaps a leprechaun. Those who believe the figure is a leprechaun have more than once questioned the wisdom of having the likeness of one of those notoriously miserly minions of Satan (most parishioners who believe the window depicts a leprechaun, Father McElarney has noted, are those who claim to have actually encountered a leprechaun back in Ireland, and to have been the worse for it) occupying such a prominent position in a Catholic church. Father McElarney has done his best each time to explain that the green figure is Saint Patrick, pointing to the snakes trailing after him, and observing that the figure is playing a flute.

In the window, Saint Patrick is depicted as a portly man with a red face. He appears to be on the brink of collapse, as if the strain of having to blow into a flute and dance a jig at the same time may at any moment prove too much, and he may crumple to the church floor. Which would not be the worst thing, Father McElarney has thought more than once, knowing that the girth of the figure and the redness of the saint's face have prompted many to refer to the parish as St. Fats rather than St. Pat's. In his youth Father McElarney himself expressed the conviction that the window must have been made by a Protestant, and he has heard some of his older parishioners say that it must surely have been erected by someone in the pay of a leprechaun, who would certainly have the gold to finance such an operation.

Although for a time Father McElarney lobbied for the window to be replaced, he resolved eventually to think about it in a positive light, as a cross that the Lord has given him to bear. So he tries, not always successfully, to look on the window fondly, the way he suspects Thomas More looked on his hair shirt—although, having had a hair shirt himself in his youth, he knows this is small potatoes by comparison. This is not any cross he imagined himself having to bear—the grieving parishioner who's lost a dear mother, the sinful parishioner who's given himself over to drink, and confessed and known his sin and sinned again—this is a stained-glass window of a leprechaun.

Victorinna, the smallest of the three children, puts up her hand.

"Yes?" says Father McElarney.

"It's about the snakes," says Victorinna.

"Lord help us," says Father McElarney.

"*Bo*," Giovanna tells her brother, "Antonio, go, ask him."

Antonio says nothing.

"Perhaps one of you could ask Antonio's question?"

Victorinna again puts up her hand.

"Yes?" says Father McElarney.

"When Saint Patrick takes his snakes out into the ocean," she says, "do they drown?"

"Yes," says the priest, "the snakes drown."

"See," Giovanna tells her brother, "I told you."

"How?" Antonio asks.

"How do they drown?" says Father McElarney. "In the water. Saint Patrick leads them out into the water, and there they drown."

"But how?"

"Saint Patrick plays his pipe, the snakes follow him, and that's the end of the story."

"But if they can't swim," says Antonio, "how do they get far enough out in the water?"

"They can't," says Father McElarney. "Saint Patrick takes them to a place where the snakes' feet can't touch."

Victorinna puts up her hand.

"Yes?" says Father McElarney.

"Those snakes," she says, "had feet?"

"Not exactly," says the pastor. "But a snake can push itself up in the water."

"So they can swim?" says Antonio.

"I wouldn't call that swimming," he explains. "It's more like walking."

"So they *do* have feet," says Giovanna.

"Not walk like you and me," says Father McElarney. He ponders this for a moment, then adds, "Snakes have their own way of walking."

"Does Saint Patrick swim out too?" asks Giovanna.

"No." Now Father McElarney squats down so he will be able to speak to the children on their level. "Look up there," he says. "Is Saint Patrick swimming?"

The children look up at the window. The snakes are only minimally depicted. There are four in all, barely visible over Saint Patrick's left shoulder, green heads peering over the barrel of his flute. The most striking thing about the snakes is the surprised look on their faces. These are snakes with eyebrows, and it is the eyebrows that convey the snakes' shock at finding themselves in the middle of the ocean: we started off listening to a song, the eyebrows say, and now here we are in the middle of the ocean (which, in the window, laps up around the snakes like the tongue of a large blue cat). Saint Patrick has lulled the snakes into a kind of drunken, senseless stupor, and they have been abruptly brought face to face with the fact of their own mortality. This is the moment being depicted, Father McElarney has concluded: the music ceasing and the subsequent silent confrontation with mortality. So it is with all of us, he thinks, then stops himself; one had to be careful not to look too often or for too long at the snakes, lest one begin to wonder about their side of the story. And once one wondered about the snakes' side of the story—any snake's side of any story—one was in real trouble.

"No, he's not swimming," Father McElarney tells the children. "God made it so Saint Patrick could walk on the water."

"How?" says Antonio.

"He just did," says Father McElarney. "Saint Patrick prayed, and then the Lord made it so he could walk on the water."

"Just like that?" says Giovanna.

"Just like that. That's what God is like," says Father McElarney. "If he decides something, it happens. He's good to have on your side, so you must always pray, so you can do great things as well." Victorinna puts up her hand. "You don't have to keep putting up your hand, child," he tells her.

"I'm sorry," says Victorinna.

Father McElarney looks at the children and the children look back at him. "What was your question?" he says, after a moment.

"Could the snakes walk on the water too?"

"No," says Father McElarney. "Because God decided only Saint Patrick could walk on the water."

"And Jesus?" says Giovanna.

"And Jesus," allows Father McElarney.

"Moses too," says Giovanna.

"No," says Antonio, "Moses moved the water, but he didn't walk on it."

"That's the same thing," says Giovanna, "except you do it with your hands."

"Giovanna's right," says Father McElarney. "Moses too."

Victorinna puts up her hand, and the priest sighs. "Yes?" he says.

"Did they ever do it together?"

"Who?" says Father McElarney.

"Jesus and Saint Patrick, and Moses," she says, "did they, you know, walk on the water together?"

"No," says Father McElarney, "they did it one at a time."

"So they took turns?"

"They lived a long time apart. Jesus died and rose from the dead a long time before Saint Patrick was born," Father

McElarney tells her, thinking that he may be on the edge of grappling with a genuine theological question. "That," he says gravely, "is the mystery of our faith."

"And what about if you're a statue?" says Giovanna.

"Statues are not people. They are images of people—not the people themselves. Don't confuse the two."

"San Bonorio is a statue," says Giovanna, somewhat defensively, "and he walked, and it was a miracle."

"Who?" says Father McElarney. He was about to dismiss the children.

"San Bonorio," says Giovanna. "The one with the chicken."

"He walked across the table where Lucio was born," says Victorinna, in defence of her sister, "and that was a miracle. Everybody says it."

"There is nothing miraculous," Father McElarney tells them, "about walking across a table."

"There is if you're a statue," says Giovanna.

"Where did this happen?" he asks.

"On Beverley Street," says Antonio. "At Lucio's house."

"And Mrs. Greico," says Giovanna, "danced. She's all better."

"She was in a wheelchair," says Antonio. "Because of the sugar. Now she can have as much sugar as she wants."

"All right," the priest tells the children, "tell me what happened."

The Bucci children say what they know: since Lucio's *nonna* saw the statue move and Mrs. Greico got out of her wheelchair, impossible things have happened on a regular basis at 187 Beverley Street. Spilt milk has arranged itself into a shape that, if you twist your head a certain way, looks like the Blessed Virgin. A young girl (whose name none of the children can recall) looked at the statue and began to cry tears of colourful thread.

A fish appeared, inexplicably, in the centre of the table. At night, the screams of a girl who died during the winter because her tongue was stuck to the fence could be heard. Cecil Altman, owner of a Jewish delicatessen on College Street, passed a kidney stone painlessly not an hour and a half after standing before the house. Guido, their eldest brother, who has always wanted to be taller, miraculously grew another half-inch right after seeing the statue—bringing him to five-seven—the exact height of Mussolini, who, the children tell the priest, is the perfect height.

"What is the name?" says Father McElarney.

"Bonorio," says Antonio.

"Not the name of the saint," says the priest. "The one who owns the saint."

Victorinna puts up her hand.

"What did I tell you about putting up your hand?" asks Father McElarney. Victorinna puts her hand down. "Whose house is it?" he says, cutting to the chase.

"Lucio," says Antonio. "Lucio Burke."

"Lucio Burke? What kind of name is that?"

"In Italian," says Giovanna, "it means light."

"No, it doesn't," Antonio tells the priest. "It just *sounds* like it."

"It means light, nearly," says Giovanna, with the air of someone settling the matter.

"Light, nearly," says Father McElarney, to himself, looking up at the window. "I wonder," he asks, having an idea, "if you would give this Lucio a message for me?"

There is not any reason why Father McElarney's suspicions should fasten onto Lucio Burke. Lucio has done nothing to deserve it. Because Lucio and his mother attend St. Costanzo's, on Bloor Street—the Italian parish near Clinton Street—this is the first the priest has ever heard of him and his strange name. The Bucci children, he soon discovers, have given him the name Lucio not because they suspect Lucio of anything, but because they have always thought of the house as Lucio's. It was simply the name that came to the little boy. But something about that name awakens Father McElarney's intuition. Lucio Burke. Lucio meaning light, or nearly light, in Italian; Burke, in the Irish, meaning fool. It is a strange name. Neither one thing or another. Exactly the kind of name you'd expect someone who faked a miracle to have.

The days following the miracle are terrible for Lucio. After Dubie ran off, and after another night came and went without Lucio and Ruthie doing it—for Lucio has not made it back to Gutman Fur—and as word of the miracle on Beverley Street spreads through the city, Lucio loses the conviction, the clear view of the situation, that made him turn back that night. The resolve has drained out of him, as if someone had pulled a plug. Once he followed everyone up the stairs to the kitchen, once he saw the statue and what it had done to Mrs. Greico, he knew he could not say anything about Dubie having been there. Because now he was implicated. When he reached into his pockets and found Dubie's matches, when he thought of the way Dubie had looked at him, he did not know what he could say, even if he made up his mind to say something. It was best to keep quiet, he told himself. And so he slunk away to his room, knowing that by now Ruthie had got up from the fur coats and had probably given up on him entirely. By now she would have returned home, heard the commotion next door and figured out that he had not been held up at gunpoint, but that it had been impossible for him to get back to her. That was what he would tell her, he decided, that it had simply been impossible—there would have been too many questions, conclusions would have been reached. So he went to bed early, closing the door behind him. He could hear the house filling up with people, however, and, looking at the sloped ceiling inches from his face, he wished that one of the animals he had imagined crawling around on the roof would finally crash through it.

Eventually the door to his room opened, and his cousin walked in.

"What's with you?" said Dante, lying down on Nonna's bed. "You got the clap?"

"No," said Lucio dissolutely, as if he wished he had. "What're you doing here?"

"What am I doing here?" said Dante. "If you think they let me miss the miracles, you got another think coming. What're *you* doing here, now that's a question. Everybody's out there. And you're in here. I heard you were sick. Is it the clap?"

"No," said Lucio.

"You know," said Dante, "I once heard of this guy, Olla was his name, got the clap and did the same as you. Right as rain, and then one day he takes to bed. No one knows why. He just comes in one night, gets into bed and that's it. Stays there for a whole month, and no matter what anyone tells him, he won't get out."

"Dante," said Lucio, "I don't have the clap."

"No, listen," said Dante, "let me finish. He stays there for a whole month, and at the end of it his dick falls off. You hear what I'm saying? His dick drops clean off."

"What're you trying to tell me?" said Lucio.

"I'm not telling you nothing," said Dante, "but if this Ruthie gave you the clap, get it looked at."

"Keep your voice down," said Lucio, sitting up. "Believe me when I tell you, there is no way I could have the clap."

"No?" said Dante. "Still no?"

"No," said Lucio. "Not yet. We nearly did."

"Not yet?" said Dante, hitting Nonna's mattress.

Lucio shook his head.

"Don't tell me you're in love with her," said Dante, "and you're waiting to get married. Because in the first place, if she doesn't now she might not then. And in the second place, everybody knows yid girls don't marry guys who ain't yids."

"You don't know that," said Lucio. "Besides, this is different—anyway, we nearly did it."

"Nearly," said Dante, "I've been *there*—what happened? She get cold feet?"

Lucio told him about having to sneak back into the house to get the condom, and finding Dubie in the kitchen.

"Lighting matches?" said Dante. "He *is* crazy."

"I suppose it makes sense," said Lucio. "He doesn't want anything to do with me, so he tries to burn down the table."

"It's not like you were on the table," said Dante. "Now if you were on the table, that'd be a different story. Who cares if he burns down the table? I was born on the table too—and what do I care? He can have it."

"Anyway," said Lucio, "that's what I think."

"It was after, then, that San Bonorio went for his walk?" said Dante.

"No, it was then," said Lucio.

Dante looked at him. "So, then, Dubie did it? Dubie did the miracle? Or you? You did it?"

"I suppose," said Lucio, "it was me who didn't put it back."

Dante considered this.

"What was I going to say?" said Lucio. "It happened fast. One minute I was there, and the next, we're all running upstairs, and then Mrs. Greico is there too. What am I going to say? Maybe she'll get sick again."

"I guess," said Dante. "But still."

"Don't tell anyone," said Lucio. "I mean, you say nothing— you know what kind of shit I'd be in if anyone found out. Nothing, I mean it."

"You ask me," said Dante, "I don't know what you got to do with it anyway—it's on Dubie."

Lucio said he supposed Dante was right, but he felt the opposite was true. That it had been up to him to replace the statue, and he had not done so.

"Lucio, take it easy," Dante tried to tell him. "Nothing bad happened."

"You call that nothing?" said Lucio. "I faked a miracle."

"Maybe," said Dante. "It's more like you were an accomplice. That's not the same thing."

"I don't know if it works that way with God," said Lucio.

Dante stared at the ceiling. "You know what you do?" he said. "You confess it."

"You're crazy," said Lucio. "That'd be the last thing I'd do. Tell a priest—that'd be the end of me."

"No," said Dante. "That's not the way it works. Once you get in that booth, they can't say anything. Take it from me. You tell the priest and then, boom, you're off scot-free."

"I don't know," said Lucio. "It's not just about saying it. You have to repent."

"Never mind," said Dante. "You don't need help in that department."

Lucio nodded, but wondered if he was beyond redemption.

After Dante was gone, he lay down in bed and thought of Ruthie lying down on her own bed, next door, but at the same time as far away as she could be.

The following morning Lucio intended to go straight to Gutman Fur to talk to Ruthie. Instead, he found the Lizzies outside in the cinder alley waiting for him.

"So, Lucio," said Goody Altman. "You'll pitch for us?"

"You don't have a choice," Milton told him, before he could reply. "We talked about it, and we need you."

Mordechai interrupted to point out to Lucio that it was not so much what he or any one person wanted, but that his pitching for the Lizzies was the best thing for the people of the Ward and, given that across the ocean Hitler was doing what Hitler was doing, Lucio pitching for the Lizzies was quite possibly the best thing for the world. Grief Henderson observed that it was clear Lucio had no choice, because it was he who had thrown the ball that had caused Bloomberg to disappear; if one looked carefully enough, Grief observed, one could see the hand of fate in motion. Ignatius Au expressed the opinion that all this talk of fate was a bad thing, an opinion seconded by Guido Bucci, the fascist, who seemed to think that Lucio should pitch simply because he, Guido, said so.

"Anyway," Izzy Au said, "we all agree on the pitching part."

"One thing's for sure," Mordechai said, "I'm not doing that again." The Lizzies' last game, he told Lucio, had been terrible. They'd won, but barely. "The whole time I was on the mound," he said gravely. "I'd throw them, and they'd hit them. Then I'd throw them again, and they'd hit them again."

"But we won," Goody told his brother, patting him on the

back. "It wasn't pretty but we're still in the playoffs—that's the important thing. This is the year we go all the way!"

"All the way to Christie Pits!" cried Spinny.

"They scored twenty-five runs," said Mordechai, staring straight ahead.

"And we got twenty-six," said Goody. He turned to Lucio. "What do you say?"

Lucio agreed to pitch and tried to continue on his way.

"Hold on," said Milton, taking his arm. "Where do you think you're going?"

"To work," lied Lucio.

"Work?" said Goody. "We've got to practise—tomorrow morning at ten."

Lucio said he'd be there, and walked quickly toward Spadina and Ruthie, turning into a back alley. He'd not taken many paces in that direction when the noise of the city seemed to melt, as if by magic, into a softened distance. Cutting through a few narrow alleys, hopping over the low fence behind Dulcimer's Milk, he soon arrived at the Darling Building. He looked up and saw there was a light on in the Gutman window, so he ran in through the doors, up to the third floor, and went right in without knocking, to find himself looking at Mr. Gutman, who was sitting behind Ruthie's desk. Mr. Gutman's face was full and fleshy, and his eyes were small and set deep in his head; there were thick veins in his forehead. He had a little nose and a large chin that seemed larger when he smiled—and when Lucio walked into the office, he was smiling. Sitting across from Mr. Gutman, on the other side of the desk, was a large man in suspenders whom Lucio recognized immediately as Leo Bernstein of Queens, New York.

"Can I help you?" said Mr. Gutman, when he saw Lucio.

Leo Bernstein turned around, and when he saw Lucio his eyes widened.

"I'm very sorry, Mr.—"

"Nonsense," broke in Leo Bernstein. "Have a seat."

"You two know each other?" said Mr. Gutman.

Leo Bernstein winked. Mr. Gutman looked at Bernstein, and then at Lucio. "We met last week," said Lucio, who could think of nothing to say except the truth.

"Well," said Mr. Gutman. "Have a seat."

"I'll stand," said Lucio.

"Never mind, take it easy on the kid," said Leo Bernstein magnanimously, winking again at Mr. Gutman. "There are worse things to do, I say."

"Did I miss something?" said Mr. Gutman.

"Ha," said Leo Bernstein, with another wink.

"You got something in your eye?" said Mr. Gutman.

"That's right," said Leo Bernstein, with impenetrable irony.

"Pleased to meet you," said Mr. Gutman to Lucio, "Mr.—"

"Lucio."

"Ha," said Leo Bernstein. "Play it that way."

"I can't stay," said Lucio. "I only came by to see Ruthie."

"She's not here," said Mr. Gutman.

"Well, then," said Lucio, walking as quickly as he could to the door, "I'll go."

Lucio was on Spadina, running home. After a few minutes he stopped, out of breath and at a total loss. He needed to talk to Ruthie, to warn her. But when he got home there was no sign of her. Nonna was sitting on the veranda with his mother, and they were both talking excitedly with some pilgrims who had come from Thorold to see the statue. It seemed to Lucio that his world had been wiped out. He had once thought of

Gutman Fur as a refuge, and now it had become the opposite. He had to talk to Ruthie, and it occurred to him that he might be able to go up the Nodelman fire escape and slip in through their kitchen window as if it were his own house. But this was too risky. Most of all because he had no idea how Ruthie would react, much less her father. So he remained on the long veranda, at his post beside the Nodelman door, until his mother told him it was time to come in for dinner. He did as he was told, but woke up early the next morning and went to sit on the veranda so he would not miss Ruthie when she went to work.

Eventually, she emerged from her house.

"Ruthie," said Lucio, taking her by the arm, "I've got to talk to you."

"What is all this?" said Ruthie, taking her arm away. "What happened to you—leaving me there like that?"

"I got caught," he told her.

"Caught?"

Lucio told her about Dubie and the matches, and his forgetting to put the statue back in the centre of the table.

"What did Mr. Diamond say?" said Ruthie.

"Asher?" said Lucio. "Nothing."

"I thought you went back to tell him?"

"I did," said Lucio. "At least I meant to. But then the miracle happened. What was I going to say?"

"Not nothing, I'm sure," she said.

Lucio looked away. "Anyway, the point is—I went to Gutman's yesterday to see you."

"Oh no," said Ruthie.

"He was with Bernstein."

She shook her head. "What did you say this time?"

"I don't know," said Lucio. "I mean, nothing. I got out of there as quickly as I could."

"Never mind," she said. "Nothing we can do now." She shook her head and seemed about to say something, then stopped. She turned around and walked briskly up the street.

Lucio followed her. "Bernstein must have told him about me being there," he said. "What're you going to say?"

"I don't know," said Ruthie. "I'll be lucky if I keep my job."

"Blame it on me," said Lucio. "Say it was my idea—or I forced myself on you."

"Lucio," Ruthie told him, "stop it."

They stood like that for a moment and looked at each other; Lucio looked sheepishly down at her feet, and saw that she was wearing the same shoes she'd been wearing that day at the Elizabeth Street playground.

"I was in a rush," said Ruthie, seeing him notice the shoes.

"You know," said Lucio, "the Lizzies want me to pitch for them."

"Is that right?" she said, uninterested.

"I won't be much good, I suppose," admitted Lucio. "At least that's what Goody says—he says I'm not any better than anyone else, but still he wants me to do it. Just in case I start throwing again the way I did that day. Anyway, that's something."

"I suppose it is," said Ruthie.

Lucio nodded at her and bit his lip.

"I should go," she said.

"Maybe," said Lucio, "we could go see *The Missing Rembrandt* some night, after all."

"It's gone. It was near the end of its run. And now it's gone for good," Ruthie told him. She was waiting with her hands on her hips.

Lucio did not know what to say. It didn't seem to him that this should be possible. "Aren't you going to wish me luck?" he said suddenly.

"With what?"

"With the game. The baseball game."

"Listen, Lucio, I've got other things on my mind."

"I know that."

"Besides, there's no such thing as luck. There's what happens and what doesn't happen. Luck is beside the point. Luck is a story you tell yourself after the fact. It's got nothing to do with me wishing it on you. Someday you'll see that."

"When? After the Revolution?"

Ruthie stared at him blankly, as if she was not sure who he was.

"Still," said Lucio, smiling, still trying to get her to smile, "I could use a little luck."

"All right," said Ruthie, looking back at him the way he had seen her look at him before, with pity. "Good luck."

"Thanks."

"Was that all right?" said Ruthie. "Can I go?"

When Lucio didn't reply, when the words he was going to say stuck in his throat, Ruthie turned and walked away. He watched her go, and it occurred to him that he had not asked her about her walkout. He should have. He had intended to. He had intended to wish *her* luck. He wanted to say much more. But when Ruthie, after only a few steps, turned around as if to give him one last chance to say something, all he could do was apologize.

"I'm sorry," said Lucio. "This wasn't supposed to happen."

"I know that," she told him.

"Be careful," said Lucio.

Ruthie shook her head and didn't answer him. She turned around and walked west toward Spadina. Lucio stood watching her, but she didn't turn around a second time.

When he couldn't see her any longer, he began walking toward Scarsdale Park, at the foot of Spadina, and went to his first baseball practice. The Lizzies, all of them, were already there. Goody had a cardboard triangle with him to use as homeplate—the same one he had used that day at the Elizabeth Street playground when Bloomberg was seen for the last time—and he squatted down in his catcher's crouch behind it. The Au brothers stood behind Lucio, where they would stand in a real game, and in the outfield were Grief Henderson and Guido Bucci.

Spinny Weinreb stood up with the bat in his hands.

"OK," Goody told Lucio, "give us a Burke Special."

Lucio threw and Spinny swung, and the ball was hit far and away over the heads of both Guido and Grief.

"Don't worry about it," Goody told Lucio. "Try again."

Lucio tried again, throwing the ball as hard as he could. It flew over Spinny's head. Goody ran to get it.

"Nice throw," said Izzy. Like many infielders, he had embraced sarcasm.

"All right," said Goody when he came back. "You all take a walk."

When they were gone, Lucio asked Goody why the Lizzies had no coach or general manager.

"My father's the coach," said Goody, "and the general manager."

"I've never seen him at a game," said Lucio.

"If me and Mordechai are at the games," said Goody, as if he were outlining a logical proposition, "who's going to run the deli? My father is who. He fills in for us at the deli, and I fill in for him as coach. Actually, the truth is there's no coach. It's democracy. We all vote, on everything."

"How can that work in baseball?" said Lucio.

"It doesn't," said Goody. "But what can you do?"

Later that morning Goody taught Lucio everything he knew about pitching: how to throw a curveball by putting your middle finger along the long seam of the ball; how to make the two-seam grip that produces the sinker; how to choke the change-up in the palm with the thumb underneath the ball; how to throw a hanger; how to lock the wrist when throwing a split-finger fastball. Soon the Lizzies came back, and while Lucio practised throwing to Goody, he listened to them talking.

"You know," he heard Spinny say, "the Swastika Club'll be there next game."

"It's a semifinal," said Mordechai. "You think they'd miss that?"

"Never mind the playoffs—they show up for everything. There's always one or two and sometimes more of them," said Spinny, who had also seen the club at boxing matches. "Always at the end they start shouting, 'Heil Hitler'—trying to get something started."

"And not just here," said Izzy, telling them how he and Ignatius had gone to see a cousin of his in a checker championship in Kitchener, a town to the west of the city, which had once been named Berlin. "There were Swastikas there."

"Playing checkers?" asked Spinny.

"Watching the checkers," said Ignatius.

"Trying to get something started," added Izzy.

"You'd have to beat the bushes pretty hard to get something started at a checker game," observed Milton.

"Were they yelling?" asked Spinny.

"No—they sat there with their swastika shirts on," said Ignatius.

"Everyone looked," said Izzy. "And they looked back—it was like a staring contest."

"Don't listen to him," said Ignatius, "it was nothing like a staring contest."

"They were staring," said Izzy.

"In a staring contest," Ignatius told his brother, "you don't think one of the guys who's doing the staring should get up and clock one of the other staring guys."

"That's what the Swastikas want you to do," said Mordechai, reaching to adjust the yarmulke on his baseball cap.

"I don't know," said Izzy, who was somewhat bitter about being corrected about its being like a staring contest. "Maybe they just like sports."

"It's not the sports they like," interrupted Little Guido, who was sitting on the grass nearby. The other boys had assumed he wasn't listening. "It's the people they like," he told them, "it's the crowd—that, they love." The others turned to look at him as he stood up and crushed his cigarette into the grass with the heel of his shoe; it was a practised, elegant gesture meant to look brutal. He wore a black tight-fitting shirt and dark pants that still bore traces of flour from his work at the bakery that morning. "In baseball," he went on, "when your team gets a hit, you cheer—you know, everybody all at once—it's beautiful. Once you got a crowd," Guido told them, "you're the one in charge, no matter who you are."

He looked up and met the eyes of the other boys. Guido had been a fascist for a little more than a year, a transformation effected during his trip to Italy, paid for by Mussolini himself. In the spring of 1932 thousands of postcards had gone out through-out the world from Il Duce, inviting all the sons and daughters of Italians abroad back to Italy, to Rome, for a grand fascist festival. The whole thing, promised the postcard, would be paid for: the steamship ticket, the food, even the black shirt Little Guido would wear to the rally in the piazza in Rome. Both he and his brother Vince, who played beside Guido in the outfield that day at the Elizabeth Street playground, went. But Vince got food poisoning and was not there that great day to stand beside Little Guido before the statue of Julius Caesar—who, like Mussolini, had also been called Il Duce—in his black shirt, sur-rounded by others in the same black shirt, singing the same song. Then Mussolini rode into the piazza on the back of a great white stallion, coming from behind, where no one expected to see him, a feather atop his helmet shining in the April sunlight. Everyone had cheered then, all at once and all with one voice, and something had happened. Because the others had not been there that day, Little Guido knew that if he tried to explain it, it would come out twisted, and that whatever he said, his words would carry in them nothing of how he had felt that day, so he tried to tell them what it was that had changed him. "Everyone, you know, you all want what you know you want"—and as if to demonstrate, he made a sweeping circular gesture with both his arms, as if he were hugging himself. The Lizzies laughed when they saw this, so he stopped talking, sitting back down on the grass and lighting another cigarette. It was not the same here, he thought; he had walked down College Street with the other Toronto fascists and they had all worn their black shirts, singing the same songs he'd sung that day in Rome, but it was not the same. People came out to look, but they weren't afraid. They were interested and entertained, and not afraid in the least.

The Lizzies left soon afterwards, but Lucio and Goody stayed on.

"So?" said Lucio, as they were getting ready to leave. "You think I'm ready?"

"As ready as you'll ever be," said Goody.

"What's that supposed to mean?"

"You're no good," said Goody, simply. "You're a bit better now, but you'll never be better than anyone else." After a short pause, he said, "What do you think it was that day? You know, when you threw like that."

"I don't know," said Lucio. "I can't explain it."

"A miracle?"

"How should I know?" said Lucio. "If it was, I had nothing to do with it."

"Well," said Goody, "maybe, if you were praying at the time."

Lucio shook his head.

"Who knows?" said Goody. "Maybe it'll happen again."

"Then it wouldn't be a miracle," said Lucio.

"Well," said Goody, "we'll just have to wait, then, and see if it was or not."

Monday's semifinal game is at Withrow Park, off Logan Avenue, in the east end of the city, at the home field of the Withrow Park Athletics. Lucio has been there, but only for baseball games, to watch the Lizzies play. It is not a park he has ever thought of going to for any other reason. Even without the recent reports about the Swastika Club in the paper, he would be hesitant about crossing over to the east side. There are no "restricted" areas in the city, nothing legally preventing him or any of the other boys from going there. There is only a feeling: places he knows he should not go, streets where he does not belong.

Only once has he experienced this invisible segregation directly, and that was when he was fourteen, in the winter of 1930—not long after the Depression hit, shortly after he began working at Michelangelo's Garage. One winter weekend he and Dubie decided to try to make money by snow shovelling. The two went up and down Beverley Street, knocking on doors, offering their services and finding no customers, before concluding they would have to cross Yonge Street, into the other part of the city. They walked east along College and got as far as Jarvis Street before a policeman stopped them. "Back you go," the cop said, taking each boy by a shoulder and turning them around.

"Back?" said Dubie.

"Where you came from."

"We're just trying to make a few dollars, sir," said Lucio.

"I see what you're doing," said the policeman.

"We're not doing anything illegal," said Dubie.

"I didn't say you were. Did I? I think I would have remembered that. Don't you think I would remember that?"

Both boys agreed.

"And," said the policeman, "if you were doing something illegal, I'd arrest you."

"Are you going to arrest us?" said Lucio, worried.

"Are you doing something illegal?"

Lucio told him they were not even thinking of it.

"Good, that's what I'm after—to avoid arrests. If someone'll do something illegal—I don't know if it'll be you two or not," he said. "But I know they'll beat two little kikes like yourselves within an inch of your life and not think about it twice. All the same," he added—stepping obsequiously out of the way, as if he were a gate to the other side of the city—"go ahead, be my guest. Only you've been warned."

Lucio was ready to turn around. Dubie followed reluctantly.

Back at Beverley Street, despite it being February, there were a number of people out on the long veranda. Ruthie's parents sat, scarves around their faces, in their cheap beach chairs; Asher, a thick jacket on, reclined on the green plastic-covered sofa; in the middle of the veranda was Lucio's Uncle Angelo, who was smoking a cigar—he had come to visit Nonna, and had been forced by his sister to smoke his cigar outside. They listened intently as Dubie told the story of what had happened.

"He had no right," said Abe Nodelman. "He could lose his badge. Did you get the badge number?"

"Badge number?" Asher Diamond shook his head.

"Once you got the number you can make a complaint." Abe was speaking to Asher. "Once there's a complaint, the man loses the badge."

"Just like that?" said Asher.

"Not just like that," said Abe.

"It takes, what, a week—two?"

"Not just like that, Asher," interjected Sadie, "you know it. What Abe is saying is, if that cop did it once you can bet he's done it before—and he'll do it again."

"So you go in with the badge number?"

"Then you make a complaint."

"Ah-ha, that's how it works."

"It's against the law," Abe Nodelman reiterated.

"You think you're the first one to think of it?" asked Asher.

"Not the first one," said Abe. "About being first I said nothing."

"Not to think of it," said Sadie, "but to do it—if enough kids go in with enough badge numbers, things change."

Asher took a breath, as if about to reply, and changed his mind. Instead he spoke to his son. "Say you did get the badge number, you want to know what'd happen? You'd go down to the police station, some anti-Semite of a cop'd write your story down and throw it out before you were out the door. And he'd write down your address—my address—and they'd come looking for us."

"You don't know that," said Sadie.

"So what're the boys supposed to do then?" Abe said, angry now. "Just go along with it? Do what they say? Get in line, keep your head down?"

"The only way around a guy like that cop," Asher told them, "is, give him a cut of what you make, find out the price—pay it."

"You ask me," said Uncle Angelo, "you don't go looking for trouble."

"But when it comes, it comes—it's up to you to make it right," said Abe.

"All right," said Asher, waving at Abe, "have a good time."

Angelo laughed, but Abe Nodelman stood up all the same. "No," he announced to the veranda. "I'm serious. If none of you'll do this, I'll take these boys to the police station myself and help them make the complaint. What do you say, boys?"

"You do what you want," interrupted Angelo. "But my nephew's staying here—it's got nothing to do with him."

Abe looked at Angelo and then turned to Lucio, who did not know what he should say. Had not Nonna come down at that moment, telling Angelo to put out his cigar and come up to help her drain the pasta, Lucio might have had to say or do something—and he didn't know what. He was of two minds: he knew the policeman had been wrong; on the other hand, he was also very frightened. It was not that the cop calling them kikes surprised him; he heard language like that every day. But never before had he felt implicated so directly. His first response had been to point out that *he* wasn't Jewish, that it was Dubie, not him, who was the kike. It was cowardly, he knew, but the words had very nearly sprung up out of him, unbidden—in the same way that, on those stolen Saturdays with Asher Diamond in the Altman Deli, he wished desperately to be Asher Diamond's son.

By five-thirty Monday afternoon, his Lizzies uniform on, Lucio is ready to leave the house and head to Withrow Park. He stands for a moment in front of the mirror, looking at himself, thinking that the baseball uniform makes him look like another person. Then he walks up Beverley Street to College, where he turns right and goes past Altman's Deli. As he walks by, the door of the deli opens and out step three of Dante's uncles, Primo, Secondo and Quintillano.

"Lucio," says Primo, surprised. "What're you doing here?"

"I live just down the street," he says. "You've been there lots of times."

"So," interjects Secondo, with the air of someone changing the subject. "Did Halloween come, and I missed it?"

"It's a baseball uniform," Lucio says. "There's a game tonight, and I'm pitching."

"Pitching?" says Secondo.

"Pitching," Lucio tells him. Primo and Quintillano are suitably impressed; as Lucio listens to them express their admiration, it occurs to him that he has never known them to be so impressed about anything. "In fact," says Lucio, not able to contain himself, "I'm on my way to the game right now."

"Where?" asks Primo.

"Withrow Park."

"You know," says Secondo, "maybe we could go?"

"We *could* go," says Quintillano. "Is there anything we got to do?"

Primo shrugs.

"Why don't we come?" says Secondo.

And just like that, apparently, it is decided.

Crossing Yonge Street, into the east side of the city, Lucio realizes what the brothers are up to and tries to lose them. He was planning to slip into the game unnoticed, as if he were just anyone. He has with him a blue pullover he will put on over his uniform when he gets closer—the reason he did not put it on before leaving the house is that he cannot help being a little proud. He *wants* to be seen in his Lizzies uniform, on his way to the game that will get the team into the finals at Christie Pits next week. Once on the east side, he will hide the uniform. But there can be no sneaking in with the Greico brothers in tow. "Why are you following me?" he asks, finally.

"It's your Uncle Angelo—" Secondo starts to say.

"My uncle said what? Go look after that *mangiacake*, the little Irish kid?"

"Take it easy," says Primo, but judging from the looks on their faces, Lucio concludes that if his uncle did not use those exact words, they are close enough. And that the three didn't just happen to bump into him while coming out of the deli. They have been sent—they are his bodyguards. When he confronts them, the brothers look guiltily away and say nothing.

"I knew it," says Lucio. "Go home, tell my uncle I don't want his help." He shakes his head and walks away purposefully. After not quite a minute of walking, he turns and sees that the brothers are right behind him.

"Didn't I tell you to leave me alone?"

"You can say what you want," Primo tells him. "But we gotta come—we told your uncle we would."

Giving up, Lucio walks with the three brothers along Gerrard Street, crossing over the Don River, where they see small boys squatting near the water, fishing for perch and wall-eye. In the middle of the river are men in work pants trying to catch fish with their bare hands, bending down in the current like catchers in a ball game. After about ten minutes of walking they arrive at Logan Avenue, where they turn north, heading toward Withrow Park. When they are nearly there, Lucio real-izes he has forgotten to put on his pullover. Now the sidewalk is crowded with people on their way to the game. Many of them have already noticed his uniform. It is too late to hide. At any moment, he thinks, something is going to happen, and he will be in the middle of it.

And then a mounted policeman rides up, and follows along just behind Lucio.

"Who gets a police escort?" Primo asks as they walk toward the baseball diamond, the crowd parting ahead of them to avoid being trampled by the horse. "King Edward, the prime minister maybe, and Lucio Burke."

Before long they arrive at the diamond. Lucio crosses the field into the Lizzies' dugout, finding that the home team, the Withrow Park Athletics, have already taken the field. The Withrow Park uniforms are light blue with a large letter W in the centre of the jersey. Looking up into the crowd, Lucio notes that more than half the crowd is wearing light blue. The other half is wearing no particular colour; Lucio assumes that these are the Lizzies' supporters, but they seem to him indefinite, undecided, as if they have come to the game without a team.

Just before the game begins, Goody addresses the team.

"All right," he tells them. "These guys aren't that good. They got no pitching, they got a little hitting and we got Lucio."

"And they got no Goody," says Lucio, as if to return the compliment.

"All right," says Goody. "Let's not celebrate yet."

"St. Peter's," says Izzy Au. "They got a Goody."

Then, as if he has forgotten what he was about to say, Goody sits down. The game soon starts, and when it does—when Goody goes up to bat—Lucio sits down next to Izzy. "Who's this other Goody?" he asks.

"His name's Elmer," Izzy tells him.

"The best baseball player the city of Toronto ever pro-duced," explains Ignatius.

"You think so?" Izzy asks his brother.

"There's no thinking about it," whispers Ignatius. "Goody's second."

It is not until halfway through the second inning, until it is his turn to bat, that Lucio realizes there is no batting order posted. There is also no first- or third-base coach. Or manager. On the other side of the field, in the Withrow Park dugout, there are at least as many adults—all of them wearing oversized Withrow Park uniforms—as there are players. Not only is there a manager, there is an assistant manager, and then two assis-tants to the assistant manager—their offices are written, instead of their last names, across the backs of their jerseys.

There is a trainer, and there are two ballboys, one bat boy, a third and a first and a pitching and a hitting coach.

"You can't run a baseball team like this," Lucio tells Goody. "You need a manager."

"What we really need," Goody tells him, handing Lucio the bat, "is a hit." Lucio steps out to the plate; it takes three pitches to strike him out. He returns to the dugout and looks at no one.

As bad as Lucio is in the early innings of the game, Goody does not pull him out, convinced that if Lucio can simply throw enough pitches, sooner or later he will begin to throw with the same deadly accuracy that knocked the bird out of the sky that day. And the Lizzies stay in the game by scoring just as fast. Other than the high score—by the time the sixth inning ends, the Lizzies are winning by a score of 13–12—the baseball game is like any other baseball game. Lucio has settled down and is beginning to throw like a real pitcher. He is no Bloomberg, but he is coming to understand that peculiar mix of tease and intimidation, indirection and suggestion, that goes into a throw that makes a batter want to swing at a ball that isn't there.

In the eighth inning, with the Lizzies still winning by a single run, two members of the Swastika Club stand up and begin to shout. One is taller, with a flat white face and small features that make his head look like an egg, and the other is a short boy in shabby clothes but an imposing shirt collar, which makes Lucio think that he has dressed up for the game, knowing he will be looked at. They stand up and begin waving a dirty white bedsheet with a dark patch in the middle, a bedsheet folded over on itself, in a seductive, weirdly playful way—but without opening it, as if the sheet is a woman performing a striptease.

"Take it off," shouts someone in the crowd, in a fierce, monotonous whine. "Take it off, baby."

"Oh, yeah, yeah," calls another. "You know what I like."

"You want it?" screams the boy with the egglike face, letting go of the upper part of the sheet so that it falls away, and it becomes apparent what the patch is—a crudely drawn swastika. But right away the taller boy covers it up again. "How's that?" he shouts to the crowd. "You want some more?"

"Sit down," someone tells him.

"Oh yeah, yeah." The egg-faced boy pulls back the sheet and shows a little more of the swastika. "I got your number."

The smaller boy squeals with delight, like a tiny stuck pig.

By the time the Bucci children arrive, Lucio is trying to close the ninth inning and win the game.

"Come on, Lucio," pleads Izzy, "*try* to throw a strike."

"Come on, Lucio," says Spinny, who is playing first base, "give him a Bloomberg Special."

"Never mind him, Lucio," says Mordechai, recalling that the last time Spinny told Lucio to throw a Bloomberg Special, halfway through the fifth inning with the bases loaded, Lucio took the suggestion and threw an underhand lob, which the batter looked at in disbelief for a long moment before smacking it out of the park for a home run.

"That's right," says Goody, who stopped giving signs to Lucio after deciding that Lucio has no control whatsoever over what pitches he throws. "You just throw away, and don't give it another thought."

Lucio goes into his windup.

The boy swings. Strike three.

Lucio's first strikeout.

The Lizzies win. The field floods with people. The Lizzies push toward the egg-faced boy who held the swastika, but cannot seem to get to him. There is more pushing and shoving and soon the sound of police sirens in the distance. And in the middle of it, Antonio Bucci runs up to Lucio and hands him a letter.

"What's this?" says Lucio.

"How should I know?"

"Who's it from?"

"The priest."

Lucio looks at the letter, and then at Antonio. He opens it. This is what it says:

> Dear Lucio,
> Repent: lest ye be as the beasts
>   that perish.
>
> Yours,
> Father McElarney

Swept up as he is in the general chaos after the game, Lucio almost doesn't see Ruthie there, standing on the edge of the crowd. As quickly as he can, he slips away and goes to her.

"You came," he says.

She lights a cigarette. "I talked to Gutman this morning."

"What happened?" he says, a little too energetically, alive with the adrenalin from the game and the thrill of seeing Ruthie.

"It's all right."

"So you're not fired?"

"I gave him some cock-and-bull story, which I don't think

he believes but, you know, we have an understanding. And besides, he needs me to model the coats."

"That's good," says Lucio, relieved. "Great."

Ruthie takes a drag off her cigarette. "Listen, Lucio," she says. "The thing is, it'd be better if you didn't come there any more."

"What, in the mornings?"

"In the mornings, the evenings."

Lucio looks at her.

"I think it'd be best."

He cannot think of anything to say; it feels as if someone has wiped a rough cloth across the inside of his forehead. "So you're calling off the walkout?"

"I didn't say that, and besides, I don't know if I could call it off, even if I wanted to—and I don't."

"What about us?"

Ruthie looks at him. "Us?" she asks.

"The finals, Lucio, you did it—you got us to the finals, in the finals!" calls Goody. "Hot dogs on us—" Then he sees Ruthie and stops.

"Yes, Lucio," she says. "You did it—beat St. Peter's next week at Christie Pits, and you really have done it."

"You think I care about that?"

"I do."

"Let's go!" shouts Little Guido, from the other side of the field.

"Go," Ruthie tells him, getting up to leave. "You love hot dogs, even I know that."

"That's it?" he says. "That's how it ends?" Then—before he knows what is happening, before Ruthie can reply—the Greico brothers are lifting him up, carrying him away, a hero.

○

Meanwhile, on the other side of the city, Father McElarney enters the kitchen at Beverley Street to find that the woman who witnessed the miracle is much as he expected her to be— withered, wrinkled, not quite eighty, in a black dress, entirely distrustful of the clergy. Her son, Angelo—Father McElarney recognizes him as one of a handful of Italian labourers who, years before, were hired to replace rotted pews in the back of the church—is there also, apparently to stand guard over the statue, as are several other people who introduce themselves as the priest moves through the house into the kitchen. One of them is a massive woman who tells him she is the one San Bonorio cured. She introduces two of her five sons (all with no wives, she tells the priest not without pride, as if their not hav-ing married were a version of priestly celibacy), both of whom hover closely around her, almost as if they are afraid that at any moment the miracle will wear off and their mother will slump down, once again blind and immobile, to the floor. Also pres-ent is Francesca Burke, mother of Lucio Burke, whom the one named Angelo introduces as his sister.

"Is Lucio here?" says Father McElarney.

"He's playing baseball," she tells him.

Father McElarney reaches into the folds of his priestly robe, producing a tiny black notebook in which he makes an entry. "Tell him, if you will," he says, "that I was asking after him."

Everyone then walks upstairs. Before saying anything, Father McElarney surveys the kitchen. It is a small, dingy place. The floor is a black and white checkerboard pattern with interleaving tiles; there is an icebox, whitewashed cabi-nets, a tiny steel sink and, in the middle of the room, a large wooden table. In the corner of the kitchen, facing the wall, is the statue. When the old woman sees the priest looking at the statue, she asserts that it got down off the table and walked across the kitchen. The priest puts his hands behind his back and walks over to the statue. The old woman goes with him, standing very close, as if there is a possibility that he may grab the statue and make a run for it. The priest sees her wariness and is unsurprised; I must be careful, he tells himself; these people call themselves Catholic but are as distrustful of the clergy as any infidel, still identifying the Church with the north of Italy, the rich end of the country, which most of them grew up never dreaming they would even visit.

The statue of San Bonorio is about three feet tall, made of greying imitation plaster, depicting a young man, prematurely bald, clinging to a chicken. "Hello, Bonorio," says Father McElarney, taking out a tiny black notebook.

The rest of them all cross themselves.

Although he did not recognize the name Bonorio when the Bucci children said it, Father McElarney realizes that this is not the first time he has seen a statue of the saint. At All Hallows College in Dublin, where he went to seminary, he was educated in the diverse and peculiar religious practices of Southern Italians. He knows, therefore, that these people are Mondorese—hardly anyone outside of Mondorio has even heard of San Bonorio. Bonorio, he recalls, as he looks carefully at the statue, performed three miracles: he restored the sight of a beggar, was able to juggle at a very early age, and made it rain while praying next to a chicken.

This is not unusual in the least. All the saints from the south of Italy have something to do with rain. The people of Mondorio claim, typically, that Bonorio made it rain during the worst drought that ever hit the region. No one is sure when this was. Some say that Bonorio lived in the twelfth century, when it did not rain for an entire year. Others that a cousin of his was on the boat with Columbus when there was a heat wave in the south of Italy and it did not rain for five and a half years. There is also the opinion that Bonorio lived in the eighteenth century and died around the time Napoleon—the French emperor with the Italian name—invaded the Italian peninsula, in 1796. Although it is impossible to specify a moment in the past when the town of Mondorio has been drought-free, it was in the midst of a great drought, and at the request of his mother (again, this is entirely typical—as Father Bertini, a Jesuit at the university, often joked, if it were not for the mothers of the saints of Southern Italy insisting their sons do impossible things, the country would be without miracles), that San Bonorio knelt down beside a chicken and prayed for rain.

"Now," Father McElarney says to Nonna, "you have no recollection of looking in the kitchen on your first trip upstairs?"

"*No, non ho guardato,*" replies Nonna, who, although she speaks English perfectly well, has decided to speak to this priest in Italian.

"You came back down the stairs—you say five minutes later?"

"*Sì.*"

Angelo lets out a sharp cough.

"What?" says Nonna.

"Ma," says the son. "Five minutes, I don't think so."

"The exact time," Father McElarney says, "*is* of some consequence."

"It's more like twenty-five," says Angelo. "She takes a while."

"Mamma," says Francesca, "he needs the facts."

"*Basta,*" says Nonna.

Father McElarney makes an annotation in his notebook.

"Getting back to the topic," he says, "you were in the washroom for somewhere between twenty-five and"—he pauses and looks at the old woman, implying that hers is the account he has decided to trust—"five minutes. Then you came downstairs. What happened then?"

"Then," she tells him, switching to English, "I look and I see San Bonorio move!"

Once again everyone in the kitchen, with the exception of the priest, makes the sign of the cross.

"You saw it?" says Father McElarney.

"I didn't see it," says the old woman, "I know it."

"How?" says Father McElarney, feeling he has arrived, relatively quickly, at the heart of the matter. "How did you know the statue wasn't moved?"

"Move, moved," says the old woman, "Francesca, what's the difference?"

"Ma," says Lucio's mother, "maybe it was moved by somebody."

"Whose side you on?" says Nonna to her daughter.

"No side," says Francesca.

Nonna, for a moment, is at a loss. But then she stands up and touches Mrs. Greico's head. "What about this one?" she says. "This is no miracle?"

The two sons of Mrs. Greico simultaneously assert that it is a miracle.

"Was there anyone else in the house?" says Father McElarney, unperturbed.

"You calling my mother a liar?" says Angelo.

"Did you or did you not see the statue move?" says the priest, ignoring him.

"No," says Nonna.

"Did you hear," says Father McElarney, "any popping noise?"

"No."

"Was there a burst of flame?"

"No."

"A great wind?"

Nonna shakes her head.

"A loud noise?"

Nonna says no.

"A smell?"

There was no smell.

"Was the ground shaking?"

Not that she noticed.

"Did anyone else notice the ground shaking?"

No one noticed.

"Were there any frogs nearby?"

"He was here," she says, "then there."

Father McElarney looks around the kitchen. He sniffs the air and looks carefully at the ceiling. Then he turns his attention to the table. "How long have you had this table?" he asks.

The kitchen becomes very still and no one speaks for what seems a long time. And by the way everyone in the kitchen looks at each other, it is immediately clear to Father McElarney that something else, another miracle perhaps, is involved here—another miracle that also has to do with the kitchen table.

"What?" he says.

"Three babies," says Nonna, "on the same day."

"When did this happen?"

"You better have a seat," Angelo tells the priest.

"I'm fine," says Father McElarney.

"You better sit down," says Angelo. "It's that kind of story."

When Angelo finishes telling the story of that day seventeen years before, when the three children were born on the same day on the same kitchen table, the moon is high and shines through the windows, casting narrow rectangles of light on the linoleum floor. In the distance Father McElarney can hear the traffic on College Street. That these people believe that something has happened, that divinity has somehow entered their dingy kitchen, there is no question. If this is a hoax, he decides, it is not one perpetrated by them.

Just as he is reaching this conclusion, he sees a face at the window, and he moves quickly across the room, crossing the floor and opening the window in a single deft movement.

"Hello, Lucio Burke," says Father McElarney, nearly pulling Lucio into the kitchen. So this is how he did it, thinks the priest as he looks at the boy. He came up the fire escape, in through the window, and out again by the time the old woman came down the stairs.

"Lucio," says Francesca, "what're you doing sneaking around out there?"

"Coming home," says Lucio, weakly.

"This is my son, Lucio," says Francesca to the priest.

"Father McElarney," says Father McElarney, extending a hand.

Lucio takes the priest's hand and shakes it, but he cannot quite look him in the eye.

THIRTEEN

WHAT STORY DID ANGELO tell Father McElarney? What other miracle? The truth is that there should have been nothing miraculous about a child being born on a kitchen table. It should have been an ordinary beginning, made more ordinary by virtue of taking place at a time when being born on a kitchen table was a common occurrence. Two babies born on the same kitchen table, and on the same day, would have been quite a coincidence, although still a coincidence. But three babies on the same day, and on the same kitchen table—that was something else entirely. By the time Father McElarney hears this story, it has become the kind of story that everyone knows and tells, and no one really believes. It has become a myth.

It began one January morning in 1916, when Asher Diamond left for work. He kissed Mazie, shook little Harold's hand and departed the house with a sack of knives and turnips slung over his shoulder, disappearing down Beverley Street on his way to the St. Lawrence Market and another day of pitching Greenstein's Remarkable Knives. Once Asher had left, a silence fell over the house. There was the noiseless sound of snow shifting on the roof, and the cracking of icicles breaking in the sunlight of the morning.

Then little Harold spoke.

"Knock-knock," he said.

Mazie sighed.

Harold did not know what to say. He had no experience of what to do when the person on the other end of a knock-knock joke sighed instead of saying, "Who's there?" On each of the previous forty-eight times he had told his mother the joke, since hearing it for the first time the day before, his mother had said, "Who's there?" just as he'd expected.

"Harold," Mazie told him, "you need to get a new joke." Harold looked at her, perplexed. "You have to make one up."

"How?" asked Harold.

This, it needs to be said, was an excellent question. Invented only three years earlier—by Alexander and Leon Lukashevsky, a father and son who owned a Jewish grocery in Jersey City, New Jersey—the knock-knock joke had arrived in Toronto only the day before, making its initial appearance at Altman's Deli when Leo Bernstein sat down beside Benjamin Nodelman, grandfather of Ruthie Nodelman, while the latter was eating a bowl of matzo-ball soup.

"Knock-knock," said Leo Bernstein.

Benjamin Nodelman passed him the ketchup.

"No," said Leo Bernstein, "I'm telling you a joke."

"This is a joke?" said Benjamin Nodelman.

"I'll start again," said Leo Bernstein. "Knock-knock."

Benjamin Nodelman said nothing. He looked at Leo Bernstein and waited. Bernstein also waited, and the two men sat and looked at each other for nearly a minute. While they did this, Cecil Altman was pouring coffee, cooking hot dogs, cracking eggs and keeping an eye on the door in case anyone tried to run out on a bill.

"This is a knock-knock joke," said Bernstein, and he explained what one says when being told a knock-knock joke.

"Got it," said Benjamin Nodelman.

"I'll do it again," said Leo Bernstein. "Knock-knock."

"Who's there?" said Benjamin Nodelman, still eating his soup.

"Boo," said Leo Bernstein.

"Boo who?" said Benjamin Nodelman.

"Don't cry," said Leo Bernstein, "it's only a joke."

Benjamin Nodelman began to laugh just as he was swallowing a matzo ball, and because he was not able to stop swallowing or to stop laughing, he began to choke. The old man turned red, then blue, and was beginning to turn purple when Cecil Altman climbed over the counter and smacked him on the back. When he was able to breathe, Nodelman thanked Altman for saving his life, and told him that Leo Bernstein of Queens, New York, had just told him the most extraordinary joke. Cecil Altman told Bernstein to tell him the joke, and while Bernstein obliged, the old man left the deli, turned west and walked toward Beverley Street. At the corner of Beverley and College, he saw Mazie Diamond and little Harold on their way home from Kensington Market, and he waved.

Mazie pretended not to see. She was in a rush. Nine months pregnant, with her hands full, she had no time to waste; in her left hand she had a paper bag full of vegetables, in her right hand little Harold's hand, and under her right arm a live chicken, which was looking down at Harold. The chicken was wrapped up in brown paper, with its feet bound and its head sticking out of the paper.

"Hurry up, Harold," Mazie said, when she saw Benjamin Nodelman waving. Harold was looking up into the eyes of the chicken. It had dirty white feathers, and its orange beak was held shut by a clothespin. But because neither she nor Harold could walk very quickly, Benjamin Nodelman soon caught up to them.

"We're in a hurry," she told him.

"A second you don't have?"

"Fine," said Mazie, "but make it quick."

"I've got to tell you what you say in this kind of joke."

"This is quick?" she said.

Benjamin Nodelman explained how the joke worked.

"Got it," said Mazie impatiently, pulling Harold along.

"OK," he said, "knock-knock."

"Who's there?"

"Boo."

"Boo who?"

"Don't cry," he told her, "it's a joke."

Little Harold burst into tears.

"With jokes like this," said Mazie, "who needs jokes?"

Because looking at the chicken only seemed to make Harold cry harder, Mazie tried to hand it to Benjamin Nodelman. Being too old to have a chicken handed to him by anyone, Nodelman grabbed at the chicken's feathers, bobbled it, juggled it, dropped it, caught it, dislodged the clothespin and had his finger bit, propelled it out of its brown paper and dropped it a second time, accidentally removing the rubber band binding its legs. The chicken hit the ground running, and ran across College Street, passing unscathed beneath a Ford Tudor.

Harold felt much better with the chicken gone and immediately began telling Benjamin Nodelman's knock-knock joke.

He told it once, twice, a third time, and did not stop telling it until the following morning, when Mazie sighed instead of asking who was there—but stop he did, for that was when little Harold, who knew nothing of Alexander and Leon Lukashevsky, found he had been brought face to face with the question of where knock-knock jokes come from, and how to get more of them. Mazie looked at her son and decided to give him what he wanted. "All right," she said. "Get ready—knock-knock."

"Who's there?"

Mazie had her first contraction. It came sharp and swift, out of the blue, and knocked the breath out of her. "Oy," she gasped.

"Oy who?" said Harold.

Mazie leaned forward in her chair as the contraction spread across her midsection. When it was finished she got up and walked as quickly as she could to the front door, thinking there might be a chance of catching Asher before he made it all the way down the street. When she opened the door, she discovered a man standing in front of the house.

"Asher, STOP!" she cried, as a second contraction began. It was stronger than the first and it bent her forward, causing her to step out onto the veranda. She gripped the railing, and the coolness of the metal on her hands made her momentarily forget the pain. This allowed her to look more closely at the man, and she saw that he was not her husband. He was Asher's height, but he was covered in mud and dirt and drying bits of cement. The only clean part of him was his left hand, in which he held a sheet of salt cod.

"Who are you?"

"Secondo," said the man.

"Secondo who?" said Harold, and laughed.

"Greico."

Harold laughed again, as if the name were a punchline, and that was when Mazie's water broke. The fluid came out of her all at once, splashing onto the veranda and onto Harold.

Secondo, the second of Mrs. Greico's unmarried sons, was one of the fifty men the city of Toronto was employing that year to dig the great hole that would one day be the Spadina Sewer. When he'd got to work that morning, the foreman—his brother-in-law, Angelo—had made him wash his left hand, and had passed him a sheet of salt cod. Angelo had told him to deliver the *baccalà* to his sister, Francesca Burke. Angelo did this every week. The delivery of the *baccalà* was considered by the Greico brothers to be an onerous task, because they knew it was simply Angelo's way of showing off the fact that he was foreman, of making it seem that he was the big shot of the family. Like his brothers, Secondo resented having to make the delivery, and complained bitterly about it when Angelo wasn't around, but each week he or one of his brothers delivered it without a word. This week Secondo felt he had made particularly good time, and he had been just seconds away from accomplishing his task when Mazie Diamond had come, pregnant and screaming, out of her house. She'd called to him, bent over and peed on her son. Not even in the old country, where once, according to his mother, a snake had crawled up into the bed and sucked on her breast like a little baby, had Secondo heard of such a thing. Not knowing what to do, he ran up onto the long veranda, past Mazie, and knocked frantically on the door of the Burke house, telling himself that if anyone knew what to do in such a situation, it would be a foreman's sister.

Francesca Burke was at the time sitting in a stuffed chair, sewing a sleeve onto a new, unbelted smock. The chair had been positioned in front of the big second-floor window in such a way as to allow its occupant a clear view of the street, and of the blind people who were at that moment making their way, as they did every morning, into the institute. The blind, to Francesca, did not seem uncertain in the least. In fact, they looked confident, even fortified by their blindness. This was why she was watching them. She imagined herself blind, her white cane collapsed and held in her lap as she sat on the streetcar, counting the stops and talking to no one except other blind people, who she knew were also counting the stops. This seemed to her the right way to do things. The blind knew the things they had to worry about. Which was what Francesca wanted more than anything else. For the whole of her pregnancy, she'd been worried. Mostly she worried about the baby, but sometimes it was something else—something shapeless and unmistakable and unshakable, something teetering just above her, something she could not see, a safe or a boulder that was about to crash down on her the way it did on the villains in the new Hap Kvidera pictures that had lately started at the Rose Theatre. She imagined herself being crushed by something strange and symbolic: a baby carriage, or a stack of hundred-dollar bills, or a statue of San Bonorio. It was only while she watched the blind that she was able to think of her nervousness as a good thing, as a kind of white cane reaching into the future and landing, as those white canes always seemed to, on solid ground.

Other than being louder than she expected, Secondo's knocking did not surprise Francesca in the least. She had been expecting the *baccalà* to arrive. Although she had told her brother to stop, the fish came every Thursday morning without fail. But because she was pregnant it took her a full five minutes to get out of her chair and down the stairs. The pounding got louder during that time, and as she was opening the door she was also resolving to send the *baccalà*, and the *gubbatost* who was delivering it, back to her *gubbatost* of a brother. We'll see how he likes that, she thought, and opened the door. She saw Secondo, Mazie, little soaking wet Harold— and the *baccalà* abandoned in the middle of the sidewalk. A moment later, at Francesca's instruction, Secondo was helping Mazie upstairs into the Burke kitchen, while Francesca made her way heavily along the veranda to knock on Sadie Nodelman's door.

"Sadie," Francesca told her. "It's Mazie—she's having the baby."

"I'll get the girls," said Sadie, and closed the door, and less than a minute later she and her two daughters, six-year-old Esther and three-year-old Ruthie, were in the kitchen too. Sadie sized up the situation, and opened one of the cupboards and took down an iron pot. She filled the pot with water and put it on the stove to boil. Then, because there was nothing else to be done at that moment, she took the opportunity to quiz her daughters.

"Girls," she said, "why is Mazie on the table?"

"Mazie is having a baby," said Esther.

"Right," said Sadie.

"Why?" asked Ruthie.

"Hi, Esther," interrupted Harold, who had followed Secondo and his mother into the kitchen.

"Hi, Harold," said Ruthie.

"Shut up, Ruthie," said Esther.

"My mom peed on me," said Harold. Ruthie and Esther were suitably impressed.

"Where's Asher?" Sadie was saying. "Asher should be here."

"He went to work," said Mazie.

"Work?" said Sadie, as if to say that, if Asher had been paying attention, he would have known his wife was about to give birth, and that any man worth a nickel should be there to watch his children being born.

"Go find Asher," said Francesca to Secondo, who had been standing, praying, in a corner of the kitchen. As Secondo pulled himself together, Francesca told him where to find Asher at the St. Lawrence Market. He was soon out the door and less than twenty-five minutes later, he was standing in front of Asher.

Who was scowling at him.

Asher was scowling because he was about to enter the most crucial stage of his pitch: the countdown. This was the moment when he told the crowd how much they would have to pay for a set of Greenstein's knives. The whole secret of the countdown, as Asher would tell his sons one day, was *not* to stop it—not ever, no matter what happened.

"I know what you're thinking," he was saying. "You're wondering how much a set of these Greenstein knives is going to cost."

Secondo raised his hand. Asher ignored him.

"Now," Asher told the crowd, "you are not going to have to pay two hundred dollars for a set of these knives. Not one hundred and ninety. Not one hundred and eighty, and not one hundred and seventy. Not one hundred and fifty. Not one hundred and twenty. Not one hundred dollars. Less than a hundred dollars. Not ninety-five. Not ninety. Not eighty-five. Not seventy-five, not sixty-five. You will not pay sixty dollars. You will not pay fifty-five. Not forty. Not thirty-five.

Not thirty. Not twenty. Not fifteen, not ten, not five, not four, not three."

Secondo tried to say something.

"No," said Asher. "I won't, I won't let you pay three dollars for a set of Greenstein's Remarkable Knives. I won't even let you pay two dollars. I will not do it. I *refuse* to do it."

Secondo said something that Asher couldn't make out, and Asher thought he was trying to prematurely purchase a set of Greenstein's Knives.

"No," Asher said, "no matter how remarkable these knives are, no matter how responsible an investment you think it is for you, your family and your future. Indeed, sir, I can see you don't know *how* we can afford to sell these knives for any less than two dollars, and I will tell you that I had similar questions *myself*. I had *doubts*."

"Mister," said a tiny woman in a black dress, in the very brief interval of silence during which Asher was taking a breath, "he don't want you knives—he says you wife, she's having the baby."

At that moment, back in the Burke kitchen, Mazie had reached cantaloupe. Labour ordinarily progresses much more slowly: from pea to grape to cherry to walnut to plum to apple to Granny Smith apple to orange to grapefruit (known in some cultures as coconut), and then, finally, to cantaloupe. But that day, miraculously, Mazie's cervix had dilated almost immediately to cantaloupe. Her contractions now came one after another, ripping through her, and they made her say terrible things about Asher.

"Don't listen," Sadie told her daughters. "That's the baby talking."

"It doesn't sound like a baby," said Ruthie.

"Mazie is going to hold her breath and push," Sadie told them. "And we're all going to count to ten. Mazie, you don't let your breath go until we get to ten. Got it?"

The doorbell rang.

"What's that?" gasped Mazie.

"It's Asher," Sadie told her.

"Asher," Mazie said, "is a *groisse farshtinkener*."

The doorbell rang a second time, and Francesca went downstairs to find that it was not Asher but Carmella, her sister-in-law, standing on the veranda with a bunch of bananas.

"Surprise!" said Carmella, raising the bananas.

Francesca did not know what to say. Carmella repeated herself and the gesture. "Come up," said Francesca. Carmella followed her, and although both women were moving as fast as they could, they were moving slowly, for both were equally pregnant.

(Indeed, they had concluded that they were pregnant at exactly the same time and, after telling their husbands, had revealed it to each other and to the family on the same Sunday afternoon, during the same dinner. "Two peas in a pod," Nonna had said, which, in Mondorio, was a way of saying that perhaps both babies would be born on the same day.)

Carmella entered the kitchen first, with Francesca just behind her.

"SHA!" Sadie was shouting. "Now—one, two, three, *BREATHE.*"

And they all did as they were told.

A moment later there was a wet shifting and Mazie gave a cry of pain, and out slid the baby. Francesca took two clothespins and the big knife out of the iron pot, and passed them to Sadie, who placed one of the clothespins on the cord between the baby and Mazie, and the second clothespin between the baby and the first clothespin, and Francesca cut the cord between the clothespins. Then Sadie handed the baby to Mazie, who held it to her breast. With the baby in her arms she sat up, propping herself against the kitchen wall. Harold stepped forward and saw the baby's newborn skin glistening white. The baby looked Harold frankly in the face, and Harold asked its name.

"Dubie," Mazie told him, "after your grandfather."

Sometime after that, after Mazie had been taken to the back bedroom and had fallen asleep with Harold beside her on the big bed, Francesca realized that Carmella was nowhere to be seen.

"She took one look at the baby, and ran," said Esther.

"She ran?" said Sadie.

"She was scared," said Ruthie.

"Scared?" Sadie asked her daughter. "Is that what she said?"

"She went to Montreal," said Esther, "—she *said* that."

"Hell," said Sadie.

This was strong language but, because she agreed with the sentiment, Francesca did not object. In fact, she echoed it: "Hell is right," she said, "to leave like that. Hell."

Sadie did not reply. "Hell" was not what she'd said. She had said, "Yael," the name of her mother's younger sister, her aunt, the pretty one who had died in Germany. Yael had married a tailor, and soon announced she was pregnant. There had been much celebration, but when by February Yael's baby still had not come, people had stopped pretending not to be worried—some said the pregnancy had lasted eleven months; others, fourteen. Finally, Sadie's mother decided to take Yael to watch another girl give birth, saying that sometimes, if a woman watched this, she went into labour herself. Sure enough, when Yael saw the baby's black hair peeking out from between the other woman's legs she began making a low, cooing sound that turned into a roar, and then she ran out into the street. She delivered her baby a few hours later, its eyes pulled shut and its skin a dark purple. It would not breathe, even when Sadie's mother put her mouth against its mouth and breathed into it. After, Sadie's mother gave the little thing to Yael, who took it in her arms, cradling it for a moment before handing it back.

Yael died two weeks later. During that time she had stayed in bed and talked only about her baby, about its closed eyes and its blue hands and how still it had been when she'd held it to her breast. And she said she did not remember running. So although Sadie guessed why Carmella had run out of the house, she said nothing to Francesca. She could not be sure, first of all, but mostly she said nothing because she hoped she was wrong, she hoped Carmella had left because she had better things to do than stand around looking at a baby. So Sadie said nothing, and her saying nothing was a kind of wish.

But Sadie, as so often happened, turned out to be right.

Carmella had gone into labour, and for reasons she would not be able to explain or remember afterwards, she ran. She ran up Beverley Street to College, where she boarded the College streetcar, paying her fare and sitting in the seat behind the driver.

The driver turned around and said hello, and when Carmella stared straight ahead instead of replying, he knew something was wrong. He applied the brake and pushed the red button under the seat, which would bring the conductor to the front of the streetcar.

"Right, Burke," said the conductor. "What seems to be the problem?"

Andrew Burke nodded toward Carmella, who was staring out the window. Every few seconds her hand would flutter up out of her lap to her lips, then down again, like a carrier pigeon.

"I've seen her before," said the conductor.

"At my wedding, Cobb," said Burke. "She's my sister-in-law."

Before Cobb could reply, Carmella spoke to him. "Excuse me," she said, with glassy eyes. "Does this streetcar go to Montreal?"

"You have to transfer," Cobb said, without batting an eyelid.

A look passed between the two men.

Burke put the streetcar in motion, as if nothing were out of the ordinary. Before long, they reached Huron Street, and Cobb stood up, announcing that anyone going to Montreal had better transfer.

Carmella went out the front doors.

Burke stood up also.

"Where're you going?" said Cobb. "You're staying with the car. Rule Number One, you know, the driver stays with the car."

Burke repeated that Carmella was his sister-in-law.

"Rule Number One is Rule Number One," said Cobb, going out the door. "Don't worry," he said. "I'll take her to Francesca, and that'll be that. She'll be fine, you'll see."

Knowing there was no arguing with Cobb, Burke sat back down in the driver's seat and closed the doors. He put the streetcar in motion, and all was well until he found himself stopped at the intersection of College and Spadina, just in front of the manhole cover that had been placed over the opening to the great hole that would one day be the Spadina Sewer. "Folks," he announced to his passengers, "I'll be back," and he stepped down off the streetcar. He ran into the centre of the intersection and lifted off the iron cover, climbing down the rope ladder into the sewer. As he climbed his left foot got tangled, and when he reached down to untangle it, he lost his grip on the ladder.

He fell backwards, into darkness. The next thing he knew, there was a light shining in his face.

"What's your name?" said a voice.

"Andrew Burke," he replied, blinded by the light. "Who're you?"

"I ask the questions," the voice told him. "You from the city?"

"I'm looking for Angelo—the foreman."

"So you *are* from the city. Did Tate send you?"

"I don't know Tate. I'm looking for Angelo. He's foreman of this job; you must know him. Angelo's wife, Carmella, is having her baby."

"Carmella?" said the voice.

"You know her?"

"I know Carmella? I known Carmella since—" and here the owner of the voice cast about for a suitably large expanse of time and, finding none, turned the light on himself. "I'm Quintillano, her brother."

"Quintillano," said Andrew, recognizing him, "you have to tell Angelo."

Quintillano did not know what to say. For as long as he could remember, he had wanted to say or do something new, something his brothers had not already said or done. And so he walked over to one of the earthen walls and flipped the alarm.

"Soon," he shouted over the ringing, "they'll come."

As if to demonstrate, he pointed the flashlight downwards, and Andrew saw that he had not fallen to the bottom of the hole, as he'd imagined. What he'd dropped onto was a plateau, a tiny earthen island directly underneath the hole's opening. He saw that the hole was not a hole at all, but a tunnel—or several tunnels—that proceeded in every direction, into the earth as well as to the north and south and east and west. Hearing a sound behind him, he turned and saw two men climbing the stiff embankment that led to the rope ladder. Then abruptly there were two more men, then more men than he could count, all climbing and running, all running and shouting, and it seemed to Andrew that the earth was heaving the men out. Hands reached for the rope ladder, knocking off other hands, until suddenly the alarm was shut off.

Andrew turned and saw that it was Angelo who'd shut it off.

"Quintillano," Angelo asked, "what's going on?"

"Listen," said Quintillano, "it's an emergency."

"An emergency?" said Angelo. "Where?"

"Wait," said Andrew. "It was me."

"*Bo*," said Angelo, seeing him for the first time. "What're *you* doing here?"

"I came to tell you—Carmella is having the baby."

"Now?" said Angelo.

"This," said Quintillano triumphantly, "is why I ring the bell."

Angelo ran toward Beverley Street, but once out of the hole Carmella's four brothers ran in the other direction, toward Clinton, where they found their mother sightlessly folding her flowers in front of the window. They lifted her and her wheelchair up and carried her out the front door, down College, past Manning and Palmerston and Brunswick and Robert, all the way to Beverley Street. The old woman sat in her wheelchair, smiling, her arms folded; the white cotton bag, still attached to the side of the wheelchair, hung open, strewing white paper flowers behind them.

Back at Beverley Street, things appeared to be going well. Carmella did what Sadie Nodelman told her to do. She took deep breaths, which she held while Conductor Cobb (who had hold of her left leg) and Francesca (who had her right) and Sadie Nodelman (who stood between her legs in a nervous crouch, trying not to think of Yael) counted to ten.

After five deep breaths, Sadie called out, "I see the head."

"Here comes the head," announced Cobb, as if it were a streetcar stop.

Then Sadie said something indecipherable in Yiddish.

"What's the matter?" said Cobb.

Sadie did not reply.

"What is it?" said Francesca. She knew something was wrong. She let go of Carmella's leg and went to look for herself and saw that the umbilical cord had become wrapped around the baby's neck. Sadie turned white and started to cry, even as Carmella began screaming, and then suddenly Asher Diamond was in the kitchen doorway with a pair of Greenstein knives in his hand. Moving with the same surety of motion, the same singleness of purpose, with which he cut turnips each day at the St. Lawrence Market, Asher inserted two metallic hands (which were on the ends of Greenstein's knives) and pulled out the baby. He unwrapped the umbilical cord and severed it, as if he were in the midst of a pitch and it was the kind of thing he did every day.

This done, Asher took a breath and went to kiss the woman on the kitchen table.

"You're not Mazie!" he said.

Before Carmella could reply, there issued from downstairs the sound of four sons pushing their blind mother and her wheelchair through the front door.

Some time after that, there was the practical question of what to feed all the people who had congregated to see the two new babies. *Olalia*—the same dish that Lucio and his mother and Nonna would be eating years later, when the Welfare Lady came to call—was decided upon.

"I'll start the water," said Francesca.

She went into the kitchen and washed out the big iron pot that Sadie had used hours before. When it was filled with water, she called to her mother to come and help her lift it onto the stove. Nonna came in and took one side of the pot, Francesca took the other, and together they lifted, and at the moment the bottom of the pot touched the burner, Francesca's water broke.

For a long moment the two women stood in silence, their feet wet.

"*Bo*," said Nonna. "*Three* peas in a pod."

It was a quick labour. "What's the name?" asked Sadie, when the baby was out.

Francesca spoke softly, and only Sadie could hear.

"Lucio," said Sadie, who made it official by telling each of her daughters to introduce themselves to the new baby. Esther and Ruthie lined up next to the table and stood on their tiptoes and said hello to Lucio, whom Francesca was holding very close to her face, rather as if he were a book with small type.

"This is the name—Lucio?" said Nonna. "This is no name."

It was only later that anyone realized Francesca had been

asking for light. She had said *luce*, not Lucio. Meaning light. She had wanted to see her baby's face. But by that time it was too late. Sadie and her daughters had already called the baby Lucio, and once a baby has been called by one name it is bad luck to call it by any other. No one except Nonna seemed to mind, and this was because, as far as she was concerned, there was only one name the baby could have—Bonorio.

"Well, Lucio," said Cobb, "I'm off to find your father."

As Cobb walked up Beverley to College Street, he looked at his watch. It was six-thirty. Andrew, he knew, should have already been home. Bobby Carlyle was to have relieved him at five, but Carlyle was unreliable, a drinker. Burke had probably been made to take a double shift. Cobb felt a deep anger welling up inside him, something like tears, but then he began to think of telling Andrew about Lucio. He imagined getting on the streetcar and sitting down, imagined that Andrew would want to know about Carmella. Carmella's fine, he imagined himself saying, but there's another thing—and he would just come out with it. You're a father, he'd say, and Andrew would not know what to say, and that would be the end of that. At College, because the streetcar was nowhere in sight, Cobb ducked into Altman's Deli and, standing at the counter, ordered apple pie.

"Knock-knock," said Cecil Altman.

Cobb looked at him.

"Listen," said Cecil, "this is a joke."

"It is?" said Cobb. "How about that pie?"

"In a minute," said Cecil, and explained what one said when being told a knock-knock joke.

"If you don't mind my saying so," Cobb told him, "it isn't my cup of tea."

"Never mind," said Cecil, "give it a try. Knock-knock."

"Who's there?"

"Boo."

"What's that supposed to mean?"

"This is part of the joke," said Cecil. "You're supposed to try to find out who I am—like I'm knocking and you ask me who I am. So I say, 'Boo.' Then what d'you say?"

"That Boo's not a name."

"Let's say it is."

Cobb shrugged.

"Knock-knock," said Cecil.

"Who's there?"

"Boo."

"Boo who?" said Cobb.

"Don't cry," said Cecil, "it's only a joke."

Cobb was not listening. The streetcar had pulled up in front of the deli. Its front doors opened and Burke emerged with the switcher in his hand. Cobb told Altman that he could forget about the pie, and began walking toward the door, looking at Andrew, who was standing in the middle of the intersection to switch the track. Cobb was laughing to himself and picturing Burke's reaction.

Then he saw the car.

It hit Andrew head on.

Later, after the police had arrived, Cobb walked out into the intersection and picked up the switcher, and returned it to its place behind the driver's seat. Then he turned around and began walking back to 187 Beverley Street.

◑

Back at the house, Nonna was angry. Andrew would be home soon, and she planned to bring up the question of the name right away. Lucio, she would tell him, would not do. The name of the baby, she would say, had to be Bonorio—after her saint, and after the boy's grandfather, her long-lost husband, who had brought her to America.

Before marrying, Nonna had spent her entire life in Mondorio, a tiny town perched on the side of a great hill, huddled into the side of the rock like a flock of sheep taking refuge from a storm. She and her brothers lived in a one-storey house with an earthen floor and a fireplace carved out of the rock itself. The centre of town was the piazza, with the police station and town hall, both of which were single-storey buildings. There was no ceiling in either building, and at night the moonlight filtered through the shingles in the roof of the jail and shone on the faces of the prisoners. On the other side of the piazza were two general stores, which had once been a single store but had been divided into two because of a quarrel between the brothers who owned them. So it was that, if you needed a nail or a piece of thread or an empty bottle, you could go back and forth between the brothers until one of them gave it to you for free in order to spite the other. Before coming back to marry her, Bonorio had been to America twice, and had made up his mind to stay. But first he needed a wife. A Mondorese wife. His plan to marry a girl from his hometown was not based on logic; he had never contemplated anything else—the certainty of it was like the ground he walked upon. There was a brief courtship, a simple wedding, and two weeks later he and Nonna—or Anna, as she was called then—began the long walk that would take them to Naples.

By the time Nonna got on the boat, she knew she was pregnant. But she said nothing—not to her new husband, not to anyone. This was because she didn't know if she would manage to have the baby—or, if she did, whether it would survive the sea passage. This thought occurred to her on only the second day of the journey, when she realized that she and Bonorio would be forced to spend the next month in the sunless room into which they had been pushed. The smell was unbearable and the air was thick with sickness. Gradually the thought that her baby would die hardened into a conviction. She went on throwing up in the mornings, but to her it was as if the baby had already been born dead, as if it had come lifeless out of her belly and the crew had already thrown the little thing into the ocean, like the old man who had died on the sixth day. It was a conviction that freed her, for once she had decided that her baby was dead, she also decided that she would not blame herself or her baby. Instead, she made up her mind to blame the men running the boat. The men who made them sleep in double-decker bunks two feet wide and less than two feet apart. The men who locked the doors of that dank underbelly of the ship, where not even Bonorio, who was less than five feet tall, could stand up without knocking his head on the ceiling. The men who locked them in that room smelling of shit and piss, the room that had already killed her baby. Better to be thrown overboard, she thought, than to be born into a room like this.

And then, just as things seemed to be as bad as they could be, they got worse.

Nonna's shoes fell apart. The sole of her right shoe came off first, and then the same thing happened to her left shoe. She put the detached soles into her pockets and for a whole week slept with them beneath her pillow, for fear of their being stolen. Then one day, when she was sitting alone in a corner of the ship, absent-mindedly turning the soles over in her hands, a man sat down beside her and asked what she was doing with her soles.

He told her that he was a shoemaker, and produced from his pocket a shoemaker's needle and a spool of rough black thread. He started with her right shoe, running the thread in and out of the leather. When he was finished Nonna walked back and forth, stomping with her one good shoe, and the man smiled. The next day he did the same for her left shoe. On the third day he sewed up the tears in the sides of the shoes as well, so that water would not get in. The man had a square jaw and, until Bonorio came over and spoke to him, Nonna was convinced that her shoemaker was an angel. This was the kind of thing she believed could happen, and although it had frightened her at first—the placid smile of the shoemaker had made her wonder if something terrible had happened and they were all already dead—she had accepted it, and watched with interest as the shoemaker fixed her shoes. Afterwards he fixed Bonorio's shoes, and played cards with Bonorio in the dim light of the room and talked about America. The shoemaker, it seemed to her, was not nearly as happy about America as Bonorio, being of the opinion that nothing really changed for the poor Italians when they came to America. They were just as poor. And who had to be poor? Nobody, the shoemaker told them. There was no good reason for anyone to be poor. At night Bonorio called the shoemaker a troublemaker—but only at night, when the shoemaker wasn't there to hear.

"No," Nonna would whisper back, "he's an angel."

Years later, when the shoemaker's picture appeared in all the newspapers alongside that of a fish peddler named Vanzetti as they were both on their way to the electric chair for a crime everyone knew he had not committed, she wondered if perhaps Bonorio had been right. But at the time he had liked the shoemaker well enough, and most nights the two would play *scopa*, with a round of *briscola* at the end. One night the shoemaker took out a pack of English cards and taught Bonorio a game called rummy. No, Nonna said, when the shoemaker asked if he should deal her in, for in Mondorio women did not play cards. Still, she watched them play, and wondered if this was one of the things she would do in America, in her *vita nuova* (which was what the shoemaker called it). When at last the boat arrived, they came down the gangplank all at once, and men with guns marshalled them first in one direction and then in the next, and then through a mazelike series of metal bars. Nonna found herself standing beside her shoemaker as she was herded along, smelling American air for the first time.

"Cows," said the shoemaker, "that's all we are to them. So many animals."

And Nonna—who had not miscarried, and knew she would not now that they were in America—giggled.

Once in New York, Nonna and Bonorio moved into a two-room flat in a tenement on Orchard Street, south of Delancey. Bonorio worked as a labourer, and she found a job as a seamstress in a sweatshop on Thirty-eighth Street. But then she had to quit when little Francesca was born. Fourteen months later came another baby, this one a boy. They named him Bonorio, after Bonorio's father, but called him Angelo. With the babies, Nonna could not go back to the sweatshop, and so Bonorio bought her a sewing machine, a Singer, so she could work at home, sewing dresses for Mrs. Vorhees, a rich woman who lived in a brownstone near Gramercy Park and spoke with an accent. Nonna had found Mrs. Vorhees after going from door to door offering her services, which was how Mrs. Seigal, the Jewish woman who lived down the hall, said it was done in America. Nonna had followed Mrs. Seigal's advice despite Silvana, a Sicilian woman who lived on the floor above, who said going door to door was like begging—or, worse, like doing housework—which Nonna thought of as the same as being a slave. The first time, Mrs. Vorhees gave Nonna the patterns and money for cloth, and two weeks later Nonna brought back the finished dress. Mrs. Vorhees inspected the seams carefully, picking at the stitching with her finger, and then disappeared into the house. Nonna thought she'd done something terribly wrong, and nearly left right there and then; but just when she'd made up her mind to do so, Mrs. Vorhees came back with a different pattern and different material, telling Nonna she could keep the first dress because it had only been a test. Then she handed Nonna enough money for both the dress she had made and the one she would make.

With cash in her pocket and a new dress on her arm, Nonna felt like celebrating, and on her way home she bought a forty-inch statue of San Bonorio to surprise her husband, and as a tribute to the saint who had taken care of them all. But her Bonorio did not come home that night. Not that night and not the next night. And not the night after that. After a week of waiting for him, she started searching. She went from door to door, first in their tenement and then in all the buildings on Orchard and Delancey streets, which were crowded with identical square, sunless buildings. She went early in the morning, before the men had gone to work, getting them out of their beds. One man told Nonna he thought he'd seen Bonorio on Cedar Street, working on the building that was to be the

Federal Reserve Bank. When she heard this, Nonna went home and brought the children with her to the building; she would show the babies to Bonorio, make them put their little faces up against his, and then she would tell him he had to come back.

Nonna soon discovered that hers was not a new story. The tenements were full of women and children whose husbands and fathers had not come home one night. No, the women replied, no Bonorio, but while you're looking keep an eye out for my Augusto, my Xacchero, my Tommaso, my Giorgio. The Italian men just disappeared. They would one day just pick up and leave. Nonna thought this was because so many of them had first come to America without women. They had seen the food, and the food had made them think it would be good to have someone to cook for them. But having a wife was different from thinking about having a wife. And then—because in America there was no one around to stop them, because a woman's brothers could not go after the husband and force him to return to the girl by breaking his arm or slicing out his tongue—the men left and did not come back.

Before long, the loneliness of the task was too much for her, and she found herself thinking of going home to Italy. But no sooner did she think of her children playing with their cousins than she thought also of the stinking room on the boat where she had pronounced little Francesca dead before she was born. She resolved to stay, and then, as if to make it official, she sold her clothes at a pawnshop on Lafayette—the bright skirts and blouses she had carried over from the old country in the cardboard suitcase Bonorio's father had given her as a wedding present—and bought a bolt of black cloth. She made three black dresses, and began telling people her husband was dead.

Yet night after night she paced the apartment, desolate and then furious, wondering what sense it made for her to be alone like this. How could it have happened? She was a good person; she deserved none of this. How could it be *allowed* to happen? The worst thing about it was that she could not be *sure* he had abandoned her at all. It was just as likely that Bonorio had been crushed under a falling scaffold, or caught in a collapsing tunnel, or injured in a thousand different ways and been taken to a hospital and, because he couldn't speak English, been unable to say where his wife and children were, or even that he had any. One night, as she was thinking this, Nonna found herself looking at the statue of San Bonorio holding his chicken on the kitchen table. Without quite knowing what she was doing, she opened the single tiny window in their apartment, a window that gave onto nothing but the wall of another tenement and the narrow gap that separated the buildings, and dropped the statue down into the darkness. Then she threw herself on the bed and fell into a fitful sleep.

The next day, in the harsh light of morning, Nonna recalled what she had done. She rushed to the window and looked down, expecting to see broken bits of the statue strewn everywhere. Retribution, she imagined, would be swift and brutal. But she saw that the statue was still intact—miraculously undamaged. More than that; it was standing upright. It had fallen six storeys and landed on its feet. Nonna understood this to be a message: San Bonorio was trying to tell her that she would be fine.

Two weeks later, when the letter came from Toronto, from Michelangelo, Nonna waited until her children were asleep, and crawled through the rat-infested alley separating the two buildings to retrieve the statue. She dragged it out after her, then bundled it up in brown wrapping paper and carried it over her shoulder, like a third child, onto the train that would take her into Canada. Michelangelo was waiting for them when they arrived at Toronto's Union Station, and right then Nonna knew it would all be fine. As she carried the statue toward their new home on Clinton Street, she understood that she owed the saint something, and resolved that it would be one of her grandchildren.

Years later, her son had disappointed her with the name Dante for his first child, but Nonna had said nothing. There was nothing she *could* say to that one, when he had made up his mind, and in any case there was another baby on the way. This one, this child of Francesca's, Nonna had promised her saint, would be a Bonorio. But all had been confusion, and somehow, absurdly, the baby had been called Lucio.

Now Francesca was asleep on the sofa with the baby beside her, swaddled, in a dresser drawer. As Nonna paced back and forth, rehearsing in her mind what she was going to say, she noticed the baby's eyes were open. Going over, she picked Lucio up and carried him downstairs so his cries would not wake his mother. She tried to rock him to sleep, and as she was swaying to and fro she looked out the window and saw a chicken on the front steps of the Institute for the Blind. It was sitting quite still. Hardly believing her eyes, she opened the front door to get a better look. Cold air rushed into the house. There was no question, the bird was a chicken. Its wings were folded but its eyes were open, and it was looking right at her, as if trying to tell her something. Nonna hurried upstairs and woke up Francesca, who looked out the window and saw the chicken for herself. The two women stared out the window, with little Lucio between them, and that was when Nonna decided that, because Saint Bonorio of Mondorio had touched a chicken and made the rain come in the driest of dry seasons, Lucio was a lucky name. She said as much to Francesca. There was the sound of the front door opening, and Francesca took the baby out of her mother's arms, holding him up because she expected her husband. But it was not Andrew who came in. It was Cobb.

He walked into the room and right away, before he had a chance to say a thing, Nonna was pulling him over to the window so that he could see the chicken, telling him it was a good omen because in all the statues San Bonorio was standing beside a chicken, with his hand on the head of the chicken, as if the chicken were not a chicken at all but a little baby. Cobb looked at them, the three of them. He began to speak.

FOURTEEN

THE MORNING AFTER THE GAME at Withrow Park, Lucio goes to see Dante at the garage.

"Lucio," says Dante, "what a surprise."

"What'd you tell the priest?" says Lucio.

"What priest?" says Dante.

"You know, the one at St. Patrick's."

"Nothing," says Dante.

"He knows," says Lucio. "I don't know how he knows, but he knows."

"Knows what?" says Dante. Lucio tells him. "I didn't say nothing," says Dante.

Lucio looks at him. "Then who?" he says, but even before he has finished speaking, they both know the answer.

"You talked to Dubie?" says Dante.

"Not yet," says Lucio. "But I know where to find him."

The Riverdale Zoo is in the shape of an L, old-fashioned and unplanned, consisting of seven animals in six cages. Lucio walks past a rhinoceros, an old, ailing animal covered in a leathery hide grown so faded and ashen grey that the animal looks as if it might blow away at any second. Next he passes a humpless camel chewing at a paper bag, and then a watery-eyed brown bear that has been donated to the zoo by the Ringling Brothers Circus because it has grown too old to ride a unicycle. A small plaque at the foot of the bear's cage, made of imitation bronze, shows a much younger, spryer bear cycling before adoring fans; the bear's name, says the plaque, is Barry. Lucio passes a penlike enclosure in which two zebras with bloodshot eyes run to and fro, throwing themselves intermittently at the wooden fence. He sees Dubie sitting in front of the fifth and sixth cages, between the cheetah and the elephant.

Lucio sits down beside him, and Dubie laughs a low, sarcastic laugh to himself.

"That's a big cat," says Lucio.

"Shut up," says Dubie.

The cheetah gets up from where it is lying at the back of the cage and walks toward them, looking out at them from between the bars. Its stare, Lucio decides, is not so much menacing as expectant. The cat paces forward, coming very close to the bars—as close as it can without hitting its nose—and then begins pacing back and forth, looking at them. Lucio watches the animal's restless movement and wonders if Dubie smells like blood, like someone wounded, easy prey.

"Is this Asher's idea?" says Dubie.

Lucio shakes his head.

"You know," says Dubie, "elephants mourn their dead— they can distinguish between a hundred different sounds of a hundred different elephants."

"Is that right?" says Lucio.

"Yes, that's right," says Dubie. "You think I'd make something like that up?"

Lucio does not reply. He looks over at Dubie, and notices that Dubie has sloppily reattached the bandage to his hand; the bandage is grubby, but at least the hand is covered.

"What I was going to say," Dubie tells him, "is that if, years later, an elephant finds a dead elephant it once knew, it kneels down right there, in the sand or the jungle or wherever the hell it happens the other elephant died, and it mourns that other elephant. *They don't forget.* That's what people say all the time about elephants. They think it's funny. And do you think they know what it means? Do you?"

Lucio says he supposes they don't.

"No, they don't. They tell that to their kids, but they don't know that what they're talking about is that an elephant, if he's wandering across the damn Gobi Desert and finds the corpse of another elephant, will kneel down right then and there."

After a minute, Lucio says, "We won—we made it to the finals."

"We?" says Dubie. "You mean the Lizzies? This is your idea of making me feel better?"

"I guess so," Lucio says. "You used to root for the Lizzies."

Dubie lets out a sharp half-laugh. The cheetah turns toward him and Dubie makes a threatening movement toward the cat, snapping the fingers on his good hand. "You remember," he says, "I was always the pitcher."

Lucio says he remembers.

"So, you think it's fair that you're the pitcher now?"

"I don't know," says Lucio. "It's not like I asked for any of this to happen."

"Really?" says Dubie. "You make this great throw, and the next thing you know, you're banging Ruthie. And here I am," he says, looking at his maimed hand. "You know what this is? It ain't evolution or adaptation—it's extinction."

"Don't say that."

"You sneak."

For a long moment the two boys sit in silence.

"I was going to tell you about her," says Lucio.

"What?" says Dubie. "You think I couldn't take it?"

"I didn't even know you liked her."

"Liked?" snorts Dubie. "I cut off my finger for her, and you say *liked?*"

"That's true?" Lucio asks. "You did it for her?"

"Yes. No," says Dubie, looking away. "I don't know any more."

"You know," says Lucio, "you had your accident and she came to get me—and the two of us came right away to the house to see if you were all right."

"You want a medal?"

"Don't be like that."

"I'll be any way I want," says Dubie. "I'll burn down that table where we were born if I want to. I'll do whatever the hell I want."

"That's what you were doing," says Lucio. "I knew it."

"Don't tell me you wouldn't do the same."

Lucio begins to say something, then stops. Instead, he tells the truth. "No," he says, "I'd not have thought of it in a million years."

Dubie shakes his head. A long while seems to pass.

"I bet you had a good laugh," says Dubie finally. "I'm such an idiot." He begins to cry. "This is stupid," he says. "So damn stupid. What do I care?" His voice is high and thin.

"But this isn't why I came," says Lucio. "I came to ask you a question."

"I don't care," says Dubie. "Do what you want—it's got nothing to do with me, you and Ruthie."

"No, not that," says Lucio. "What do you say to being the Lizzies' manager?"

"Because I'm no pitcher? That's a consolation prize?"

"It's not nothing. I thought you'd want to do it."

"Why would I want to be manager?" asks Dubie. "When have I ever said anything about wanting to be a manager of anything?"

"I thought you'd want to be there, on the field. I thought you'd want to be part of it."

"Of what?" Dubie looks away derisively.

"Of the whole thing," says Lucio, and gestures ambiguously, as if to suggest that nothing he can do with his hands can convey the size of what he's talking about. "Or at least," he says, stopping himself, "that you'd want to be one of the Lizzies, on the day of the big game—Christie Pits, you know, for all the marbles."

"It's just a baseball game," says Dubie. "It's not that big a deal."

Lucio stares into the middle distance and doesn't move. Neither boy speaks. Then Dubie looks at Lucio. "You serious?"

Lucio nods.

"You asked Goody?"

"Goody's the one who asked me to ask you," lies Lucio.

"Is that right?" says Dubie, because he can see Lucio is lying.

"That's right."

"Manager," says Dubie, half to himself.

"Take it or leave it," says Lucio.

The two walk out of the zoo, and Lucio asks Dubie if he told anyone about the statue.

"What statue?" says Dubie.

Father McElarney is meanwhile making it his business to talk to everyone connected to either the miracle of the moving statue or the miracle of the three births. He begins with Asher and Mazie Diamond, who cannot agree about what occurred on that morning seventeen years ago, when the three children were born on the same day, and on the same kitchen table.

"You," Mazie says, "kissed us when you left for work?"

"You were pregnant," says Asher.

"There was none of this kissing back then," Mazie tells Father McElarney. "I can tell you that much."

"The kissing," Father McElarney says, "is of secondary importance."

"Maybe to you," says Mazie.

"What I'm interested in," says Father McElarney, "are the details of the miracle."

"Miracle?" says Asher. "Who said miracle?"

"If he'd kissed me," says Mazie, "that would've been a miracle."

"I'd like to know," says Father McElarney, "if either of you saw the chicken."

"If you want to know about that day, talk to Harold," says Asher. "Harold saw the chicken. The first one, not the second."

"They're the same chicken," says Mazie.

"That is yet to be determined," says Father McElarney.

"I'll tell you one thing," says Mazie. "That chicken scared Harold."

"Perhaps," says the priest, "it was not a chicken."

"Then what?"

"The Holy Spirit," says Father McElarney.

The Diamonds do not know what to say to this.

Stranger things, the priest knows, have happened. Saint Thomas Aquinas believed that the Holy Spirit manifested itself in the shape of a sphere, that the perfect age was thirty-three and that in heaven everyone was a thirty-three-year-old sphere. If Aquinas could say such things, thought Father McElarney, who was he to say there could be nothing divine about a chicken?

He finds Harold at the St. Lawrence Market.

"That chicken," Harold says, "it was horrible. Its eyes were worst of all. I remember looking into those dead chicken eyes."

Father McElarney takes the black book out of his robe and writes down, "dead eyes."

"Dead chicken eyes," corrects Harold.

Father McElarney makes the emendation. "Did it say anything?" he asks.

Harold looks at him. "It didn't talk; it looked at me and ran away," says Harold. "I remember watching it go—under the wheels of a car. It ran like it knew what was going to happen."

"And what was going to happen?" says Father McElarney, his eyes narrowing.

"We were going to eat it," says Harold. "For dinner."

Father McElarney does not make a note of this.

"I always wondered about it, about that chicken," says Harold. "Sometimes I'd be walking and I'd turn the corner and I'd expect to see that chicken there, waiting for me. But it never happened, and I forgot all about it, more or less, until a couple of weeks back, when Bloomberg was giving away that baseball. There was this bird that landed—from the way people talk about it, it doesn't sound like it was a chicken. My brother,

Dubie, says it was a mix between a bald eagle and something a bald eagle should've kept its hands off in the first place. But I think it was that chicken. Who knows what seventeen years in the wild can do to a chicken? I think it came for me, but it made a mistake and went after Dubie. I wasn't there, mind you, but that's what I heard. The bird landed right in the middle of the baseball game and sat on the ball. Dubie was the next one up when it landed."

"And this, you think, is the same chicken."

"From what I heard, it was horrible. And then it took Bloomberg's glasses."

"His glasses?"

"Right off his face," says Harold, "and from what I heard, it would've got clean away if it hadn't been for Lucio throwing the ball, and hitting the bird just so."

"Lucio Burke?" says Father McElarney.

"That's right," says Harold. "The ball rolled his way, and he threw it like it was nothing. He knocked the bird out of the sky, like he did it every day. It was a miracle he hit the bird so perfect."

"A miracle?" says Father McElarney.

"It was way the other side of the playground. I didn't see it myself, mind you," he adds.

"Just one more question," says Father McElarney. "Where were you when the statue moved off the table?"

"On a date," says Harold, and then adds emphatically, "with Esther Nodelman—and I don't care who knows it."

Father McElarney then tries to find Bloomberg. But like everyone else who's tried to do this, he finds nothing. He finds only Bloomberg's father, a lens grinder with a shop the size of a closet on Walton Street. Except for his eyes and the thick glasses he wears, which are the same as his son's, Bloomberg's father is the last person you'd expect to father a Bloomberg. He is a bent, downtrodden man, scant of flesh and scant of hair, a man who has no interest in even touching a baseball.

Bloomberg's father, when pressed, admits that he cannot recall exactly the last time he saw his son, only that there was a time recently when he didn't see him at all and that this roughly coincided with people coming by and asking questions about him. Being asked about his son seems to be an entirely new and disorienting experience for Bloomberg Senior, who explains to Father McElarney that his wife, who died some four years ago, was the one who dealt with people. She died quite suddenly, he says, in the middle of a coughing fit, falling to the floor right there in their little shop. He gestures at the place where Father McElarney is standing, as if to indicate where it happened. There is a moment of silence between the two men, in which it is plain to the priest that something is expected of him, so he crosses himself and says a small prayer for Bloomberg's mother. Bloomberg's father watches and bows his head but does not cross himself. When Father McElarney has finished the prayer, the old man explains that he has long ago ceased wearing a *kippah* because it is too dangerous. The thugs will come over from the east side and knock your windows in if they see the *kippah*; Altman on College, he says, is crazy in these times for letting his kid wear his *kippah* the way he does. Trying to steer the conversation back to Bloomberg, Father McElarney asks if the other man remembers who came by asking for his son. A number of people, he says; one even who had the glasses and the baseball his son tried to give away; that one, who was tall like his son, gave him the baseball and the glasses.

"I keep them," he says, and Father McElarney sees the two items on a shelf just behind the counter, the glasses positioned in front of the baseball, as if the baseball is wearing them, magnifying the stitching on its side to an alarming size. "I didn't want to take them but that *goy*, he insisted."

"Why didn't you want them?" says Father McElarney. "Don't you think your son might want them when he comes back?"

"Zack's as likely to go to that kid as to me," says Bloomberg's father.

"Zack?"

"Zack," says the man. "My son."

"Of course," says Father McElarney.

"He hates that name," he tells the priest, turning and walking to the back of the dusty room. "And he hated those glasses. Ever since he was a boy, that one, always breaking the glasses, which cost money. What does he think? That I make him wear the glasses because I like them? That I wear the glasses because I want to, and because I got to, I make him? This is what my son thinks. Even when he's older and he knows better. This is what he thinks. He's nineteen, Zack is. When I'm nineteen I came to this country. So he's gone. He'll be back. And then I'll say, you don't want to wear the glasses, you don't got to." There is a stout four-legged stool behind the counter, and the old man sits down on it resolutely, his knees pointed outwards.

Father McElarney mutters a thank you, and turns toward the door.

"He always wanted to be a big shot, that one," says Bloomberg's father. It seems to Father McElarney that he is speaking to himself. "Always with the baseball, telling people he's something special. See what it did."

On Beverley Street, odd things continue to occur in the Burke kitchen. A second blind woman regains her sight by kissing the statue. A woman with shingles finds her disease miraculously gone after rubbing her hand against the underside of the table. A man enters the kitchen and confesses to adultery, prostrating himself on the kitchen floor in front of the statue. People arrive from Walkerton and Penetang, Fergus and Port Credit and Ancaster, and as far away as Montreal and Halifax and Vancouver. And Father McElarney talks to Sadie and Abe and Esther Nodelman, to Cecil and Goody Altman, to Carmella and her five unmarried brothers, to Angelo, to Dante and even to the Au twins.

But not to Lucio. For him, Father McElarney has something special in mind.

After what Ruthie says to him after the baseball game, Lucio goes back to working his shifts at the garage just as he always did, as if none of his time with her ever happened. He has not seen her since that day at Withrow Park, and knows nothing about what was said between her and Gutman other than that she has not lost her job. He wonders if she has given up on the walkout, or if perhaps Gutman is somehow in on it now—perhaps he makes the sardine sandwiches each morning. Anything is possible, thinks Lucio, as he waits each night on the veranda for her to come home. When there is no sign of her, he goes around the house into the cinder alley and waits for her there. But he never seems to be able to catch her. The simple thing, he knows, would be to go to Gutman Fur and ask for her. But he cannot make himself do it. Partially because he is afraid of what Gutman will accuse him of, but mostly because he is afraid that Ruthie will want nothing to do with him—that she will say again what she said that day after the baseball game.

"Never mind," Dante tells him. "There's lots of fish in the sea."

Lucio shrugs.

"And not just lots of them, there are a lot of *different* fish."

"Different kinds of fish—I know."

"They got these fish, they make their own light—and then there's a little pole around the fish's nose that it uses to get other fish."

"Dante, listen, you don't have to make me feel better."

"It's called the anglerfish, the one with the light—it lives near the bottom."

"The bottom of what?"

"Of the ocean."

Lucio looks at him. "I thought you were talking about girls, and trying to make me feel better."

"It started out that way, but then we got onto the fish thing."

"What do you know about fish?"

Dante looks at him, and Lucio, in spite of his low mood, laughs.

"You know—I never found out what happened with all of that," says Dante, after a moment.

"We didn't do it." Lucio hears the bitterness in his own voice. "There, now you know."

"Not that, the other thing, the walkout."

"It hasn't happened yet," says Lucio. And then he realizes: "It's tomorrow, August twelfth."

"Never mind," says Dante. "I'll take the shift."

"No—she doesn't want me there; she said so."

Dante shook his head. "Of course she wants you there."

"You should have seen her," says Lucio. "If you had seen her, you wouldn't be saying that."

"OK," says Dante. "Do what you want."

"I will."

"I'll come, just in case."

Lucio looks at him. "All right," he says. "I'll go."

Dante shrugs. "Never mind, she'll be glad to see you. One thing about dames, they're always glad to see you. Even if they don't want to see you, they're glad to see you."

"What's that mean?"

"Never mind," says Dante. "Listen to your cousin."

Early the next morning Lucio finds himself standing on the third floor of the Darling Building, listening to the sound of sewing machines hammering away on the floor above. He is standing in front of Gutman's frosted glass door, and once again he is trying to decide what to do. Finally he knocks, and the sound of his hand on the glass makes him think that he shouldn't be here. That it has all been a mistake and he should leave, that he had no business being here in the first place. He turns and starts walking down the hall, but then the door opens and Ruthie is there. She has been waiting for him, he realizes, standing on the other side of the glass door and watching his shadow. It is the first time in a week that he has seen her, but it feels much longer, and he is struck again by her beauty; it makes him helpless the way it did when she waited for him that night by the garbage cans. She is wearing her grey dress, and looking very like a shop girl. For a moment both stand and look at each other. In the distance there is the sound of the newsboys with the morning papers, beginning their rounds.

"You're pretty," he tells her.

"You sound like you mean that," she says. He looks down, embarrassed; she is right, the compliment leapt from him as if he had been thinking it for a long time and had only now got around to saying it. "Gutman's gone," she tells him.

"Dead?"

This makes her laugh, and when she laughs she seems to change. "No," she says, "to Queens, with Leo Bernstein."

"That's good."

"You want to come in?"

He steps inside. Her desk is as orderly as it ever was, a copy of *Das Kapital* in the centre, like something on display. "You know," he tells her, "I thought you'd be different, you'd be running around. More excited. This is a big day for you—you've been waiting for this a long time."

"I know, that's the problem. Now that it's here, I don't know." She walks inside, and he follows her to the big window at the far end of the room, standing beside her as she stares down at Spadina Avenue. "Five minutes," she tells him, and now he can hear how nervous she is. "When Mr. Gutman left a couple of days ago, I went straight back to the shops with my sandwiches. In and out, you know, ten shops in a day. Some of the time I had no sardines, nothing, just bread. The girls took them anyway." She turns away from the window. "The word got out—now we'll have to see." She realizes that Lucio is not listening to her. "What is it?" she says. "What's wrong?"

He doesn't reply. Head cocked to one side, he doesn't move. "Listen," he tells her. "They stopped."

Then she hears it. Nothing—the hammering of the sewing

machines upstairs has stopped. She makes a small choking sound, which makes Lucio think the shock has been too much, that she has become ill. Then she turns and looks out the window, down at the wide street below, which is slowly filling with people. They hear the sound of feet on the stairs of the Darling Building, running from the fourth and fifth and six and seventh floors, on their way out of the building and into the street. Voices whispering as they pass the door of Gutman Fur, nervous laughter, and out on Spadina Ruthie sees an old man with a bagful of groceries caught on the sidewalk, unable to get through the crowd, which soon extends into the middle of the street. The sound of police whistles. There are now so many people that they are stopping traffic, standing in front of cars and streetcars, and even the police horses cannot move. Circles of women and men, smoking, standing with their arms crossed, waiting, most of them holding leaflets.

"You did it!" Lucio shouts.

He kisses her, and just as he finishes kissing her, while his lips are still touching hers but they are not quite kissing any longer, the sewing machines in the shop upstairs start up again. And just like that, the people out on Spadina don't matter to Ruthie in the least.

"It can't be," says Lucio. "It must be a mistake."

On Spadina there is silence, as if not just the traffic but time itself has come to a halt. But that is outside. Inside the Darling Building it is again a day like any other. It is business as usual. Before long the demonstration below begins to break up. The girls have walked out of the shops but, as there is no one there to speak to them, no one to lead them to anything, there is nothing to do but go back inside and work. An hour later, except for a number of Ruthie's leaflets littering the street, there is no sign that anything happened.

"It was still a big deal," says Lucio. "You did it. You did what you wanted to do."

"That's the problem—it wasn't what they needed."

"I mean what you set out to do—you made it happen."

Ruthie shakes her head.

"It was big," he insists. "It'll be in all the papers tomorrow."

"Yes, the papers were there. I called them." Ruthie sits on the window sill, her back to Spadina. "Otherwise it's like it didn't happen."

The two remain like that for a long time, Ruthie sitting on the window ledge and Lucio standing in front of her with his hands spread, trying to think of something to say. Then he walks over and lifts her down from the window. He picks her up and carries her over to the desk. With a single sweep of his arm he knocks everything—the telephone, the pencils, the copy of Das Kapital—onto the floor. She says nothing as he lifts her grey dress up and over her head. Underneath she has on only her rough, homemade linen underpants, and he slips them off as she lies back on the desk, and then there is nothing separating them.

That night Lucio falls asleep immediately.

Despite Nonna's snoring, despite the sound of raccoons making their heavy way across the roof, despite the fact that the following Monday he is going to have to pitch for the Lizzies in the Toronto Junior Championship at Christie Pits, for once he sleeps soundly—until he wakes up with a start to find Father McElarney sitting in a chair next to his bed.

"What are you doing?" whispers Lucio. "How did you get in here?"

"How do you think?"

"How should I know?" says Lucio.

"How?" says the old priest. "Indeed."

Lucio looks over at Nonna's bed. She is still snoring away. Father McElarney puts a finger to his lips. "It's no problem to get inside, you know, just up the fire escape and in through the window. Even an old man like me can do it. There's really nothing to it."

"What do you want?" says Lucio, suddenly afraid.

"No," says Father McElarney, "it's what do you want?"

"Listen," says Lucio, "it's not me who snuck into my room."

"Maybe not," says the priest, "but I think it's you who wants to talk to me." Nonna shifts in her sleep, and says something in Italian. "So? What've you to say?"

"What do you want me to say?"

"Are you going to make a confession?"

Lucio looks at him.

"Now," says the priest, "before you do, before you say anything at all, let me say that I know you were the one to move the statue of San Bonorio, and that you snuck in up the fire escape."

"You know that?" says Lucio.

Father McElarney shrugs, and cannot quite stop himself from smiling. "The Church must examine the circumstances of every miracle before anything decisive is done about it. I must make it my business to know."

"But you haven't done anything," says Lucio. "You haven't told anyone."

"There's where you're wrong. Not telling anyone about your

involvement, not saying anything—these are both examples of my doing something."

"Then you know it wasn't a miracle," says Lucio.

"I don't know," says Father McElarney. "What's a miracle?"

"How should I know?"

"A miracle," the priest tells him, "is an event that creates faith. That is the purpose and the nature of miracles. They may seem very wonderful, entirely inexplicable even, to the people who witness them, like your *nonna*, but very simple to those who perform them. Like yourself, I'm sure. I'm fairly certain that the movement of the statue was an inadvertency on your part. You simply forgot to replace it. But that is beside the point. What matters is what that inadvertency produces. If it creates or confirms faith, then it is a true miracle."

"Even when it's a fake?"

"A fake is something that deceives," Father McElarney tells him. "An event that creates faith, an occurrence that brings those it touches closer to God, does not deceive. Therefore it is not a fake. It is a miracle."

"So," says Lucio, "are you saying you're not going to tell anyone about it?"

"And," says Father McElarney, "that you've nothing to confess."

Lucio does not know what to say.

The priest stands up, makes a slight bow and turns toward the door. Then he turns back. "If, however, you do decide to say something," he says, "if you decide you must tell people that it was you who moved the statue, I will have no choice but to say that I knew it all along, and to demonstrate"—he holds up his black book—"that all along I have been building precisely that case. Then I will have no choice but to prosecute you to the fullest extent, which I will allow you to imagine. Are we understood?"

"You're not going to tell anyone?" says Lucio, very softly.

"Not if you don't," says the priest. "This is, after all, the Depression. The Church needs all the miracles it can get."

Lucio looks at the priest for a long moment. "Deal," he says.

Father McElarney smiles. "Good luck at the ball game. It's been a long time since the Lizzies made it to the finals at Christie Pits."

"Christie Pits," whispers Lucio, nearly to himself. "Do you believe in luck?" he asks, turning back to Father McElarney, only to find that the old priest has disappeared—gone, out the open door like a wisp of smoke, or a ghost.

FIFTEEN

NAMED AFTER WILLIAM MELLIS CHRISTIE, co-founder in 1861 of the Christie and Brown Cookie Company, Christie Pits is located at the corner of Christie and Bloor, near the city limits.

It was once a gravel and clay mine, but the mineral reserves of the pit were declared exhausted in the winter of 1909, and Mr. Christie—who was then known as the man in charge of the Christie Mining Company but would, in the latter half of the twentieth century, gain a reputation with children in Southern Ontario for making "good cookies"—donated the pit to the city of Toronto.

Finding itself in possession of a large, empty gravel pit, the city of Toronto did the only reasonable thing: it turned the pit into a baseball diamond.

With the exception of a single large hill in the northern corner of the park (which was thereafter mysteriously referred to as the "camel's hump"), the city levelled the ground at the bottom of the pit, planted grass, installed a backstop and put in bleachers, a scoreboard and two dugouts.

It was not long before people forgot all about the Christie Mining Company. Still, Mr. Christie's name stuck, despite the city's attempt to rename the place Willowvale Park. Soon known as the best baseball field in the city, it was the site where the Toronto Junior Championships were played every year. And the more people forgot about Mr. Christie, the more remarkable the park seemed—like a natural wonder created millions of years before, along with the Grand Canyon, in the meteor shower that wiped out the dinosaurs.

On the day of the finals, people begin to arrive at the ballpark just after noon, for it is well known that by six in the evening, when the game is scheduled to start, not only the bleachers but the hillsides behind them will be filled. So people make their way there early, coming from all over, from the east and west of the city, from the suburbs to the north, from Kingston and from Hamilton, the great steeltown to the west, and from as far away as Ottawa. They come with umbrellas, wide-brimmed straw hats and fedoras, with checkered table-cloths and lawn chairs. They spread the tablecloths on the sloping grass hillsides and eat cold chicken or boiled eggs or cheese sandwiches, or *fritata* in doughy Italian buns bought from the Bucci Bakery, or *challah* left over from *Shabbes* dinner, or sardines on onion-rye bread, or peaches that chicken trucks ferried in early to Kensington Market from Niagara. There is also a good deal of smoking going on, and even drinking, despite two policemen walking back and forth across the diamond on the lookout for anyone in violation of Toronto's newly declared temperance laws. Many in the bleachers are carrying tiny flasks somewhere in the folds of their clothes, filled with a substance they call rye, which is really raw alcohol flavoured with brown sugar and tea—the kind of stuff that burns the throat going down, making you jubilant at first but mean as a snake later.

Just beyond right field, on the camel's hump, are amassing a number of boys wearing brown shirts.

Michelangelo and Nonna arrive just after two-thirty, and sit down behind home plate. They are both carrying briefcases, which Michelangelo has contrived to borrow from some of the bootleggers at the garage. In Michelangelo's briefcase there are four Coca-Cola bottles filled with homemade wine; in Nonna's briefcase there is the following: a large dried Calabrese sausage, a one-pound hunk of salty cascaval cheese, several tomatoes and an onion.

"Lucio," Michelangelo shouts, as they sit down.

Lucio has arrived earlier and is standing on the mound, partly because he has never stood there before and he wants to have a chance to do so before the game begins. He looks over and sees that they have brought the statue with them. San Bonorio has a seat of his own, propped up on the bleachers, facing the field.

Lucio goes over. "What are you doing here?" he says.

"*Bo*," says Michelangelo. "We brought San Bonorio."

Lucio looks at the statue; like the chicken he is holding, San Bonorio has about him a placid self-confidence that comes, Lucio supposes, from being a statue, from knowing that, no matter what happens, at the end of it he will still be a statue. "Well," says Lucio, "I need all the help I can get."

Which are the same words he used earlier today, when he informed Goody that he'd asked Dubie to be manager. "It was Dubie," he said, "who moved the statue."

"So it was Dubie who did the miracle?"

Lucio nodded.

"You think it could happen again, like your throw?"

"Who knows?" said Lucio. "But I need all the help I can get."

"Then manager he is," said Goody.

The two policemen stand with their backs to the field, scanning the crowd for troublemakers. There is every reason, they know, to expect trouble. Word is already out around the city that something is going to happen, and boys from all over are making their way to Christie Pits. During the night, the group of toughs who call themselves the Swastika Club snuck onto the baseball field and painted a swastika on the top of the clubhouse. When it was discovered this morning, the city rushed to paint over the emblem, knowing that if it was still there when the crowds arrived, there was no telling what would happen.

Dubie arrives an hour and a half before the game in his manager's uniform. He is looking considerably better than he did yesterday; when he returned home, Mazie went quickly to work, despite his protestations, changing the dressing on his hand and replacing the grey, torn bandage that had fallen off at Altman's Deli. But more than that, Dubie is steadier, rejuvenated at finding himself in a Lizzies uniform on the morning they take on the great St. Peter's team—the team of which even Goody Altman is afraid—for the championship. Dubie lay awake last night, imagining himself into his new role of manager—his missing finger, in such a situation, is an advantage, he tells himself, because it confers upon him the kind of wizened authority that settled upon the veterans of the Great War when they first returned. So it is that, in his first act as manager, he posts a batting order. Other than the appearance of Lucio at the end of it, it is no different from the batting order the Lizzies have used for the whole of the season, and Dubie—like the rest of the Lizzies, like most everyone in the Ward—knows who is up without having to consult the list.

Still, he writes it down; the act of posting the list, of pressing the thumbtack into the soft plaster inside the dugout, gives him the sense that he is taking charge of the situation.

This is the batting order:

1) IZZY (Shortstop)
2) IGNATIUS (Second Base)
3) SPINNY (First Base)
4) GOODY (Catcher)
5) GRIEF (Left Field)
6) LITTLE GUIDO (Right Field)
7) MORDECHAI (Third Base)
8) MILTON (Centre Field)
9) LUCIO (Pitcher)

As he is doing this, Dubie hears a sound behind him, coming from the top of the dugout. He looks up and sees his father setting up a lawn chair on the roof. Asher, he sees, has with him the black bag with the word Greenstein embroidered on it.

"Dad," says Dubie. "What're you doing?"

"What's it look like?" says Asher. "I'm here to watch a baseball game."

"You're not going to sell the knives here," says Dubie.

"How's the hand?"

"The hand's fine," says Dubie. "Don't think I don't see the bag."

Asher looks at the bag and shrugs, like an addict. "You never know," he says.

"Not here," says Dubie. "Not during the baseball game. There's no selling in baseball."

"You ask me," says Asher, "it's all selling."

Dubie looks at his father.

"Fine," says Asher. "You say no selling, I say no selling. You won't be sorry."

"Good," says Dubie, uncomfortable that he, who has never won an argument with his father, has won this argument so easily. He steps back into the dugout and sits down to think about it. Mostly, he is worried about what his father meant when he said Dubie wouldn't be sorry.

Meanwhile the Lizzies are arriving. One by one they step into the dugout, see the batting order and see Dubie standing there authoritatively. Because they know the story about Ruthie and Lucio, and how Mordechai hit him, they acknowledge his presence with oblique, awkward nods, glancing surreptitiously at him and his bandaged hand.

"Dubie," says Spinny Weinreb, finally, "you all right?"

"Other than the hand, I can't complain," says Dubie, holding up the bandage.

The Lizzies, uncomfortable at being made to look directly at his hand while he is watching them, laugh unanimously.

"So," Spinny asks him, still with a smile on his face, "what're you doing here?"

"I'm your manager."

There is silence in the dugout; the last game of the season is no time to break in a new manager. They got this far without a manager, why do they need one now? What does Dubie know, anyway—has the chopping off of his finger caused him to lose his mind?

"Hold on," says Spinny. "Does Goody know? We don't have a manager usually, is all—the way it works is, we all make the decisions."

"Goody's the one that told me," says Dubie.

Goody is behind home plate, taking throws from Lucio. But Goody is not watching Lucio; he is catching the pitches and returning the ball to Lucio without looking right at him. Instead, Goody is staring at a tall, athletic boy in the outfield with jet black hair, wearing a St. Peter's uniform. This boy is named Elmer Querques. Elmer is eighteen years old, and already he is what he will always be: the best baseball player the city of Toronto will ever produce. He is also, however, one of the dumbest baseball players ever produced anywhere.

And Elmer is a virgin.

Suffice it to say that Elmer Querques is able to throw a base-ball at a hundred miles an hour, but if you were to ask him, at any given time, what the count was on a batter, how many balls and how many strikes, he would be at an utter loss. Elmer can hit anything, and can throw with deadly accuracy with his eyes closed, but often runs directly to second base. Still, in an absolute sense, in terms of pure ability, Elmer is the best, and Goody knows this.

"If you want," Dubie tells Spinny, "go ask Goody."

Spinny looks over and sees Goody watching Elmer. Spinny was there during the regular season when Goody batted against Elmer—who, as well as being St. Peter's best hitter, is also their pitcher—and Goody struck out three times in a row. Spinny was sitting on the bench when Goody came walking back into the dugout after he struck out that final time, and found himself unable to look at him. After the game, which the Lizzies lost, Goody went straight home without speaking to anyone. Spinny felt relieved, for the whole time Goody had been up at bat, Spinny had been trying to think of what he was going to say about Goody being second-best—and he had come up with nothing.

"That's OK," Spinny tells Dubie. "I believe you."

By five the bleachers are full, and people are beginning to sit on the grassy hillsides. One of the last seats in the bleachers goes to Father McElarney, who finds himself sitting beside Harold Diamond and Esther Nodelman. Not caring in the least who sees them, the couple are already kissing when the priest sits down. Harold is wearing a bright tweed suit that Esther picked out for him from the Timothy Eaton's catalogue, and a squat fedora that is instantly recognizable anywhere in Canada in 1933 as a King Clancy hat, named after a hockey player recently purchased by Conn Smythe and the Toronto Maple Leafs for the monstrous sum of thirty thousand dollars. When Esther throws her arms around Harold, the King Clancy hat is knocked off his head, landing in Father McElarney's lap. For the duration of the game the discomfited priest sits with the hat on his lap, holding it gingerly, as if it were the couple's child.

In the dugout, Milton Weathervane is looking at the batting order. "Whose idea was this?"

"Mine," says Dubie.

"What're you doing here?"

"I'm manager," says Dubie.

"Manager of what?" Dubie lets out a laugh. "Of us?" says Milton. "Of the Lizzies? What do we need a manager for?"

"It's Goody's idea," Spinny tells him.

"Fat chance," says Milton, who is about to walk across the field to ask Goody why he wasn't consulted when there is a commotion behind him.

"I can't do it," Mazie Diamond is saying. "I can't reach—it's too high."

"Well," says Asher from atop the dugout, "what am I going to do?"

Milton makes a quick, angry movement with his hands, as if he is going to pull his hair out of his head.

"Hold on," says Dubie. He puts out his hand but remembers the bandage, and gets down on all fours, turning himself into a stepstool.

"Thank you," says Mazie, stepping onto her son's back and reaching up so Asher can pull her the rest of the way.

Dubie is about to get up when he feels a second foot on his back. Abe Nodelman is hoisted up, and after him, Lucio's mother.

"Well," says Sadie when they are all seated, "this isn't Beverley Street."

Dubie returns to the dugout, sitting down on the bench with his head in his hands. Guido Bucci sits down beside him. "Dubie," he says, "I just want you to know, you need to get rid of anybody, I'll do it."

"Can you get rid of my father?" says Dubie.

Guido stands up.

"No, listen," says Dubie. "It was a joke."

Guido sits back down. "Listen," he tells Dubie, more intensely, taking hold of Dubie's arm. "I know you're a Jew. That's OK, nobody's perfect"—Little Guido stops himself, considers this statement, then rephrases it—"I see what you're doing, and I respect what you're doing. Before you came, we were like a bunch of babies in the desert, you know, going here and there, and any time we needed to do something, we had to have a big talk. *Basta,* I say, *basta!*"

Dubie looks at him.

"I say, *basta,*" says Little Guido, still with his arm on Dubie's.

"I hear you," says Dubie.

"I've seen you with the knives, the way you talk, and I

know you got the same love for the engine as me. The engine of progress."

Dubie smiles an awkward half-smile.

"You are going to take us onto the engine, and into the twentieth century."

"I'll try," says Dubie.

"Just remember, if anyone says anything you don't like," he tells Dubie, taking out a cigarette and walking down to the far end of the dugout, "you tell me, and I'll take care of it."

"It's good to know," says Dubie.

From near third base there is applause. Dubie looks over and sees Grief Henderson, wearing a flowing black cape. He is doing a magic trick that consists of pulling mice out of a large soup bowl, which Grief has painted black in order to make it look like a bowler hat. It is not a particularly impressive trick, for the mice are small and dirty and Grief is quite plainly pushing the mice up through a false bottom in the bowl. But the woman he is performing it for does not mind. This is because she was blind until recently. She is standing in the middle of left field, on her way to the bleachers behind home plate, where Michelangelo and Nonna are saving seats for her and her five unmarried sons, all of whom make no secret of their feeling that their mother is being far too appreciative of the trick.

"Ma," says Primo, "he's pushing them up through the bottom."

"Look at the little mouse," says Mrs. Greico. "Such a cute little mouse."

"You should make the mice disappear," Secondo tells Grief. "Now, that's something I'd pay money for."

Lucio and Goody return to the dugout.

"So," Mordechai asks his brother. "What's this I hear about a manager?" Goody shrugs. "Who made you king?"

"Nobody," says Goody. "That's the whole point: I'm not the king, Dubie is."

"Hear that?" Asher can be heard saying atop the dugout.

"Why they would want a king," says Abe Nodelman, "you'll have to tell me. You ask me, it's the ones that want a king that's the problem."

"Watch it," says Asher. "That's my son you're talking about."

Inside the dugout, Mordechai is saying to Goody, "The point is, we don't need a manager."

"That's what you think," Dubie says. "I got a few tricks up my sleeve."

"What kind of tricks?" says Grief Henderson, who has just come in.

"Not those kind of tricks," says Dubie. "Baseball kind of tricks."

"You're *meshuga*," Mordechai tells him. "And a *schmuck*."

Before Dubie can reply, someone stands up in the outfield and shouts, "*Heil Hitler*."

Mordechai turns. The two police officers walk in the direction of the shout, but there are so many people milling around that they cannot tell who said what, or even where the shout came from. "It must be the Swastikas," says Mordechai. "I'd like them to come here and say that. Then I'd show them."

"I'd start with the nose," says Milton, who considers himself an expert on such matters. "I'd take the nose, and I'd pull it to one side. And I'd say, how do you like that?"

"The nose is good," says Mordechai. "But not as good as the fingers."

Before this discussion can progress very far, the umpire walks onto the field and the crowd hushes. Goody walks out for the coin toss, and Lucio watches him making his way to the mound. Then Lucio throws up on Dubie's shoes.

"What the hell?" says Dubie.

"Sorry, Dubie," says Lucio, straightening up. "I didn't mean to."

"What's going on down there?" says Francesca, from atop the dugout.

"I'm fine," says Lucio.

"Hold on," she says, "I'm coming down."

A moment later, she is lowering herself into the dugout. She is wearing a black skirt that bunches up at the waist as she climbs down, to reveal a set of knees that are quite spectacular. All the boys, but most especially Spinny Weinreb, watch.

"I don't think you should play," Francesca tells her son.

"Please, not now," says Lucio. "You have to go. You're not allowed in the dugout. The rules say that the only people allowed in the dugout are the people on the team." He turns to his teammates for support, but finds that they do not seem at all inclined to tell her to leave.

"I hate to say it," says Spinny Weinreb shyly, "but he's right. The Babe, they say, got so nervous he puked before every game."

"Well, I don't know this Babe," says Lucio's mother, "but if he jumped off a bridge, would you?"

The Lizzies stare back at her in admiring silence.

"If I can't get an answer from the rest of you," Francesca says, "I'm going to talk to Dubie. Now listen," she tells him. "You're supposed to be in charge of this outfit, which means that if anything, and I mean anything, happens to Lucio, it's your fault."

Dubie looks down at his dirty shoes.

"You hear me, Dubie?"

Dubie says he does.

Feeling she has made her point, Francesca asks for someone to help her return to her seat up top. Spinny jumps up and lifts her. "Thank you," she tells him. "That was thoughtful."

"I'm Spinny," he says.

"I'm Lucio's mother," she says.

Spinny blushes and cannot speak.

Out on the field, the ump is introducing Goody Altman (the second-best baseball player the city of Toronto will ever produce) to Elmer Querques (the best baseball player the city of Toronto will ever produce), and getting ready for the toss.

"You call it," says the ump to Goody, knowing from experience that it is next to impossible to explain to Elmer Querques how a coin toss works.

"Heads," calls Goody.

The coin comes down and the ump catches it in the palm of his hand, slapping it on his forearm. Inside the dugout on the other side of the field, the St. Peter's team—who know how difficult it is to get from Elmer an account of what happened during a coin toss—watch, and decide, when the Lizzies emerge from the dugout with their gloves on, that they are up first.

"Play ball!" calls the umpire.

The crowd cheers, and all around there is the whispering that is the prelude to all baseball games. Lucio heads out to the mound, staring at the ground as he walks and taking small, delicate steps, as if he is making his way along a narrow, barely floating plank. After he has finished swinging the bat, St. Peter's first batter, a lanky kid named Gord Noble with hair parted down the middle of his head, steps to the plate. Goody pulls his catcher's mask down, and the umpire leans forward on the balls of his feet, anticipating the first pitch.

Lucio throws, and the batter swings.

It is a high line drive over third base.

Base hit.

There is a cheer when Gord Noble reaches first—a number of St. Peter's supporters are sitting along the first-base line—and a disappointed silence from the crowd of Lizzie supporters who are sitting across from them behind third base. The boys in the brown shirts are cheering fiercely, and do not stop when the ball is thrown back to Lucio. No one expected a no-hitter, but they did not expect this either. Lucio kicks at the dirt on the mound.

"All right, Lucio," calls Goody over the cheering. "Don't worry about it."

"Play ball," shouts the ump.

The second batter for St. Peter's is a tiny boy named George Lunt. Lucio recognizes him as the boy with the fancy collar at the previous game, who bobbed up and down with the swastika flag. Lucio gets into his stance and throws the ball. It hits the boy in the ear.

"Take your base," says the ump.

"I'll get you, kike," the boy says to Lucio as he is walking to first base. "You watch it."

"Oh, yeah," Spinny, the first baseman, says, "we're scared." After he says this, Spinny looks up at Lucio, smiles and winks, but Lucio does not smile or wink back. Lucio, it seems to Spinny, *does* look scared.

"Kike," the tiny boy says. Then he turns to Spinny. "You too," he says.

"Play ball," calls the ump.

Lucio is rattled. He was not trying to hit the boy, but the thought had crossed his mind, and it happened. He does not regret having hit him, but wishes there weren't two men on base. He also wishes he could throw with that kind of accuracy on purpose. Nothing to do about it now, he tells himself, and takes a deep breath. He gets into his stance and checks the runner at first. While he is doing this, the runner on second takes off for third, and he is already there, standing up, by the time Lucio realizes what has happened.

"Lucio," calls Goody, "just throw the ball."

Feeling that he is losing even the tiny bit of control he has on the game, Lucio goes into his windup and throws the ball as hard as he can, without even looking at the man on first, or at the batter or even at Goody.

This is, as it turns out, the wrong thing to do. For as the ball leaves his hand, Lucio notices that the batter to whom he is throwing is none other than Elmer Querques.

Elmer hits the first home run of the afternoon.

A moment later, the scoreboard clacks into place:

| 3 - - | - - - | - - - | (ST. PETER'S) |
| - - - | - - - | - - - | (ELIZABETH STREET PLAYGROUND) |

After a miraculous catch by Grief in left field and a complicated play at third base in which Mordechai reaches blindly behind his back to tag out a runner, the inning ends. "Looks like it's going to be a long night," says Goody, not quite to himself, as the Lizzies run into the dugout.

Izzy Au, the leadoff batter for the Lizzies, steps to the plate. Elmer Querques throws three strikes, then three more strikes to Izzy's brother, Ignatius, then one ball (low and outside, just missing the strike zone) and three strikes to Spinny Weinreb. End of inning. The Lizzies, all of them, have struck out. Three up, three down.

St. Peter's comes up to bat.

Lucio walks the first batter. The second hits a short blooper over Ignatius Au's head for a base hit. There are runners, again, on first and second. Worried that this is going to be a repeat of the first inning, Lucio does not check the baserunners, and instead pitches as quickly as he can. The St. Peter's batter con-nects, sending a low dribbler toward second base. Ignatius Au fields it and flips it to his brother, who steps on second base and throws to Spinny, who throws to Mordechai at third.

Triple play.

"Now that's more like it," shouts Dubie, standing up in the dugout. The Lizzie supporters finally have something to cheer about.

But not for long.

The Lizzies come up to bat again, and this time Elmer Querques throws thirteen pitches: three strikes (to Goody), three strikes (to Grief), four balls (to Little Guido—who, being considerably shorter, even than the Au twins, has an almost non-existent strike zone) and three strikes (to Mordechai).

Just as the Lizzies are emerging from the dugout, a voice calls, "Get used to it, sheenie, you little piece of shit."

A fight breaks out on the hillside behind the bleachers. The umpire stops the game, and Lucio watches as two police-men march up into the bleachers. A moment later the policemen return, each pulling a boy by the scruff of his neck. One of them is Meyer Rubin, the boy who was fourth in line that day at the Elizabeth Street playground, just behind the Bucci chil-dren. Meyer's lip is bleeding, and he appears to be missing one of his front teeth. Still, he looks very happy.

"Give them hell, Lucio," Meyer shouts as he is being hauled away.

By the time the bottom of the sixth inning arrives, the Lizzies are losing by seven. This is what the scoreboard looks like:

3 0 1   1 1 1   - - -   (ST. PETER'S)
0 0 0   0 0 -   - - -   (ELIZABETH STREET PLAYGROUND)

Since the triple play in the second, St. Peter's has managed to score each time they have come up to bat. The Lizzies, on the other hand, have yet to touch a single one of Elmer's blistering fastballs and, except for Little Guido (who walked a second time) and Izzy Au (who bolted to first base after one of Elmer's pitches was dropped by the catcher), they have yet to get on base. Now they are up again, and back at the top of the batting order. Izzy Au goes out for his third at-bat.

"Listen, Izzy," says Goody as Izzy walks past, "he's throwing fastballs. Very fast fastballs. So this is what you do—the moment he starts to move, you start to swing."

"At what?"

"At nothing, but right down the middle," says Goody. "He's throwing the balls right down the middle. But don't worry about that. Don't worry about seeing the ball. Just pretend it's there and swing, and by the time the bat's there, the ball will be there too."

At the plate, Izzy gets set and lifts the bat to his shoulder.

Elmer goes into his windup, throws, and even before the ball is out of his hand, even before Elmer can bring up his leg, Izzy is swinging, and connects, sending the ball over the head of the second baseman.

The Lizzies have a hit.

This brings up Ignatius, who does the same thing—swinging at an empty space over the centre of the plate, where he believes the baseball will eventually arrive—and hits to the opposite field. A grounder that goes between first and second, a base hit. There are now men on first and second. Elmer is looking worried, but all the same throws the same pitch to Spinny Weinreb, who sends one over the head of the shortstop. The bases are loaded. And then Goody steps up to bat. Elmer winds up and delivers. Goody sends the first pitch over the fence. The scoreboard clacks. It now reads:

3 0 1	1 1 1	- - -	(ST. PETER'S)
0 0 0	0 0 4	- - -	(ELIZABETH STREET PLAYGROUND)

As dull as Elmer Querques is, it does not take him long to understand that the Lizzies have figured out how to hit his fastballs. And just like that, with the facility that makes him the best baseball player the city of Toronto will ever produce, he changes the way he is pitching. Instead of fastballs, Elmer throws breaking balls that veer wildly off to the left at the last minute. Curveballs that appear, at first, to be heading away from the plate. Split-fingered fastballs that sink, at the last moment, below the knees. And so, after Goody's home run, it takes Elmer only nine pitches to end the inning.

Which is to say that, with the game half over, the Lizzies are still losing by three. As the seventh inning begins, things start looking very bad. After managing to get the first two batters for St. Peter's to fly out, Lucio walks the next three, loading the bases once more. The crowd grows quiet with anticipation, knowing that if four more runs are scored against the Lizzies the game is as good as over, and the batter—a thin boy who plays right field for St. Peter's—steps into the box, swinging the bat menacingly.

Lucio gets ready and throws. The pitch travels toward home plate, right where the batter wants it, and that is when Asher stands up, as he has been planning to do since he arrived and installed himself atop the dugout, despite his son's protestations. He has waited and watched, and now he moves quickly, and in the time it takes the pitch to travel from Lucio's fingertips to home plate, Asher not only produces the pineapple from the black sack with the word Greenstein embroidered on it, but puts it on his lawn chair—which turns out not to be a lawn chair at all, but a whitewashed pedestal, a smaller version of the one that stands beside the Diamond booth at the St. Lawrence Market.

"In a minute," says Asher in his booming salesman voice, when the pitch is some five feet away from the batter, talking to everyone but really addressing the batter, "I'll get to *that*."

The batter looks. The crowd looks.

"Strike one," calls the umpire.

Dubie sees everyone at Christie Pits looking at his father, and says nothing. Then Goody throws the ball back to Lucio, and Lucio goes into his windup.

"Now," says Asher, turning the pineapple on its side, "*this* is going to be something."

"Strike two," calls the ump. He, too, is looking at Asher.

Goody throws the ball back to Lucio, who gets ready and throws.

Asher is now standing with the knife over his head. He freezes for a moment, poised, and then brings the knife down on the pineapple, which makes a hollow, plastic sound, and the batter, along with everyone else present, realizes that Asher Diamond's pineapple is not a pineapple at all.

"Strike three," calls the umpire.

The top of the seventh ends.

The crowd—the Lizzies' side of the crowd, anyway—goes wild. But then the umpire calls time out and marches over to the Lizzies' dugout. "You're out," he yells up at Asher.

"What?" says Asher. "What'd I do?"

"Get walking!"

"All right, all right," says Asher, taking Mazie's hand, "we're leaving."

There's a growing sense of impatience in the crowd while Dubie's parents are helped down from the roof of the dugout.

"Good luck," Asher tells Dubie. Dubie seems about to say something to his father. "Never mind," says Asher, before he can. "We're going."

Dubie, standing outside the dugout, watches his father and mother make their way up the side of the hill toward Christie Street, on their way home. His father carries the heavy bag filled with knives, and turnips and carrots and fake pineapples, and *The Complete Works of William Shakespeare,* and a hundred other things necessary to sell Greenstein's Remarkable Knives. He sees the two of them stop to rest for a while, his mother standing on tiptoe, fanning his father with an Oriental fan he bought for her years before Dubie was born, at the Canadian National Exhibition, when Mazie was still living with her father in Richmond Hill and Asher was still a broom salesman.

"Play ball!" calls the ump.

It is the bottom of the seventh; the Lizzies are back up at bat.

This time it takes Elmer only four pitches to end the inning: Milton flies to centre field, Lucio strikes out (swinging

wildly at pitches that are nowhere near the plate), and Izzy, trying to bunt, hits a tiny popup right into Elmer's glove. The
eighth inning is no better. Although all three St. Peter's batters hit long pop flies into the outfield for easy outs, the Lizzies
still cannot score. Ignatius strikes out, and then Spinny
valiantly steps in front of one of Elmer's fastballs. The ball hits
him in the middle of the back, and the umpire tells him to take
a base. With Spinny at first, Goody gets a second hit—but
then Grief strikes out to bring the inning to a close.

"We've got to do something," says Goody, as the Lizzies
take the field for the top of the ninth inning. "If you've got any
tricks, now's the time."

"Don't worry," says Dubie.

"We'll see," says Goody, taking his glove. On his way to
home plate he says, "Come on, Burke, show them what we've
got."

We, thinks Lucio, and throws his first pitch. The batter
connects for an easy base hit to right field, but Lucio doesn't
seem to mind. He is trying to imagine what it would be like if
this were true. If there were a *we*. This is no easy thing. He has
always been the kid with half a name: not quite a wop, but not
quite anything else either. A kid from nowhere in a country
where everyone is from somewhere. If Lucio had been born in
another time, he would have considered himself Canadian. He
was not born in another time. He throws another pitch. The
second batter swings and hits a quick line drive toward third
base. Izzy knocks it down and throws to Spinny at first.

"One out," calls the ump.

"All right," says Goody. "Now we're cooking with gas."

Lucio is thinking back to those Saturday mornings when
he sat across from Asher in Altman's Deli, wishing himself a

different person. He wished himself a Jew. And it has happened; he has become Bloomberg. In a manner of speaking. Lucio still does not know why or how it happened—why he was able to throw the baseball that one time with such deadly accuracy and precision, and then never again. Not in his wildest dreams had he imagined himself capable of such a thing. But he also had never imagined himself not capable of it. He had dreamed of other things. He had dreamed of Ruthie, and of the animals on the roof, and sometimes of the tiny room where Nonna once lived with his mother and uncle in the New York tenement, a room he has never seen. But the ball rolled toward him and he picked it up. Now all he wants is to get out of the inning.

"Play ball," calls the umpire.

Lucio sends a pitch, low and inside but in the strike zone.

The batter swings.

It is a short hopper between second and third. Izzy fields the ball, tags the man who is on his way to third for a second out, and throws to first in time to catch the batter.

The top of the ninth ends. The crowd is restless. Noisy. Wanting a winner. Wanting the game over. The scoreboard creaks into place, flipping up a final zero for St. Peter's. This is what it reads:

3 0 1   1 1 1   0 0 0   (ST. PETER'S)
0 0 0   0 0 4   0 0 -   (ELIZABETH STREET PLAYGROUND)

Which is to say that, as they go up to bat for the last time, the Lizzies are *still* losing by three runs.

Now it's the second half of the batting order, and Little Guido is the first one up. He gets a hit, and then so does

Mordechai, hitting an infield squibber that stops halfway down the third-base line and gets him on first base. Milton is up next, hitting a shallow blooper to left field. Base hit. The crowd is standing. The bases are now loaded, and the Lizzies are at the very bottom of their batting order.

Lucio Burke is next up.

Nobody is out: the Lizzies have three chances to win the game. Or to lose it. But none of this occurs to Lucio. So worried is he about having to get a hit, so convinced is he that he will not be able to hit the ball, to even touch it, that Elmer will blow three pitches past him without his even moving the bat—so shocking is it to him that in years to come the only thing anyone will remember about this baseball game is that he, Lucio Burke had a chance to win the game and then did not—that he doesn't realize until he is standing at home plate that he has been pulled out of the game.

"Hold on," the umpire tells him, looking in the direction of the Lizzies dugout. "There's a pinch-hitter coming in."

"A pinch-hitter?" says Lucio, turning around. "Who?"

Ruthie Nodelman walks out from behind the dugout.

"Ruthie?" says Lucio.

"Hello, Lucio," says Ruthie, walking past him.

Lucio turns to see Dubie coming out of the dugout, and understands that it is not he who has pulled Lucio out of the game. Nor is it Goody or Mordechai or any of the Lizzies. He realizes it is Ruthie herself who has made the decision. She has put herself into the game, decided that it is her moment to step up to the plate. Dubie comes out of the dugout in his role as manager, with the intention of putting a stop to it all, but then halts, and for a moment he and Ruthie stand together, not talking. Lucio walks over to them, and hands the bat to Ruthie, who is still looking to do the kind of thing that will make people think. "Good luck," says Dubie, and before Ruthie realizes it, he has leaned forward to kiss her, once and very nearly chastely, while Lucio looks on like a silent lover in a silent film.

And she lets him.

The crowd goes wild.

Inside the St. Peter's dugout there is a great deal of commotion. This is the first time in the history of the Toronto Junior Championships that a girl has ever entered the game. The St. Peter's coaching staff conclude that her coming into the game is not only a violation of the rules of baseball—you can't just throw anyone in at the last minute, much less a girl—but also a violation of propriety itself. So it is that as Ruthie takes the bat into her hands and approaches the plate, the St. Peter's manager emerges from the dugout with the clear intention of protesting her entrance into the game. His face is set. He paces purposefully over to the umpire, but just as he is opening his mouth, he looks at the scoreboard, looks over at Ruthie and changes his mind. "Never mind," he tells the ump. "They want a girl to bat, they get a girl." And he turns around and heads back to the dugout.

The ump shrugs as if to concede the point. Ruthie steps to the plate, takes a practice swing (hitting the bat off the underside of the beautiful, entirely bourgeois shoes she is wearing), and blows a kiss to Elmer Querques.

Who throws the ball straight up over the backstop, and into the lap of a statue.

"*Bo*," says Michelangelo. "It's a miracle."

"Ball one," calls the ump.

The Bucci children, who are watching the game from behind the backstop, fall to their knees.

There is a good deal of shouting when the umpire—and after the umpire, several members of the crowd—and after the crowd, the police—attempt to get Michelangelo to return the ball so the game can continue.

"Listen," says the umpire, "we need the ball to go on with the game."

"Over my dead body," says Michelangelo.

"And," says Nonna, "over my dead body."

"And my dead body," adds Primo, standing up out of the seat in front of the statue.

"And my dead body." Secondo stands up beside his brother.

"Also mine," says Scevola.

"And if the ball is moved, over my dead body," says Tommaso, already standing.

Quintillano is about to stand up and declare that the ball will be moved over his dead body also, when he sees that his mother is smiling and looking in the wrong direction.

"Mama," says Quintillano, waving his hand in front of her face.

"Sì," asks Mrs. Greico.

"Ma's blind again," Quintillano tells his brothers.

There is then a terrible moment when the brothers look, ready to dismiss this as impossible, and find that it isn't; their mother's eyes have clouded over once again.

When he sees this, Primo turns around, and reaches up to Michelangelo behind him, and takes the ball away. He lobs it back onto the field. Then he turns back.

"Bo," he says, breaking off San Bonorio's nose with his fingers, the plaster snapping with surprising ease, "see how you like that."

"Primo!" cues Nonna. "What're you doing?"

Primo tells her that his mother is blind again, and Nonna, who realizes she has again made the mistake of putting her faith in the old, unreliable saint, takes the statue in her arms and throws it off the side of the bleachers, head first. The statue hits the ground and bounces and rolls down the grassy hillside, unbroken.

"Anna," exclaims Michelangelo, "That's valuable."

"Sit down," Nonna tells him. "Nothing's going to happen to that thing."

"Play ball," calls the ump, throwing the ball to Elmer Querques.

Ruthie Nodelman steps back into the batter's box, and as she does, she lets down her hair. She runs her fingers through it, and at that moment the ballpark lights snap on, shining down on the field, catching the redness of Ruthie's hair, just as the sun did that morning at the Elizabeth Street playground.

Helpless, Elmer throws the slowest, weakest, easiest-to-hit pitch of his life.

Ruthie's swing starts, and it starts from the centre of her being. It starts twenty years before, when Abe and Sadie Nodelman are trying to convince the Timothy Eaton Company to pay its employees a living wage. It starts some sixty years before that, when Marx writes of a spectre sweeping through Europe, with the streets of Paris on fire, with revolution everywhere, and with Mary Wollstonecraft on the other side of the English Channel, pregnant but still vindicating the rights of women. I suppose it begins even before that, hundreds of thousands of years before, when people started telling each other stories with happy endings.

Elmer Querques's pitch does not have a chance.

The crowd rise to their feet, gazing at the ball as it soars over the centre-field fence, even over Bloor Street, blown by the wind all the way to College Street, where it bounces off the roof of a streetcar.

The Lizzies, all of them, are standing. Dubie is jumping up and down in the dugout, with Lucio beside him. Guido is skipping from third base toward home plate, dancing a partnerless tarantella. Mordechai takes off both his baseball cap and his yarmulke and throws them in the air, like someone graduating. Milton Weathervane is weeping like a baby, and the Au brothers are dancing with each other. Spinny cannot stop laughing. In the middle of it all, Ruthie is rounding second base, looking at the crowd—half of which is cheering and half of which is groaning—and thinking to herself that maybe, just maybe, it *is* baseball that is going to make people think. And at that moment, just beyond the home-run fence, along the side of the westernmost hill—the camel's hump—a group of boys in brown shirts unfurl a massive swastika flag.

Ruthie notices that the cheering has stopped. The crowd stand silent, staring. Realizing that something has happened, that something is happening, she stops running, turns around and sees for herself. The swastika is waving in the August wind—a much bigger swastika flag than she's ever seen. It is billowing, held aloft by a number of boys in brown shirts, and all around those boys there are more boys in brown shirts. Nobody says a thing, and then there appears a short red-haired boy who tries, single-handedly, to tear the flag down. From where she is standing, the boy looks impossibly alone, as if he simply happened to be walking by the baseball game, an innocent bystander who, confronted by the sight of a massive swastika, decided to do something about it. The red-haired boy takes hold of the flag, and a second later he is felled by an act of decisive violence. A heavy object—to Ruthie it looks like a brick—that one of the bigger brown-shirted boys is holding in both fists is smashed into the red-haired boy's Adam's apple, lifting him off his feet, several inches in the air.

And then, after the silence, the explosion.

All at once, people are shouting. The crowd spills onto the field, but Ruthie cannot tell what the shouts mean—whether the crowd is outraged or cheering, whether the sight of the red-haired boy's blood has produced a guttural, spontaneous howling. Still with her foot on second base, she is suddenly surrounded by the people who, a moment before, were watching the game, and she understands that all day long, waiting for the game to begin, a crowd has been trying to form. That for those not on the teams, the experience of the day has been one of anticipation, of being frustrated and contained, and that the appearance of the swastika has set them free—just as those waving the swastika have themselves been waiting, sitting for hours with their massive flag balled underneath them like an egg.

It is not any one person who decides that the swastika must be ripped out of the hands of the brown-shirted boys and torn to pieces. But that is the decision. All at once, the brown-shirted boys are running. As they move, Ruthie sees glinting sunlight, sees that many are carrying broken wine bottles. It happens in a moment, and in that moment everyone understands. All at once they move, their goal known and clearly marked, and near. Not far from her Ruthie sees Milton Weathervane break away from the pack, running, a bat in his hands, a grey blur headed toward the swastika and the home-run fence, which is in the process of being taken apart by the boys in brown shirts, the slats of wood handed out as weapons. Behind Milton are a number of boys she does not know, big and brawny and also running, vicious. Ruthie watches as a smaller boy catches his heel, tripping. Falling forward, he rolls and covers his head. His chin is popped back by a boot and he is knocked forward as another of the brown-shirted boys kicks him from behind. On the far side of the field she can see Mordechai bringing a baseball bat down hard into the centre of a boy's back. All around there is more of the same, and more and more people. Behind her in the bleachers she hears the sound of wood splintering. Turning, she sees that Dante's five unmarried uncles have lifted up their mother and have put her down in the space between Michelangelo and Nonna, where until recently San Bonorio had been. The brothers then tear out the bench itself, splintering the wood and carrying it up the steep hill toward Christie Street. As they run, the brothers nearly knock down a priest in a King Clancy hat, and a moment later, Father McElarney is lifted up as well and placed onto the bench beside Nonna, and the two sit placidly like an old married couple.

The crowd now carries Ruthie forward, and a moment later there is a sharp movement in the opposite direction. Pushed backwards, she understands that the boys carrying the swastika have changed direction, that they are intent on carrying the flag out onto the streets of Toronto. Something stings her, a sharp pain at the side of her head. She reaches up and sees that all around her people are doing the same—the other side has taken to throwing bottle caps with sharpened edges. Still the crowd is lurching forward. In a last-ditch attempt to find Lucio, she glances back at the Lizzies' dugout, where she sees Little Guido calling for silence and shaking his head at the disarray.

On top of the dugout she sees Lucio's mother, a worried look on her face, also searching for Lucio. There is a tiny mark on Francesca's face, a bit of blood, like a tear. Ruthie waves to her frantically, but just as the two make eye contact, Francesca is picked up by Spinny, who has leapt onto the dugout and taken her in his arms to carry her to safety. Ruthie is pressed forward and finds herself sandwiched against the brown-shirted boy who is carrying the swastika flag itself, holding the white fabric with both his hands. The world narrows, and Ruthie reaches for the flag, ripping at it, tearing a bit of it away. The boy pushes her back, hard. She falls and looks at the piece of cloth in her hand. It is yellowed and jagged—nothing at all— but there is something about the sight of it that causes her to get up quickly. She pushes forward, unafraid, joining the crush. Now she is one of them. Now she is out to make a point. Now it does not matter. In the distance she sees the flag, still borne aloft but with its centre ripped out, even the arms of the swastika gone. The boys holding it are mindless of everything except the fabric in their hands. The sight of the flag with nothing in the middle of it fills Ruthie with wild excitement: once we have it, she thinks, we can put anything in the middle. To Ruthie, it feels as if she's in the centre of something coming alive, of cells dividing, and then suddenly they are moving. She doesn't know why the flag is travelling in any given direction, but she moves with it. There are faces in the crowd she hasn't seen before—older men, men in their forties and fifties who have turned up expecting violence, knowing that the Swastika Club was going to try something, determined to stop it.

From somewhere behind her she hears her name, and she turns. It is Dubie. She calls to him and presses forward, and just then a bottle sails over the crowd, crashing into his head. Dubie falls, rolling down the hill. Ruthie tries to stop, and it is as if she is waking up, as if she has been asleep while pushing through the crowd. Dubie is hurt, and she must help him but she cannot, and she is instead pushed forward and turned around. When she tries to get her bearings, not only has she lost sight of Dubie, but she can't tell what direction he fell in. Beside her now are a number of boys in black shirts, fascists, Little Guido among them, singing. Up the hill the crowd begins to run, and faster now, on Bloor Street. They pass Palmerston, Manning—they are moving east through the city. Somewhere in front of her is the swastika and somewhere behind her is Dubie, wounded again. She must go back, but she cannot go alone, so she tries to speak to Little Guido. "Something happened to Dubie!" she screams. "He's hurt!" Guido stops, unable to understand her in the chaos, and she stops with him. A number of people behind them stumble into them, one of them a tall boy in a baseball uniform. He swears and she mumbles an apology, and when she looks up she sees an astonishing sight: it is Lucio, and he shakes his head when he sees her, too out of breath to speak.

"Back there, it's Dubie," she tells him. "He's hurt."

"Where?" Lucio manages to say.

"We have to go back."

"He's not hurt," Little Guido tells them. "He's in front of us, I saw him."

"He got hit," says Ruthie.

"You sure?" Lucio asks.

"It was a bottle," shouts Ruthie. "We have to go back."

A moment later they are on their way. By the time they get back to Christie Pits the riot has moved on, into the streets of

Toronto, and the baseball diamond is an abandoned mess. Broken bottles and rocks and planks of wood with nails sticking out and trash and ripped pieces of clothing are everywhere. But not Dubie.

"You sure it was him?" asks Lucio.

Ruthie is walking back and forth across the diamond, kicking over loose pieces of newspaper and broken bits of lumber, as if there is a chance Dubie might be under one of them. They stay there for a long time, the two of them, looking for him. Eventually they give up and walk home to Beverley Street, thinking that someone there will know something, or that, if he has been hurt, he will be brought to the long veranda. But he is nowhere to be seen, and no one seems to know anything. Dubie, it seems, has disappeared like Bloomberg. For a little while, anyway, both Lucio and Ruthie wonder if they are ever going to see him again.

SIXTEEN

BUT DUBIE HAS NOT DISAPPEARED. Not long after he gets hit in the head by the bottle, he finds himself being shaken awake by a twenty-two-year-old girl named Martha Crowley.

"Are you all right?" she asks him.

"I suppose," says Dubie. "My head is killing me."

He opens his eyes to find that Christie Pits has been turned into a wasteland. There is no sign of any of the Lizzies or St. Peter's or anyone else. Off in the distance, on Bloor Street, he can hear shouting, sirens blaring, the screeching of brakes, but near him he hears nothing. Christie Pits is silent, cut off once again from the rest of the world.

"You're bleeding," she says, and takes a hanky from her pocket. She wets it in her mouth and dabs at the matted hair on Dubie's head.

"Ow," he says. "That hurts."

"Come on," she says. "We better get you to a hospital. You might have a concussion."

"You think?"

"It could be," she says. "I'm training to be a nurse."

"Is that right?" he says. "You think I have a concussion?"

"Let's see," she says, holding up three fingers. "How many fingers?"

"What fingers?" he asks, looking in her eyes.

"You seem fine to me, but we better have you looked at." She leans down and takes him by the arm, and Dubie lurches to one side as if he's drunk.

Martha catches him. "Here," she says, "lean on me."

Dubie puts his arm around her and they begin to walk up the hillside, toward Bloor Street.

"I'm Dubie," he tells her.

"I'm Martha," she says. "Actually, Katherine is my name. But it's also my mother's name. Katherine Crowley. All my life, whenever someone said Katherine Crowley, I'd turn around and think my mother was behind me. Finally I said, enough. Call me Martha. Some people do it and some people don't. Would you call me Martha?"

"OK, Martha."

"What position do you play?" she asks.

"Position?" he says, then realizes that she's looking at his uniform. "Nothing. I mean, I'm the manager."

"Well, you did a good job."

"I did?"

"Sure," she says. "You won."

"Right," says Dubie. "We won."

They walk like that for a while, and are almost out of the pit when Martha sees Dubie's hand. He has his arm over her shoulder, and he notices that his new bandage has fallen off and the stump of the index finger, bloody and unsightly, is inches from her face. He tries to take his arm away, but Martha, her arm around his back, keeps him where he is, saying that if she's ever going to be a nurse she'll have to get used to much worse.

"What happened?" she asks.

"I had an accident," says Dubie, after a moment.

"What kind of accident?"

"Actually," says Dubie, "I cut the finger off myself. I'm a pitchman. I mean, my father has a booth at the St. Lawrence Market, and he and my brother, all three of us, sell knives. It was that kind of accident."

"Greenstein's Remarkable Knives?" says Martha.

"You know it?"

"That's where I know you from," she says, amazed. "You probably don't remember it, but last week you gave me a turnip rose."

"I'm sorry," Dubie begins to say. "There are a lot of—"

"Never mind," she says. "I went right home and put it in water. I love it."

"Really?" says Dubie. "Can I come to the wedding?"

Martha stops. "Now, that is just being terribly forward," she tells him.

"No, no," says Dubie, explaining that it's a joke. "If you love it so much," he says, "you should marry it."

Martha laughs.

And Dubie laughs as well. "That's an old one," he says.

"I've never heard it," she says, moving a little closer to him.

"I got a million of them," says Dubie, then adds, "from my father."

Martha is getting a good look at Dubie's hand. "At least," she says, "it's healing."

Dubie sees that she is right. Already there is skin beginning to grow over the knuckle, and soon there will be a smooth place next to his thumb, as if there had never been a finger there to begin with.

They walk down Bloor Street, toward the hospital, with a divided city all around them, horns blaring and men shouting at each other. But the doctors find nothing wrong with Dubie, and the two come home, safely, to the long veranda on Beverley Street.

EPILOGUE

My grandmother Martha Crowley—the girl Dubie left with—is now ninety-one years old and a resident of West Park Hospital, in Toronto. She is a widow with two children (my Uncle Asher and my mother, Mazie) and two grandchildren, of which I am the older. My mother, as my grandmother (who is a goy herself) likes to say, went out and married a goy. My grandfather, who the reader will have figured out by this point is none other than Dubie Diamond, died nearly thirty years ago. The death certificate reads pneumonia, but the truth is lung cancer. They cut him up, but the cancer came back. They did it again and he never had a chance—at least, not in 1973. Today they would be able to keep him going for years, says my grandmother, the way they do her. She has told me most of this story while propped up in a hospital bed; she has a failing heart, obstructed lungs, hardening arteries, a weak stomach, unpredictable kidneys, negligible hair, cracked knees, wobbly ankles, and liver spots. She is an old girl nearly done. Kaput. Fatto. Those words are hers, as is the list of ailments.

"And that's it?" I said to my grandmother. "That's how it ends?"

"Of course," she said. "They were all there, waiting, when your grandfather Dubie and I got back to Beverley Street. Lucio certainly was no tough guy, and he and Ruthie went straight home. People acted like they were surprised to see them, but by that time almost everyone had either heard or figured out they were a couple. And there was so much happening—people were angry or frightened or both, and there was a lot of confusion. Dante drove around in one of those chicken trucks for a while, looking for a fight, but eventually everybody got back. It was Dubie they were worried about. Only a few people got seriously hurt that night, and Dubie was one of them. Everyone was glad to see him, I can tell you that much."

"What happened to Ruthie?" I asked.

"Well, she died, of course."

"I suppose she'd be pretty old by now."

"Probably she would be, but she never made it much past twenty. She died in '34, before the war even. She had tuberculosis."

"Was there an outbreak?"

"No," she said. "But Ruthie got it somewhere—probably in one of those sweatshops, when she was handing out her sandwiches—and then, you know, she passed away."

"I can't believe it," I said.

"Oh yes, it was very sad. She probably had it already when she hit the home run. Lucio was a wreck afterwards—they both were."

"Both? You mean Lucio and Dubie?"

"The two of them—your grandfather was still in love with her."

"I thought he was in love with you."

"He was, but after."

"No, I mean, in the story, at the end—it ends with him falling for you."

"It ends with him meeting me, which was a step in the right direction, but there was a ways to go after that. There was a courtship, as we used to say. Your grandfather and I didn't get married until after the war was over. It wasn't like today, you know, Steven."

"Weren't you jealous of Ruthie?"

"I might have been, if I'd known what happened. But it was only after Ruthie was gone that anyone really told me any of it. If anything, I wish I'd got to know her better. Your grandfather made her sound like quite a girl."

"She must have been," I said.

"Now don't you go getting any ideas—she's long gone."

I laughed.

"Never mind," she told me. "I've seen that look before. You're like your grandfather, and Lucio, no different."

"What about Lucio?" I said. "I mean, after she died."

"He fell apart. I remember him crying, but mostly it was like he didn't believe it. So many people came for the shivah that it spilled out of the house onto that long veranda, and it was like the whole world was there. The Lizzies, all of them, weeping the whole time, along with Comrade Biro, even Elmer Querques. I went too, like everyone else. But not Lucio. People started asking where he was and eventually your grandfather found him in the cinder alley under the fire escape. He said he looked like something plastered up against the side of the house by the wind." She stopped speaking and shook her head. "It was like a part of him had been cut off, is what your grandfather told me. And I suppose that's right. I suppose your grandfather knew what he was talking about."

"And after that?" I said, after a long moment.

"He got drafted and went overseas. He disappeared."

"Disappeared? You mean he was killed?"

My grandmother paused and tilted her head. "Well," she said, "there were stories. People said things. But you know, people are always saying things."

"People?"

"Dante."

"Dante saw Lucio get killed?"

"Dante was the one who told the story. Mind you, we're not talking police facts here. Not the kind of thing you can take to the bank, as they say. But both Dante and Goody Altman were there with Lucio. You know, Goody was—"

I cut her off. "The second-best baseball player the city of Toronto ever produced."

"Goody went on to play for the Red Sox," she said. "Then he enlisted in the army, which sent him to France. Lost his leg, came back and never played again. The three of them, Dante, Goody and Lucio were part of the famous Canadian 3rd Infantry Division that stormed the beach at Bernières-sur-Mer on D-Day—but you probably don't know anything about that. Why would you? It was a great thing at the time, though: pictures in all the papers of our boys in their flotillas. One of the pictures was of Goody, Dante, and Lucio. They were sitting in a little row, their helmets on, looking at something in the distance. We all couldn't believe it. Front page of the Globe and Mail, eh?"

"When was that again?"

"June, of course," she told me, incredulously. "June sixth, 1944, Steven. It was one for the books."

I felt myself reddening.

"Afterwards, Dante came home," she said, "and not long after he was back, he came for a visit with us. Your grandfather, because of his hand, couldn't get into the army, but he wanted to know what had happened, what it felt like, so he sat there drinking beers with Dante for hours waiting for him to get around to it. By that time Lucio's mother'd already got the cable from the government saying he wasn't coming back. So finally your grandfather just came out and asked what had happened."

"What'd Dante say?"

"That he didn't know. It was all confusion, of course. There'd been an explosion to one side and then a great rush of air from the other—and when Dante turned back, Lucio was gone."

"Gone?"

"That's right."

"He was probably thrown overboard," I said.

"Could have been." She paused. "But that wasn't what Dante thought. He said Lucio was taken. He saw the bird."

"The bird?"

"Like Bloomberg's glasses," she said. "Up and away."

"Let me make sure I've got this straight," I said. "Dante said that, in the midst of their storming the beach at Normandy on D-Day, the bird from the Elizabeth Street playground came down and took Lucio."

"And carried him away."

"This was what Dante told you?"

"He said, 'I turned and there was a shadow and I swear to God it was that bird. Lifted him up and out of the boat, and carried him away.'"

"Away where?" I said.

"Who knows?" she said. "Maybe all the way up."

"You mean, to heaven?" I said, before I could stop myself.

My grandmother shrugged. "Is that what you want to think?"

"And this is in the photo?" I said, ignoring her question. "This is in the Globe and Mail?"

"I'm not saying that," she said. "But Lucio is—oh yes, and the sight of him on the front page very nearly killed his mother. If it hadn't been for Spinny, who knows what would have happened to her?"

"Spinny?"

"Spinny was smitten, and they hit it off after that ball game. Which is kind of funny, when you think about it. Your grandfather—

who knew all about Lucio's wanting a father so badly—used to laugh and say, who could have guessed that Lucio's father should turn out to be Spinny Weinreb?"

"And what about you?"

"Well, you know that," she said. "I lived happily ever after."

The next day I go to the Robarts Library at the University of Toronto, and look at all the Toronto papers from the week of D-Day. And there is Lucio, right where my grandmother told me he would be, on the front page some three days after the invasion. I know what Goody looks like, because I have seen his baseball card, and that makes it easy to find Lucio. In the photo he is twenty-eight and unshaven; his hair, which has been closely cropped by the army, is hidden beneath his helmet, but his eyes— the blue eyes that Ruthie could never seem to stop herself from looking into—are staring off into the distance. This is the only surviving picture of Lucio Burke. It's not a picture of him—it's supposed to be a photo of the massive assemblage of equipment brought together for that day. But there is Lucio. Squeezed together with Goody and Dante into the lower left-hand corner. If you look closely enough, you realize that you can't see Lucio's right shoulder. But not because the photo has been cropped. Because there is something else in the way. You can't see it clearly, but it's there all the same—something touching Lucio's shoulder.

A moment later, bird or no bird, Lucio Burke would be gone.

AUTHOR'S NOTE

A COUPLE OF YEARS AGO, in connection with a different story I'd written about a different baseball game, a journalist asked me, "Was the game real, or did you make it up?"

Some readers, having arrived at the end of *The Secret Mitzvah of Lucio Burke*, may ask the same question. And there are other readers who will have noted the frequent and sometimes great liberties I have taken with the historical record.

First, and most crucially: the riot at Christie Pits did happen. On the evening of August 16, 1933, just as a playoff baseball game was ending at Christie Pits in Toronto, a group of about twenty boys, supporters of the local Pit Gang and the Swastika Club, unfurled a white sheet on which a vivid black swastika had been painted. A number of Jewish spectators in the crowd rushed the flag-bearers. It was by no means the first time that "Heil Hitler" and anti-Semitic insults had been shouted in Toronto, but on this occasion word spread fast throughout the city, and the Jewish boys from the downtown core—along with a number of Italians who considered themselves allies—decided to organize in response: boys across the city piled into trucks and raced down to Christie Pits. Mayhem ensued, sparking a riot that stretched into the night.

This incident was the culmination of several years of growing anti-Semitism across the country, most particularly in Montreal, but evident in Toronto too where Jews were banned from specific areas, such as parks and beaches, hotels and golf courses, with large signs noting "Jews Keep Out" and "Jews Not Allowed." Jews were also barred from many universities and from the professions themselves—prevented from practicing law or medicine, architecture and engineering, for example, as well as excluded from many commercial and industrial places of employment, or from renting apartments. Fascism was also a subtle but invidious element in Toronto at that time.

But *The Secret Mitzvah of Lucio Burke* is a work of fiction. While some of the characters are based on real people and some of the incidents portrayed here did happen, they have been altered—like the city of Toronto itself—to suit the strict purposes of storytelling. These characters and incidents, despite their resemblance to actual persons and known events, are therefore the products of my imagination. Even the names of the teams that were playing have been changed: the actual baseball game (which was not a championship game) was between the team from St. Peter's Church and Harbord Playground (St. Peter's won); the Elizabeth Street Playground team, the Lizzies, did exist but they were an amateur baseball team in Toronto—my own grandfather, Clifford Hayward, who does not appear in the book, pitched for them—and were not involved in the game that led to the riot. The Lizzies, as I have invented them, are a decidedly more ethnically diverse group than was the Harbord Playground baseball team, which was composed almost entirely of Jewish boys. My aim was to make the Lizzies a kind of microcosm of the Ward at the time and, by placing so many different kinds of new immigrant Canadians on the same team, to suggest the alliances that existed between them in a more direct manner than the historical record might allow. I've also suggested that everyday life often goes on unnoticing of historical events that we only see in retrospect as significant, and that those who were at Christie Pits that day were, undoubtedly, first and foremost, the protagonists of their own stories.

Other matters: the words Emma Goldman speaks in the novel are largely hers, culled from her writings, but, while it is true that she did live for a number of years in Toronto after being exiled from the United States, she does not seem to have been in the city that summer; there were a number of wildcat strikes on Spadina Avenue in the 1930s, and a boy named Elmer Querques (pronounced "Kirk" in my imagination) *did* play in the game that night at Christie Pits for St. Peter's, but he was most certainly not the best baseball player the city of Toronto ever produced, and might not even have been a virgin.

I wish to acknowledge with gratitude the help and inspiration I received from *The Riot at Christie Pits* by Cyril H. Levitt and William Shaffir (Lester & Orpen Dennys: Toronto); *A Coat of Many Colours* by Irving Abella (Lester & Orpen Dennys: Toronto); *The Darkest Side of the Fascist Years* by Angelo Principe (Guernica Editions: Montreal); *Call Me Sammy* by Sammy Luftspring (Prentice Hall of Canada: Scarborough); Rick Salutin's introduction to *Spadina Avenue* by Rosemary Donegan (Douglas & McIntyre: Toronto); *Italians in Toronto: Development of a National Identity, 1875–1935* by John E. Zucchi (McGill–Queen's University Press: Kingston and

Montreal); *The Great Depression* by Pierre Berton (Penguin Canada: Toronto); and *A Toronto Almanac* by Mike Filey (Mike Filey: Toronto).

Thanks also to those who helped in the writing of the book: Paul Pellizzari, Norman Ravvin, Mark Hayward, Peter Kvidera, Gena Gorrell, Derek Cohen, Elin Diamond, Phyllis Rackin, Richard Carlstrom, Frances Carlstrom, John Lawson, Michael DiFranco, Barry Hayward, Debra Rosenthal, Glenn Starkman, Nathaniel Starkman, Ariana Starkman, Jimmy and Rique Sollisch, Scott Shane, Wendy Simon, Chris Roark, Tom Pace, George Bilgere, Rich Rosfelder, Suzanne Brandreth, Samantha North, Eilseen Turoff, Angelika Glover, Deirdre Molina, Fr. Francis Ryan, S.J., Fr. Oliver Rafferty, S.J., the members of Cleveland's East Side Writer's Group (Maureen McHugh, Sarah Willis, Jim Garrett, Amy Bracken Sparks, Erin Nowjack, Charles Oberndorf and Lori Weber) and, finally, my students at John Carroll University in Cleveland, who saw early drafts of this work and offered many excellent and valuable suggestions.

I also want to thank my mother, Phyllis Hayward, for her love and support, but also for providing me with a fine written account of what it was like to grow up on Beverley Street and of the house in which she and my grandparents lived. I must also mention the dearly and recently departed in my family, people who were here to ask questions of when I started writing and now, somehow, are not: my grandfather, Costanzo DiFranco, my grandmother, Anna DiFranco, and also her brother, my great uncle, Paul Greico. I miss you all.

My two most particular debts of thanks are due to my editor, Louise Dennys, whose patience and editorial genius can be witnessed on every page of this book, and to my agent, Dean Cooke, for believing in and nurturing this book from the first.

I must say hello to Frances and Edward, who will one day read this and want to see their names here. And, finally, this book is dedicated with all my love and gratitude to their mother, my wife, Katherine Carlstrom, who bears all the burden, is the best and wisest of readers, and makes everything possible, each day.

STEVEN HAYWARD was born and raised in Toronto. His short fiction has won awards at the University of Toronto, the University of North Carolina and the University of Arkansas, and his first book, *Buddha Stevens and Other Stories*, a collection of short stories, won the Upper Canada Writers' Craft Award. He currently lives in Cleveland Heights, Ohio, with his wife and two children where he is Assistant Professor in the English department at John Carroll University.